Melissa Kite is a British journ for the *Spectator* magazine. She has also written articles for several other newspapers including the *Daily Mail*, and was Deputy Political Editor of the *Sunday Telegraph*. She is the author of a memoir, *Real Life: One Woman's Guide to Love, Men and Other Everyday Disasters*. This is her first novel. She lives in London with her spaniel Cydney.

The Girl Who Couldn't Stop Arguing

Melissa Kite

corsair

CORSAIR

First published in Great Britain in 2015 by Corsair

Copyright © Melissa Kite, 2015

The moral right of the author has been asserted.

A CIP catalogue record for this book
is available from the British Library.

ISBN: 978-1-47211-536-2 (paperback)
ISBN: 978-1-47211-537-9 (ebook)

Typeset in Sabon by Initial Typesetting Services, Edinburgh
Printed and bound in Great Britain by CPI Group (UK) Ltd.,
Croydon, CR0 4YY

Corsair
An imprint of
Little, Brown Book Group
100 Victoria Embankment
London EC4Y 0DY

An Hachette UK Company
www.hachette.co.uk

www.littlebrown.com

The Girl Who Couldn't Stop Arguing

Court 38, The Royal Courts of Justice, London 2014

The sound was deranging, like chalk on a blackboard.

As the lawyer known as the Chair-Scraper leapt to her feet, she made a toe-curling squeak so that everyone in the courtroom winced as if in pain.

'M'Lord!'

'Sit down!' yelled Mr Justice Juniper, wiping away the beads of sweat that were already accumulating on his brow. 'Please at least let me begin the session before you start your funny business. The other parties have not even managed to make it into the court, so far as I can see.'

Juniper nodded to the clerk, who walked to the door and called into the corridor: '*All* parties in the matter of Taylor *and* Taylor . . .'

He said it sarcastically, as if to emphasize that some fool had already tested the judge's patience by being incompetent. Amateurs.

Sure enough, a greasy-haired, bespectacled solicitor with a cheap imitation-leather briefcase and an armful of scruffy lever-arch files trotted into the courtroom followed by a tall, blond beefcake of a fellow dressed curiously in what looked to be a crumpled morning suit, with a petrified corsage still pinned to the lapel.

The pair gulped helplessly before the clerk showed them to their seats.

Even if they had not been, respectively, Britain's worst lawyer and the most hapless gold-digger ever to try to fleece a rich widow, they could be forgiven for looking so woefully disorientated. The courtroom looked like a scene from the Mad Hatter's tea party.

All the furniture was oversized with strange walls around it. The judge was sitting in a vast throne high above the rest of the court. Random officials walked around passing bits of paper to other random officials sitting in seats behind big walls. It could hardly have been more disconcerting if the fat, rosy-cheeked tea lady in a pinafore posted outside the court with a trolley came in and started serving everyone Darjeeling in oversized teacups. Or if the clerk brought in a set of hoops and mallets and instructed all the assembled parties to start playing croquet. There seemed to be no rhyme or reason to how or why any of this strange scene fitted together.

The bespectacled solicitor sat down for a few seconds, then rose gingerly to his feet and began to speak very quietly. 'M'Lord, we [cough] would first like to tell the court that—'

'M'Lord, I must object!' The girl was on her feet again.

'We still haven't started yet!' bellowed the judge. 'Nothing starts unless I say it starts!

Juniper dabbed at his head more vigorously. His pores seemed to be perfectly incontinent today.

The Chair-Scraper was still standing. 'Counsel cannot be heard properly. He is speaking in an inappropriate manner so as not to be fully audible. If we cannot hear him we cannot be expected to proceed.'

The judge sighed and nodded at the husband's solicitor. 'Will you please try and speak up, and speak clearly, so as not to cause my wooden floor to be scratched by *her* chair?'

'M'Lord?' She was on her feet again.

The judge dabbed at his head.

'You make certain assumptions that the floor will be marked as a direct consequence of the chair movement when clearly there are other factors which might easily impact on the integrity of a floor of this type. I will outline those factors now if it pleases the court.'

'It does not please the court. Sit down, woman, or I will have your backside coated in glue.'

And that was when he noticed that the client sitting next to her, a very overdressed woman in her sixties with a shock of frizzy red hair standing out from her head in a halo, had taken the opportunity, while her lawyer's attention was elsewhere, of committing the cardinal sin of fiddling with her phone. As her heavily bejewelled fingers stabbed at the keys she giggled at something on the screen which evidently had nothing to do with the proceedings.

'Switch that off in my courtroom!' he yelled, before turning to the clerk and muttering: 'I've just about had enough of this lot and we haven't even begun.'

The clerk gave him an arch look.

The judge turned to the other lawyer. 'Mr . . . ?'

'It's Mr John, sir. Elden John.' Juniper looked him up and down. 'Well, you don't look anything like Elton John to me.'

'Not Elton, sir. Elden. With a d, e.'

'I see,' said Juniper, as if this was typical of the sort of thing he had to put up with. 'Well, get on with it.'

'I would like to begin by, er . . .' And he stopped speaking and started staring into space. 'By, er . . . by, er . . .' His eyes glazed over. 'By . . . er . . .' He gave every impression that he might go on like this indefinitely.

'Frankly we don't care how you would like to begin. Just begin.' Juniper sighed and then took a big cleansing breath through his nose, in the way he had been taught to at the drug and alcohol rehabilitation unit from which he had just escaped.

'M'Lord!' The sound of scraping pervaded the room. The girl was on her feet again. It set Juniper's teeth on edge. He suddenly felt the overwhelming urge to run to the nearest off-licence.

Instead he breathed in, blew air ostentatiously through his mouth, then mopped away a stream of sweat running down his head.

The clerk looked up at him nervously from where he was sitting at a table beneath the judge's bench.

He knew this was Juniper's first case since his incarceration for his little problem. He was too fragile to be working again, let alone presiding over a high-profile divorce case that was already attracting international media attention.

With any luck he would have one of his attacks and be stretchered out of the courtroom before the end of the day. A new judge who was not teetering dangerously on the brink of a homicidal breakdown exacerbated by delirium tremens would be brought in (hard to find though they were), and then they could all get on with what would no doubt turn out to be a gruelling marathon of divorce wrangling, as the lawyer known as the Chair-Scraper did her worst . . .

1

The Cotswolds, 1973 (nearly)

New Year's Eve was foggy that year, and Madison Flight decided not to venture out.

As the muffled revellers poured through the streets, she dug in her heels and refused to move.

'Come out, come out, wherever you are!' joked the midwife, but the joke wasn't funny, because everyone knew exactly where she was. For Madison's mother, it was an especially poor choice of moment for irony, as women in childbirth are not well disposed to it.

The doctors tried everything, including a suction device which slightly elongated Madison's head, and a huge pair of forceps, which was wielded far too enthusiastically, inflicting on her, as she lay curled in the womb, two deep cuts, one behind each unborn ear.

Six whole days she had been holding out, suspended upside down with her thumb in her mouth, eyes squeezed shut. Now the doctors would prepare for an emergency caesarean because her mother, the already long-suffering Cynthia Flight, was three tanks of gas and air beyond trying to persuade her daughter diplomatically to launch her attempt at the business of living.

It had been Christmas Day when she went into labour. Now it was getting on for next year and if Cynthia Flight had one New Year's resolution it was to get this baby out before the clock struck 1973.

'Come out, come out, wherever you are,' twittered the midwife, in the general direction of the space between Cynthia's knees.

But Madison clung onto unbornness, like a hedgehog refusing to uncurl. Upside down, suspended, trying to pretend nothing was happening.

If we give some thought to what was waiting for her we can perhaps gain a better appreciation of her attitude.

The world on the brink of a new year is always daunting, but 1973 was going to be a humdinger. The UK was about to enter the EEC and the first ever episode of *The Last of the Summer Wine* was shortly to be broadcast. If you could get over that, a volcano called Eldfell on the Icelandic island of Heimaey was going to erupt, a Boeing 747 was going to crash in Nigeria killing 176 people and the ribbon was going to be cut on a complex of skyscrapers called the World Trade Center.

Perhaps Madison simply didn't fancy Edward Heath faffing about with prices and incomes policy, or Tottenham winning the cup final, or George Foreman defeating Joe Frazier (especially since the main thing Foreman chose to do with his fame was to market an eponymous meat grilling machine).

Possibly she had mixed feelings about the state of Ohio posting weights in metric for the first time, which would one day make Hackney greengrocers whinge endlessly about being forced to re-write all the white plastic signs sticking out of their fruit and veg.

We cannot know whether she agreed or disagreed with the abolition of the monarchy in Greece, or the shooting down by snipers of left-wing supporters of Eva Peron in Buenos Aires.

Maybe she knew the first mobile phone call was about to be made, by a Motorola executive in New York City, and that this would end thousands of years of human freedom and pave the way to the total enslavement of mankind to technology and, ultimately, the end of everything at a much later date in the future when, in a multi-billion-to-one incident, every single person alive would decide to update their Facebook status on their smart phone at exactly the same moment, creating a catastrophic surge in network activity which would blow the earth out of its orbit. Maybe Madison looked way into the future and foresaw that there would be one single, ecstatically awful moment when everyone on the planet knew exactly how everyone else on the planet felt, or in the case of most of the updates, knew what they felt about something irrelevant, like their dinner, or their downstairs toilet being blocked. And then it would end.

That being said, there were some things to be cheerful about in 1973. A chestnut horse called Secretariat, or Big

Red to his friends, won the triple crown of thoroughbred racing.

Richard Nixon ended the Vietnam War. And more people than watched the Apollo moon landings tuned in to a stupendously good concert by Elvis Presley in Hawaii.

But Madison, it seemed, weighed all of this up and decided that, on balance, she wanted nothing to do with it, thank you very much.

Maybe the clinching factor was that somehow, whilst curled up snugly in utero, she had gleaned the knowledge that her mother was planning to leave her father for a club singer called Hilton Valentine just as soon as she was old enough to go on the road with them.

In any case, she curled herself smaller in her upside-down cradle and pushed her thumb further into her mouth.

Then, as the midwife commenced another round of 'Cooey! Where are you?' she pulled her thumb out, and, using her arms as paddles, whooshed herself through 180-degrees in one smooth, effortless underwater somersault so that her feet were pointing downwards. And then she pressed her hands against the sides of her mother's womb, so that she was completely wedged.

'Breech!' shrieked the midwife, as she realized what was happening. She meant breach of protocol as much as anything. The midwife ran the miracle of birth with a rod of iron, and woe betide the foetus who gave her any funny business. A week overdue was one thing, but a baby suddenly turning the wrong way up midway through delivery was beyond a joke.

So the doctors put on masks and wheeled poor Cynthia down to the operating theatre as her husband Mitchell trotted behind.

It was quite out of the question that Mitchell would watch his daughter being born out of a makeshift opening in the front of his wife. Quite, quite out of the question.

A man's place at sixteen minutes to midnight on 31 December 1972 was on the plastic seat just outside the delivery room, so Mitchell watched Cynthia wheeled into theatre on her trolley followed by a clatter of drips, and waved with faux cheerfulness. 'I'll be waiting for you when you come back!' he said, much as if he were seeing her off on a day trip to Torquay.

In the end, it took two hours to get the recalcitrant baby out. As they pulled her legs, several of the team swore they saw her little hands trying to monkey climb back up the umbilical cord in what they could only assume was an attempt to get back in.

Holding the wrinkled human piglet aloft, Mr Archibald Sinclair was astounded when it began making the strangest noise he had ever heard coming from a baby.

'Naaaaaaaaaaaah! Naaaaaaaaaah!'

'Is she saying no?'

The midwife looked at him with contempt.

'Naaaaaaaah! Naaaaaaaaah!'

Then Dr Sinclair noticed for the first time the two bleeding inch-long slashes behind the baby's ears. He really would have to get a better pair of forceps.

'Naaaaaaaaaaah! Naaaaaaaaah! Naaah!'

'She just said no! Didn't you hear it?' said Sinclair. 'Why would she be saying no? Can babies say words at . . .' He looked at his watch, doubtfully, '. . . seventeen seconds old?'

'Of course she's not saying no,' said the midwife. 'What would she be saying no to?'

And then all the monitors started beeping and pandemonium broke out.

When Cynthia woke from the anaesthesia, the surgeon was standing at her bedside, shaking his head.

'I'm afraid I've some bad news,' he said. 'There were problems.'

Sinclair was standing with his arms at his side, looking entirely wooden and useless. If any expectant mother had seen him at that moment, they would never have trusted him with the job of safely extracting an infant from them. And they would have been right, by and large.

'Problems?' said Cynthia, trying to snap out of the drowsiness. 'Where's my—?'

'Sometimes, there are complications that mean we have to do certain things.' Sinclair leaned forward and stroked her awkwardly on the arm in an attempt to appear sympathetic, but it came off as something else. Cynthia snatched her arm and hid it under the covers.

'What things? Where's my baby?'

She started to pull herself up. She scanned the room through bleary eyes. There was no cot. No baby. And what sort of doctor tries to seduce a woman as she's coming round from anaesthesia, for the love of God?

'Your baby was very stuck. When we got her out . . .'

'Her?' said Cynthia, and then again, 'Her?' thinking that if she just repeated the word often enough the 'her' would materialize. 'Where's my baby?'

And at that very moment, just as Cynthia was about to start slapping Sinclair around the head, a nurse breezed in with a parcel of blankets wrapped tightly around a tiny pink face.

She placed the bundle on Cynthia's lap. Dr Sinclair looked down, squeamishly. He had never liked children. This one was particularly suspicious. 'Oh, the baby is fine – seven pounds, five ounces. She's finally asleep, I see. After giving us a good demonstration of the best pair of lungs we've heard in a while.'

'She's a troublemaker all right,' said the nurse. 'You're not going to have a moment's rest, I'm afraid, Mrs Flight.'

Dr Sinclair turned his nose up. Suspicious thing number one: the baby had had its eyes open when it came out. Suspicious thing number two: he could have sworn its eyes were focusing, and that it was making eye contact specifically with him. And not in a nice way. In an accusatory way. Suspicious thing number three: its mouth appeared to be in the process of forming words. Words that somehow had to do with telling him off for cutting its ears. No, surely not?

The whole thing was very disconcerting. Whatever was up, he disliked this baby more than any baby he had ever pulled out of a womb.

Cynthia, however, was transfixed as the little lips pursed

and unpursed as if the baby were having an animated conversation with her.

She didn't even notice Mitchell knocking cautiously on the door even though it was open and asking timidly if he might come in. Standing just outside the scene, as he usually did, Mitchell did not hear as the doctor announced: 'But the bad news is you won't be able to have any more children.'

Mitchell did, however, hear Cynthia shrieking with delight, and then pain, as she burst several of her stitches.

If the bad news wasn't bad news to Cynthia, it was still bad news to Archibald Sinclair, because he strongly suspected his lack of forceps dexterity had almost got him into hot water again. And that made him nervous. And that made him need a stiff drink.

The other bit of bad news that he reflected upon as he walked back down the corridor to have a well-earned cup of whiskey with a splash of tea, was that the Flight baby had probably missed being the first born of the year in the county and probably only by a matter of ten minutes. Delivering the first born of the year would have earned him the honour of appearing on the front page of the local newspaper. Doctors in the seventies loved getting their picture in the local paper, almost as much as they loved drinking whiskey with a hint of PG Tips.

2

Most women wanted a *baby*. But Cynthia Flight wanted *a* baby, with the emphasis on the *a*.

She wanted *a* baby because two babies would have made a total of three of them and three would have been a crowd. As it was, it would be very cosy. Her husband Mitchell spent long periods away from home and Cynthia wanted to keep it that way.

Mitchell Flight was a pilot. How it made the passengers giggle with delight when his steady, monotone voice came over the intercom to announce: 'Ladies and gentlemen, this is Captain Flight, welcoming you aboard this Boeing 747 . . .'

They never minded if a flight was delayed on the tarmac by an air traffic hold-up, or if the plane was shaken for hours by extreme turbulence, because you couldn't feel bad when you were being flown across the Atlantic by a man called Captain Flight.

Mitchell had always wanted to be a pilot, because all his friends always told him when he was a young boy how fantastic it would be if he did become a pilot because then he would be called Captain Flight.

His parents, Mitchell Senior and Beryl Flight had rather hoped their son would help run the family business, a thriving pork pie and sausage factory called Mitchell's Meats – Food You Can Trust! (an ironic title if ever there was one).

But it soon became clear that Mitchell was mechanically minded to the extent that it would have been a travesty to confine him to the mechanics of mechanical meat extraction.

He proved precociously able to drive his father's car at the age of seven – first, up and down the long sweeping driveway of the Mitchell family home, then out of the driveway and onto the public roads, because his father saw no reason why the boy shouldn't make himself useful and drive him to work.

Mitchell Senior gave up on the idea that his son would one day take over the meat business, and Mitchell Junior duly became a pilot for one of the world's leading airlines.

I should explain that the Flight men always had the same name as their father, apart from the senior bit, obviously. They only got that when one of them dropped off the end of the chain. They passed down the name Mitchell because of an inflated sense of their own grandeur coupled with a lack of creative energy.

It was this same failing that meant that, because the Flight men couldn't name their female offspring Mitchell, no matter how much they would have liked to, they always gave them names that began with M, like Madison, as a sort of consolation prize. Mitchell's two sisters were called

Maureen and Marjorie, and his aunts were Muriel and Margo. The Flights did not have unbridled imaginative powers and whilst they liked names that began with M, they never seemed to tire of running out of ideas for them, nor did they ever give way to an urge to pick up a baby-naming book – or indeed a book of any other kind – in order to replenish their stock of approved monikers. It was Cynthia who came up with Madison. Mitchell had wanted to call her Maureena.

And since we are on the subject of names, Mitchell's Meats was named Mitchell's Meats and not Flight Meats because Mitchell's great-great-grandfather Mitchell Thaddeus Flight, who founded the pork pie and sausage-making empire in 1853, was a man who set a lot of store by alliteration. He also set a lot of store by adultery, but that's not an issue we shall delve into here. Suffice to say, he considered Mitchell's Meats more conducive to launching a fledgling sausage meat firm into the public consciousness than Flight's Meats, which sounded downright ridiculous.

But we digress. By the time Mitchell met Cynthia he had gained his captaincy and was spending a lot of time on long haul.

Since their marriage, he came home to the smart house he had bought for his family in the village of Little Fougham only periodically, sometimes not for months on end.

That didn't bother Cynthia at all. Marriage was over-rated, if you asked her. She had always known it. Never had she nursed a single hope or delusion that marriage would be anything other than what it was, which, according to her mother before her, was not much, when it came right down to it. Actually, that's not quite right. Years ago, she had nursed just such a delusion. But she had had to get over it by the time she got herself married to Mitchell, because Mitchell was not a man you could be romantic about. He was way, way too practical for that.

By the time she was preparing to walk down the aisle, Cynthia had joined the realms of the disappointed and decided she couldn't afford to believe any longer in anything so fickle as love.

'I can't see why on earth women make all that fuss about white dresses and bridesmaids,' she said to her friend Shirley as they planned the special day by looking at the Kay's catalogue. But whether or not Cynthia was truly being realistic or whether she was simply putting a brave face on the crushed idealism she still felt deep down was not completely clear.

That said, no one went to town on weddings in those days. The practice of spending thousands of pounds on designer dresses and lavish receptions featuring enormous ten-tier cakes is a relatively new invention.

Cynthia and Mitchell married at their local church, St Ignatius, with Cynthia wearing a knee-length, very plain dress made by Shirley, Mitchell in a hired morning suit that didn't really fit, four family members who were at least wearing their own clothes, and a friend taking pictures with a Kodak Instamatic camera. Two pictures, to be precise. No point going over the top. One of Cynthia on her own in front of the graveyard before the ceremony.

One of Cynthia and Mitchell in front of the graveyard after the ceremony. The two pictures were identical in almost every way, except for Mitchell being in the second one, smiling with one side of his mouth.

Cynthia really could have had more pictures taken, given how long she waited there in front of the graveyard dotted with too-tidy arrangements of primroses. With her bobbed yellow-blonde hair she looked a little like a primrose herself.

I hate spring flowers, she thought, because the blasted things look so bloody hopeful.

Mitchell didn't turn up for three hours and they had to send someone to look for him. He was hiding in a shed full of old pork pie casings at the bottom of a debris-strewn plot of disused land behind the factory where the stables had been, years ago, when Mitchell's Meats – Food You Can Trust! had made deliveries by horse and cart to all the best grocery shops, and quite a few of the worst.

He was smoking a cigarette and swigging from a bottle of whiskey. He had barely been able to stand at the altar long enough to say his vows, and his best man had to keep leaping up from the front pew to push him straight as he veered from side to side and staggered slightly backwards. But apart from that, it all went off very well.

3

When Cynthia got her baby daughter home she realized almost at once that something was wrong.

It wasn't just that Madison would not stop crying. It was the sort of crying. In fact, it wasn't crying, it was yowling, like the sound of an outraged hyena.

Cynthia tried milk – not breast milk, because breast milk wasn't at all fashionable in 1973 – and she tried singing. She tried walking her around. She tried putting her in the back of the car and driving her around. She tried soothing, and clucking, and cooing and then she just put the baby down and contemplated suicide.

A few hours after getting her home, she telephoned her next-door neighbour and best friend Shirley, who had been a district nurse until a spot of political bother over her baby-soothing techniques, which were evidently a bit behind the time. 'I'm telling you, Shirl, I'm ready to throw myself out of the window.' Or the baby. She didn't know which, to be honest. But she was assuming either would be a mistake and not strictly how she was supposed to do it according to those parent technology books Shirley lent her (which, I have to tell you, she hadn't got around to reading yet).

Shirley came over and found Madison so frothed up by her yowling that she had to take all her clothes off to get her temperature down from 103.

'What on earth is the matter with her?' said Cynthia, lighting a Silk Cut cigarette, in a long, black holder. Cigarettes in holders, unlike breast milk, were terribly fashionable in 1973.

'I don't know,' said Shirley, staring disapprovingly down at the naked baby wriggling on a sheet like a marooned platypus, paddling the air. There was nothing Shirley liked less than a misbehaving newborn. A baby she couldn't stop crying challenged her sense of what she had devoted her entire professional life to knowing – and reminded her of the unfortunate incident that had ended her career – which was not a comfortable thing. 'She seems to have taken against something, lord knows what. Never in all my years as a nurse have I heard a baby with a mouth on it like this one.'

Eventually, Mitchell came home one weekend from a five-day stopover in Miami to ask how it was going 'with the baby, and all that'.

'I'll tell you how it's going,' said Cynthia, her sleeves rolled up and baby sick down the front of her Biba blouse (very, very fashionable in 1973). 'That baby you gave me is the most foul-mouthed infant that ever drew breath.'

It was true. Madison Flight, aged three months and two days, just went on protesting until Cynthia and Mitchell didn't know whether they were coming or going that fraught weekend when they tried to share a house for the first time, all three of them being just the crowd Cynthia had anticipated.

Nothing was right, so far as the protesting newborn was concerned. They offered her a bottle and she booed. Rocked her in a crib and she hissed. It all seemed to confirm to Mitchell that he was right to live out his married life in various popular holiday and business destinations throughout the world. Family was not something a man should have any more to do with other than paying for it, he thought – which, to be fair to him, was a fashionable notion in 1973. But Cynthia begged him to hold out a little longer and stay.

Apart from anything else he owed it to the baby to try to stop its mother from extinguishing it.

Then one day, just as Cynthia was about to throw in the towel and eject herself from the window, possibly with the hullaballooing babe in arms – for truly, it was the only clean-cut solution she could think of – the racket of baby yowling was suddenly replaced by the alien sound of gurgling.

Cynthia ran to the nursery and stared down into the crib to find Madison contentedly playing with her toes.

She stared and stared in astonishment, wondering what manner of miracle had occurred. Then she realized that Mitchell, who had taken it upon himself to do some DIY to make up for all the time he had been away, had just moved the crib from the wall by the door to beneath the window so that he could paint some scuffed skirting.

He straightened up with the paintbrush in his hand, scratching his head.

'You don't suppose,' he said, 'she prefers being by the window? Maybe she was trying to tell us she wanted us to move her bedroom round.'

'Nonsense, Mitchell, a baby doesn't have opinions about interior design. How ridiculous. If they did, some expert would have written a book about it by now.'

But inside she knew full well she was kidding no one, including herself. Clearly there was a book about babies who argued about where they wanted their crib and she just hadn't heard of it. Tomorrow she would ask Shirley.

'Don't be an imbecile, Cynthia. You really do test my patience sometimes. Of course there isn't a book . . .'

In truth, everything tested Shirley's patience, particularly her husband Ralph not parking the Austin Princess correctly: 'right beneath the car port, not protruding out of it – that's the way to get rust on the bumper'.

When Madison was one, Cynthia and Shirley took her on her first foreign holiday, to the then killingly fashionable Mediterranean resort of Benidorm (seriously, it was fashionable).

They asked Mitchell if he would like to come. But their tone, being more one of sorrow than of genuine invitation, imparted adequately enough to him that what was really wanted was his 50 per cent family discount on flights and not his actual presence.

He had thought he hadn't wanted to be wanted, but when it was made clear to him that he wasn't wanted, he wasn't all that sure that he didn't want to be wanted, after all.

To cheer himself up, Mitchell had an affair with an air stewardess called Cheryl, in room 303 of the Djibouti Palace after the pair staffed a flight to Ambouli International Airport.

That was Mitchell's one and only foray into the world of spontaneity and he was happy not to repeat it. Cheryl, who was beautiful but mad, demanded he leave his wife and marry her, and even threatened to take pills. Or more pills than she usually took, in any case.

Meanwhile, Cynthia and Shirley got liberally drunk in Benidorm, and at one point almost got Madison drunk because, as usual, she wouldn't stop crying.

'I mean it, our Cynth,' said Shirley. 'I used to put whiskey in the bottles all the time when I was doing my rounds. There's no harm in it.'

Cynthia looked doubtfully at Madison, who was roaring from the bottom of her lungs about something she found deeply unsatisfactory and getting herself into a sweat which would have been life threatening even if the air conditioning had worked.

'Well, maybe just a touch of something . . .' said Cynthia, resplendent in a long pink kaftan, casting her eyes about the hotel room for the half-empty bottle of sangria she had brought back from lunch.

And then she said it. Madison said her first word. Well, not so much said as yelled.

She opened up her little pink mouth, as her mother ransacked the room looking for the sangria bottle, and shouted: 'No!'

'Bloody hell, Cynth,' said Shirley in a panic. 'You'd better not give her a drink if she doesn't want it. There'll be hell to pay.'

'Her first word!' exclaimed Cynthia, and then simpered up to the bed where Madison was holding court. 'Nooo, nooo, we won't give the baby girl boozy wooze if she doesn't want it. Does the baby girl want milky?'

'No!' shouted Madison. Then she yelled even louder: 'NO!'

'Oh dear, Cynth,' said Shirley, looking squeamish as she peered. 'I do hope that's not going to be the only word she says.'

'Say "mama",' said Cynthia imploringly. 'Ma-ma!'

Madison looked inquisitively at Cynthia's mouth making the M shape and then gurgled ecstatically as she declared: 'NO-NO!'

Madison was delighted with her new word. She said it at dinner fifty-seven times that evening, to offers of pretty much everything from the waiter, and she said it 399 times by the pool the next day.

She said it when people bent down and said, 'What a sweet baby!' She said it when people knelt by her pram and said, 'What a beautiful little girl!' And she yelled it at the top of her voice when a lady in a huge sunhat who was showing off to her rich boyfriend stooped down and said, 'Babies just love me, Frank – you watch, now: what have we here, sweetie-pie? Can I pick you up and give you a nice cuddle? . . . well, how rude!'

She said it when Cynthia was dressing her in a crisp white smocked dress for dinner and she said it when she tried a pair of candy-striped romper pants instead.

She said it and said it and said it and said it until the proud resort of Benidorm concluded that it had never suffered so much rejection from one person in the space of two weeks, and hoped it never would again.

But the proud resort of Benidorm had got off lightly, considering what happened next.

On the plane journey home, Madison hit upon the idea of saying no repeatedly at speed, without any sign of stopping ever.

'No no no no no no no no no no no no no no no no no no no no no no no no no no no no,' she said, as the plane crossed southern Europe.

'No no no no no no no no no no no no no no no no no no no no no no no no no no no no,' she said, as the plane flew north over France.

'No no no no no no . . .'

If you listened hard you could almost hear the squeak of the chair of the future Madison as she leapt to her feet in a packed courtroom, stamping her right stiletto so hard on the floor that it sent shudders back through the decades.

The future Madison, in dark suit and severe, tortoise-shell-rimmed spectacles, was taking shape, you see, as the baby Madison was screaming on that plane.

Cynthia and Shirley sat in their seats with rictus grins

as a hundred holidaymakers tutted, ordered them to 'do something about that brat', complained to stewardesses and finally booed in unison.

As the plane landed, the passengers burst into cheers and clapped, as if Madison's tantrum had been an ordeal on a par with a hijack.

'Really,' said Cynthia, smoothing her long, rainbow-coloured dress as they collected their bags at the carousel, 'you would think they would lay on more amusements for children on those flights.'

'It's a bloody disgrace, is what it is,' said Shirley, trying to avoid the eyes of accusing passengers and reaching into her bag to sneak her third Valium in an hour. (Valium was incredibly popular in the seventies. No fashionable handbag was without it.)

Mitchell was there to meet them at the airport in one of the airline's big silver chauffeur-driven executive limousines.

'How was the trip?' said Mitchell, smiling. He looked genuinely pleased to see them. He even tried to kiss Cynthia, although she pushed him away.

'Don't be silly, Mitchell, thank you. The trip was fine.'

'You're looking tanned,' said Mitchell, though in truth they were looking like all British female holidaymakers circa 1975 – in the era before SPF was invented, and when the sun oil Bergasol was used primarily as a basting lubricant – which is to say, like lobsters wearing lipstick.

'And how is Daddy's princess?' Mitchell, to his credit, was always genuinely pleased to see his daughter, unlike some fathers in 1975 who couldn't distinguish one end of their child from the other. 'Have you enjoyed your holiday?'

'Don't start her off, Mitchell,' said Cynthia. 'It's been no this and no that. She doesn't like anything, do you?'

But Madison shook her big blonde sun-bleached curls in a vigorous nod and said: 'Yes!'

4

It is a truth universally accepted that you cannot get into a packet of scissors until you have a pair of scissors.

Whatever force is at work here is the same one ensuring that money makes money, and nothing succeeds like success.

That force was also at play where Cynthia Flight's quest for love was concerned. As a young girl, Cynthia had wanted someone to love her. But she soon realized that in order to get someone to love her, she would need to be the sort of sunny, loveable individual that people fell in love with. And she wasn't. So she couldn't. And around it went.

Mitchell Flight was the only man who didn't seem to mind the fact that she was in a bind in this respect. He seemed to be completely impervious to all her moods. This was because he was an impervious kind of guy.

As such, he was very good in a crisis. If a warning light went on mid-air over the Atlantic, he barely blinked. And it was the same if Cynthia started screeching about not being able to get into a packet of scissors.

Despite his immense capacity for tolerance, however, he wasn't what you would call one of life's natural-born bon-viveurs.

He did love Cynthia in his quiet, calm, unflappable way, but he was so quiet and unflappable about it that it was impossible for anyone, including her, to tell.

She married him anyway because a) he didn't mind that she was not a happy person, b) he was in a secure job with a big salary, and had a huge inheritance to come, what with all the dodgy pork pies being churned out at Mitchell's Meats – Food You Can Trust! and c) she figured that the way she would make everything all right was by having *a* baby.

In any case, she got all the romance she required from novels by a popular author of the time called Genevieve Sanderson, who wrote sweeping number-one bestsellers about working-class heroines who went from rags to riches.

Whenever she could, Cynthia had her nose in a book with a flowery cover depicting a pretty girl in tattered clothing who was about to meet a rich, powerful, Heathcliffian man – depicted in a billowing shirt standing proprietorially in front of a country estate, sometimes alongside a gleaming black horse – who would whisk her away from her dull, difficult life to a world of prosperity and everlasting domestic fulfilment.

'Cynthia Marie Rose, do you take Mitchell Walter Gerald to be your lawfully wedded husband?'

As we contemplate the solemn moment in a small church on a rainy Thursday when Cynthia and Mitchell Flight had become man and wife, after someone dragged Mitchell out of the shed where he had been hiding, plied him with more whiskey and then bundled him into a car, it may be a good time to pause and reflect on why the happy couple had such silly names.

Young couples in the 1970s had silly names because they had been given them when their parents were celebrating the end of a world war that they thought they would never survive. Also, following this war, they had just started getting access to things like butter and bananas.

The celebratory mood was all too much for them, and the butter and the bananas combined to form a potent cocktail forcing the release of larger than usual amounts of endorphins from their brains, making them go a bit over the top.

It was not unusual at this time to come across children with three Christian names, all of them preposterous.

Cynthia was Cynthia Marie Rose – 'like the cocktail sauce,' Cynthia would say, whenever she tried to explain it.

Cynthia's best friend and next-door neighbour Shirley was Shirley Norma Barbara.

And it was just a totally random coincidence that Cynthia Marie Rose and Shirley Norma Barbara had a friend called Rosemary Norma Cynthia. Honestly, it was a coincidence. No one planned anything in the 1970s. The decade was a complete hotchpotch.

In addition, Cynthia's mother Peggy was called Peggy Marcia Shirley.

And Peggy had a friend called Wendy Cynthia Rose.

What are the chances of all that? A million to one. But million-to-one things were fashionable in the 1970s.

Also fashionable was the practice of doubling or even trebling the fanciness of one's own name where naming one's daughters was concerned. Hence Peggy produced Cynthia who gave birth to Madison. We can only presume, therefore, that if Madison brought a daughter into the world, and if the trend continued exponentially, the little mite would be called Savannah.

As for the men, well, Mitchell Walter Gerald's father Mitchell Senior's full name was Mitchell Leonard Bernard Bartholomew Flight.

I can't furnish you with too many other male names in Mitchell's circle because it was impossible to say who Mitchell's friends were. We do know he was quite matey with one of his co-pilots, and he was called Terence Jeremy Kenneth Price.

But Terry Jerry Kenny very wisely told people to call him Jim. (Another popular practice in the seventies was to ignore all of one's names and pick another one which was entirely different, claiming that it was a short form.)

And then there was Ralph, Shirley's husband, who Shirley told off every day without fail at 6.35 p.m. when he returned from his office at the General Electrical Company because he always parked the Princess in slightly the wrong place, igniting Shirley's fears about the integrity of the Sand Glow exterior paintwork and the Walnut vinyl roof.

Ralph didn't have any middle names. Ralph was just Ralph Perkins. His parents can't have had that much fun, or eaten too many bananas.

5

The advert had said: 'Princess: Not The Car For Mr Average.'

But this was clearly a trades' descriptions violation because there was no one more average than Ralph Perkins.

There had either been an oversight when the car was sold to him, or Austin Motors were lying in their promotional literature.

If the Princess was Not The Car For Mr Average, then someone had to explain why Ralph Perkins had got hold of one and was suiting it so absolutely.

Shirley tried to believe the posters. And she liked the Princess well enough until Cynthia Flight got a Ford Cortina.

At this crucial juncture, the Princess was put under more pressure than it was ever realistically going to cope with. It had never been destined to set the world on fire. But in Shirley's estimation, the very least that could be expected of it was that it should be kept clean and rust-free by being parked under the car port. But it wasn't. Again. It was protruding a full five inches from beneath the plastic, see-through awning.

'Ralph! Move that bloody car!'

She called and called but Ralph didn't answer. So she grabbed the keys and went outside to move it herself, knowing full well how this would annoy him, because she couldn't drive and always ran into things when she tried. But she didn't get far before she stopped dead in her tracks.

There were two feet protruding from beneath the Princess.

Inside the house next door, Cynthia and Madison didn't hear the screams because they were watching Larry Grayson's *Generation Game*. They were laughing so hard at a contestant failing to memorize twenty-six items on a conveyor belt, including a cuddly toy, that they didn't hear a thing until Shirley threw herself screaming at their front door and hammered on it with her bare fists.

She pressed the bell for good measure. 'Ding-dong ding-dong, ding-dong ding-dong' it went, as it played its cheerful little cover version of the chimes of Big Ben.

The bell had been Madison's idea. Cynthia had wanted a simple chime, a more classical ding-dong, if you will.

At this time, the tuneful electronic bell was the latest must-have accessory, shortly to be followed by the Teasmade with its groundbreakingly metallic-tasting tea, and the travel iron – never knowingly used by anyone. Until the tuneful electronic bell, people had been alerting each other to their presence at doors by means of a crude buzzer, or even knocking the knocker above the letter box, like barbarians. Now, thank heavens, technology had advanced mankind out of the swamp into the civilized uplands of a piece of classical music connected to the electricity.

The problem was, what sort of tune did one have? The options were endless. Which was why the Flight family ended up having a ding-dong about the ding-dong.

As usual, Mitchell was caught in the middle, unable to decide whether it was more painful to side with his wife against his daughter, or his daughter against his wife. Either way, there would be ructions. As he always did when he was back for a few days between jobs, he started to regret ever trying to live with his family, even if it was only on a part-time basis.

'Why can't we have a long tune?' said Madison, appealing directly to Mitchell.

'Why can't we have a long tune?' said Mitchell, looking pathetically at Cynthia.

'Charmaine Finkelstein's front doorbell plays Toccata and Fugue,' said Madison, folding her arms as if to emphasize that that ought to settle it.

And indeed it did, because Cynthia said: 'Just fit us a bloody bell, Mitchell, and have done with it. I don't care what length of tune it plays.'

It was not unusual for Madison to drive her parents to the point where they just gave up and let her have her way.

She had very set ideas about everything. Once she had a concept in her head it was very difficult to shift it.

She was mechanically minded, like her father, and if she

couldn't get what she wanted, she made it. She patented her first invention when she was five years old, hitting upon the idea of making things to solve problems that could not be put right with existing appliances after a series of early frustrations.

The world's first pet-tracking device, for example, was invented after her Norfolk terrier Scruffles went missing for three days, only to be found residing with a family of gypsies on a traveller site. As Scruffles seemed to be very happy in his new home and even cried when they took him away, Madison resolved to make sure this treachery was not repeated.

Her early precursor to the GPS petfinding device, provisionally entitled Waggy Tails! ©, a sardonic title considering the sorry look on Scruffles's face when they dragged him home, was one half of a battery-operated children's walkie-talkie set strapped to poor Scruffles's neck. It was a cumbersome gadget and way ahead of its time. But it worked, mainly by slowing the dog down so much that he never strayed very far while wearing it.

Also aged five, and after deciding she no longer wished her Wellingtons to become muddied, she invented Wellybags ©. These were plastic bags shaped like feet and lower legs with elasticated tops that formed a protective covering over boots.

As the copyright signs suggest, Madison registered her various inventions with the patent office. She did this by making her parents drive her down to the bank and lift her up to the counter so she could hand the teller a piece of paper with the details of the invention written on it to put in the safe.

Madison was not just precocious in a practical sense. She was also spiritually conceited from an early age. Aged six, she informed her parents she did not agree with death, as presently construed, nor with the concept of heaven, nor indeed with any of the arrangements for the afterlife, as they currently stood. In fact, she disagreed comprehensively with pretty much everything laid down by the Lord God Almighty and his emissaries on earth. She became very argumentative during church services.

The priest would raise the chalice in the air and say: 'When supper was ended he took the cup . . .'

And a little voice would whisper, too loudly: 'They should have drunk that with the meal!'

Arguing with Scruffles was all very well, but arguing with God was too much.

In the end, Cynthia, a very superstitious Catholic, had to take her to see the priest.

Father Matthew was supremely confident that he could talk a six-year-old child out of her spiritual difficulties. But midway through their little talk, in the robing room at the back of St Ignatius, he began to have doubts.

'So you see, Father, if we really are going to live forever and ever, it won't be much fun,' explained Madison. 'Far better if God put some sort of time limit on it. Think about it, Father, forever, and ever, and ever, and ever . . .'

'Yes, well,' Father Matthew said, laughing, 'I don't think we need to think about the exact details too much.'

'Oh, but we do, Father! It's terrifying to think that you and I are going to be sitting around in heaven talking like this for all eternity. Why, isn't it bad enough now, sitting here in this horrible, boring little church? But forever, and ever, and ever, and ever . . .'

Father Matthew felt a tightness in his throat and chest. He pulled at his dog collar to loosen it.

'All these things will be revealed to us in the afterlife,' he said, twitching. He felt like he was suffocating. 'We don't need to know the answers just yet.'

'Nonsense. It's going to be too late when we get to the afterlife. We're going to be stuck in all eternity then. Wouldn't you rather give it some thought now, and then if you don't fancy living forever you can commit some mortal sins and get yourself out of it?'

'I hadn't thought of it quite like that,' said Father Matthew, as he began thinking of it precisely like that and finding the thinking of it precisely like that a very sobering, and at the same time strangely invigorating experience indeed.

Father Matthew had long fancied the idea of committing some mortal sins, but he had managed to put this aside in the interests of enjoying heaven in the hereafter. Now that he had been forced to think about heaven in a negative light, it didn't seem at all sensible to continue denying himself.

After Madison left, he got to work that very night, opening himself a bottle of whiskey and settling down in a comfy chair to read William Blake's *The Marriage of Heaven and Hell.* Of course, it's obvious now I think about it. I am one of those super-humans Blake talks about who doesn't need to worry about morals. Morals are for weaklings, he thought.

Sunday services were never the same after that, because he started to tell his congregation that nothing enjoyable was wrong in the eyes of God, and that it would, in fact, be a sin against nature if they did not get out and start grabbing life by the throat before they were too old to get a bit of it. It was advice that most of them gratefully and speedily took, I am sorry to say.

And so Madison had an incredible impact on the world for a child of her age.

In one afternoon she triggered the metamorphosis of the character of an entire community, plunging large segments of it into a moral chaos from which it never really recovered.

Following her intervention, Father Matthew's congregation would do all sorts of things to each other that they really ought not to have. The swinging parties in Little Fougham are, to this day, quite legendary.

And Madison was little more conducive to public order than she was to public morals. The day she decided to tell the other children at St Ignatius Roman Catholic School for Girls about the way pork pies were made is a particular case in point, although we must draw a veil over that incident, for now, for taste and hygiene reasons.

6

People often say that some children are born difficult. And Madison certainly was in that category.

She inherited her mother's cynical genes, for a start.

But then there was the matter of her growing up in the town of Little Fougham, a truly godforsaken rural idyll where a child born difficult might be well and truly hot-housed into a state of pure belligerence. London was too far one way, and Birmingham was too far the other, to be of any use to the poor, marooned inhabitants of this picture-postcard corner of the Cotswolds.

Worse, in one ten-mile radius of un-prime commuter belt featuring nothing of any note to save people from boredom or unemployment, there were four small towns with the word Fougham in the title. There was Little Fougham, and there was Great Fougham and there was Market Fougham and there was Fougham-on-the-Water, for good measure. To make matters worse, people often just said Fougham when they were talking about any of them.

All the Foughams eked out a living as minor irrele-vancies, except Market Fougham, which was a major irrelevancy as it was bigger than all the other Foughams but no longer had a market, on account of an Asda opening up five miles down the road.

Great Fougham had Great Fougham Equestrian Centre (GFEC) and a 100-seat theatre named after Harold Pinter, for no good reason.

Little Fougham had a heritage motor museum and a crafts centre with cream tea facilities and coach parking attached, and this, even if it did not attract tourists, made the residents of Little Fougham feel just that bit special. Fougham-on-the-Water had a small stream.

But the deepest problem all the Foughams had was an endless debate about how one should pronounce the word Fougham. Posh Tory-voting sorts said it was pronounced Foam, while left-wing people opted for Form. The consensus among Liberal voters, such as they existed, was Fowum. Total weirdos called it Foom. But there were also dark murmurings from some very intellectually adventurous residents who had done research, and they claimed the authentic way to say the name, as it had been said in the Middle Ages, was something involving a 'ck' in the middle.

This was, obviously, the very last thing the people of the Foughams needed to hear. Madison's parents came to an accommodation with their consciences and decided early on to call it Fokkam – telling themselves it was a bit like Fokker, the plane.

But by and large people tried to ignore the whole sorry business.

They concentrated on keeping their houses well maintained and as a result it was a very neat part of the country indeed, consisting of roads with perfectly square grass verges giving way to driveways leading to moderately sized brick houses, a lot of them bungalows. They were called things like Trelawney and Sandy Banks and Belmont and Little Foxes. One was called Lusty Glaze, causing the onlooker to ponder all sorts of horrible possibilities as to what might be lusty about it. Another was called Chimera. Possibly this was meant to invoke the mythical fire-breathing monster which was part lion, part snake, part goat, because the house featured a series of hideous extensions to the back and sides.

Some of the homes had car ports; some had little ornamental wells in the front garden, some with small figurines wielding fishing rods sitting on the walls of the wells, fishing for nothing in particular.

Madison's house did not have a well with a figurine with a fishing rod because Cynthia thought them vulgar. Madison had been distraught about this. She saw no good reason why she shouldn't be allowed to keep carp in a pond like her best friend Charmaine did. As such, she carped about the carp issue on and off for several years until Cynthia agreed to a pond with some goldfish in it.

But carp or no carp, none of the residents of Little Fougham were happy, not even the garden gnomes, who had anguished expressions on their rosy faces.

Perhaps it simply was not fashionable to be happy in the 1970s. Who knows?

But certainly her mother was not happy. Her mother's best friend and next-door neighbour Shirley was not happy. And neither was Shirley's husband, Ralph Perkins. In fact, whilst remaining consistently uncomplaining throughout his life, Ralph Perkins was the unhappiest of them all.

Which was why he made an extraordinary bid for freedom.

7

Ralph Perkins had been in an advanced state of extreme unhappiness for as long as he could remember. His was not just the usual, run-of-the-mill unhappiness, the low-level dissatisfaction felt by all residents of houses with strange names and windmills in the front garden. His was the deep, brooding, turbulent misery of the truly repressed. The sort of misery felt by those who are not only unhappy, but who pretend not to be unhappy, in order to try to make those around them more happy, which is the surest route to despair on an epic scale.

Commuting to Birmingham every day for more years than he cared to remember had taken its toll, but it was also the one thing that almost preserved his sanity because it kept him away from Shirley.

When he was called in to the managing director's office and told about the cutbacks he took it harder than most.

Liberated from the 100-mile round journey he might have gone home and put his feet up, but in fact he continued to get up at 6 a.m. to make the commute, parking in the same space in the car park of his former workplace, getting out and walking to the nearest pub where he sat in a corner and drowned his sorrows with pale ale – which wasn't even stored at the right temperature and had gone off, he always noted – before driving home again with a blood-alcohol level fifteen times the legal limit.

Shirley didn't notice anything amiss, except that his domestic habits got more slapdash and his car-port negotiation was sloppier than ever. This she put down to age, and the fact that he was probably going senile, as she assumed he surely must do one day, condemning her to a life of even greater penury.

Ralph waited patiently until things had gone beyond unbearable – two drink-driving charges and a pending prison sentence for something that happened when he stopped off near some woodland one evening, which would be impossible to explain to Shirley without coming clean about all of it – before he connected a hosepipe from the exhaust and fed it inside the car where he sat at the wheel with the engine running.

But the car port being an open-ended affair, enough of the fumes escaped and he merely fell unconscious.

He also fell out of the car because he hadn't shut the door properly, on account of the hose being fed through the hinge, and ended up lying slumped by the side of the Princess with his feet poking out from the side so that it looked, at first glance, to Shirley as if he had run himself over.

This she considered a thoroughly rum way for Ralph to try to finish himself off. It had to have been quite a feat of ingenuity to start the motor, put the car into gear, let it roll forward then jump out and throw himself in front of it, and even then it would have been a very low-velocity collision. In all probability, he would simply have sustained a slipped disc.

Later, when she found out what had actually happened, she concluded that her husband's attempt to 'fumigate himself', as she called it, was even more ridiculous.

Other men threw themselves off bridges or drank themselves to death after losing their jobs, but not Ralph, oh no. He had to try to inhale carbon monoxide in an open-ended car-port.

'Typical. He even makes a holy show of himself committing suicide,' she said to Cynthia. 'Anyone might have seen him lying on the ground as they walked past. Who is this going to reflect on badly? Me, that's who.' Her humiliation was such that she pulled out of rehearsals for the Angel Lady Players' forthcoming production of *The King and I* at the Harold Pinter Memorial Theatre in Great Fougham, with the express intent of becoming a social outcast therewith.

To add insult to injury, the Princess was still sticking outside the car-port because the police ordered Shirley not to touch it until they were satisfied that Ralph had not been drugged and forcibly dragged to the car by someone – i.e. her – and made to breathe CO_2. 'As if I would be so stupid. If I wanted to do away with him I would have laced his tea with that poisonous herb that mimics natural causes.'

'You mean deadly nightshade,' said Cynthia.

'That's the one. There's loads of it at the bottom of my garden.'

The fact that Shirley envisaged deadly nightshade as a fitting method of despatch for the husband who had been faithful to her for forty years (bar one evening in a woodland car park) says much about her. But it also says quite a bit about Ralph, because you really have to push the boat out some to make your spouse so fed up with you that they end up wanting to poison you.

Ralph's problem was that he was too laid back. He was so laid back he was horizontal, Shirley said. She was the one who wore the trousers – reluctantly, she would have you believe. She had to nag her husband to do anything. It was like pulling teeth just to get him to decide what he wanted for breakfast in the morning.

In truth, it was impossible to say what came first, the nagging or the need to nag.

Ralph was too tired to do anything because of all the nagging Shirley subjected him to so she had to nag him to get him to do anything.

And he never listened to her because she was always nagging, which made her nag him even more, which made him even more tired and unable to do anything. He couldn't make a decision because Shirley made all the decisions for him. In any case, he had either lost or never had the ability to make decisions, so Shirley had to make them.

Thus were they destined to perpetuate each other's worst habits ad infinitum, or until one of them finished off the other, whichever was sooner.

Ralph often looked as though he might strangle Shirley as she was mid-sentence, ordering him to do something or arguing about how he ought to be deciding what she was deciding. But if you had to put money on which of them would murder the other in cold blood first, you would back Shirley all the way, if only because Ralph had very little initiative left to do anything of his own volition, let alone kill Shirley. If he had attempted it, he would probably have asked for her permission first, and her opinion on the best way to accomplish it.

As it was, he simply sat and brooded on his plight, which made him all the more despondent. Things had definitely got worse lately, he reflected, when Shirley began taking an experimental treatment for the change of life, called H-R-something or other, which had made her even more aggressive than normal. 'This drug is going to change the world,' he heard her telling Cynthia over the garden fence one day, as she persuaded her to give it a try too. 'Honestly, Cynth, it's made me feel like a new woman.' Ralph had often wished she were a new woman, but not this sort. Not the sort that was so emboldened she felt she could do without him altogether.

One day, when Ralph went off to his pretend job, Shirley looked up the symptoms of deadly nightshade poisoning in a book called *Gardener's Companion*.

If there had been a magazine article in *Woman and Home* entitled 'Exciting new recipes with which to poison your husband this spring!' she would have read that too.

As it was, she settled down at the pale blue Formica

kitchen table with a cup of tea and a saucer of Nice biscuits. She nibbled one as she read:

'Dilated pupils, hallucinations, blurred vision, loss of balance, staggering, a sense of suffocation, paleness followed by red rash, flushing, husky voice, extreme dry throat, constipation, urinary retention, confusion, and death . . .' She read the list out to herself as she sat alone in the kitchen. Shirley often talked to herself, even when Ralph was in the house. She said it was the only way she could guarantee a decent conversation.

'Don't knock talking to yourself,' she said, paraphrasing Woody Allen in *Annie Hall*. 'It's conversation with someone you love.'

She often chatted to herself as she washed pots, or watered plants. She particularly enjoyed talking things over with herself as she sat in the kitchen, drinking her mid-morning tea.

'What bothers me most about that list of symptoms,' she said, as she perused the chapter on poisonous plants, her reading glasses perched diligently on her nose, 'is the constipation.

'The idea that you should be dying in agony and not even be able to go to the loo is a step too far. Also, I don't see how a husky voice helps the process either way. If I were trying to kill someone off, I wouldn't bother making their voice husky, it doesn't seem worth the candle. And if you ask me, the urinary retention is also surplus to requirements. I wonder, does it happen in that order?'

She took another sip of tea and removed her glasses.

'Wild eyes, visions, falling over, struggling for breath, then you call out for help and you're pleasantly surprised because your voice sounds like Joanna Lumley's. Excited by this discovery you suddenly feel as if you need to go to the loo, only to realize that you can't go, which is obviously very confusing – "Why can't I go to the loo?" you wonder. "Or can I? Maybe I've just been. Oh dear, I can't remember." Then you keel over and die on the floor of the toilet.

'Am I reading this right? Is that death by deadly nightshade? Because if it is, then barring the constipation, it ought to do all right for Ralph. I don't want him to suffer too much. He has always been faithful to me, after all. And he's always been very good about unblocking the drains . . .'

But in truth Shirley would never have poisoned her husband, she just liked to fantasize about it in an escapist way, the way you would dream about going to Disneyland or winning the football pools and going to live in Marbella.

In reality, she was more bonded to the misery of living with the most boring man she knew than she knew. After he filled himself full of exhaust fumes, she felt a strange disquiet at the lack of him.

8

For Madison, listening intently from the top of the stairs as her mother comforted Shirley on the evening of Ralph's little accident, it was the first time death, or something very much like it, had come into her world.

The ambulance had been called and a dreaded hush had descended. Days later the whole horrible truth became clear in whispered conversations heard from her post on the top stair.

Ralph wasn't dead, but detained in a psychiatric hospital, where, according to Cynthia, he sat in a chair staring at the window all day – not out of the window, at the window – and might as well have been dead. For Madison, the fact that Ralph had survived did not mitigate the suicide attempt but rather made it worse. She thought it was simply outrageous that a man should live and as good as die, having enjoyed so little of what life ought to have had to offer.

She listened from the top of the stairs as Shirley talked intemperately about finishing the job. And she listened as her mother said, 'Don't be stupid, Shirl. You'll end up in the clink.' And then she ran down the stairs and started bawling her eyes out at the horror of it all.

They told Madison to stop making a fuss. Ralph had made his own bed and he would have to lie in it. Besides, the police had let him off the drink-driving charge, so it wasn't all bad. But Madison wouldn't give up. She couldn't accept that Ralph was to be confined to an insane asylum and her indignation was not relieved by Shirley's insistence that 'The Pines is most definitely not an insane asylum. It's a private rest home with bespoke twenty-four-hour nursing and state-of-the-art occupational rehabilitation therapy'.

Madison formulated her plan to take matters into her own hands as she lay in her bed one night under her Bambi quilt.

She had suddenly remembered an incident from her childhood . . . she couldn't have been more than three or four . . . the rabbit in the pet shop . . . walking past the window . . . her mother taking her inside and how the shop scared her with all those little animals looking out at her from their prisons . . . bringing the rabbit home, feeling bad she could only rescue one . . . setting it free . . . catching glimpses of it every few days running around the garden . . . finding it again after the fox had killed it . . . and feeling not guilt, but great relief and satisfaction that it hadn't suffered by being kept in a box . . .

Madison couldn't think of anything worse than the misery of being kept in a box. She was glad the rabbit was dead. She was glad she hadn't even given it a name. She didn't want it to suffer just so she could look at it.

She didn't want the poor rabbit to be lonely and miserable for years in the name of making her happy. And neither did she want any human being to be either.

All she wanted was to relieve people in perpetual torment of their suffering and despair. That was her vocation, she decided.

From around that time onwards, whenever questions surrounding her future were asked, Madison was ready with an answer.

'What do you want to be when you grow up?' was not a question that usually elicited very exciting responses from children in the 1970s because the options were pretty limited back then.

When the other girls in her class at school were asked, they said 'ballerina' or 'nurse', or declared their intention to marry a prince and have his babies.

But Madison would say: 'I want to be a solicitor.'

'Don't be silly, Maddie,' said her mother. 'Tell Mrs Finkelstein what you really want to do.' And Cynthia turned to the neighbour having tea in her living room and said: 'She's going to train as a make-up artist, Rita. To work on film sets.'

'How lovely!' said Rita Finkelstein. 'And do you practise putting make-up on Mummy?'

'No I don't! I hate make-up! I want to be a solicitor and help people get divorced. I've read all about it at the library. I'll do you a divorce if you like. Or do you want to spend your entire life pretending to be happy while Mr Finkelstein cheats on you with that secretary of his?'

Mrs Finkelstein gasped and put her hand to her chest.

'Madison!' Cynthia blushed purple and gave her the 'wait till I get you on your own' look.

'I'm only trying to help.'

And to Cynthia's surprise, Mrs Finkelstein put down her teacup, wiped her eyes and said: 'You're right, of course, dear. I ought to do something about it. But I was rather hoping he might pop off soon and leave me all his money.'

It was not a fad. Madison was deadly serious. Divorce inspired her. She wanted to get people free of each other. She decided it was the noblest of callings.

And she was shaping up to be one hell of an advocate. She felt the desperate urge to prove she was right at all times and that made her almost impossible to challenge.

Madison was incredulous when the head teacher at St Ignatius asked her: 'Do you want to be right, or do you want to be happy?'

'I want to be right, of course,' said Madison, thinking the woman was clearly stupid. She had been rowing all morning with another child over the matter of three Love Heart sweets, which had been swapped for a candy stick but the candy stick had not materialized. And now she had been called to the headmistress's office because a fight had ensued in which the offender's candy stick had been forcibly removed and confiscated, and the offender's pigtails summarily pulled.

'Young lady, it is not up to you to settle injustices. You

must leave these things to the good Lord upstairs. Those who steal will get their comeuppance in the afterlife,' said Sister Mary Aquinas.

'The afterlife is ages away,' said Madison. 'This needs sorting right now.'

'Well then,' said the nun, 'I feel it is only fair to point out to you that if you continue taking matters that are none of your business into your own hands, fighting with everyone and everything to prove every conceivable point that has ever entered your head, then you are not going to have a very happy time of it.'

'Sister, there is nothing further to discuss,' said Madison, with a pomposity belying her seven years, 'because, if you ask me, happiness is overrated.'

She had heard her mother say this, of course, but the fact that she saw it as ripe for repetition gives us some insight into her state of mind as she stood, all three foot five of her, in front of the fearsome Sister Aquinas. Instead of cowering before her, as all children naturally did, she stood bolt upright with her hands on her hips and her jaw jutting determinedly.

And she carried on in this defiant vein no matter how much those in authority tried to dissuade her.

As all the other children chanted their times tables, Madison sat in her little chair with a scowl on her face, refusing to chant anything and thinking, 'Are two twos four? How do we know they are?'

Her belligerence extended to absolutely everything, including things she ought to have been pleased about.

If someone told Madison they liked her dress, for example, she would throw herself in the nearest puddle and roll around until it was black. If you told her you didn't like her dress she would wear it for weeks on end, and insist on sleeping in it.

Madison would submit to neither compliment nor criticism, but she detested the former far more, by a long chalk.

'What is the matter with you?' her mother would say.

'Why are you so darn difficult?' her father would say.

'Why won't you play with the other children?'

'Why aren't you like the other children?'

These were all questions that were routinely asked of Madison but the answers were never particularly forthcoming. In the end, those who knew her best simply concluded that she was that most elusively infuriating of things, A Difficult Child.

She was difficult about everything.

But she was particularly difficult in her attitude to the truth. She absolutely refused not to tell it, even when not telling it was the right thing to do. And so I can hold off no longer. I must tell you about how she came to cause a riot in Little Fougham.

It all began when, as a project for English class one summer term, the children at St Ignatius were told to prepare a talk.

It was to be on a subject they knew something about – a hobby or interest, for example. Cynthia naturally assumed that Madison would want to do hers on ballet, or ponies, or one of the many other nice hobbies in which she had been enjoying expensive instruction.

However, Madison had other ideas. She began asking her father for information about her grandfather's pork pie factory and insisted on him taking her there so she could have a good look round. You see, just as some of her contemporaries had become curious about the facts of life, Madison had become curious about the facts of mechanical meat extraction. She was, to all intents and purposes, becoming pie-curious.

Mitchell was at first delighted that his daughter was showing an interest in the family business and one day, after a particularly tedious three-night stopover in Bogotá, he came to collect her and take her on an outing.

Madison was dressed as she was always dressed by Cynthia for outings, in her best red polka-dot dress and matching red coat with red velvet collar, pristine white ankle socks and black shiny patent-leather shoes. A very jolly afternoon was had by all at Mitchell's Meats – Food You Can Trust! Mitchell and Madison did some long over-due father–daughter bonding and all the staff thoroughly enjoyed having a little one about the place.

'Isn't she just an absolute poppet!' said Mrs Overstrand, Mitchell Senior's personal assistant.

'Is she?' said Mitchell, who thought this doubtful. She was up to something.

He was right, of course.

The school talks were grouped into sets of two, with each child instructed to speak for about ten minutes.

When it was time for Madison's talk, she followed a girl called Emily, who spoke movingly without notes on the subject of 'My bunny rabbit Tinker'.

Madison, by contrast, consulted her notes copiously as she told the story of pork pie production in great detail and from the *very* beginning, taking as her starting point the moment when the unsuspecting pigs were pushed out of their pens and herded into the back of a lorry.

Standing on a chair at the front of the class she opened her lecture by asking rather sarcastically: 'Have any of you ever wondered how a piggy-wig became a porky-pie?'

The teacher thought of stopping her there but she couldn't quite get her head around what was happening until the talk had got beyond the point of no return, which is to say, the pig was well and truly out of the bag.

The scene that greeted the mothers who had to be called to the school to collect their children early that afternoon was one of complete chaos.

Dozens of infants stood screaming on the playground in front of the school as teachers knelt at the feet of those they could comfort and tried to offer kind lies to put things right, whilst those who were beyond help simply lay on their backs screaming and kicking their fat little pink legs in the air.

The hysteria was exacerbated further by Madison, who would not be silenced and stood in the midst of the children shouting that she knew lots more, including a thing or two about sausage rolls. Like a street preacher on fire with zeal she stood amid the wailing masses, relentlessly telling her truth.

The first parents to arrive on the scene begged her to desist, but the more they begged the worse she got.

'I know all about Santa Claus too!' she shouted.

'No!' screamed a mother. 'She must be stopped! Stop her, somebody! For the love of God, stop her now, before it's too late!' And several of the parents ran at her as if to throw their bodies over her, but they didn't get there in time.

'Santa Claus doesn't exist!' Madison shouted, and there was a brief, stunned cessation of wailing as the children all gasped . . . which was quickly followed by an even louder eruption. The mothers now turned and ran back to their children, putting their hands over their ears as they dragged them to their cars.

'The Easter Bunny's made up! And some people called Muslims don't believe in Jesus! Noah couldn't have got all those animals in the ark. And God didn't create the earth in six days. It's just a metaphor!'

At which point several of the parents demanded the police be called.

Unfortunately, Cynthia was out shopping with Shirley and so didn't arrive until the usual time of 3.45 p.m., with Shirley in tow, to collect her daughter. By then, the infant animal rights riot had been raging for two hours and had descended into a public order situation.

Cars dumped by parents who had rushed to the school in a panic were backed up all the way down the road, causing a bottleneck. A police officer was trying to direct traffic. The parents themselves were fighting pitched battles with the teachers, who they blamed for the unfolding atrocity and the loss of their little ones' innocence. And all the while the children wailed bitter, disillusioned tears.

Cynthia and Shirley ran through the crowd and grabbed Madison, who was at the centre of a baying mob. One took the legs and one the arms as they bundled her into the back of the Ford Cortina. Truly, no pig had ever been manhandled into a meat man's lorry so unceremoniously. 'Drive!' shouted Shirley, as the screaming mothers pounded on the windows with their fists.

9

In the aftermath of the Little Fougham pork pie riots, Mitchell began spending more and more time at home.

This was not just because of how complex the clean-up operation was, although that was bad enough. There was a tense stand-off with the headmistress of St Ignatius, which resulted in the Flights only just persuading the school not to expel Madison.

'She's a troublemaker,' said Sister Mary Aquinas, a look of thunder on her face. 'She doesn't know the meaning of obedience. Metaphor indeed!'

'I'll have you know she is a very well-brought-up child,' said Cynthia, resplendent in her best fur coat. 'She just has very good bullshit detectors. The six days thing is clearly unfeasible. I mean, He couldn't even have put Fougham together in six days.'

'Well!' gasped Sister Aquinas. Cynthia had pronounced Fougham in the lewd way.

'Cynthia, leave this to me,' said Mitchell, before persuading the indignant nun that Madison was overwrought because she was the child of a broken home on account of his being away so often. 'And, as you may be able to tell,' he said, nudging Cynthia to collude in this humiliating but urgently needed explanation, 'my wife is going through a very bad time at the moment. She suffers with her nerves.'

Cynthia squeaked.

'I see,' said Sister Aquinas, looking much relieved. She knew where she stood now. 'And might you see your way to spending more time with the poor child in future?'

'Oh yes,' said Mitchell. 'I envisage spending much more time with her, starting imminently.'

Cynthia looked askance at Mitchell, and later turned on him in the car on the way home: 'You didn't tell me you were going to be at home more often. I hope you're not thinking we're all going to play at happy families.'

But that wasn't what Mitchell thought at all. And Madison's welfare wasn't the real reason he was expecting to be at home.

A recent random blood-alcohol test performed on him and a number of other pilots at the airline was the real reason for his newfound love of domesticity.

He wasn't going to go into it any more than he absolutely had to for the purposes of explaining to his wife, who was chain-smoking in the passenger seat beside him, that she was going to have to make up the spare bed on a permanent basis from now on. Well, he couldn't very well expect her to let him climb into her bed, except on very special occasions when the mood took them, could he?

In the event, she took 'the drink-driving incident', as she called it, on the chin. Her attitude was one of long-suffering resignation, as if this was always how she had expected his career to turn out.

But she hit the roof when he told her he was going to start working at Mitchell's Meats.

'Why can't you get a job with another airline? Why on earth are you even thinking about going to work in that hideous place?' she demanded, incredulously. 'I suppose I'm to tell my friends my husband is a pork pie maker now, am I?'

'Tell them what you like. That hideous place has been good to us,' said Mitchell, reminding her of all the extra luxuries they enjoyed because of his family's wealth. The big house, the car, the gardener, the charwoman, the private school that Madison went to, the ballet and elocution and horse-riding lessons – none of it would have been possible on his pilot salary alone.

'Fine, you go your own way, Mitchell, you always do,' flounced Cynthia. 'But you had better not speak of this. As far as I'm concerned you're flying private planes now. I will not tell my friends that my husband makes pork pies.'

As Mitchell had neglected to tell her the full story, including the bit where the aviation authority had confiscated his licence, he was in no position to argue. He had told pork pies about the reason for his having to make pork pies, and as such he could not take the moral high ground.

And that was how Mitchell Flight became a pilot in a pork pie factory, and the only airline captain in history to operate a conveyor-belt pastry roller, so far as it is known.

His father wanted him to stay in the office, to work on the accounts and help formulate a new marketing strategy.

There were plans for a new logo featuring a pig in a World War Two flying jacket and airman's goggles, for some reason. Perhaps it was Mitchell Senior's silent tribute to his son, who had been forthright with him about the reason for his return. The slogan was to be changed to Mitchell's Meats – Best of British!

Creating a marketing strategy to sell pork pies using a pig dressed as a fighter pilot ought to have been enough of a challenge for anyone, even someone used to flying a 747.

But Mitchell preferred to get his hands dirty. He spent all his time on the shop floor and when he got home, and collapsed onto the sofa, Cynthia would scream the house down about the smell of raw sausage meat.

They would argue late into the evening, all variations based on this theme, and Madison would listen from the top of the stairs.

'Those bloody pork pies will be the death of me! I can't shift the smell of them from my three-piece suite!'

'Those bloody pork pies have been good to us! Those bloody pork pies will be there for us when all your fancy friends have turned their backs!'

'Rita Finkelstein cancelled lunch yesterday. She didn't say anything, she's too polite. But I know it's because she doesn't want to go home reeking of pork after she's been sitting on our soft furnishings. Our sofa isn't kosha, Mitchell. Do you know how that makes me feel? After all the years I've been friends with Rita…'

And she wept a little, to emphasise the point, but Mitchell was impervious.

'Rita Finkelstein thinks no such thing. She probably doesn't want to come round here because your sponge cake is inedible. I bet she'd love a pork pie instead. I bet she's got our full range in her larder.'

'Mitchell, how could you!'

'Well, who doesn't like a nice pork pie now and then?'

'I don't! They're cheap and nasty and I hate them!'

'They may be cheap and nasty but they make money. Come good times or bad, Cynthia, people will always want pork pies.'

'But people shouldn't want pork pies! The poor idiots who buy the rubbish you make don't know what they're eating!'

Cynthia had visited the factory, you see, shortly after Mitchell took to working there. He wanted to reassure her that it was all very high-tech and impressive, not so much a humble pie-making plant as a food empire, over which he presided as his father's heir apparent.

Together, Mitchell Senior and Mitchell Junior proudly showed off the ten lines of production, featuring women wearing little blue hats and white overalls. Each line was making a different kind of pie or pasty.

A strange, almost military-style pecking order appeared to be in place, whereby the women in blue hats were governed by one woman on each line wearing a red cap.

It reminded Cynthia of a Butlins holiday camp, which made her very bad-tempered indeed.

But it was more surreal than that, because every now and then a fat man in a white coat and a trilby would walk along the lines and bark orders at one of the red caps, who in turn would bark at the blue caps.

And humming above it all, the fruity stench of overprocessed meat. Cynthia watched the pastry being rolled and the pork being mulched in machines whilst trying her best not to visibly heave. She found every aspect of it unbearably revolting and humiliating.

But nothing compared to the horror of the gala pie processing line. Like most people who are innocent of such matters, Cynthia had never really given much thought to how the eggs got into the middle of gala pies. But now she stood staring at huge buckets of eggs – dozens, maybe hundreds in each bucket, like so many eyeballs without pupils stacked together in mound upon mound. Cynthia shuddered as she thought that someone had had to shell all those eggs. Or were there chickens somewhere specially designed to lay shell-less eggs? Hideous mutated chickens . . .

Transfixed in horror, she watched as the ladies in the blue hats reached into the buckets every few minutes to take a boiled egg and then began to roll the egg into a flat wodge of processed pork until the wodge formed a ball with the egg inside.

'I hope they've washed their hands,' she whispered, barely able to speak for shock, at Mitchell, who was beaming with pride.

'Of course they have. It's all being scientifically monitored, I can assure you.'

'To think I ate one of those damned things a few days ago. Mitchell, I had no idea . . .'

But Mitchell wasn't listening. Mitchell had left her side and was talking with one of the men in trilbies about quality control, and then he started rolling an egg into a patty of pork with his own bare hands in a part of the line where they were short staffed. He had a daft smile on his face as he did it. He obviously found it deeply therapeutic.

She marched over to him and barked that she was leaving. 'Is the car outside? I don't want to be seen standing around out there. Someone might drive past and see me.'

'You can't leave yet,' said Mitchell, looking up innocently from his egg rolling, 'you haven't seen the jellying section. We've just started using a new type of gun to squirt the jelly into the pies. It's really something to see . . .'

Cynthia came away and didn't eat meat for three months afterwards.

Imagine her horror, then, when seventeen-year-old Madison one day announced her intention to do her sixth-form work experience at the factory.

'You can't be serious,' said Cynthia.

'Why not?' Madison shrugged. 'I need to find a work placement and this is as good a place as any. Saves me writing a load of letters. Anyway, there isn't anywhere else that comes close to qualifying as a major employer for about ten miles. If you won't let me go to work with Daddy I'll have to get a placement in London and then I'll probably end up living on the streets.'

'Don't be smart, young lady. You know very well how

much this upsets me.' Cynthia had been harbouring fears that Madison would abandon her plan to become a divorce lawyer – which was bad enough in itself – and follow her father into processed pig production.

She had witnessed a strange sort of axis developing between Madison and Mitchell. It wasn't exactly affection, more like expediency. The sulky teenager and the dispirited husband were colluding in an attempt to defy her. She wouldn't put it past Madison to make a living out of pork pies just to spite her.

But Madison said going into sausage meat was most definitely not her intention and that she merely wanted to get some experience of managing a business to tick a box on her business studies coursework module.

Whether or not she achieved this was a matter of debate. But Mitchell's Meats certainly got some experience of trying to manage a Madison.

Naturally, she took issue with a few things.

It wasn't just that she didn't agree with the way the pork pies were being made; she didn't agree with the finished product either. She wanted to make a more ambitious pie. A pie fit for the twenty-first century. A fat-free pork pie.

She pressed her point of view about this so vehemently on Grandpa Mitchell that in the end the old man sighed and said they were to give Madison's scheme a chance. 'After all, we need some fresh ideas breathing new life into the place.'

The first crustless pork pie rolled off the production line a few weeks later, amid threats of industrial action from the pastry-rolling line. But the ladies in the blue hats needn't have worried. It was an immediate flop. It turned out that people who bought pork pies did not want pork pies to be anything other than extremely unhealthy.

Madison declared that she had learned a valuable lesson about human nature and went back to school.

Mitchell's Meats went back to making lardy, gelatinous mounds of pastry filled with the most questionable cuts of pig and everyone agreed that the fat-free pie experiment had been the worst episode in the company's history.

However, it would not always be so. The food safety scandal which erupted at Mitchell's Meats a few years later would make the disaster of the fat-free pie pale into insignificance, but we shall have to return to that at a later stage, when my stomach is feeling a bit stronger.

For now, peace reigned in the Flight family because Madison had had her fill of cheap meat production. Thankfully, she was as good as her word to Cynthia and as soon as she passed her final exams, she applied to law school. Cynthia, once so devastated that her daughter was eschewing make-up artistry for the law, now grudgingly embraced Madison's career choice as infinitely preferable to making pies.

10

When Madison was in her twenties, there was nearly a wedding. The residents of Little Fougham nearly got excited. But didn't. Because they knew Madison. And they knew better than to accept as a foregone conclusion that she would go through with the happy event, even when they had received their gold and white invitations announcing that:

Captain and Mrs Mitchell Flight
have great pleasure in inviting you to celebrate
the marriage of their only daughter
Madison to Simon Pugh
on Saturday, 15 March at 10.30 a.m.
At the church of St Ignatius, Little Fougham
and afterwards at The Saville Hotel and Country Club
for a champagne reception with dinner and dancing.

RSVP
Mrs Cynthia Flight, Sandybanks,
Rosewood Way, Little Fougham

Cynthia and Mitchell were nearly ecstatic. Even if they knew they couldn't relax until Madison was walking back down the aisle with the ring wedged firmly on her finger, they were nearly relieved of a burden they had thought would never be lifted – the burden of worrying that no one else in the world would ever be able to cope with their daughter.

The prospective groom – a boyfriend from university – was perfectly adequate in every single way, and especially, so far as Cynthia was concerned, in the way that he was now a management consultant. Perhaps she imagined that an aptitude for management might mean he could manage Madison. And perhaps he might have been able to, given half a chance. But Madison approached the enterprise with the same zeal to find fault that she applied to every other aspect of her life.

She argued about the wedding dress not fitting properly, and she argued about the bridesmaids' dresses being a shade too dark.

'This is not Victorian Jade T3104516, this is Vintage Jade T4679324.'

'But it's nicer!' pointed out Cynthia.

'I don't care if it's nicer. It's not the colour I ordered. There's a mistake and they need to correct it.'

She argued about the band not sending adequate demo tapes to demonstrate their capability in the country and western genre.

'This tape is Sounds of the 60s,' she told the booking agent. 'I don't want them to play Sounds of the 60s. I want them to play Country Classics, like it said on the website. And until you send me evidence that they won't tarnish the memory of Johnny Cash, I'm not paying the outstanding balance.'

She argued about the corsages containing one, not two sprigs of gypsophila – 'You're defrauding us out of twelve sprigs of gypsophila!' She argued with the venue for not getting the seating plan right – 'We always made it perfectly clear Great-Auntie Margo couldn't be put anywhere near Aunt Maureen! Are you going to pay the medical bills when they scratch each other's eyes out?' And she argued about the cars – 'Not the white Jaguar, the cream Jaguar.' 'But the white's nicer!' 'That's not the point!'

And when she had finished arguing with the individual component parts of the wedding, she argued with the wedding industry in general for making so much money out of people who were stressed and clearly not quite themselves.

She registered complaints with all the trade bodies about direct marketing techniques, and she called the Office of Fair Trading about the sharing of customer data between wedding retailers, and she sparked a government inquiry into rogue wedding planners.

And when she had finished bringing the wedding industry to its knees, she got stuck into the holy estate of matrimony itself. Unfortunately, she didn't start doing this until the moment she was standing at the altar, which was cutting it a bit fine.

'Madison Maureena Margo, do you take this man to be your lawful wedded husband?' said Father Matthew, nervously, as the pair stood in front of him beneath the gothic arches of St Ignatius.

Madison looked a bit peaky and said: 'Er, I do.'

'Will you love him, honour him and, forsaking all others, keep only to him as long as you both shall live?'

'Well, erm, the thing is . . . Oh, fine, go on then.'

'Repeat after me: "For better for worse, for richer for poorer, in sickness and in health, till death do us part."'

And there was a horrible silence, until Madison said:

'When you say worse . . . Worse than what? I mean, it depends on your definition . . . Hang on. I need to think. I'm not sure I agree that the whole concept of worse should be included in this.'

And the ceremony ground to a halt. There was an almighty groan from the congregation, for all the guests who knew Madison even slightly had known all along that it would probably come to this. Father Matthew cursed and declared that he had missed the 3.30 at Epsom. He had fifty quid on.

The fiancé stormed back up the aisle and the guests went to the hotel and ate the food anyway and Madison's parents declared it the worst day of their lives. 'How could you do this to us?' said Cynthia, as Madison changed out of her wedding dress, threw the offending garment down on her mother's bed and stood with her hands on her hips in her white wedding underwear, complete with a some-thing-blue garter around the top of her left leg.

'I'm sorry, I just can't.'

'But why on earth did you wait until we were all there?'

'Because I didn't know until I got there.'

'Could you not just have pretended you wanted to get married to Simon and divorced him later like a normal person? Rita Finkelstein's daughter's been divorced three times now and no one in Fougham thinks any worse of her. It's what all the young people do nowadays.'

'I suppose,' said Madison. 'It's just that it suddenly struck me that it wasn't at all fair.'

'What?'

'All of it. Simon wanting me to live in Surbiton. The vicar telling me I had to love and honour him when he's really a colossal moron, as you know. And worst of all, me having to change my name. I was standing at the altar thinking about it and I realized that no woman has ever had her own name. Ever. I mean, when did a woman actually have her own name? Have you never wondered about that?'

'No,' said Cynthia, sitting wearily down on the bed.

'Maybe there was once a woman living in a cave, before the dinosaurs came, and she had a name that was her own but then some caveman came along and beat his chest and decided she had to have his name . . .'

Cynthia was taking the pins out of her huge, elaborate pink hat and starting to detach it from her head. It was a complicated construction and the hair wouldn't quite come free until she started yanking it.

'And her name was lost and all subsequent women's names were lost and thousands of years later I'm losing Flight, a perfectly nice name which wasn't even my name but I'd just got used to it, to become Mrs Pugh, and all so

I can cook Simon's dinner in Surbiton. And do you know what the worst of it is? The bloody bridesmaids' dresses weren't even in Victorian Jade.'

Cynthia finally pulled the hat free, set it down on the bed and stroked it, longingly. Her manhandled hair stood out from her head like a scarecrow.

'And as for that thing there . . .' Madison picked the wedding gown back up and shook it by the scruff of its neck, as if it were an errant puppy, before throwing it back down, '. . . it still doesn't fit under the armpits.'

Her mother sighed and picked the wedding dress off the bed and held it close to her, as if to protect it, poor thing. If it had been a simple matter of her daughter realizing she didn't love her fiancé it would have been a lot easier to avoid a cancelled wedding. But of course, Madison didn't realize she didn't love her fiancé. She realized the whole concept of marriage was flawed. From top to bottom. And she was going to fight it.

From that day forward, she would not worry about what everyone else did, including Rita Finkelstein's daughter, who had gone through four surnames and was now called Charmaine Shufflebottom, which was probably exactly what she deserved. No. Madison would do things her way. Even if that meant doing them on her own, with the whole world against her.

And so as the guests of the aborted wedding partied long into the night at her parents' expense, she went to bed that night feeling curiously free, with a great sense of the world and all its many torments lying tantalizingly at her feet . . .

11

London, 2014

Madison slammed the palm of her hand down on her phone, hitting the snooze key, and pulled the covers back over her head.

The opening bars of Toccata and Fugue really ought not to have come as an unpleasant surprise at 6.45 in the morning, because they had come at 6.45 every morning for the past twenty years of her working life. Nevertheless, they were always a bit of an assault on the senses.

She was never quite sure whether waking up to angry organ music put her in an angry frame of mind for the day, or that she naturally woke up in the sort of mood that was in tune with angry organ music. Either way, she felt it was as well to have the right soundtrack playing from the get-go.

There it went again. She slapped it, missed the snooze button, threw the phone at the wall and stuck her head back under the pillow.

'You utter bastard!' she shouted, at Johann Sebastian Bach, or possibly the BlackBerry Corporation, or the World. She swung her legs out of bed, located the phone on the floor under a chest of drawers and found the dismiss key.

She sat back down on the bed, a black look on her face. Then she reached for her dressing gown, pushed her feet into a pair of slippers that turned out not to be the fur-lined ones she liked, and wouldn't go on properly anyway. So she shouted at them, 'Get on! Get on to my feet properly, you evil swines!' and stumbled down the hallway.

As she entered the kitchen, a cat made a mewling sound and threw itself through the catflap.

Fumbling around the units, she started a dispute with the coffee-grinder. 'What's the matter with you? Why won't you go . . . ? Oh, not plugged in. Well, that's just bloody typical . . .'

'Where is the cup I usually put under here to catch the grinds? It's that cleaning lady again! I told her, never, never, never move the cup from under the nozzle . . . how many times? I don't want the cup washed up. I want the cup left under the nozzle . . .' And she found the cup and slammed it under the nozzle, turning on the horrible-sounding grinder at the same time.

The sound of the loud grinding seemed to soothe her momentarily and she stared out of the kitchen window into the meticulously manicured garden with its box hedges shaped into perfect oblongs, and lavender bushes in perfect orbs.

After a shower in which she argued with the shower head – 'What's happened to the pressure? You didn't do this yesterday . . .' – she dried off with a towel she found to have deliberately eroded its own fluffiness: 'Damn thing's as crisp as a loofah! I may as well dry myself on a piece of sandpaper! I'm always buying new towels and then they're never there. Why am I always buying new towels which are never there?' Then she pushed her feet back into her slippers – 'Aargh! Where *are* the fluffy ones? Get on my feet! Now!' – and trooped back into the bedroom.

There, she sat on the bed for a good half hour, nursing her second cup of coffee and brooding over the day ahead. Finally, when she could put it off no longer, she stood up.

Opening the wardrobe doors, she argued vociferously with her autumn clothes collection. 'I have literally nothing suitable in here. NOTHING!' she ranted. 'And I don't suppose I'll be able to find my black cardigan, will I? Oh no. That would be too much to ask.'

She wrestled a particularly obstinate navy blue skirt suit out of the wardrobe, and forced a white blouse to come out and cooperate.

'Come on! Come on!' she said as she struggled with the buttons. 'Oh, why are you tormenting me like this?'

When she had finished arguing with her outfit, she rowed with the handbags in her handbag closet, who were deliberately secreting the one she wanted, like French peasants sheltering a member of the Resistance. 'I know you're in there! You're only making it worse for yourself!'

But it wouldn't show itself. So she grabbed another bag,

threatened it with serious consequences if it didn't behave itself, stuffed it with her personal effects, and slammed out of the flat.

Down the pathway into the street she went, and all was going suspiciously well until she found a traffic warden ticketing a car.

'It's not eight o'clock yet. Control hours are 8 a.m. till 5 p.m.,' she informed the warden.

'I'm getting the ticket ready.'

'You'll get the ticket ready when the car is parked there illegally.'

'It's two minutes to eight. I'm getting the ticket ready now.'

'Then I'm going to stand here and make sure you don't issue it before 8 a.m.'

'Is this your car?'

'That's irrelevant. But no, it's not. I park my car three streets away so I'm out of the control zone.'

'You could buy a permit.'

'I could. But I don't agree with the council's pricing system for permits. So I don't buy one. I park my car somewhere else, nowhere near my house.'

'That sounds like a bit of a palaver.'

'It is.'

And she sat down on a wall and watched as the warden stood looking at his watch and waiting for the hands to tick past 8 a.m.

When they did, he wrote out the ticket and slapped it on the windscreen.

'Happy?' he asked, as Madison walked away.

This was a very good question. Whether Madison was happy or not was a matter of deep philosophical conjecture.

She certainly was happ*iest* when challenging parking wardens about issuing tickets at two minutes to 8 a.m.

But whether that constituted happ*iness*, per se, was a more complex issue. Of course, it was perfectly possible that she was secretly happy behind her darkly glowering face as she stomped her way to the station, although it seemed unlikely.

Standing in front of the self-service ticket machine, Madison wasn't at all satisfied with the range of options offered on the screen.

She queued at the kiosk and then told the man behind the counter: 'That machine still isn't offering a Day Return by overland train alongside the options that come up on the home screen.'

'And?'

'And that's misleading. Because if you chose from the options you were offered you would order the Day Return to London terminals but that's a full £1.50 more expensive than the Day Return to London Blackfriars using only the overland, which doesn't come up unless you search the station finder, which takes a long time because you have to go to L and then go through all the Ls.'

'And?'

'Give me a Day Return to Blackfriars.'

The man stared.

'P-lease,' she said, sarcastically.

'Why don't you just get an Oyster card?' said the ticket man, wearily, as he punched in the ticket details. 'You know, like everyone else who uses the train every day? Instead, you go through this same row with me every single morning . . .'

'I don't get an Oyster card, as you well know, because I don't want the train companies, Transport for London and the government to know where I am at any given time. It's an issue of civil liberties. I do not wish to be tagged and tracked like a sheep in transportation. I am a human being. And I will not be counted.'

'How exhausting for you.'

'Yes. It is.'

As she queued to walk through the barrier, the man in front of her put his ticket in the slot and the word 'Child' flashed up.

Madison pushed her ticket through at speed and ran after him. 'Excuse me!'

She came up panting behind him and tapped him on the back.

He turned round: 'Yes?'

'I think you have the wrong ticket.'

'Sorry?'

'I noticed your ticket was a child ticket.'

'So?'

'So you're not a child. You're thirty-five. Maybe thirty-seven.'

'I'm thirty-two, actually.'

He turned to walk on.

Madison caught up with him. 'Really? You look older. I think it's your hair. Well, anyway, you've purchased the wrong ticket. So you might want to go back.'

'Go away.'

'Thief!' Madison called after him as he ran towards a waiting train and jumped on as the doors closed. A woman waiting on the platform looked at her accusingly.

'Don't look at me. It's him who's ruining things for everyone. The system can only work if we all recognize our responsibility to do the right thing.'

The woman looked her up and down as if she smelt funny and walked away.

On the train she found herself sitting amongst a party of school children playing music on their iPhones.

She tapped the 'Quiet Carriage' sign on the window. They laughed. So she removed the earphone from the nearest ear of the nearest schoolboy and shouted into it.

'I don't want to listen to that. I don't even enjoy hip-hop when I decide to listen to it and I don't want to listen to it now.'

'Get lost, bitch!' he said and replaced his earphone. She took it out again.

'I tell you what,' she said, 'I won't get lost and, further to that, if you don't turn your music off, I'll pick up that emergency phone and notify the British Transport Police that you are breaking Section 19 of the Regulation of Railways Act 1840: it is an offence to cause noise or nuisance in a public rail carriage detrimental to the peaceful enjoyment, safety and comfort of other passengers. This offence is punishable by one month's imprisonment. In your case, that means you will be sent to a young offenders' institution where you will doubtless have to share a wing with delinquents who have beaten their own grandmothers to death.'

At which point the boy turned up his iPhone. The passengers were frozen in trepidation for the next few moments, eyeing Madison to see what her next move would be.

But she didn't seem to have a next move, or if she did it was just to move.

She pushed her way up the train to the opposite end of the carriage. 'Excuse me, excuse me!' she shouted, as she squished everyone out of the way. The other passengers moaned. 'Don't blame me, blame the budding delinquent over there. Excuse me! Coming through!'

Once at the other end of the carriage, she commenced a brief argument with a girl who was sitting in the 'disabled, old or pregnant' seat but appeared to be none of these things. After uprooting her, she installed an elderly man there by manhandling him into the seat as he protested wildly. 'I'm perfectly happy standing, thank you. I'm not that old!' he kept saying. 'You are old, sir, I think you'll find. Sooner you face facts the better,' said Madison, forcing him into a sitting position.

She then had about thirty seconds to look around for any other anomalies before the train rolled up to her stop.

When she got off and started marching towards the

street, she noticed that the information sign by the exit barriers was not displaying the travel news for the day.

Instead, some cheerful soul had written the words:

> If you want the rainbow
> You have to put up with the rain
> – Dolly Parton

She marched up to the kiosk. 'Excuse me, is there any information about train running times?'

The rail employee shrugged.

'Because if there is, it should be on that board there. Not the wit and wisdom of Dolly Parton.'

'That's just a joke. To cheer people up,' the man said.

'Well, it's not cheering me up,' said Madison. 'Number one, I'm not a fan of Ms Parton, although I do concede that anyone who manages to make a theme park out of themselves deserves some credit for ingenuity. Number two, I'm a taxpayer and I want the proportion of my tax that goes towards rail services to fund, in part, the posting of relevant travel information on that board to improve the quality of my journey.'

'Why are you arguing about this? What difference does it make?'

'Fine. I will take it up with your superior later,' said Madison.

'Killjoy!' shouted the rail employee, as she marched off.

'Misuser of public funds!' she called back over her shoulder.

'Uptight bitch!' he shouted.

Two insults before 9 a.m., she thought. Not bad going.

She made straight for her usual coffee bar where she ordered her usual black Americano, of which she took her usual one sip before handing it back saying: 'You've made it wrong. It's too weak.'

The barista gave his usual sigh, tipped the coffee away, made another that was exactly the same and put it down on the counter.

'Mmmm, lovely,' said Madison, as she sipped the identical coffee, which tasted infinitely better. She paid with the exact change.

Marching back down the street, she walked past a perfectly functional pedestrian crossing and got herself across the busy square at the spot she desired, just opposite her office building, by climbing the four-foot-high barriers and dodging six lanes of horn-beeping traffic.

The big red door with gold letter box and entryphone of Wilde and Sawyer was reassuringly heavy. She swiped her card and pushed. It bounced back and shut behind her with a decorously soft click.

Inside the foyer, she swept past the beige suede sofas bearing anxious-looking people reading bad magazines and said good morning briskly to the Amazonian woman who sat at the reception desk. She said it in a voice that left the woman in no doubt that a good morning was the very last thing Madison hoped she would have.

She carried on down the plush, thick-carpeted hallway, past her boss's office. His door was shut. She saw him in her mind's eye, snoozing happily in his big chair. Or possibly playing computer games. To the door at the end of the ground floor hallway she went. 'Madison Flight', it said simply. She didn't ever put letters after her name. If people couldn't work out that she was qualified without being told so by letters on a sign then she didn't want them as a client.

As she landed at her desk she checked her watch. Just after 9 a.m. Not bad.

Madison factored time into her schedule to argue because she didn't want to be late for work or keep clients waiting. Especially not new clients.

And a new client was waiting. She had been there for half an hour, boiling with indignation on a beige sofa.

Today was the day she had come to start telling Madison the story of her marriage. The story of her broken heart.

12

If she had gone with her very considerable instincts, Belinda Bilby would have worn a more expensive suit and bigger jewellery for her first meeting with the lawyer.

As it was, she had decided against an outfit that might be construed as a gratuitous display of easy wealth.

This was tricky, because if Belinda Bilby was anything, she was a gratuitous display of easy wealth.

She was no good at modesty or understatement and it never came off well when she attempted it.

This particular stab in the dark entailed her wearing only her second most preposterous Vivienne Westwood suit: a ripped-hemmed *Les Miserables*-inspired strumpet frock made of silk imprinted with a pattern of CND logos and recycled bottles. Normally this outfit would have been accessorized with a shepherd's crook, but she had left that in the car in order to look businesslike.

She cursed her austerity now, as she sat feeling dowdy on the edge of a pristine beige suede sofa in a law firm's waiting room, nervously flicking through the dull as ditchwater in-house magazine.

After ten minutes, she gasped with exasperation, put down the magazine and snatched a complimentary nail file emblazoned with the firm's name out of a holder on the table beside her and started filing her long purple nails.

Her hands were a clash of rubies, garnets, amethysts and pink sapphires. She blew as the dust from the filings fell onto her outfit. The skirt showed off too much of her knobbly knees and the bodice too much of her ample wrinkled bosom. Like everything about Belinda Bilby, the outfit defied both gravity and belief.

As a young woman she had been quite ravishing and extremely chic. She had been born into an aristocratic family of Anglo-French-Brazilian ancestry called the Montagu-Santos-DuLally-Gaseuse who were dizzyingly well connected and impossibly grand. The women were also very beautiful. There had been an era in her life when she could be in the same room as Jackie Kennedy and hold her own quite comfortably.

But her response to age had been to wrestle with it clumsily. Some women grow old by letting themselves go. Belinda Bilby was letting herself go all the way. Her taste in clothes was veering towards what you might call desperation couture – absurdly expensive and aesthetically very unpleasing.

She performed a double whammy with her dress sense because at the same time as letting it all hang out, she was also attempting to cram it all in. Her eclectic taste in outfits was always a catastrophic mistake, not least because the hourglass figure of her heyday was no longer even vaguely discernable amid the marauding flesh.

Ten years ago, as she approached her fifties – or when she was well into them, depending on your view of her current vintage – she had enlisted the services of the world's foremost cosmetic surgeon, who was well known for giving all his patients the same face. Now in her sixties, she had regained something of her old face back, and so the two faces of Belinda Bilby were now fighting each other for control of the territory between her chest and her hairline. It was not a happy sight. She had it on her to-do list to have it all nipped, tucked and plumped again. But her accountant had made it very clear: either she could renovate the country house again this year, or she could renovate herself. Not both.

She had chosen the house, and until she could get around to her own bodily schedule of dilapidations, she resorted to the old trick of drawing her lipstick over the actual line of her lips, which made her look as if a seven-year-old child had done her make-up.

Also as part of the undignified battle she fought with Mother Age, Belinda Bilby had acquired the habit of dressing mainly in purple. She dyed her hair purple, too. Why, it cannot be said.

Perhaps she was throwing caution to the wind and pleasing herself in a free-spirited way. Or perhaps she had ideas about the specific properties of purple and its capacity to promote good health and fortune. If so, the strategy seemed to be working all right.

She had been left very well off by her arthritic, asthmatic first husband Marcus, a shipping magnate, who died suddenly one summer – some say of a broken heart, some say of a chronic bout of hay fever. In any case, his heart broke, and stopped, after a good deal of sneezing.

The pollen count was often cited as an explanation because no one could work out why his heart should have broken otherwise, as he was living a most conducive life with his glamorous wife and three teenage sons in a huge house in Holland Park. Nothing seemed amiss, except that behind the Bilby family's perfect, stucco-fronted exterior, Mrs Bilby had a young lover – a Spanish waiter called José, which she refused to pronounce with an H sound, thus making her lover Portuguese, despite his protestations – and his children, whose names escape me now as they always escape everyone, were ungrateful delinquents who, when they were not sitting about the house smoking marijuana paid for with their father's hard-earned money, were out selling it and getting themselves arrested because they were not very bright.

That little package of domestic bothers, you might suppose, could break a man's heart just as surely as a volley of fifty-seven sneezes. In any case, when the funeral directors came to take the body away, they found an envelope which his wife hadn't found because she hadn't gone near him, even when he was dying, and so had failed to notice the leaving of a last will and testament in a package beneath his orthopaedic pillow.

It didn't change much. But it did contain a cassette tape in which Mr Bilby voiced all the anguish of thirty years, culminating in the declaration that 'now you've got all my money you vile bitch, I hope you spend it all on drink and it kills you'. It had been recorded over a copy of a Queen *Greatest Hits* album, and when Mr Bilby stopped speaking there was a squeak of the cassette and then the voice of Freddie Mercury sang the chorus to 'Fat Bottomed Girls'.

'Charming,' said Mrs Bilby, as her husband's lawyer, Lawrence Loonie, of Loonie, Loos and Leithall, played her the cassette at the reading of the will.

Loonie sang along and insisted on playing the tape long after Mrs Bilby had lost patience with it. 'Oh yeah, rockin'!' he said, improbably, as he switched off the machine.

Mrs Bilby screwed up her nose and shifted uncomfortably in her seat. In truth, none of it, including the fat bottoms, bothered her that much because she *had* got all the money. And she also had husband number two lined up in the shape of Seth, a handsome young artist who had come to the house a few months earlier at her husband's bidding to paint a portrait of him to hang in the offices of Bilby, Bilby and Bilby (Logistics) Ltd.

He did a good enough job, although Mrs Bilby felt he might have rendered the slightly liverish hue and deep worry lines around her husband's features a little less realistically in order to maximize customer satisfaction.

Seth said he thought it a good likeness, which brought out her husband's spirit and his inner truth.

Mrs Bilby didn't care much for her husband's inner truth. She might have cared for it a long time ago, but not now. Now, she told Seth how hard it was being married to a bad-tempered, stubborn, unforgiving, embittered, angry, power-crazed, at times violent shipping magnate who callously and ceaselessly cheated on her with young boys and neglected her in every possible way.

And Seth understood. He really did. He didn't say so explicitly but you could tell by the look on his face when she was pouring out her heart to him.

They married in a beautiful ceremony in the grounds of the Bilby country residence in Surrey, which was a vast red-brick pile punctuated by faux turrets, the largest of which proudly flew the St George's flag.

The wedding was a lovely garden party. And Belinda, dressed in girlish white Vera Wang, kept the lid on her ardour until right after they cut the cake, at which point she couldn't help playfully grabbing her new husband's bottom: 'Let's go upstairs and fool around,' she said. Alas, the fooling around was all too short-lived.

After three years of wedded bliss, Seth had decided he wanted out. He didn't want a penny of her money, he said, as he broke the news to her one night after dinner. They were sitting in the vast kitchen with its black granite surfaces and poured white concrete floor gleaming like serenely bottomless pools of water. Mrs Bilby had been smoking a Marlboro Light as the housekeeper cleared the plates away. She had intimated how nice it would be to get an early night. And he told her he wanted to get a divorce. He wanted to return to his old life as a struggling artist with nothing, he claimed.

Belinda didn't believe a word of it. She was distraught.

She began to panic. She sensed that a betrayal was being practised upon her. Everything she believed in suddenly came crashing down. Her identity faltered, her ego crumbled, and out of the wreckage came a deranged creature of the night.

She got up from the table and began pacing up and down, muttering like a mad woman. The housekeeper beat a hasty retreat to the servants' quarters.

Seth got up and said something about packing his things and being gone by the morning. 'You can't leave me,' she said, her eyes glinting like the granite worktops.

She grabbed the first thing she could lay her hands on, which was a cheese knife. A chase ensued, and Seth came off the loser.

Stabbed through the left buttock, he ended up skewered like a piece of Cheddar. He managed to pull the knife out and dived, howling, for the garage, where he kept his beloved motorbike.

But when he got inside, someone had removed the saddle. Perhaps, sensing the end was nigh, Mrs Bilby had instructed one of her workmen to vandalize it to prevent him ever leaving her. Perhaps it had simply fallen off. Who knows? She couldn't remember. It was all a blur. But whoever had done it, Seth's only means of escape was now a motorbike without a seat. Reflecting on it, she supposed this wasn't necessarily a completely bad thing, considering the state of his left buttock.

Belinda sighed as she thought about it now. With no word from Seth, who she called and called in the days after his departure, and only the briefest of notes from his solicitor a few weeks later spelling out his intention to divorce her, Mrs Bilby had been left with no choice but to get herself a lawyer.

She looked up at the tall, unfeasibly beautiful girl at the reception desk of the room where she was now sitting, who was on the phone ignoring her, and sighed again, more dramatically.

Then, when that didn't work, she gasped. She had been waiting for twenty minutes in this godforsaken place in the back of beyond – or just off Holborn, in her view a dingy arrondissement she would hope to have avoided all her life if it had not been the venue for the headquarters of the law firm that had been recommended to her.

She perched on the edge of the sofa, noticing that the nail file she was using was emblazoned with the words 'Wilde and Sawyer – Experts in Family Law'. She couldn't even begin to work out the connection between divorces and nail files. Except, she supposed, that one *filed* for divorce. Could that be it? If so, it was in very bad taste.

She was pondering what sort of people made jokes like that, when the receptionist put the phone down and addressed her: 'Miss Flight will see you now.'

And before she could ask where to go, Miss Flight appeared from a door at the other end of the waiting area and stood in front of her. She wasn't exactly what you would call beautiful, but she was certainly striking. She had all the component parts of attractiveness: long, tousled, honey-blonde hair, blue eyes, a good figure, shown off by a well-fitting navy pencil skirt and elegant white blouse. But the slightly too-big nose, the rather manly hands and the strong jaw seemed to warn one off from thinking, 'Ah, I know how to handle this one'.

Her face was at first almost obscured by a large pair of brown tortoiseshell glasses, which she took off and allowed to fall around her neck on a cord in order to greet her client. As she did so, it was clear that the most striking thing about her was her frown. Mrs Bilby had not thought those kinds of deep furrows had survived the era of Botox.

She looked as if something about standing in her own office waiting room receiving a new client who was going to pay her a lot of money was a major inconvenience. She held out her big hand and said: 'Mrs Bilby-Taylor . . .'

'Bilby,' said Mrs Bilby, archly.

'Mrs Bilby. Of course. So pleased to meet you. I'm sorry if I kept you waiting.'

But her tone suggested that she wasn't pleased at all. And she wasn't sorry either. Not one bit.

13

'Have a seat,' said Madison, as she shut the door behind her new client and showed her an uncomfortable-looking leather chair in front of a desk.

Mrs Bilby surveyed it suspiciously. Then she sat down extremely slowly and cautiously, as if the chair were booby-trapped with an explosive device. She looked around her.

The pictures on the walls were charcoal sketches of nudes. Mrs Bilby judged them to be amateurish. The hands weren't very good. People who couldn't really draw properly always drew fingers like pointy blades. She began fretting that her choice of lawyer was not going to be expensive enough. Also, this Flight woman looked a bit bloodless. She was thinking she should have gone to the other top divorce lawyer who had been second on the list prepared for her by Lawrence Loonie – the big, busty woman who, according to the articles about her in the press, had three ex-husbands, five children, an enormous townhouse in Belgravia and drove everywhere in a red 1980s Mercedes – when Madison suddenly slammed her right hand down on the desk.

It came from nowhere, a show of violence so shocking that Mrs Bilby jolted back in her seat.

'Meat fly,' said the lawyer, sweeping the dead creature off the table into the wastepaper basket. 'There's a steak restaurant a few doors down with questionable refrigeration practices.' She nodded towards the open window and beyond. 'I'm having a long-running dispute with them about it. Their right to rot food versus my right to breathe nice-smelling air, broadly. I'm hoping we will end up in the European Court of Human Rights.'

'Oh, I see,' said Mrs Bilby, feeling slightly but by no means totally relieved.

Madison placed the wastepaper basket back on the floor, cleaned her hands with a wet wipe and put her spectacles back on her face. She then started reading a file while saying, in an utterly dispassionate voice:

'My associate, who you spoke to yesterday, I believe, says you have just been contacted by the lawyer acting for your estranged husband, Mr . . .' She flicked over the papers, '. . . Seth Taylor.' She looked up over the top of her glasses. 'I thought it would be useful if we used this meeting today for me to talk you through the process that will now unfold.'

Mrs Bilby's eyes had already started to well up with tears. 'It's all so brutal,' she sobbed, thinking of the poor little fly as much as the divorce. In her spare time, she was a deeply misguided animal rights campaigner.

Wearily, Madison did her smiley face. Divorce lawyers needed to be counsellors as well as solicitors, so she had learned to smile quite convincingly. If you looked closely, you could see that only her mouth was smiling, while her eyes remained beadily contemptuous. But it didn't really matter because Mrs Bilby's tears were mostly fake also.

Almost as soon as they appeared, they vanished, and Mrs Bilby snapped: 'I'm not getting divorced.'

Madison sat back in her chair. This was slightly unusual, though not unheard of.

'Oh?'

'I don't want to. Are you listening to me?'

'I'm listening. This is an entirely normal reaction. Divorce is an emotional time, involving an internal process a little like grief. There are five stages. First, shock – I'm guessing that's where you are now . . .' Madison began to open her desk drawer to take out a 'So Your Husband Has Left You For A Younger Woman – Now What?' leaflet.

'Miss Flight. I understand that you think I have come to you for a divorce. To save my money, or something vulgar like that. But I have not. I have come to you to stop a divorce.'

Madison started leafing through Mrs Bilby's file again.

'I have read the summary of your case my people prepared for me. I have to say, I think if your estranged husband does petition first, based on your unreasonable behaviour his petition will be looked on favourably by a judge. The cheese knife in his buttock rather clinches it.'

'Even so, I want to stop this divorce, Miss Flight. Money is no subject.'

'You mean money is no object.'

'Do I?' said Mrs Bilby, who was prone to snatching precisely the wrong word or phrase out of the ether. 'Yes, perhaps that is what I mean. In any case, there must be something you can do. Are you going to help me, or should I go to that woman with the big hair and shoulder pads. What's her name? Tina Tuna, is it? Something to do with fish, anyway.'

'Anna Pirana,' said Madison, grimly. She knew the name only too well. As she said it, it struck like a blade of ice into her very soul. She was damned if she was going to let a high-value client like the Bilby woman walk out of her office and make her way to the golden mile to see that grasping, greedy, fame-hungry bitch-of-a-bitch.

If it meant embarking upon the almost-certain-to-fail strategy of defending a divorce petition to try and stop it, a course almost never ventured upon by any kind of lawyer, good or bad, because it so infuriated judges, then she supposed she would have to do that. The only consolation was that it would get her a cheap headline.

She pushed the leaflet back into the desk drawer and fixed Mrs Bilby with a stare. 'I need you to be very clear about what you are asking me to do. And what you are going to need to do in return.'

'Yes, yes,' said Mrs Bilby. 'If you can stop the man I love divorcing me, I'll do anything.'

'Good, because you may need to do something about your taste in outfits, for a start. And then we'll have a think about that hair.'

Mrs Bilby put her hand to her head and smoothed her mane. 'He always said he loved my hair,' she said, becoming tearful. 'You think he would prefer it another way?'

'I'm thinking mainly about the judge preferring it another way, to be honest.'

'You want me to make a play for the judge?'

Madison spoke very slowly and loudly: 'I'm thinking you need to present a more conservative image to the judge for the purposes of getting on his good side. We're going to have to persuade him that when you stuck a cheese knife in your husband's bottom you were having an off day.'

'All right, all right. You don't need to shout. I'm eccentric, not deaf.'

Madison stood up. 'I think this has been a very productive meeting. Now, if you will excuse me, I have another appointment.'

'No, you don't. You're just trying to get rid of me.' There it was again, that intractable look.

Was it her imagination, or had Madison met some kind of horrible match?

The sensation stirred in her of meeting a kindred spirit. But that was impossible. Mrs Bilby was a silly person.

She shook Mrs Bilby's hand and assured her she would be in touch. Then she watched her flounce out of the room after picking a fight with a chair that wouldn't move out of the way.

And as Madison watched her client wrestle with it, as if

the chair were a sentient being to be scolded and put in its place, she had the sensation of watching herself.

She wasn't at all shocked when the door slammed.

The light knock at the door a few hours later meant it could only be Madison's boss, Christopher Wilde, standing on the other side – probably in his socks. Since his nervous breakdown, when he ran amok in his bare feet shouting obscenities one afternoon, Wilde had taken to padding about with no shoes on as a sort of halfway house between sanity and lunacy. The local theory was that he did it as a sort of warning to all that he was teetering dangerously close to the brink and might, at any moment, whip his socks off and go tonto again.

He also went about with his shirt hanging half out of the top of his trousers, with one button undone so you could see a small patch of his stomach.

He opened the door and peeped in. His expression was sheepish. Everything about his body language said he appeared at Madison's door not as a boss, but as a supplicant.

'We need to talk about Mrs Bilby,' he said apologetically, visibly cowering slightly, as if the mere mention of a request might lead to Madison pushing a button on her desk to empty a tank of gunge onto his head.

He had given her the Bilby divorce partly because Mrs Bilby had come to his firm requesting Madison, but also because he had decided upon meeting Mrs Bilby that she was quite, quite mad. Even if she had requested him, he would have had nothing to do with it. She was going to be more trouble than he could handle, especially now he had the kids at weekends and, to all intents and purposes, just wanted a quiet life.

'We've got a big client,' he had told Madison, after he got the call from Lawrence Loonie, sounding him out.

'How big?' She gave him the bored look that said it was a liberty his even daring to speak to her.

'Big. Could be really big. Could be The Big One.'

'The Big One? Really?' Sarcasm now.

He tried humour. 'Yes, this is it. The one that cements you as London's leading divorce lawyer. Knock that woman with the red Mercedes into a cocked hat once and for all.'

'I see.' She did not look impressed. He had often tried to palm difficult cases off on her by saying this. It was seldom true.

'Yes. This one, and then we're off to the Bahamas. Or possibly the west coast of Ireland. I can't decide. You decide. I'm happy, as long as we're together.'

Madison took off her glasses and looked at him. 'Do you realize you've been asking me to run away with you since I got here nineteen years ago? It's inappropriate bordering on actionable.'

'Never mind. Read that.' And he threw a thick file on the desk and pushed it towards her.

'So, you've got a difficult client, an older woman, who you can't picture yourself in bed with, and you want me to take her case because you can't be bothered.'

'She requested you, actually. And she's not just a difficult old woman, although that is undoubtedly the case. She is also the widow of Marcus Bilby. The shipping magnate? If we succeed in defending her assets from an assault by her toyboy second husband, it will be a very big feather in our cap. In your cap, I mean. Don't thank me. For giving you the case, I mean.' He tapped the file. 'I had the girls prepare this. She's a devil to deal with, I warn you.'

Madison raised one eyebrow. 'Hmmm. I might be able to set up my own firm after this. Flights: Britain's top divorce lawyers. With offices overlooking St Paul's Cathedral, I expect.' She put on her glasses.

'I'll just go, then. Forget the thank you bit.'

'I will.' And she waved him out with one hand, while she turned the pages of the file with the other.

He scuttled away. The dynamic between them always conformed to the prototype that had been carved out many years earlier when she was a young trainee and he, a partner, who should have known better, first set his sights on her while mentoring her and requested that she come to the Savoy with him for some afternoon sex.

She refused, whilst holding out the frosty possibility that if he kept her on as a trainee and promoted her generously as and when she deserved it, which would be often, she wouldn't cut up rough and ruin him.

She had been wiping the floor with him ever since, and as such they had grown together, like an old married couple. She only ostensibly treated him with contempt, but underneath quite liked the fact that after all the years they had been needling each other, he knew her better than she knew herself. He always had her back and, secretly, though she would never admit it, she had his.

Because of this, every now and again, she looked at him in a way that he interpreted as meaning she might one day, after all, offer him something other than scratchy intolerance.

She would refute this. But the occasional look of slight fondness – like the fondness one has for a puppy covered in mud making a mess on the carpet – was enough for him.

Christopher Wilde, who wasn't very wild, but wished he was, was obsessed with Madison. He didn't just want to take her to the Savoy. He dreamed of marrying her, and walking into the Bahaman sunset with her. Was it Bahaman? Or Bahman? Because Barbados became Bejan in the adjectival, he knew that much. In which case, did Bermuda become Buman? This, and many other inconsequential wonderings in the mind of Christopher Wilde was one of the contributing reasons for his extreme unattractiveness to women.

Knowing this was partly why he knocked so gently on Madison's door now.

'What about the Bilby case?' she said, affecting the bored pout she did so sexily, and looking so wonderfully like Catherine Deneuve in her *Belle de Jour* days, only with a slightly – OK, maybe significantly – bigger nose.

Her face had become more childlike because she had pulled her long hair casually back into a knot as she worked, and a lock of it was falling across her cheek.

Wilde, standing there in his stockinged feet, patch of stomach exposed, groaned almost audibly with desire. He knew he was a middle-aged loser who had long since ceased to be anything to write home about, but it didn't stop him dreaming.

He had once been described by Madison, in one of her philosophical moments, as looking 'a bit like Alec Baldwin gone to seed'.

'But Alec Baldwin *has* gone to seed,' he had pointed out.

'Well, if Alec Baldwin went more to seed, then that's what you look like,' she said.

'How much more to seed, exactly?'

'Quite a lot.'

Later, he decided that she had been trying to be complimentary.

Despite being in his fifties, he did have a good head of thick hair that was flecked with silver and stood charmingly on end, a somewhat Irish face which might have been described as boyishly good looking – or was before his ex-wife Isobel had spent fourteen years wiping the smile off it – and a paunch, which Isobel informed him was not a prosperous paunch but a paunch born out of chronically irresponsible overindulgence and moral turpitude. He supposed that that was where the resemblance to Alec Baldwin ended.

'I just had a call from her. She was hysterical.'

'Oh yes?'

'Yes. Ranting about how she's going to sue you and

report the firm to the Law Society. No need to worry, apparently. Lawrence says she does this all the time.'

'Oh? Why is she upset?'

'She says you insulted her.'

'I thought we had a very productive meeting.'

'She says, and I have no reason to disbelieve her, that you told her she would have to sleep with the judge.'

Madison was calmly surfing the net, reading her emails. She didn't flinch. 'Actually, I told her to dress appropriately when we get to court. Did you see the outfit she was wearing?'

'It was a little eccentric.'

'Eccentric? She looked like Elizabeth I would have looked if Alexander McQueen had got hold of her. When she's in the witness box, as she will be if she persists with this insane idea of defending the petition, I don't know how I'm going to work her from the back. This case could quite easily be a car crash. And not a slow one.'

'Remember the golden rule. Only ask questions that can be answered yes or no.'

Madison carried on typing, and didn't even look up as she said: 'The golden rule, as you well know, is only take on cases you can win. Now if you don't mind, I have a lot to do and you are obscuring my view of the blank wall I like to look at to help me think.'

14

After being despatched from his employee's office and told to mind his own business, Christopher Wilde, founding partner of Wilde and Sawyer, spent the rest of the day sitting at his desk playing *Grand Theft Auto* and wondering whether there was any chance, if a complicated chain of coincidences were to be contrived, that Cara Delevingne might somehow be persuaded to sleep with him.

The only scenario he could envisage that would lead him to this happy place involved a change in both gender and sexuality on one or other of their parts (or possibly both), a total revamp of his personal finances and a good deal of his person being subjected to liposuction and reconstructive surgery. Still, he thought, it might happen.

Whether or not Christopher Wilde had good reason to so trust in the benevolent nature of the universe was debatable. In some ways, life had been cruel to him, in other ways kind.

He had set up his own legal practice after walking out of one of the biggest law firms in the City – the ubiquitous

Henchmann's – following a mid-life crisis brought on by a bad divorce.

His co-founding partner Mr Sawyer was a difficult man who rarely, if ever, came into the office. He had never been seen by anyone currently working there, nor had anyone ever got hold of him on the phone.

To be precise, Mr Sawyer did not exist.

Christopher had happened upon the idea of an invisible partner one day whilst reading *The Adventures of Tom Sawyer* in his new office. He was a meagre sole practice then, with no clients and nothing else to do. But it suddenly struck him that a partner might change everything.

The choice of Mr Sawyer was apt, because he wanted to have adventures. He suspected his whole life had been leading up to an adventure – well, it had to have been, because he had never had an adventure yet and so one must be on the way sooner or later, surely?

'Christopher Wilde. Wilde by name, wild by nature!' he used to say to women he tried to pick up in bars, unsuccessfully.

But if he couldn't have adventures as Christopher Wilde, then maybe his alter ego, the elusive Mr Sawyer, would have them for him. Mr Sawyer certainly did broaden his horizons.

As if by magic, as soon as there were two names on the door, the clients started to come through it, along with more lawyers, and a young graduate, Madison Flight, looking for a job as a trainee. His practice had taken off.

But he still kept Mr Sawyer on because he needed his

protection. This was because of how things had ended at Henchmann's. When he thought of it, he still felt tears pricking his eyes. He had turned up to work one Tuesday not wearing any shoes or socks and had had to be taken home, and then put on gardening leave for a month, and then sacked. He had been lucky not to be disbarred, his former partners had said, because he did some terrible things while running about the office that morning in his bare feet. Specifically, he had lost them several important clients who had happened to be in the waiting area as he ranted about things that the general public was not meant to know about the legal profession. Things about billing, and leaving the clock on while going out for a slap-up meal.

But there were mitigating circumstances. Running amok barefoot in the office had been very much precipitated by his wife leaving him for a woman (or 'another woman' as she put it), commencing transgender reassignment and then trouncing him in a bitter divorce battle in which she had represented herself.

'Partner at Top Law Firm Beaten Hands Down in Court Showdown by Sex-Change Wife' was the headline in the *Law Society Gazette*. And so it was understandable that Wilde would have a complete mental breakdown, lose his job and be forced to start over.

Aside from occasionally padding about in his socks, he was on the straight and narrow again now.

If anything, he was on the too straight and narrow, and as being on the too straight and narrow (his wife called him boring) was how he'd got into trouble and lost everything in the first place, he thought it prudent to try to become more irresponsible.

Which was where Mr Sawyer came in. Mr Sawyer was very unreliable and capricious. He drank a lot, often during office hours. Whenever anyone rang and asked to speak to him he was always unavailable. But he was a shit-hot lawyer.

Everything nasty that needed to be done was done by him. Any threatening letters, Mr Sawyer would dictate them. Anything ruthless that Wilde lacked the courage to do, he delegated to Sawyer, and Sawyer did it with aplomb. Anyone who had ever been sacked had been sacked by Mr Sawyer. The letters from him in which he despatched people by telling them their shortcomings were legendary.

Wilde built quite a successful legal practice in this way. His expanding staff and client base meant he soon had to move to bigger offices off High Holborn.

And it was around that time that the riddle that was Madison walked through the door and asked for a traineeship.

She was late, she said, as she sat down in front of Christopher without being invited to, because she had been arguing with a man outside selling the *Big Issue*. She had bought one and then he had asked her if she wanted one.

'I don't get it,' Christopher had said.

'Exactly,' said Madison, jutting her jaw out. 'He took the money and then asked if I would like the magazine or not. If I didn't take the magazine he could make more money by keeping it to sell to someone else.'

'Well, I suppose it's a good cause.'

'That's not the point. If he does that with the next person, and the next, it defeats the whole object of the exercise. Because then he is not someone trying to better himself by providing a service for money, but someone simply begging on the streets.'

'I suppose he's hungry.'

'That is possible, but beside the point I'm trying to make. I'm going to phone the magazine's head office and see what they have to say for themselves.'

Christopher had to tell her she was right in the end, or they would have been there all day debating the pros and cons of homeless magazine mis-selling.

She was a most singular person, he thought. And so attractive. Her blue-grey eyes made you want to stare into them until you felt yourself disappear. He loved everything about her, including her big, bold nose.

For some reason, he decided to tell her, there and then, about the invisible Mr Sawyer. 'Can you keep a secret?' he had said, feeling an uncontrollable urge to reveal himself to her instantly.

When he had told her all about his alter ego, and his nervous breakdown, she looked at him enigmatically, as if deep in thought.

'Aren't you going to tell me how wrong that is?' he said, expecting a long lecture about deception.

'Not really. It's your business how you run your firm,'

she said, before negotiating a deal in which, in return for keeping her mouth shut about the irregularities of his practice, she would be seated with him for a two-year traineeship in his specialism, matrimonial law, after which she would become a salaried partner with bonus and additional commission as a cut of the profits.

That was nineteen years ago and apart from a six-month sabbatical when Madison left Wilde and Sawyer to do pro bono work overseas for the UN's 'women in conflict zones' programme – which she did to give herself a bit of a break – the pair of them had been working together in the firm's family law division ever since.

He had the curious sense of knowing her better than anyone, and yet not knowing her at all.

He had found out, after years of trying to extract the meanest pieces of personal information, that there was a boyfriend of sorts, who she simply referred to as The Banker.

This international man of mystery, whom nobody had ever met, was evidently married to someone else. Wilde had ascertained that The Banker had once tried to leave his wife in order to marry Madison, and Madison had told him in no uncertain terms that if he did, she would never see him again.

Being the other woman, having her boyfriend call in on her occasionally, then sending him home to his wife, was exactly how she wanted it.

There was never any talk about whether she was sad about not having children. She never seemed to have emotional longings like other women.

She was still living, so far as he could make out, in a modest two-bedroom flat in south London when she could afford to live in a townhouse in Chelsea. She said she didn't like change. She said she liked the grimy south London neighbourhood with its criminal gangs and grafittied walls. She said she felt safe there. 'You know where you are with anti-social behaviour' was a saying of hers, along with 'You know where you are with a married man.'

The only other thing he knew about her private life was that she owned a cottage in the country, several hours from the city. She drove out there at weekends to paint.

He pictured her playing a scratchy version of Miles Davis's 'Blue in Green' as she sat at her easel conjuring the sunset. He had no reason to believe she listened to Miles Davis, or that she painted sunsets, but he liked this image and he played the reel often in his head.

He dreamed of being invited. He dreamed of the two of them lingering together in this picturesque hideaway. Then the needle scratched across the vinyl and the music stopped as The Banker appeared in an expensive suit, swirling a glass of red wine in his hand, a fiendishly rakish look on his face. Damn him.

When Madison turned forty, she announced it as she and Wilde were about to leave the office one evening to walk to the Tube station. 'How about a glass of champagne for my birthday?' she said, matter-of-factly. 'I know I don't look forty so don't feel you have to start giving me embarrassing compliments.'

'Aren't you doing anything special?' he asked her, horrified.

'Why would I do that?'

'Well, you know, people celebrate forty, don't they?'

'Why?'

'I don't know, really. They just do. It's a milestone.'

'Are you insinuating that forty is some kind of halfway point? Are you saying I'm going to be dead when I'm eighty?'

Wilde gave up trying to find things out about Madison; it only ever ended in her being appalled at his impertinence.

But that didn't stop him falling more and more in love with her. In fact, if anything, the mystery only made him love her more.

As such, he indulged Madison in everything. He lived for the day they would walk off into the sunset together. If not her, he would settle for Cara Delevingne.

He looked at his screen and realized that his character, a rich kid cruising the badlands in a sports car, had been murdered by a prostitute kicking him to death. Dammit! That was the wrong way round, according to the blurb on the game instructions. He couldn't even do virtual life properly. He looked at his watch. 3 p.m. Only one more hour of pretending to work and it would be time to pick the kids up from his ex-wife's new wife, a nice enough woman called Geraldine. He actually liked her more than his ex-wife. She was relatively straightforward. Why couldn't his ex-wife have just become a lesbian? That would have been too simple, of course. His ex-wife didn't even have a name at the moment because he was still trying to decide what to call himself. He had been Ian at first but now felt that was giving in to socio-economic stereotyping. Apparently, it was currently a toss-up between Presley or Kendal. Christopher was at a loss to make any sense of it. Every time he thought about it his head ached. He could see why one might want to pay homage to Elvis. But why you would want to name yourself after a type of mint cake was a mystery to him.

15

'Just drive, please,' said Madison to the taxi driver, who had begun to claim he couldn't take her south of the river. 'I'll pay extra, whatever you want.'

It had been an exhausting day. The last thing she needed was one of those argumentative black cab drivers who refused to go any further south than Waterloo Bridge.

'I'm on me way 'ome, love,' said the cabbie, doing his best apples-and-pears impression. 'You're miles out me way.'

'Double fare,' said Madison, who didn't buy it for a second.

'Sorry, love. I promised to take the missus to the cinema tonight. She wants to see that new Iranian film.'

'Triple fare. And the Iranian film's rubbish. I've seen it. They all die in the end.'

The cabbie, swore, slammed the dividing window shut and drove. Everyone had their price, even cab drivers who liked obscure foreign-language films.

As she watched the lights and the gloss of the City fade behind her and the desertion of dark, southside London come to greet her like a gloomy old friend, she felt calm and reassured.

But half an hour later as she neared her flat, a modest garden apartment in a red-brick Victorian block, she finally succumbed and engaged with the nattering cab driver.

It was a protracted, existential row she could have done without. It hinged on whether the cabbie should have wound down his window and thrown frozen sausages out of it for the foxes as they drove alongside the park near her home, or whether this only encouraged predators to venture closer into civilization and torment human beings by rampaging through their bins.

'Foxes are vermin,' she said. 'They eat babies.'

'Nonsense. Foxes are gentle creatures. Besides, they keep the rats down.' And the cab driver threw another string of sausages out of the window.

'So, they're gentle creatures but they also kill rats. How do you explain that, then?'

In the end, she had to stop because the cab driver had stopped outside her house and was demanding £59.80.

'Make it sixty,' she said, handing him three twenties.

'Sixty? A 20p tip. For coming all this way.'

'I already allowed you to triple it.'

'Yeah, but that doesn't include tip. Twenty pence is an insult.'

'Fine. Forget the 20p. Make it £59.80.'

'What?'

'That's right. I'm not moving until you give me my 20p

change. I'll call the cab office and register a complaint against you if you refuse.'

'I knew you'd be trouble!' he shouted, throwing a twenty pence piece out of the window at her, closely followed by a string of sausages, then roared off.

They lay on the pavement looking forlorn until a fox came and tucked in. He looked at her as if to say thank you.

Madison sighed and let herself into her flat.

Somewhere in the dark recesses of the kitchen at the back of the apartment, a cat made a mewling sound and threw itself out through the catflap as she entered.

Madison walked into the kitchen and picked up a note from the table. It was written, as usual, in the form of a haiku:

> *'I came
> but you weren't here
> ah, loneliness . . .'*

The note was signed, as the notes always were, 'W x'.

She crumpled it into a ball and threw it absent-mindedly into the recycling bin.

She walked through the apartment meticulously putting things away as she discarded them: coat on the coat rack in the hall, on a hanger, handbag in a handbag closet, shoes in a special shoe cupboard, on shoe holders that ensured they would not lose their shape. Before long she was putting things away by pushing them into cupboards and then arguing with them when a piece of fabric poked its way between the doors as she shut them. Exasperated, she poked at the offending garments and slammed the wardrobe doors, nearly trapping her fingers. She was aware she had to have some form of OCD, only it wasn't exactly about tidying. More about making inanimate objects do exactly what she wanted them to do. I suppose I'm mad, she thought, not much bothered by this.

When everything was pushed out of sight and she was satisfied that not a single bit of fabric was defiantly peeping at her, she put on her favourite sweat pants and looked at her watch. Five to eleven. Perfect.

She didn't like to have too much of the evening left to spend doing nothing before it was time for bed. She didn't really do relaxation. If she tried to sit around doing nothing she just ended up thinking of people to argue with and then if it was too late to ring them she had to add them to her list of people to argue with the next day.

She went into the kitchen and heated a bowl of tomato soup. She put down cat food for the missing cat then carried her meal into the living room where she flicked on the TV, which was tuned to the same channel it was tuned to every night. She sat balancing the soup bowl on her knees, ladling her frugal meal into her mouth while watching re-runs of old cop shows.

She liked watching the good guy wrestling the bad guy to the floor, punching him violently.

That was what Madison would really like to be doing.

Madison believed that if you believed in something, you fought for it. A lot of people didn't agree.

Earlier that day, she had fallen out with a girlfriend who had made the mistake over lunch of telling her that she had just been caught by a ticket inspector for not putting enough credit on her Oyster card. 'See! Those things are designed to catch you out. I've always said it. Lulling you into a false sense of security. They want you to forget to top them up. And they're a gross intrusion of privacy, giving the state the means to track your movements like you're some kind of—'

'Madison, leave it! It's just a bloody train fine,' said her friend, as Madison got to work.

'It's not *just* a train fine,' she said. She had got that far-away look in her eyes. The look that said she was going to be studying the relevant legislation all afternoon and hounding the train company until they gave up and not only refunded the fine, but gave her friend a free season ticket, just to make it stop.

As usual, lunch in their favourite Sicilian bistro was going to be ruined because her friend had stupidly forgotten the rule – never tell Madison about your problems. Not unless you wanted her to commence solving them immediately, to the exclusion of all other considerations, including the peaceful eating of spaghetti.

She was already on her iPhone, Googling the train company involved, its policies, rules and regulations when the waitress arrived at the table. Glasses perched on her nose, she looked archly over the rims at her friend: 'If we allow a wrongful train fine to go through, what next?'

'Well, it's not exactly next stop Nazi Germany. It really isn't worth busting a gut for.'

Madison gave her the arch look again.

The waitress coughed. 'Ready to order?'

Her friend told her they wanted two spaghetti bottargas and two green salads. Madison waved her hand as if to say the matter of eating lunch was now irrelevant. Arguing always suppressed her appetite.

'I need to check the signs at the station where you got on. You say they not only served you notice of a fine, but also deducted the £1.50 your Oyster card was short. I fail to see how they can charge the fare then fine you for not paying the fare. You were not travelling without a ticket. You touched your card at the barrier. You have broken no statute that I can see. You stand a reasonable chance of getting the fine overturned when the case proceeds to a court hearing. There may even be a human rights issue.'

The waitress came with a bottle of mineral water.

'That's not fizzy,' said Madison, still looking at her iPhone as the waitress poured it into her glass.

'I'm sure you said still water, madam. I have it written down here.'

'We said sparkling. A large bottle. Take that one away, please.'

'How can you even tell the water's still? You're not looking at it,' said the friend.

'I can hear it. I can hear the distinct lack of carbonation as it's being poured.'

'I don't mind still water,' said the friend, 'in fact, I prefer it. In fact, I think I might have asked for it.'

As soon as she said this, the friend realized her mistake. The arch look was coming at her. 'Well, maybe we can have one of each,' the friend said.

'One of each. A compromise. Yes, why not? And while we're at it, let's just compromise on wanting to have water at all. How about liquid plutonium instead? Not much difference.'

'It's just fizzy water,' said the friend.

'It's just fizzy water. It's just a train fine. It's just the Pope telling Galileo he can't say the earth is revolving around the sun.'

'For heaven's sake!'

'For heaven's sake what? You want me to sit here and deny the Copernican model of the solar system now?'

The friend whimpered, then let it go. Madison wasn't a bad person. On the contrary, she was a very good person. One of the most loyal and kind people she knew. She just couldn't see the wood for the trees. In her view, if you didn't fight for everything, you fought for nothing.

A coffee with not enough coffee in it, a train fine, the lack of civil rights in China, or Burma or North Korea, inconsistencies in the evidence that man had landed on the moon, water that wasn't fizzy – for some reason it was all the same to her.

She didn't even begin to grasp the concept of 'pick your battles'. To her, life was one big battle. You got up in the morning and started fighting and you fought all day, every second of every minute of every hour until you arrived home at night after a nightmarish journey in a black cab, during which the cab driver never stopped telling you how far from anywhere civilized you lived, and how upset his wife was going to be that, because of you, he hadn't got home in time to take her to see the new Iranian film at the Curzon. And when you were driving alongside the park near your home, this same cab driver wound down the window and threw a packet of raw sausages out of the window for the foxes, forcing you to have another argument with the last ounce of strength left in you.

Did these things not happen to other people too? Probably. It was just that Madison didn't let a single one of them go.

And so, as she put the key in the door that night, she knew she would have dark circles around her eyes, and new worry lines on her forehead that had come up that very day.

But when she looked in the bathroom mirror she gasped as she saw a huge thick vein bulging on the right-hand side of her head. Later, she fell asleep watching TV in bed. But her eyes pinged open a few minutes later, and she lay wide awake for hours worrying about the fact that there was a squawking fox outside ripping the rubbish to pieces, and she really ought to ring the authorities and report the fox-feeding cab driver.

And if the authorities wouldn't do anything, she could always get a gun.

She imagined herself patrolling the streets with a .22 rifle, in a dirty tank top, bandana around her head, camouflage on her cheeks, firing shots into the air.

She would tell the startled residents who came out of their homes to object, 'Stand back! Someone has to deal with this. Step away from the string of sausages!' Pow!

Lying stiffly in bed, precisely at the meridian point, her arms by her sides over the sheets, the pillows arranged symmetrically and the duvet smoothed so that there wasn't even one crease, she tried to send herself off to sleep by counting foxes.

When that didn't work, she opened the bedside table drawer and took out a strip of pills she kept for sleep-related emergencies and swallowed one, then another for good measure. And when, after ten minutes, they appeared not to have worked either, she reached over the side of the bed and grasped the Bilby folder and began to read.

16

Behind every moderately successful man is a deeply dissatisfied woman.

And behind every deeply successful man is a moderately dissatisfied woman.

Belinda Bilby went from deeply to moderately dissatisfied on the day her husband floated his first company – Bilby Logistics – on the stock exchange and made £250 million pounds.

To celebrate their new super-wealth, they moved from a large house to an enormous house, from a Jaguar saloon to a Bentley Turbo, and from a frightful relationship to a merely fraught one.

In fact, they splashed out in every conceivable way. Mr Bilby set up a new company called Bilby and Bilby and placed most of his assets in his wife's name, registered to a home address in Monaco, where she apparently spent most of the year in a one-bedroom cupboard-sized apartment because the weather there helped her arthritis. She had never seen this apartment – just as she had never seen her arthritis – but she trusted it existed because her husband had told her all about it, right down to the pattern on the rug by the sofa, in case she ever needed to describe it to the people from Her Majesty's Revenue and Customs. Thankfully, the people from the Revenue never did ask her to describe either her arthritic joint problems or the carpet, because she never could remember whether it was pale blue and red, or deep pink and pale green. The carpet, I mean, not her arthritis.

Over the next two years Mrs Bilby gave birth in rapid succession to two more children, both boys, to add to the sullen and uncommunicative son they already had. Once divested of them, she oversaw the installation of a very flash swimming pool, Jacuzzi, sauna and gymnasium complex in the house in Holland Park.

This house was a beautiful forty-seven-room Queen Anne-style mansion built in 1875 to a design by Norman Shaw. An estate agent would have called it elegant and commodious.

As well as sixteen bedrooms and a labyrinth of staircases, it had the aforementioned swimming pool and leisure complex in the basement, as well as a private cinema and a triple-height ballroom.

Unfortunately, Mrs Bilby let her dogs shit all over it.

She had three chihuahuas, an Afghan hound and a Lhasa apso called Wonky-Poo, which was appropriate as his poo was in evidence everywhere, although whether it could be considered wonky depended on how closely you looked. It was probably no wonkier than the poo of any other Lhasa apso, but that didn't stop Marcus Bilby sticking his foot up the dog's backside and sending it arcing through the air at speed whenever his wife wasn't looking. He even drop-kicked it once, to no obvious detriment. The darn thing was as tough as old boots.

The matter of the poo did not detract much from the house's reputation, especially as it had become known rather hysterically as the largest in London (although in truth there were about 120 of those). It was rumoured to be worth an unfeasible £60 million, which was a living nightmare for all involved, especially the accountants.

Mrs Bilby, however, moved to the country place in the latter years of her marriage. This was a vast pile on a shooting estate called Tankards Reach, in a well-heeled village in Surrey which was so small that hardly anyone apart from the fifteen people who lived there knew it existed, and the people who did live there often wondered whether they really existed or were a figment of their own imaginations.

The Bilby country residence, it may be noted, had a very silly name. This was not lost on Mr Bilby when he bought it and indeed he even tried to haggle the estate agent down because of it. As he said, 'A Tankard does not have a reach.' But they wouldn't budge on the price and as Mrs Bilby had apparently, for some reason, fallen in love with it, Mr Bilby was forced to acquire it for £10.5 million. After completion, he tried to change the name but the district council wouldn't let him, nor would they confirm whether the missing apostrophe in the ancient sign for Tankards Reach at the bottom of the driveway should be before the 's' or after it, so the blasted place was not only metaphorically absurd, it was grammatically incorrect as well. Mr Bilby was distraught that he could move ships across oceans but he could not make the paperclip-counters of a Surrey council discuss an apostrophe.

As such, the house was tainted. Mr Bilby refused to go to Tankards Reach, which made it even more perfect for his wife.

'What does she do all day?' was the question a retired gamekeeper in the village called Bert asked his wife Margaret, who was Mrs Bilby's housekeeper, when she returned home tired and emotional in the evenings.

'I'll tell you what she does. She shops. She shops and she shops and she shops and she shops. And she buys so many clothes she has to have new cupboards built for the clothes. And when she's tired of shopping for clothes and building new cupboards for clothes she has new chunks stuck on the house so she can fit more new cupboards and new clothes in them.'

'Sounds a bit pointless to me,' said Bert, proving there was much truth in the old adage 'Out of the mouths of babes and gamekeepers'.

But what Margaret told him wasn't the whole truth, and she knew it. Mrs Bilby didn't just shop. She also went out for coffee. Every morning at 11 a.m. she dressed in vintage Alexander McQueen, or else Moschino, Missoni, Roberto Cavalli or Valentino, and met her friends in Cobham for coffee at coffee shops that were next door to boutiques selling more designer clothes, and sequinned

T-shirts and knick-knacks and not quite antique artefacts and every kind of daft novelty silver-plated spoon or fork she didn't need. And beyond the boutiques were beauty shops that did tanning, waxing, exfoliating facials and seaweed wraps. Or stripping and sanding, as Valmir and Vasilis, her two sinister, Eastern European bodyguards, called it, whenever they dropped her off there.

She also exercised her grey matter by helping to run various animal charities, including The Micro-Pig Foundation, and she read a lot. She toiled away for hours in her vast bedroom with its own elegant sitting-room area reading cheap thrillers in her La Perla dressing gown whilst drinking Moët.

She was not a slouch when it came to the grocery shopping, either. Twice a week she went to Waitrose, from which she emerged both times with three trolleys piled high with everything she could get into them. She was always driven by Valmir or Vasilis in a blacked-out Range Rover, number plate BOB1, for Belinda Ophelia Bilby, an abbreviation which spawned the codename 'Bobi', used by the bodyguards, in fondness, for they loved her dearly, but also in the same spirit of efficiency and diligence used by guardians of the President of the United States when they refer to him as Potus. So, for example, when one of them was helping her shop in Waitrose, the other would sit in the car and wait, and when the great lady was emerging from the supermarket, the one pushing her trolleys would say into the hidden walkie-talkie mike in his right cufflink: 'Bobi en route to car park. En route to car park.

Over.' Sometimes they said this in English, to reassure the boss of her tight security arrangements. Sometimes they forgot and said it in Albanian, which always prompted Mrs Bilby to complain bitterly: 'English, please! Don't talk as if I'm not here. I like to know what you're saying. You might be talking about assassinating me.' They did all this because they took their job seriously, but also because they wanted to relive the inglory of their previous lives in the war-torn Balkans, the truth of which we shall have to leave shrouded in mystery for now or we shall become seriously sidetracked.

Suffice to say, Valmir and Vasilis had begun working for Mrs Bilby after she found Valmir mending a roof on Kensington High Street. She had never delved too deeply into their origins but suffice it to say, she did have a sneaking suspicion they were ethnic Albanian rebel leaders who may have taken part in the odd small to medium-sized uprising back in the day. Having said that, one mustn't be petty, or indeed racist, when employing household staff and they were terribly good at frightening people away.

They were also very good at drinking champagne, and on the basis that one could never have enough people with whom to drink champagne, Valmir and Vasilis were a godsend. They were able to down several bottles of Moët, with or without vodka, in any one session.

In the same spirit, she made friends with the endless stream of builders who came every few months to add on the new chunks to the house, and they were more than happy to sit around the kitchen with her sharing the champers and telling her she was 'wasted'. She was wasted, though not in the sense she liked to think they meant, which was to say, a wasted treasure or a pearl cast before swine.

The thing that was well and truly wasted in that sense of the word was the fruit of her husband's labour, which, despite her efforts to despatch it in Cobham High Street, largely languished in a Monaco bank account, of which she had full control.

Meanwhile, the newly re-established Bilby, Bilby and Bilby (Logistics) was now administered very efficiently by a board of directors appointed in her husband's will, whilst being notionally controlled by her three sons, who were too lazy to do the slightest thing to contribute to the running of it, thank goodness.

In total, taking into account the funds from the liquidation of Bilby and Bilby, her small stake in Bilby, Bilby and Bilby, the house in London and the rest of the property including Surrey, Monaco and a charming little island somewhere off Scotland that her husband had acquired from a drunk viscount during a card game at Aspinalls, her assets, her lawyers informed her, were in the region of £15 billion.

'Numbers bore me, darling,' she told her drinking companions, sighing heavily. 'I care nothing for money. Money is of no importance to a woman of earthy passions and simple, artisanal tastes. If you ask me, money doth not happiness make and that no man is an island, no matter how he might try to force himself through the eye of a needle, like a camel.'

Mrs Bilby mixed metaphors and made them meaningless.

That she cared nothing for money was true, in a way. Like all rich people who proclaim their wealth and privilege irrelevant, Mrs Bilby was supremely unbothered by money so long as she had plenty of it. She would have started caring about it pretty darn quick if she had run out.

Indeed, once she got her head around the extent to which she would soon be losing it, she quickly came to the view that she would do anything she could to stop the idiot artist boy getting a single penny of the fortune that was hers by right, through years of putting up with Marcus and his horrible offspring, as she called them.

You might suppose she could just as easily have called Truman, Fitzgerald and Ernest *her* horrible offspring, especially since she had gone to the trouble to name them all after her favourite authors. (Strictly speaking, they weren't her favourite authors. Her favourite authors were Dean R. Koontz, Stephen King and Sidney Sheldon. But those names didn't really work for her social purposes.)

She resolutely refused to call them *her* horrible offspring because she passionately believed that Truman, Fitz and Ernie had come out wrong because of the way her husband had insisted on conceiving them, whilst dressed up in her best leopard-print Roberto Cavalli underwear, listening to 'Bohemian Rhapsody'. If she had had her way, it would all have been quite different. She didn't ask for much, but soft lighting, a little romantic classical music and her husband not wearing her G-string would have been nice, and would have spawned a far classier and more intellectual trio of brats, in her opinion.

Madison lay in bed with the Bilby file on top of the covers and thought about her new client, and her new client's poor children. It could not have been easy for them growing up in a vast mansion in Holland Park with the eccentric Mrs Bilby as a mother.

Come to think of it, she thought, as her eyelids grew heavy, it could not have been easy for anyone living with Mrs Bilby.

17

After three years living life in the fast lane, Seth Taylor's adventures with Mrs Bilby led him, rather sadly, to the Citizens Advice Bureau in Croydon, where so many dreams must end.

The nice lady there recommended a cheap lawyer. Free divorce lawyers did not exist, dearie, she explained, because pro bono was not allowed in divorce cases, and neither were conditional fee arrangements whereby the lawyer took his cut from the settlement he won his client at the end.

So Seth ended up with a lawyer he could afford, which was the worst lawyer in Croydon, and that was saying something.

'Is he any good?' he asked the nice lady, who wore her glasses on an actual piece of string and had a rubber finger-protector on the index finger of her right hand to protect it from getting ink on it from her cheap biro.

'Who, dear?'

'This lawyer you're recommending. The one whose

name you've just written down on this bit of paper.' He turned it over in his hands. 'Is he any good?'

'Him? Oh no, dear. Goodness me, no.'

Elden John ran a small sole practice, with experience mainly of immigration, conveyancing, insolvency, personal injury and other 'no win, no fee' compensation work to keep the wolf from the door. He had absolutely no experience whatsoever with divorce, but had taken on Seth when the lady from the Citizens Advice Bureau called him because he was in a bit of a tight corner, financially. As usual.

In his last personal injury case, his clients Wayne and Tanya Dawson had not only lost what they'd thought would be an open and shut claim for whiplash in a rear shunt they had faked on Streatham High Road, but were also sent to prison for perjuring themselves. Since then, the work had not been forthcoming.

And then there was the matter of the slight conveyancing mistake he had made, in which he had borrowed money from another client's holding account to pay his mortgage one month when he was a bit short. He had always meant to put it back.

The Law Society investigation would probably exonerate him from wrongdoing, eventually. It was his contention that an internet banking error had made the money disappear mysteriously from the escrow account before re-appearing three weeks later.

And if they didn't let him off, well, then he would cross that bridge when he came to it. He could always play the piano in cocktail bars. He would have to learn the piano first, of course, but that shouldn't be too much of a problem.

I feel I should balance all of this by telling you the good things about Elden John: I mean, the good thing, singular.

He was cheap. Well, let's not gild the lily – he was free. He had offered the penniless Seth a not-strictly-kosher deal whereby he would give him his services at a nominal rate – 25p an hour, to make it legal – in return for a nod and a wink with regard to him getting a huge cut of the dosh if and when he took Mrs Bilby to the cleaners.

'No fleece, no fee, you might call it,' he joked. But Seth looked a bit queasy.

The first thing they needed to do, the lawyer explained, was lodge the divorce petition citing Mrs Bilby's unreasonable behaviour.

'You have done this before . . . haven't you?' Seth asked him as the pair of them sat in Elden John's sparse office space, the euphemistically entitled Suite 23 – it really wasn't a suite, more a cupboard with an Ikea desk, some Ikea shelves and an Ikea filing cabinet – in the Whitgift Shopping Centre in Croydon.

'Not exactly, per se, so to speak,' said John, who tended to insert phrases which added nothing to the meaning of what he was trying to communicate.

Seth frowned. 'What do you mean, exactly, by *not exactly*?'

Seth was not an argumentative man. He was a conciliatory sort. He would give anything for a quiet life. He was a doormat, a fact he had already explained to his lawyer.

He had only married Mrs Bilby because she told him to. All he knew, looking back, was that he had finished the portrait of Marcus Bilby, delivered it to the back door of the Bilby residence in Holland Park, whereupon, as he stood there waiting for a servant to take the unframed canvas from him, Mrs Bilby's hand came out of the back door and pulled him inside the kitchen. She sat him down at the kitchen table, where the servants were having their dinner.

She was wearing a very strange ensemble by Issey Miyake, though he could not have known that, of course. All he knew was that her Aladdin-inspired costume featured chiffon pantaloons that were entirely see-through, displaying her red knickers. His eyes were fixed to this unfortunate spot as she led him to the table and sat him down.

'Darling, you've done wonders with the old badger,' she said, apparently referring to the portrait. 'Now, come and drink a teensy glass of bubbly with Mrs B, so that we can celebrate your very great genius.'

'Is Mr Bilby coming?' Seth looked around frantically for signs that the shipping magnate might appear and make everything safe, for Mrs Bilby appeared to be undressing him with her eyes.

'Oh, I'm afraid not. My husband is taking supper in bed with Simon Cowell.' And Mrs Bilby popped a cork and filled a glass with an excited explosion of froth. 'I mean to say, he's watching *The X Factor*. Poor Marcus. He has never been a cultured man. I don't like to complain but I have spent my entire married life feeling stifled by him. Spiritually, intellectually . . .' There was a dreadful pause. '. . . sexually . . .'

About one hundred seconds and three flutes of champagne later, Mrs Bilby communicated to Seth that they were now, and irreversibly to all intents and purposes, having an affair.

Seth explained all this to Elden John, as they sat together in his office in Suite 23 of the Whitgift Centre.

'And a few months later the poor old man died, would you believe?' he explained, and Mrs Bilby had informed him that they were to be married. This altercation took place in the kitchen of the country residence where she was now living, as she and he sat at the table drinking champagne.

Like the start of the affair, the onset of marriage was an irreversible process, so far as Seth could make out from what Mrs Bilby was saying.

'Well, if you're sure,' said Seth, not arguing, because Seth never argued. And so they were married at Tankards Reach and the rest was a horrible blur of unspeakable things happening, and not happening, which was worse, all culminating in him trying to renegotiate the terms of their arrangement.

'Really, it's my fault, Mrs Bilby, I'm truly sorry.' He thought if he went back to calling her Mrs Bilby he might turn the clock back to the point when the relationship was just about manageable.

But that had not been possible. Eventually, he had found

himself on the wrong end of a cheese knife, and had been forced to escape from Tankards on a seat-less motorbike.

'You see,' Seth explained, as Elden John's eyes all but popped out of his head in astonishment, 'I could hear Mrs Bilby inside the house crashing about in the kitchen drawers.'

He had come to the only conclusion he could, Seth explained, which was that she was looking for a bigger knife. She later maintained she had been looking for first aid equipment. But how was he to know this?

So he did the only sensible thing under the circumstances. He drove at the security gates with his eyes closed, hoping they were on automatic open, and not night mode. Fortune smiled on him because they opened, with just one minute to go to the cut-off time, and he made his bid for freedom.

Those who saw the motorbike making its stately progress around the M25 that night must have had to do a double take.

Seth stood up on the pedals going very, very slowly, occasionally letting go of the handlebars with one hand to clutch his backside. All the way into south London he went like this, until he reached his father's house in Thornton Heath.

The next morning, he rode the seat-less motorbike one last time, to the Citizens Advice Bureau in Croydon.

'Can I help you, dear?' said the nice lady behind the counter.

'Er, yes,' said Seth, taking off his helmet as he sat down at the desk, then winced, and got back up again. 'I think I need a divorce, please. A rich heiress I sort of accidentally married when I was at a low ebb is probably going to cut my throat with a cheese knife if I ever go back to get my things out of her house.'

'Right, I see,' said the nice lady, pulling out forms 55b and 37ii. 'Fill these out.'

As he finished his account of these sorry circumstances, he looked pathetically at the lawyer.

Elden John licked his lips. Clearly, if he tried, he could wrap Seth around his little finger. Elden John hadn't been able to wrap anyone around his little finger before.

He imagined it. He envisaged Seth like a string of Play-Doh, being stretched longer and thinner until he was nothing but a shoelace being wound round and round, squealing . . .

Elden John was overcome by a sudden belief that he could manipulate Seth Taylor into just about anything.

And so when Seth asked him if he had done divorces before, he leaned forward and said: 'Not exactly. But I did have considerable experience of a case like yours when, er . . .'

As Seth's face lit up, John trailed off and stopped talking. Then he began to stare out of the window. About three minutes later, for no particular reason that Seth could make out, he turned back around and concluded his sentence. '. . . whilst working as a paralegal during my gap year for a firm of solicitors called Wright Hassell.'

'Oh,' said Seth, trying to digest the full extent of the awfulness of his situation. 'And since then?'

'Nothing. As I say, you're my first divorce. I was terribly excited when the Citizens Advice Bureau rang me to ask if I would offer you my, er . . .'

This time, Seth felt obliged, as most people did, after about ten awkward seconds, to help Elden John finish his sentence. 'Services?'

'Thank you.'

'You're welcome,' said Seth, trying, as usual, to make the best of a bad situation.

18

Seth Taylor first learned to make the best of a bad situation in 1975, when he was aged three months and five days. His mother Louisa Mary Taylor plopped him down on his grandmother Eunice Taylor's lap as she was sitting in a bus shelter in a dreary suburb of south London and said, 'You'll have to look after him. I'm not cut out for this.'

Eunice had been minding her own business waiting for the number 197 bus, so we can forgive her for being a bit hostile towards the Moses basket containing her grandson and now foster son.

At first she refused to take it. She argued. She told her daughter this was really not on. But Louisa had made up her mind.

'I'm desperate,' she said. 'I can't go on. I feel like every day the walls are closing in on me and I'm suffocating.'

'Is this about that gardener you've been having it away with?' said Eunice. 'Because if it is, you're a fool. If you're really leaving Geoffrey and all his money and that nice house in Glendower Gardens for that good-for-nothing scrubber . . .'

Louisa leaned into the basket and kissed her son. And then she crossed the road to the stop for the number 37, because that went to where she was planning to meet the good-for-nothing scrubber, with whom she was planning to elope.

There then followed an embarrassing twenty minutes as the two women sat waiting for their respective buses on either side of the street, Louisa sitting alone in the shelter for the 37, while her mother sat in the shelter for the 197, tending the bawling infant, whose suspicions had been raised and who was wondering more feverishly by the second why Louisa had decided to take a different bus to the one he was queuing for.

Naturally, the two buses were both late, and then came along at the same time, as buses are apt to do.

As Eunice got up to board her bus, she shouted at Louisa Mary: 'Louisa Mary,' she shouted, shaking the Moses basket at her as if it were a sack of potatoes, 'you won't get away with this. I won't pick up your pieces.' And she got on the bus holding the baby basket with a very angry expression in her eyes.

Whereupon Louisa, who was already crying genuine tears of sadness and regret, shouted: 'He's due a feed at four, Ma. Tell Geoff I'm sorry . . .'

But Eunice was on the bus, looking for a double seat where she could store both her shopping trolley and the baby. There wasn't one. So she had to pile everything up on the floor in the tiny space between her feet and the seat in front of her. It was all deeply annoying.

Louisa got on her bus crying bitter tears and sat with her face pressed against the window waving as the two buses passed each other and drove away.

Nowadays, of course, we would say she was suffering from post-natal depression, but in the mid-1970s post-natal depression had not really been invented.

Seth adapted as best he could to life with his grand-mother Eunice, who was not a woman who easily gave away affection, although she did feed and care for him methodically and fulfilled her duties as a caretaker in every technical way.

But after a year and no sign of Louisa, despite extensive investigations, Eunice decided to outsource the problem herself, and so she marched into Glendower Gardens, up the driveway of Squirrel's Leap, knocked on Geoffrey's door and said: 'You'll have to look after him. I'm too old for this.'

Geoffrey Roberts was not in the best of places, his wife having run off with the gardener.

He had visited the child often enough at Eunice's and paid towards its keep, but had largely accepted that Seth would be subsumed back into Eunice's side of the family and had even agreed to his name being changed to Taylor. He never thought it feasible to take his son back and bring him up on his own. Men simply did not do that in the seventies. The man-mummies you see now in Starbucks, coddling their toddlers in papooses, are an entirely new invention in that respect.

Once Geoffrey did try to raise his son on his own he proved how unfeasible it really was.

Although he was a very good turf accountant, as an early prototype of the man-mummy, he didn't function at all well. In fact, he dysfunctioned in every single way. There was no method to his parenting, and quite a lot of madness. But he showered the baby with love.

Indeed, he loved the little boy so much you would have thought he more than made up for any deficit in the love department left by Eunice and Louisa.

'Will Master Seth have beans on toast tonight or pilchards?' he would say, as he peered into the cupboard at the store of easy-to-cook comestibles his various female neighbours put in there for him every week when they did their own shopping.

'Beans!' Seth would shout, banging his fork on the table.

'Right you are, sir. Coming up on the double.' And Geoffrey would run around the kitchen pretending to be a servant until Seth would be laughing so hard he couldn't breathe. 'Come on, lad, calm down. Help your old dad make the toast.'

And the two of them would butter the toast together. Then, after tea, Geoffrey would read to his son from *World of Dogs* magazine or else they would watch a TV movie, usually something starring Clint Eastwood and involving a good deal of sex and violence. Sometimes they played cards, usually blackjack.

Geoffrey taught Seth all his best gambling tricks. He gave him some other tips too.

During the day, when he went to work at the bookmakers, he taught him how to tell people who knocked on the back door things that made them stop asking for money. And also how to lie to the police, if they asked why he was not at school. He never went to school. Geoffrey was too worried about the teachers asking questions and wanting to take his son away.

And so the two spent their every waking hour together, and Seth learned the bookies' trade and a lot about the form of horses and greyhounds.

He was not especially deprived by his lack of formal education. He taught himself to read by studying betting slips and listening to the TV sets on the walls of the betting shop, and this gave him a more varied vocabulary than he might have acquired at pre-school. His favourite phrases, aged four were 'Lady Pimpernel's coming up on the outside!' and 'Boomshackerlacker by a length!'

His innate artistic talent was also well nurtured. One of his favourite things to do by the time he should have been at school was to sit in the shop sketching pictures of the people laying bets. They were well-worn faces, lined and craggy. Their skin seemed to sag as if pulled down by invisible weights.

The old men had deep, dark half-moon shapes beneath their eyes and big red noses that made him think of the sadness of clowns.

Later, when people started to commission him to paint portraits, he remembered the betting shop punters with fondness and a sense of sadness that they were probably no longer around.

But the most important, most striking, most definite

advantage Seth Taylor enjoyed was that he was incredibly easy on the eye.

People always said he was blessed with good looks because his sandy blond hair, olive skin, bright blue eyes and Adonis-like physique really did look like the work of the angels.

This meant that despite his many other disadvantages, including little or no education and a personality that was by and large borderline autistic, he got away with it.

He quickly worked out – more by accident than design – that older women in particular were a good port in a storm.

As he began to make his own way in the world, there was always some rich divorcée or other who took him under her wing. There was always a lady with a room in her house where he could lodge and eat free and become a member of the family.

He didn't use these women, exactly, he just allowed them to use him to cheer themselves up.

Whilst living this carefree lifestyle, he put cards up in shops advertising his portrait business.

There weren't many people in the suburbs of south London who wanted a painting of themselves and he ended up drawing a lot of family pets. Cats, dogs, ferrets, that sort of thing.

The Bilby commission had been a godsend. He had been retained through the recommendation of a friend of his father, for whom he had painted a very nice whippet.

The portrait of Marcus Bilby had been a triumph, in his view. The sittings at which his subject had posed whilst

propped up in bed had been quite tricky, because he had
kept sneezing. Seth had offered him antihistamine pills
at one point, only for him to shout: 'It's not hay fever,
it's those damned dogs. I'm allergic but she won't get rid
of them!'

But despite the challenges, the finished work had been
one of his best, in his opinion.

Such a shame when the old man died. Sneezed his head
off, they said.

He was waiting for payment when Mrs Bilby offered
him her hand in marriage and he didn't feel he was in any
position to refuse. He might not get the money in if he said
no. He thought with his usual vagueness that he might be
able to get out of it later.

Seth's father was distraught. He could see his son was
just taking what Mrs Bilby was offering because he was
still searching for his mother.

After everything he had done to make it up to his son,
he could never fill the hole in Seth's soul that opened up
the day Louisa ran away on the number 37 bus.

There was something unhealable about that hole. Like
a scar that hadn't been stitched, its edges never knitted
properly together.

19

Seth certainly looked like a lost soul as he sat holding a plastic bag, containing his wallet and house keys, in front of Elden John of Elden John Associates in Suite 23 of the Whitgift Shopping Centre in Croydon.

Poor Elden John also looked pretty lost. 'People come to see me but they don't retain my services once they realize I have difficulties expressing myself and a concentration . . .' He began to stare at the space beyond Seth's head.

'Problem?'

'Yes.'

'We all have our ups and downs,' said Seth, tightening his grip on the bag and trying to disguise his mounting sense of panic.

'The concentration problem is pretty much under—' said Elden, stopping abruptly mid-sentence.

'Control?'

'Hmm?'

'You were saying you had the concentration problem under control.'

'That's right. But I have another problem.'

'Another one?'

'My main problem is a form of Tourette's that makes me shout out one particular swear word when I'm under a lot of stress.'

'I see. Can you give me some idea of the sort of swear word we're talking about?'

Elden John had a childish look of guilt on his face.

'Oh. You mean the C word?'

'As in King Cnut, yes.'

'Oh dear.'

'It can be very inconvenient. Male judges are usually pretty understanding about it but women judges hate it.'

'You mean you've shouted it in court?'

'A handful of times. Seven, tops. When I was an intern with Wright Hassell I was jailed for contempt. You're not going to hire me, are you? I knew I shouldn't have been honest. I should never let anyone know there's something wrong with me.'

Seth reflected on the situation for only a second before he made his decision. Obviously he had to hire the worst lawyer in the world because that was the kind thing to do.

He could hardly string the poor chap out to dry. If Elden John didn't get a proper case soon he would never make his way in the legal profession and all those who had sought to keep him down because of his affliction would be proved right. He owed it to him to give him a chance. So he said:

'Can you start work on my case straight away?'

'C***!' shouted Elden John. 'Sorry, I forgot to say – sometimes I say it when I'm happy.'

As the pair got down to brass tacks, Elden John's initial euphoria wore off when he discovered that Seth really did not want to take Mrs Bilby to the cleaners. This was very disappointing.

The beauty of such a high-profile case was going to be that, so long as he didn't say the C word too often in the courtroom, he would get so much exposure he would never need to put an advert in the *Croydon Sentinel* again. And if he won, he would get paid a huge sum out of the settlement.

But if Seth didn't want to go for it in a high-value case, it wouldn't be much use at all. It would be the briefest of divorces with no publicity value. He felt his big moment ebbing away.

His only chance lay in convincing Seth Taylor that he had a right – no, a duty – to extract the settlement he deserved from Mrs Bilby.

'You have a right – no, you have a duty – to seek what you are owed under the, er . . .'

'Law?' Seth finished his sentence.

'Very good!' said Elden. 'You're getting the hang of this.'

'But I don't want any money. I just want one of those quickie divorces.'

'Look, it's not up to you. You must think of the bigger picture.' Elden sounded distinctly ratty now.

'What bigger picture?'

'If you let this rich, predatory woman off the hook it will set a dangerous precedent, Mr Taylor. A dangerous legal precedent.'

'Oh?'

'Yes. If you give in and walk away with no money, you will have established, in the eyes of the law, a firm principle upon which all future divorce cases involving young, penniless, helpless men separating from rich, selfish, predatory women will be decided upon. To wit, Mr Taylor, if you get no money from this divorce, neither will any other poverty-stricken young man who comes after you. And those men may really need the money, Mr Taylor. They may not have the artistic talent you have, the ability to scratch a living by drawing pictures of people's cats.

'They may need alimony to survive, to pay the bills, to heat their home, to eat, to live, to feed their starving children. Have you thought how selfish it would be to deny those poor men the very means of existence? To take food out of their children's mouths? To rob them of the very means to survive?'

'Oh dear. I hadn't thought of that.'

'That's why I'm here, Mr Taylor. To think of things. Of things you can never imagine in your wildest dreams. Things that are entirely of another plane of experience. That is why we lawyers charge a lot of money. We deliver a service that is absolutely indispensable. We take care of problems that the client cannot even conceive of until we point these problems out. I am here to guard your back, Mr Taylor. And not only your back, but the backs of all those helpless victims who are relying on you to do the right thing. Can they rely on you, Mr Taylor?'

'Yes, they can rely on me,' said Seth, gloomily, staring down at his feet. 'So what do we do?'

'First we lodge a petition for divorce citing her unreasonable behaviour. I will do that right away. It should be easy enough. She plunged a serrated-edge cheese knife into your . . . your . . . er . . .'

'Backside.'

'Thank you.'

'And then?' prompted Seth, wondering how much more Elden John he could take before he went completely mad.

'And then we ask for money, Mr Taylor. I think we should apply for an interim maintenance order so you can pay me something towards your legal fees and other costs. We might need forensic . . .' He trailed off.

'Scientists? Will there be a murder?'

'Forensic accountants. Sorry. And private investigators. To find the money. She will hide it.'

'Oh dear. I'm not sure I'm really up for this.'

'And then we will need to go through various hearings while the judge decides how much she has to pay. She will fight dirty, of course. She has appointed a very slick lawyer. Madison Flight, of Wilde and Sawyer. She was *Vanity Fair*'s twenty-sixth most frightening woman in the world of 2013.'

'Oh dear.'

'She will try to make you look like a cruel and abusive gold-digger.'

'I don't like the sound of that.'

'Don't worry about it. I am going to work night and day on your behalf and I have every intention of proving that you are totally and utterly guilty . . .' Elden was staring at the space beyond his head again.

Seth squeaked. Elden snapped back to attention.

'. . . of nothing more than being in love with a woman who manipulated you and used you and cast you aside.'

Fine, thought Seth. So I'm going to have to finish my lawyer's sentences. It could be worse.

20

The family law team at Wilde and Sawyer usually declared half-time at 12.30 p.m. and left the office to walk the short distance through the packed streets of Holborn to their regular luncheon venue.

Christopher and Madison went for lunch together at the same restaurant most days.

Christopher often said he wanted to go somewhere new, but Madison didn't like new places.

So they went to The Lobster Pot, a dingy budget diner serving simple home-microwaved food at preposterously low prices. It couldn't possibly be making any money and some said it was a front for a sinister criminal racket of some sort, though no one knew quite what.

It had wooden tables and chairs and a hatch through which the steaming plates of food appeared and were slammed down, and then announced to the waiting staff by a loud clap of the chef's hands. The menu was extremely large – too large, one might say. They can't possibly be cooking all that stuff out the back, the customers all thought silently to themselves as they looked down the unfeasibly long list of culinary possibilities. In fact, history will recount that there was only one thing The Lobster Pot had never attempted to serve, and that was lobster.

Because their office contained a pale, thin bespectacled secretary called Judith, who whispered everything and was permanently on the verge of tears – that's when she wasn't obstructing their every request by claiming that it couldn't be achieved, no matter how small or insignificant it was – Christopher and Madison spent a lot of time in The Lobster Pot. Often they took their work there, spread it out over the table and got much more done than they would have with Judith nagging them.

Their fellow diners were a mixture of tourists, taxi drivers, professionals on a budget, students, and local bohemian minor aristocrats who had fallen upon hard times and, when they were not in Kerala for the winter, wanted their meals cooked for them as if they still had household staff.

Every few months or so, the owner, Luigi Rizzo, a very small neat man in a Lacoste polo shirt, chinos and brown brogues would come up to Christopher as he ate his lunch and say, in a low, conspiratorial voice: 'I might need you. I don't know I need you yet. But I might need you. Soon.' And he would wink, and tap his nose. He had been saying this exact sentence, and winking and tapping his nose, in the same place, just on the side of the right nostril, for about seven years now, ever since finding out that Christopher and Madison were lawyers.

Christopher would nod and say they could be relied upon to do whatever was needed and on that basis, ever since they first promised this, he and Madison had always been able to get the big table in the far corner with the comfortable banquette at any time of day or night. They were never any the wiser about what Luigi might one day need them for, and tried not to think too much about it.

Once, Rizzo got pulled over for drink-driving and nearly secured their services. He had a cast-iron defence, he informed them, as he had been taking his disabled mother out for dinner. Quite why he was taking her out for dinner at 3 a.m. and needed a claw hammer in the boot and a suitcase full of cash, was a small technical matter he would like Christopher and Madison to help him iron out. But thankfully it never came to that, as mysteriously, after two court appearances, the Crown Prosecution Service suddenly dropped all the charges.

Whether or not Rizzo had turned informant they never found out, but so long as there were old favourites like prawn cocktail on the menu, Madison saw no immediate need to panic. Drive-by shootings at restaurants were rare, she assured Christopher. Crime lords usually settled these things by coming for their enemies at home, in the dead of night. And in any case, a drive-by shooting was unlikely to disturb them so long as they were sitting at their banquette table at the back.

They sat at this table now, and picked up the huge menu cards. Madison looked at the specials on a blackboard on the wall. In truth, there was nothing special about the specials, for this blackboard always bore the same offerings, including Madison's favourite, 'minestronez soup', always written with a z, and always pronounced minestron-*ez* by the waitress. It reminded her of her unfashionable 1970s childhood, when meals often began with thin genteel gruels almost always featuring croutons.

'Where's the soup?' The tone of Madison's voice was the one that made Christopher's chest tighten.

'I'm sure it's there.' Christopher was staring over the top of his half-moon specs at the laminated list of delicacies, from 'scampi and chip' to 'spaghetti with meatsball'.

'It's not. It's not on the board. It's not there.' Madison's face took on a frozen look. She peered closer at a suspicious-looking smudged area where the soup had been but where now there was only a ghost of a chalk mark, and all but shrieked: 'It's been rubbed off!' She waved manically at the waitress, who lurched towards them with empty plates balanced all the way up her arms. 'Where's the minestron-*ez* soup? What have you done with it?'

'Good afternoon to you too. It's nice to see you. Thank you for asking about me, I'm fine today,' said the waitress.

'Yes, yes,' said Madison impatiently. 'Where's the minestron*ez*?'

'We've a different soup today. Leek and potato. I haven't got around to writing it on the board yet. It's very nice.'

Madison suddenly found herself lifting the waitress off the floor by her neck with one hand. Possessed of an almost supernatural strength, she dangled the woman in the air as her feet kicked helplessly and she made gurgling noises through her half-closed throat.

The other diners totally ignored this scene and went on eating, seemingly in total oblivion. Christopher had opened up a copy of the *Evening Standard* and was reading the classified ads for the latest West End theatre shows at the back. He fancied going to see *Slash!* – although he wasn't sure if it was a stage biopic about the band Guns N' Roses or the story of Jack the Ripper. Either would be entertaining, he supposed. The waitress wiggled and turned purple. The she started to look a bit blue.

Madison wondered if it might not be a good idea to throttle her after all. Was it really her fault that the minestronez was off the menu? Yes, thought Madison, it bloody well was. The waitress had been mocking her with all that talk of leek and potato. She knew what a terrible disruption this would be to Madison's life, and the routine she relied on to make everything all right.

She tightened her grip a bit more. And then a bit more. The waitress went purpler. And then her eyes started to bulge. She made a series of terrible gagging sounds and then . . .

'So do you want the leek and potato or what?' The waitress had her head on one side and was waiting for her answer.

Madison's expression had assumed a rictus grin as she fantasized about murdering the woman. Christopher had indeed picked up the *Standard*, to pass the time during the ensuing brouhaha. 'Fasten your seatbelts,' he muttered under his breath.

'No. I don't want leek and potato. I want minestronez.'

'No minestronez,' said the waitress, with a determined look that said she was going to try and enjoy the next few minutes.

'Why have you taken off the minestronez? I don't understand. That board never changes. Never. Why now? Why today? For the love of God, why today?'

'Chef thought it might be nice to have a change.'

'A change? A *change*?' Madison was doing her best impression of Lady Bracknell. 'But I don't want a change.'

'I seem to remember you complaining yesterday that the menu was boring and never had anything new on it. You said you were sick of prawn cocktail and minestronez soup.'

'I never said that. I would never say that.'

'You should try the leek and potato.'

'I don't want the leek and potato. I want the minestronez. Tell the chef. He must have some out the back.'

'We don't have anything out the back. There is no minestronez.'

'Where's Luigi?'

'Luigi's off today.'

'Listen to me. We've been coming here for—'

'Three years, five months and twenty-seven days. A very long time.'

'Yes. And I've been eating minestronez soup for a very long time and there's no good reason why I shouldn't eat minestronez soup for even longer than very long.'

'You could always go somewhere else to eat it.'

'I don't want to go somewhere else to eat it! It's bad enough eating it here!'

'You know, you should really try the leek and potato. Always eating the same thing isn't healthy. Besides, this happens in restaurants all the time. Chefs change menus. You need to relax. Chill out.'

'Uh-oh.' Christopher took his glasses off, as if he feared he might get punched in the face in the crossfire.

But Madison didn't throw a punch. She walked away from the table and paced up and down very melodramatically, holding one hand to her temple, from which protruded an ostentatiously pumping vein. Christopher took the opportunity to put in his order.

'I'll have the pâté to start, and then the trout with *seasfood* mix and *chip*. And she'll have the same.'

Madison came storming back to the table.

'How much?'

'Sorry?'

'How much do you want to put the minestronez back on?'

'It's not about money.'

'Can you hear yourself? "It's not about money"! This is a business, isn't it? Of course it's about money. And if you want to get money from me you have to give me minestronez. How much do you want to go out now and buy a 50p can of minestronez soup and bring it back here and heat it up and put it in a bowl and bring it to me?'

The waitress walked away.

'Just once I would like to come out for lunch without having a huge row over something incredibly small and insignificant,' said Christopher.

'That's what my needs are to you? Small and insignificant? There are tribunals I could take that to.'

'Yes, there are. But you won't. Now, I'm going to listen to you moan about the minestronez soup for ten more seconds only . . .' and he laid his cheap wristwatch on the table 'and then I want to discuss something important. Ready? Your ten seconds begin . . . now!'

'You think you're funny, but you're not funny. That minestronez soup is an important part of my daily—'

'I'm sorry, your time to moan about the minestronez is now up. No more minestronez moaning for you today. Same time tomorrow?'

'What was it you wanted to talk about?'

'Hmm?'

'Something important, you said.'

'Oh, yes, well, the thing is—'

'Oh my God.'

'What now?'

Madison had taken a swig of the mineral water in her glass.

'This is still water, not fizzy.'

'We'll send it back. Don't panic.'

But she was panicking. 'Luigi goes away for one day and the place falls to pieces. Come on, come on!' she said, looking for the waitress who had entirely disappeared. 'Where is she?'

'I don't understand why you always have to get so worked up about every little thing,' said Christopher. 'One minute it's minestrone soup and the next minute its water. Next thing you'll be arguing about interest rates, or tax, or saying you're furious about the Pope. Or something. Don't you ever get tired of arguing about everything?'

Madison thought for a minute. It was a very good question. She thought a bit more. And then the answer came. 'That's the funny thing,' she said, as she waved at a waitress. 'I never do seem to get tired of arguing. I always think I'm going to. But it never actually happens.'

Sometimes she suspected that arguing was her engine room. It was the generator that made the heat and energy that was keeping her alive.

Christopher persisted. 'The thing is, I wanted to ask you if you would consider . . . I have to go to this hideous play of Chloe's this evening, as you know, and I'm dreading it. Oh, I may look tough, and in control and suave and self-possessed . . .'

At this moment, Christopher, who had been fiddling neurotically with his glasses, tried to put them back on his face but one of the side arms came out in his hand. Madison looked at him blankly, at his glasses sitting lopsided on his face, the stray arm in his hands, his hair standing up on end, his collar undone, his badly knotted tie skew-whiff. He put the broken-off arm in his pocket and poked his glasses, which fell into an even sillier position.

'. . . but beneath this cool, calm, self-assured exterior there's an awkward, shambolic nervous wreck, believe it or not.'

The glasses now fell off his face entirely. He put them away in his pocket and squinted.

'Since Isobel left me and became a man I haven't been very good with social occasions. The truth is, I feel horribly alone all the fucking time, Mads. After what she did to me, that's not surprising. But you know, despite it all, the pain, the hurt, the years of torment, the affair, the divorce, her taking the kids away, the loss of the house and the money, having to pay for her gender reassignment surgery as the final bloody insult, and then the nervous breakdown, the cognitive behavioural therapy, the cluster headaches, the foot eczema, the endless fucking foot eczema, and Isobel telling everyone it's not eczema, it's athlete's foot – it's not athlete's foot – God knows, it's difficult enough having your feet itch all the time without your ex-wife telling everyone it's fungal . . . and Isobel not even being Isobel any more because she's now calling herself Jefferson – after Jefferson Airplane, apparently...

'But despite all of that, a part of me still believes in love. I still believe there's someone out there . . . and sometimes I wonder whether . . . I wonder if that someone isn't someone right under my nose, someone I see every day, someone who is . . . here . . . right . . . now . . .'

'Do you know what I think?' Madison was leaning forward and staring deep into his eyes.

'Please. Tell me.'

'I think she's gone to find that can of soup.' Madison turned around and began scouring the restaurant for the waitress, who was all she had been thinking about for the three and a half minutes during which Christopher had poured out the long-concealed contents of his heart and soul.

'She knows I'm right,' said Madison. 'She knows it. And she's going to get me my minestronez because that is what she should have done all along. And here she is. Yes! I do believe that's a thin, brown, tasteless, over-processed gruel in the bowl that is making its majestic progress towards me now. She shoots, she scores!' And she held up her palm for the purpose of high-fiving.

Christopher felt a pang of hurt at first, and then relief. It was probably best she hadn't heard.

21

A few months earlier, the senior staff of Wilde and Sawyer had attended a legal conference at the De Vere Heron's Reach hotel and conference centre just outside Blackpool. I'm not going to apologize for that. Sometimes the truth is boring. It still has to be faced up to.

'Eat Drink Sleep Chill Meet Party' is the slogan of that particular establishment, as displayed on its website. A more honest slogan might have been: 'Turn Up Get Drunk Sleep With Someone From The Office Go Home With A Hangover'.

Madison and Christopher were enrolled to take part in a compulsory refresher course called 'Leave to Remove and Schedule 1 – Detecting Trends', which meant arrangements for divorcing couples where one parent wants to abduct their children and take them to a foreign country.

In between studying divorce cases where husbands, or wives, had run away to Australia with their infants, they were forced to partake in the organized 'fun' that was laid on as part of the occasion.

They were paired off together for a team-building exercise in which they were supposed to build a model of the hotel out of Lego. This made them even more angry and depressed than they already were and they got even more drunk as a result.

That evening, in the romantic surrounds of the Heron's Reach 'Village Urban Resort' bar, whatever that was, they both got steaming drunk and sat watching the other lawyers networking at a Surf and Turf 1980s-themed 'buffet and boogie' evening.

'I hate solicitors,' said Christopher. 'They're fuckpigs.'

'I'm going to buy more drink,' said Madison, heaving herself up from her chair.

'I should have been a barrister,' said Christopher. 'My father was right.'

While she was gone, REO Speedwagon came on the sound system and some of the lawyers in suits started to slow dance, the men with their ties pulled askew, splodges of surf and turf remnants down their shirt fronts, the women with their skirts hitched up and askew, tottering on high heels, their black stockings laddered beyond repair.

Christopher sat in stunned drunkenness – the sort of drunkenness that involves rocking backwards and forwards whilst making little 'hurr, hurr, hurr, hurr' sounds – and watched Madison at the bar talking to a lawyer with spilled Marie Rose sauce down his front.

Christopher was feeling decidedly stirred up, which was unusual for him, as, since his nervous breakdown, he had become expert at pushing down all emotion to a level where it could never again get back up.

But he found the drink and the music and the traumatic

team-building exercises, and perhaps even the Marie Rose sauce, to be extremely provocative. He imagined being able to tell Madison his feelings for her.

No, that wasn't it. He wanted Madison to tell him. He wanted to be sitting at the bar chatting up a drunk female lawyer with laddered stockings, and her to walk up behind him and tap his shoulder and say: 'I need to speak to you. It's urgent.' He would be polite to the woman at the bar, of course he would. He would say, 'Do excuse me.' And he would follow Madison to the quiet corner she was taking him to, and he would affect to be casual, at first, until she said: 'I can't fight this feeling any more.'

And, with any luck, he would then land his ship in her shore. So to speak.

But Madison couldn't stop arguing long enough to notice that Christopher had fallen in love with her. Madison couldn't even stop arguing long enough to enjoy her minestronez soup. Or indeed anything.

She came back from the bar now with two triple vodkas and a can of Red Bull. 'Down the hatch,' she said, grimacing as she gulped a mouthful.

If Christopher got drunk to forget his divorce, Madison got drunk to forget that she was very nearly the country's leading divorce solicitor. But not quite.

Madison had nearly become the country's leading divorce solicitor by building her reputation steadily so that after ten years at Wilde and Sawyer, and in her mere mid-thirties, she was the only matrimonial solicitor ever to be rated Solicitor of the Year by both the *Law Society Gazette* and *The Times* Law Supplement.

She had a couple of lucky breaks early on, including a famous case called Grey v Grey, the outcome of which had greatly contributed to the pre-nup becoming all but enshrined in British law. 'Princess of Pre-nups', the *Sun* had called her.

For a few months she was the go-to person whenever the media wanted a quote on divorce. She sat on the sofa on breakfast news and on the *Lisa* show at lunchtime on ITV.

She had been on *Newsnight* and *Channel 4 News* commenting as an expert on developments in divorce law. She had written an article for the *Telegraph* headlined 'The End of Love as We Know It', which sparked a Twitter storm and thirty million hits on the newspaper's website. 'The woman who killed love', was how the *Guardian* rather hysterically described her.

And then just as her tabloid celebrity was peaking, it all came to an abrupt end when another female divorce lawyer, called Anna Pirana, represented the wife of a rock star and got her the biggest settlement in legal history.

The *Daily Mail* dubbed Pirana the 'Doyenne of Divorce', the *Sun* screamed from its front page that the rock star had been 'Bitten by a Pirana!' and that was that.

The media focus switched completely. Pirana was the go-to rent-a-quote lawyer for the primetime shows now, and the truth of it was, she made a better go-to rent-a-quote than Madison had been.

While Madison was cool and classy, Pirana was a pushy, full-of-herself, loud-mouthed tart – a technical term used by Madison's mother, who had phoned her daughter to deliver her verdict on the competition after Madison's nemesis had appeared on the news one night during an item on pre-nups.

'I thought you reinvented the pre-nup anyway?' said Cynthia, incredulous.

'I did. But it doesn't matter who reinvented it now. That woman is going to claim all the credit.'

In the final analysis, Madison went back to being a serious lawyer, mentioned occasionally and with respect in *The Times* Law Supplement, and Pirana got on with being a celebrity. They bumped into each other often in court, and Pirana would always greet everything that Madison said with the same words: 'Hey! What can you do? It's showbiz, baby!'

Madison worked even harder and was even more joyless than she had been before, making her incredibly if quietly successful.

The Times' legal pages noted that she won more cases than any other matrimonial lawyer. 'Tenacious. Uncompromising. Relentless.' And before she knew it, she had a new, rival media profile to Pirana's.

An article on 'the new generation of young female divorce lawyers' in *Glamour* magazine described Pirana as 'the Warmonger of Wedlock!' but Madison was 'the Ice Maiden'.

It didn't take long before they were both involved in the same case: Barker v Barker. She would never forget it.

Madison thought about her nemesis as she raised her glass of vodka again. She would get even, somehow.

Christopher had watched her knock the vodka back with a mounting sense of hopefulness. Maybe tonight, he had thought, with his customary lack of realism.

22

When Christopher and Madison got back from their lunch at The Lobster Pot, Mrs Bilby was sitting in the waiting room fidgeting.

She was wearing a pinstriped jacket over a voluminous white blouse with a gigantic, oversized pussy bow, and a way-too-short mini skirt teamed with white knee-socks and platform heels. This ensemble was normally worn with a *Hunger Games*-themed bow and arrow set sling bag, but she had been having trouble carrying it so had left it in the car.

'Thank God you're back,' said the Amazonian receptionist, 'she's been upsetting the other clients.'

Mrs Bilby had been telling everyone in the waiting room how corrupt the legal system was and how they were all going to end up penniless. She knew this because she had been Goggling it.

'You mean Googling,' said a gentleman who had come in for some conveyancing.

'I mean Goggling. Don't you do the Internet?'

The man gave up, which was what most people did after a few seconds of trying to row with Mrs Bilby.

'I do not want to get divorced, Miss Flight,' said Mrs Bilby, as Madison escorted her to her office.

'Nobody wants to get divorced. It's just that realistically, you're going to have to get divorced, I'm afraid. Now they've served the petition. Did you read the pamphlet I sent you explaining the process?'

'To hell with the process!' shrieked Mrs Bilby. 'I'm not getting divorced. There must be a way.'

'There isn't a way.'

'There's always a way.'

'Well, OK, maybe there is a way. But it's a virtually unheard-of way. No one defends a divorce petition and I cannot advise it.'

'But I refuse to be divorced,' said Mrs Bilby.

'Well I refuse to let you refuse,' said Madison.

'And I refuse to let you refuse to let me refuse.'

'This could go on for some time,' said Christopher, who had padded in in his socks to try to act as mediator, but now made his excuses and left. The children were being dropped off tonight and he wanted to knock off early.

'You are my lawyer and you will do as I say,' said Mrs Bilby.

'You are my client and you will take my advice. I cannot let you make a fool of yourself like this.' Any more than you will anyway.

'No, no, no. I cannot let it go down in history that I, Belinda Bilby, married a younger man who was only after my money. It's not true. I do not accept that this marriage has inconceivably broken down.'

'Irretrievably.'

'That's what I said. And I do not accept that I have behaved unseasonably. If anything, my behaviour was in perfect keeping with the seasons. It was spring. And I got a bit frisky. Call it March madness.'

'You mean unreasonably.'

'Well, it wasn't unreasonable either.'

'Mrs Bilby, I want you to listen to me very carefully. You put a cheese knife in your husband's buttocks. That is unreasonable behaviour by any standard of proof. And the judge only has to examine it on the balance of probabilities. As such it is my solemn duty as a sworn officer of Her Majesty's courts to urge you to desist with this line of thinking.'

'You wouldn't say it was unreasonable to put a cheese knife in his buttocks if you knew what that man did to me.'

'It is unreasonable no matter what he did to you.'

'I disagree. I wish to prove I have not been unreasonable. I will not have it go down in history that I, Belinda Ophelia Bilby—'

'Nothing is going down in history. Really. It is simply a matter of getting a decree nisi issued with the least fuss and expense. He says you're unreasonable, you confirm this in an affidavit. It doesn't mean anything. Nobody cares. A thousand couples a day register the fact that one of them has been unreasonable in order to get shot of each other. It really doesn't matter which. Pick a card, any card. We send back the acknowledgment pack, we argue about money. And hey presto, that's it. You're done and dusted.'

'I don't want to be done and dusted. The entire process sounds perfectly immoral.'

Madison sighed. 'You will be divorced, at some point, nothing is more certain. Mr Taylor will be granted his petition. A decree nisi will be issued. Financial arrangements will be made. The only question is, how much money do you want to give away? If you follow my advice I can limit the amount to something bearable. If you play silly games, get all high minded and morally outraged, set yourself on fire with righteous indignation at the injustice of the system and so on and so forth you will irritate the judge so much that he favours your ex-husband. And you will lose so much money you will wish you had never been born.'

'That's a pretty speech, Miss Flight. But . . . but . . . I am a woman in love. And I'll do anything . . .'

'Are you quoting Barbra Streisand?'

'Now look here. You were recommended to me as the most argumentative lawyer in London. I was told you were the sort of person who would do anything for a fight. I was given to understand, on very good authority, that you would argue any case no matter how hopeless or complicated.'

'And so I will. But no lawyer worth their salt will defend a divorce petition. It is my duty to tell you this is the most stupid thing in the world you could possibly do. You won't win. The judge will hate you. He will be furious with me for not talking you out of it. Read my lips, Mrs Bilby: no one refuses to be divorced. Your marriage is over if one of you says it's over. You need to grasp that and move on. Allow us to do our job here.'

'Very well. I shall have to find someone else.'

She got to her feet and smoothed her tiny skirt.

'In the name of all that is decent and true I intend to fight for my marriage. I wish to argue with every bit of strength left in me, even if it does mean I lose all my money, or even if it kills me. I wish to stand up and be counted.

'I was told you were the person to fight such a fight on behalf of the broken-hearted, but obviously I have made a mistake in coming to you. That other woman with the big shoulder pads will jump at the chance of taking my case.'

She walked to the door, then suddenly turned round and fixed Madison with a withering stare.

'I believe that if you believe in something, you stand up and fight for it. Justice doesn't happen on its own. Good day to you.' And she began putting on her gloves.

Madison rose too. Mrs Bilby, picking up her Birkin bag to leave, saw that the lawyer was changing her mind.

'If I agree to do this, I want you to be honest with me. And I want you to answer me one question entirely truthfully, off the record, right now. Are you doing this because you love this man, or because you hate him? Are you a woman in love? Or are you looking for revenge?'

Mrs Bilby answered in her own way, by allowing a tear to sneak out of her eye, which she dabbed strategically with the corner of her silk Hermès scarf.

Madison intended to talk Mrs Bilby out of defending the petition so she could do something that would irritate the judge only marginally less.

Her plan was to lodge a cross-petition for divorce on Mrs Bilby's behalf, citing Seth's unreasonable behaviour. This would make Mrs Bilby feel a lot better about the whole thing. She needed to feel she had got one up on him, which was all anyone really wanted in these situations. Once Mrs Bilby was satisfied she was humiliating him, Madison figured she would be able to get on with the business of getting her client divorced.

It was only a shame the husband had already filed and she would not be able to get their petition in first.

Whoever lodged first was in the better position as the other party was psychologically on the back foot. As such, there was often a race to lodge first. Sometimes an actual physical race . . .

Barker v Barker. He was a banker and his wife a Dutch former lingerie model. It had been a close-run thing between her, acting for the wife, and her nemesis, Anna Pirana, who was acting for the husband.

By coincidence, she and Pirana had chosen the same day to lodge and were both making their way from Holborn Tube to the Principal Registry just after 9 a.m. with their files in their arms.

Pirana spotted Madison first, and started to jog, hoping she hadn't seen her.

But Madison had spotted Pirana and was now jogging too.

As they started up High Holborn, Madison picked up the pace and started to run in the direction of the courthouse. Pirana, who was a good deal heavier than Madison, with huge bosoms, began to run too.

Much to Pirana's credit, they were soon running side by side, faster and faster until they were sprinting at breakneck speed up High Holborn.

Pirana hugged her files to her chest, as much in a bid to hold her vast bosoms down so she could run as to keep her petition safe.

At one point, Pirana, who was on the inside of the pavement, held her files with her right arm and reached over and pushed Madison hard with her left hand. The number 17 bus rattled past within a hair's breadth of her.

Christ! She's trying to kill me! thought Madison, as she recovered her balance and picked her speed back up. Pirana had got ahead.

They raced faster up to the court steps, where Madison tripped slightly and fell. But she recovered quickly as they scrambled up the steps. Pirana was beginning to flag, the inevitable consequence of the extra weight she was carrying, and her liking for eighties-inspired fashion, a consequence of her childhood obsession with the TV show *Dallas*.

She slowed down for a second to catch her breath and Madison seized the advantage.

As they hit the stone floor of the courthouse, the two women clattered in their high heels like deranged meerkats.

Madison skidded the last few feet and fell over the tops of her shoes as she hit the counter.

She slammed down her bundle at the hatch.

Pirana slammed her bundle down on top of Madison's.

'No you don't, Pirana,' said Madison, pulling her bundle out and pushing it onto the top.

Pirana did the same.

They repeated this a few times as the clerk looked from one to the other.

'Shall I just take those from you?' said the clerk, looking bored.

'You can take mine first,' said Pirana and, quick as a flash, she pushed her bundle into the clerk's arms.

Madison was put on the back foot from the start and the wife only won a paltry share of the banker's fortune as a result – reduced even further to just £400,000 on appeal. The poor woman had to go back to Holland and take her clothes off all over again . . .

Madison would have quite enjoyed another race up High Holborn to try to exorcize the ghost of Barker v Barker. But sadly, none of this was going to be necessary. Mrs Bilby wouldn't hear of it.

'I want to defend the petition. This marriage has not broken down. Help me fight this or I will go to the fish lady. Whatshername, Tessa Tunafish. Look, I've got her number on my phone. I'm going to call her right now. I'm calling her . . .'

And Madison could hear a voice saying 'Pirana and Clutterbuck, can I help you?' on the end of the line.

And that was how Madison, against her better judgement, snatched the phone off Mrs Bilby and got herself involved in trying to prove that an eccentric, rich woman had not been unreasonable, and that her marriage to a toyboy had not irretrievably broken down, even though she had put a cheese knife through his buttocks.

23

'What now?' said Seth, as he sat like a damp rag in Elden's office in the Whitgift Centre.

'I don't know. This isn't in the book,' said Elden. Every inch of his desk was covered in papers and pamphlets and law books and files. He threw the book he was reading down and picked up another. 'It says here no one defends divorce petitions . . . Oh, hang on, apart from in exceptional circumstances where because of blah blah . . . extreme bitterness and bad feeling the parties may both decide to . . . Oh dearie me, I didn't see that bit . . . What do we do now?'

'I don't know. You're the lawyer, remember?' said Seth, sounding testy as the panic mounted in his chest.

'Ah, here we are. It seems we wait. There will be a hearing. The judge will have to decide whether your marriage has irretrievably broken down or not. He will have to decide this on the balance of probabilities, a lower burden of proof than in criminal trials, which is in our favour.' Elden was leafing through a law journal.

'Are you looking all of this up as we go along?' said Seth, clutching his plastic bag.

'I'm just checking. I do remember some of it from my law degree.'

'Yes, of course, I keep forgetting. You do have a law degree,' said Seth, reassuring himself. 'Where did you graduate from, by the way?'

'Cambridge . . .'

Seth's eyes lit up.

'. . . Poly. East of England University, I think they call it now.'

'Oh.' Seth picked up his file and leafed through the papers gloomily. 'Irretrievably broken down. It seems more depressing now I see it in black and white. Maybe she's right. Maybe it was me who was being unreasonable.'

'Don't even think like that. She's a conniving bitch.'

'I'm sure you're not meant to say that. God, I'm depressed.' And he clutched the plastic bag containing his little wallet tighter.

'Everything is going to seem more depressing now,' said Elden. 'Apparently before we get to the end, you're going to lose an entire . . .'

Elden had gone off into his own world and was now standing staring out of the window with no apparent intention of finishing his sentence.

'An entire what? What am I going to lose?'

Elden was in a sort of reverie, staring onto the dreary streets of Croydon as his eyes glazed over and his head slipped to one side.

'Tell me! Tell me, for God's sake! What am I going to lose?' And not for the first or indeed last time, he grabbed

Elden and shook him until he came back to himself. 'You were telling me what I'm going to lose, remember?'

'Oh yes,' said Elden. 'You're going to lose an entire stone in weight.' He sat back down.

'Maybe we should withdraw our petition.'

'Never.'

'Do we have to accuse her of being unreasonable?'

'She stuck a cheese knife in your backside.'

'Yes, but Mrs Bilby doesn't like people accusing her of things. I'm sure she will be more understanding if we just say I got cold feet and wanted to be on my own again. No hard feelings.'

'Let me explain something to you. There are five grounds for divorce, none of them particularly appealing. They are called the five facts but they might as well be called the five fictions. It's not about what actually happened, it's about what the two of you can eventually agree might just as well have happened in order to get yourselves free of each other.'

'So there are other options?'

'Yes.'

'Thank God. What are they?'

'Did she have an affair?'

'I don't know. I think she might have. There were always lots of men coming and going from the house. And those bodyguards looked awfully sure of themselves.'

'It's not as simple as that. You have to prove she had sex with them. Not just sexual activity. Sex sex.' Elden stuck his nose in a law book. 'One way of proving sex

sex would be if she got pregnant by one of these other men.'

'Mrs Bilby is in her sixties.'

'Then you're right – you can't go down that road.' Elden slammed the book shut.

'What are the other options?'

Elden started reading from a pamphlet entitled 'Divorce: A Quick Guide': 'Adultery – can't have that. Desertion – well, you deserted, technically, so not very helpful. Unreasonable behaviour – you don't like that. You've been separated for two years with consent. Or separated for five years without consent. Neither of those are valid. Nope, you're stuck with it. Either you've been unreasonable or she's been unreasonable. That's your lot.'

'The divorce process is an outrage,' said Seth. 'Something should be done about it.'

Elden was inclined to agree. After a few weeks of grappling with it, it did seem thoroughly capricious. But he didn't say that – it was his job to inspire his client with confidence. Instead he said: 'Have you noticed how there are always either five or seven of everything?'

'Hmm?' said Seth, reading a pamphlet.

'Yes. Everything nowadays is grouped into low prime numbers; three, five or seven, most popularly. The three Rs, for example. The five election pledges politicians always seem to have. The skin cream adverts go on about the 'seven signs of ageing'. You never get two or four of anything, in ad speak. Have you noticed that?'

'I can't say I have.' Seth was now staring at the pamphlet

and clutching his plastic bag with an expression of extreme resignation.

'Well, it's definitely a thing. There must be some secret research somewhere showing that human beings are more receptive if you give them low prime numbers to think about.'

'Why do they call it no-fault divorce?' asked Seth, suddenly staring at Elden with bleak, almost tearful eyes. 'The idea that couples are not blaming each other or saying who's most at fault seems a little ridiculous, when you think about it. In practice, that's precisely what everyone is doing.'

'Don't think about it. We just have to make the system work for us. The less we worry about the rights and wrongs of it, the better.'

Elden John had long since given up on worrying about the rights and wrongs of the system.

He had never been married himself. And girlfriends had been few and far between. Elden was that very particular thing, the confirmed bachelor. He belonged to the realms of the disappointed. He wasn't bad looking, although he hadn't a clue how to dress. And he hadn't a clue how to talk to women.

It didn't help that he couldn't finish his sentences. This was largely due, he suspected, to the fact that his mother Doris had always finished them for him. After a few years of her doing it, when he was aged about five, he just gave up trying to speak for himself and adopted the practice of saying half a sentence and letting her do the rest. When Doris passed on and he was finally left alone, in his mid-thirties, with his own sentences, he had to get used to doing whole ones, but he never really perfected the art.

And this really did cramp his style in many ways, not least with women.

There had been a woman once, with whom he had been in love. He pursued her for years. But every time he tried to ask her out he could only say, 'Would you like to have dinner with . . .' And she was happy to avoid the issue by leaving the last word hanging and replying, 'Honestly, Elden, I don't know what you mean.'

One day, she told him she was getting engaged to be married. Not to him, obviously. Apart from anything else, he wouldn't have been able to propose. He would have got as far as 'Will you marry . . .' and then the thing would have become mired in confusion.

So that was all he knew about love, and it wasn't much.

But from what he had read in the last few weeks while preparing for this case, it seemed obvious to him that the more a spouse felt they had been wronged, the more they claimed in spousal maintenance. A financial settlement in a divorce was a form of damages in that sense.

People wanted revenge. So much so that they were prepared to spend tens of thousands or even millions of pounds on lawyers, forensic accountants and private investigators. People wanted to win. They wanted to vanquish their ex-wife or husband and reduce them to a quivering, penniless wreck.

Elden had an idea why this was. People were waking up to the fact that love was a thoroughly awful experience.

Disappointment. That was the cause. People wanted revenge for the disappointment they had suffered.

In his view, you could probably make every divorce going on right now into one big class action. Disappointed Men and Women Everywhere v Love Inc.

It all fitted with his theory that love pulled you in and then spat you back out again.

24

Elden John was definitely on to something. Indeed, all the latest research in the field would seem to suggest that it is every man's destiny to disappoint women, whilst it is every woman's destiny to be disappointed by men.

Even as Adam stood in the garden, thinking himself a happy sort of chap, Eve was starting to feel the first pangs of resentment. She knew there was something better out there, if only Adam would pull his finger out and become more go-getting.

'It's just typical of you not to want to get out there and see what more Satan has to offer,' Eve scolded. 'Here I am stuck at home all day in this bloody garden, and all you can do is tell me to be happy with what I've got.

'And don't get me started on your behaviour the other day in front of Lucifer. He comes over here to try to offer us a great deal on the Tree of Knowledge and what do you do? Whinge that you're really not sure if we should eat apples from a new supplier. I was so embarrassed.'

'*You* were embarrassed? What am I supposed to tell the kids when they ask where mankind's innocence went?'

said Adam, fiddling with the loincloth Eve had made him wear, which felt very uncomfortable and unnatural.

'It was too good a deal to turn down. Until he came along all we had to eat was nuts. I'm sick of nuts. Get a grip, Adam. Are you a man or a mouse?'

Whereupon Adam reminded Eve that if it hadn't been for him donating a rib she wouldn't exist at all. And so on.

Eve, it is thought, had at least twenty-three daughters, and one presumes taught them a fair amount about how limited and unexciting life would have been had it been left to their father. And those daughters passed on these tales of dissatisfaction to their daughters. In effect, female disappointment spread like a genetic mutation. Since Adam and Eve, essentially, all couples have been having a version of the same argument.

With Cynthia and Mitchell it all centred on whether Mitchell would ever stop flying long haul and put his family first.

Cynthia, who had been more than happy, or so she thought, to marry a man who was away all the time, had come to the opinion over time that what she actually wanted was a husband who came home every evening and took her 'out', for example to dinner. 'I'd also like to go to the garden centre every now and then. Have you ever thought about that?'

But evidently he hadn't. Mitchell refused to switch to European destinations by the deadline Cynthia had set – her thirty-fifth birthday – and so she carried out her threat and ran away with her paramour, the club singer Hilton Valentine.

'I'm leaving you, Mitchell,' she told him. 'I can't take it any longer. There has to be something more to life than this.'

Logic is not always the leading factor in a woman's decision-making processes. Leaving her husband because he wouldn't spend more time with her, when she knew damn well she hated spending time with him, was definitely a decision of the heart, not the head. And considering that she had been threatening to leave him for the past seven years, her packing her bags and driving away one evening cannot have been much of a surprise to Mitchell.

Nevertheless, he was a little shocked to be left looking after a seven-year-old child.

On the first night they were alone in the house together, Mitchell and Madison sat on the settee with a TV dinner and tried to watch *Last of the Summer Wine*.

Thankfully, they didn't have to do this again. She came back two nights later. Hilton Valentine was a pig. It turned out there was no more chance of him ever taking her to a garden centre than there was of finding life on Mars. Mitchell welcomed her home, without argument. 'Come on in, Cynthia, love,' he said. 'Let me make you a nice cup of tea.'

Sitting on the top step of the staircase looking down over the banister as her mother wiped her feet on the mat, snivelling and dabbing melodramatically at her eyes, Madison sighed with relief. She didn't rush downstairs because she thought it would be a good idea if Cynthia and Mitchell had some quality time alone together.

25

Madison sat with her back to her desk, staring out of the window of her office, which overlooked a small courtyard. The workman who was doing something to their building was out there smoking a cigarette in the sun with his over-alls pulled down to his waist. Madison suddenly found herself thinking thoughts that were quite confusing. One of the thoughts was: Maybe it's that simple. She wasn't even sure what this thought meant.

She was almost relieved when Judith, the secretary, crept through the door and up to her desk, making her jump.

'I couldn't find those cases you were talking about,' she whispered, in a squeaky little voice that sounded like it was on the verge of a sob. 'Are you sure they happened?'

'Quite sure.'

'It's just that I can't find any such divorce as Schneider v Schneider . . .'

'That's because I asked you to find Shlesinger v Shlesinger. Never mind. Can you just get me a coffee?'

'Er, not really. Well, I could. But it won't be easy. It's just that the cups all need washing and I haven't had time.

I mean, I could wash them but I'd rather let the cleaner do it because my carpal tunnel is playing me up.'

'No. Please don't. Just pop out and get me a coffee from Starbucks.'

'Oh. You want one from Starbucks, do you? It's up to you, but I wouldn't want coffee from there if it were me. I'd go to that independent coffee shop further up on the right. The organic, fair trade one. It's very good. Although it's quite a long way and I have got quite a lot to do, what with printing out these case histories . . .'

Madison sighed. There were can-do people and then there was Judith.

Judith was a can't-do sort of person. She was also a can't-sack sort of person. They couldn't sack her because she was struggling financially, her husband had left her, her children never called her, and she had carpal tunnel, which in all probability had been caused or made worse by whatever it was she had been doing for them all these years, which was bordering on nothing.

She stood there now, bent over Madison's desk, her one good hand supporting her perennially bad back. She was wiry and very tall, at least six foot even when she was wearing flats and bent double with her various aches and pains. She had poker-straight bobbed hair which sat flat against her sharp, pale, worried little face. And just to confirm that she had no sense of self-awareness or sense of humour at all, she teamed these unhelpful physical characteristics with a pair of horn-rimmed Harry Potter-style spectacles. All that was needed was a scar on her forehead to show where the lightning bolt had struck. I could put a scar there by biffing you over the head with my empty coffee cup, is what Madison sometimes thought when Judith was pushing her towards the edge.

'Please, Judith, just ... please, don't worry about anything.'

'But I want to find the papers.'

'No, really. Forget the papers.'

She and Christopher had been known to cancel whole cases because they couldn't bear to press Judith to dig out files and research legal points.

She was supposedly a qualified paralegal, but this didn't make her any more capable or effective when it came to doing something that might reasonably be called 'a job'.

What she seemed to spend her entire time doing was a form of worrying so tangible that the worry seemed to take a physical form and hang like a big viscous cloud in the middle of the office.

Inside Judith's worry cloud were all the worries of the world, plus some really silly things that ought not to be worries at all, but which worried Judith all the same, such as the exact ingredients of Starbucks coffee, the reason Gmail had changed the look of her inbox so that the delete button, which used to be at the top of the screen, was now a dustbin icon in the bottom right-hand corner, the likelihood of her breaking utterly worthless mugs from the 99p shop every time she washed up, and (one of her favourites) whether Christopher was looking a bit peaky and should go to the doctor because there were several bugs going round, including Ebola: maybe she should just nip out and get some Beechams Powders, or maybe she ought to go home because she couldn't afford to pick up a potentially lethal flu-like plague, not with her weak larynx.

Chief amongst the proper worries she tormented herself with were her anti-social neighbours, who were always making her life a bigger misery than it might otherwise have been with their relentless noise and littering.

Judith would come into Madison's office each morning with a cup of badly made almost-cold coffee, which she carried with a quivering hand.

And in her timid voice, aggressively quiet, would complain of a headache because her neighbours had kept her up all night again.

She was no match for the tattooed, beer-swilling ne'er-do-wells – her phrase – who lived behind half-closed curtains in the house next door and who seemed to spend their entire lives listening to very loud television and shouting at each other.

Madison had trawled through the Anti-social Behaviour Act. She had rung Judith's local council. She had rung her local MP. Christopher had told her, 'Don't interfere. Don't stress yourself out. Judith will have to sort it herself. She's quite capable. She only feigns helplessness.'

'I will just have to cope, I suppose,' Judith would say, spilling coffee all over the desk with her shaking hands as if to demonstrate that her trying to cope would necessarily involve a lot of not coping that would impact badly on everyone else. 'But I just wondered if you had had any luck with ringing the noise people?'

'I'll try them again later,' grumbled Madison. 'I'm going to sort it.'

Judith twittered about these things all day long, without pausing for breath. I mean twittered in the original sense. She didn't have a Twitter account. If she did she would worry about who each and every one of her followers were, and when and where she had originally met them.

'Judith, why don't you go home early today?' said Madison, thinking of the only thing that would release them from the background hum of Judith worrying so they could get some work done.

'Really? I wouldn't want to leave you in a mess without those papers.'

'I can find the papers.'

'No,' Judith shook her head solemnly. 'No, I don't think you will. I think you'll find I'm right in saying they've either disappeared forever or they didn't exist in the first place. Oh dear. I hope it doesn't completely ruin the case you're working on.'

Pessimism is a funny thing, isn't it? Madison thought as she looked at Judith's furrowed face. I like a bit of pessimism as much as the next man, but when I'm bombarded with it I suddenly became an eternal optimist.

This wasn't so surprising given Madison's propensity for playing devil's advocate. Her natural scepticism was quite capable of evaporating if someone else was saying everything was pointless. Then she would come over all optimistic and start arguing, Obama-like, for a 'yes we can' attitude, and the fierce urgency of now.

Besides, there was something aggressive about Judith's worrying. Something that made you think maybe she was exaggerating her anguish to annoy you.

'I'm sure the papers are here somewhere. It will all be fine.'

'But what about Christopher?' Judith fretted, sounding tearful suddenly. 'He doesn't look well to me. Do you think I ought to pop out and get him some Beechams Powders before I go?'

'Trust me. Christopher is fine. Nothing that a good night's sleep and a week off the booze wouldn't sort.'

'Oh dear. Are you saying he's got a drink problem? I don't think he's got it in him to handle a drink problem. He's not one of these people who gets over things, is he? I can't see him getting help. He's too proud. Oh gosh. He'll probably just drink himself to death . . .'

And Judith was away with the fairies, staring into space thinking about what she would do when Christopher was found choked on his own vomit in his sad little studio flat one morning soon. Would Madison keep her on? Probably not. Miserable bitch. She would have to go back to working in the library, which might be closed down any day now that books were becoming obsolete . . .

In her mind's eye, Madison saw Judith look up solemnly before beginning to sing 'I Dreamed a Dream' from *Les Miserables*. She was standing on the stage at *Britain's Got*

Talent. Simon Cowell and Piers Morgan were gurning in front of her.

'Judith!'

'Hmm?'

'Go home.'

Judith fingered the edge of the desk. 'Well, if you're sure . . .'

'I'm so sure you would not even believe it.'

Judith got her mac and umbrella. 'I think it's probably going to rain. It'll probably start just as I'm walking to the station,' she said, as she limped towards the door. She had no actual physical reason to limp but she did limp, probably to emphasize the invisible weight that hung around her shoulders as she shuffled her way through the world. Poor Judith, thought Madison. Not because she was feeling compassionate, but because 'Poor Judith' was Judith's official name whenever Madison or Christopher referred to her. And because Poor Judith was now on the other side of the door and no longer on her irritation radar, so she could afford to be magnanimous.

Where was she?

Yes, the interesting thing about this Bilby case was that the usual facts were rather the other way around to the traditional fleece job, on the face of it.

Here was a man, an innocent-seeming, youngish, naive and impressionable man who had fallen for an older woman, or at least the idea of her, and appeared to have been manipulated by that woman, who had no ideals about love at all.

And yet was this really about the exploitation of the toyboy? And could you even be a toyboy at thirty-nine? When you looked at it, was this not about Mrs Bilby thinking she had cracked the age-old dilemma of female loneliness by finding herself a young man who wouldn't give her any trouble and winding up with more trouble than she could ever have bargained for? She put a hard face on it, but maybe Mrs Bilby was just another lost soul looking for a companion. A good woman gone bad through disillusionment. Was this, after all, yet another case of a woman's disappointment?

Madison put her glasses on and re-opened the file.

26

There is organized chaos, which is how most people live, and then there is the way Belinda Bilby lived, which can best be described as disorganized tedium.

Never had so much of a mess been made of the business of achieving so little until Mrs Bilby walked the earth.

Despite enjoying every logistical advantage money could buy, her life had no onward or upward momentum at all. It ground almost entirely to a halt after she moved to the country, leaving her three teenage sons and her husband in the house in Holland Park. And since her husband had died, three months after the move, she had even less to do once hating him was off the agenda.

She didn't need to sell the London house, as she simply left the three boys, now aged seventeen, eighteen and twenty-one, living there.

'Do you think I'm being neglectful, leaving them to their own devices in town?' she asked a friend during a coffee date in Cobham.

'Not at all,' said the friend, a tall, bleached-blonde, over-Botoxed woman called Georgie, who was married to the local Ferrari dealer but who had much more money than even a Ferrari dealer ought to have. 'I should think they're having a wonderful time. How many teenagers would give their eye teeth to be left alone in a house like that?'

And indeed they were having a wonderful time, smoking weapons-grade skunk and selling it to all comers from the back door of the huge stucco-fronted white mansion. In addition, the two boys who had reached the age of majority and assumed control of the majority share their father had left them in the company, occasionally signed papers pertaining to international shipping matters brought to the front door by the men on the board of Bilby, Bilby and Bilby.

Suffice to say, there was a period of at least six months when the business being done at the back door produced profits almost rivalling the business done at the front.

But there, for now, we must draw a veil over the activities of the notorious Bilby brothers, who eventually embroiled themselves in a vicious turf war with a rival skunk syndicate in the Royal Borough of Kensington and Chelsea, called the Kensington Wildcatz, which culminated in a shoot-out in Hyde Park just by the Albert Memorial.

We shall return to that at some stage, if there is time. For the moment, our concern is with their mother. She had been left astronomically wealthy, but with no controlling shares in her husband's company or role on its board, and thus divested of anything to worry about, she turned to spending as her main outlet. Shopping was her big passion. She would shop for absolutely anything. Animal, vegetable or mineral.

She hoarded everything, from tins of chopped tomatoes to llamas. She purchased literally anything she set eyes on. If she was in Waitrose she swept a shelf full of ready meals into a trolley. If she was in Peter Jones she bought the entire cushion department. If she went past a furniture store and saw a sofa she liked she would end up ordering two of them and everything else in the display as well, including the plastic apples on the display coffee table. If she drove past a llama sanctuary she would put a deposit down on three llamas and an alpaca and demand they be delivered by 9 a.m. the next morning. And then realize she had nowhere to put them.

'Oh, they can roam about the lawns,' she told the man who brought them in the lorry. And they did, until they wandered all the way around the lawns and out onto the road where they chased a girl on her horse, spitting great blobs of llama spittle at her until the horse reared up and deposited the girl in the road. She came up the drive later to complain.

'You need to put them in a pen,' she told Mrs Bilby.

'Oh, but darling, that's so cruel, the poor little things. They can't be locked up in prison.'

'Either those llamas go in a prison, or you go in a prison,' said the girl. 'Because if they have me off my horse again I'm going to call the police.'

When Mrs Bilby wasn't hoarding exotic animals that couldn't be used for any purpose other than frightening the neighbours, she immensely enjoyed stocking up on food she didn't ever eat.

She did her big food shop of the week on Monday, and by the look of her three groaning trolleys you would think she wouldn't darken the doors of Waitrose again for another three months.

But a few days later, she was at it again, piling up her trolley, and the two trolleys pushed by Valmir and Vasilis, with things she evidently thought she needed to stockpile in catering quantities.

But as she rarely consumed anything apart from champagne with the odd bit of cheese on a cracker, the food accumulated, and every now and then Valmir and Vasilis would go to find something to eat and the double-door walk-in ice room would be so packed, there would be a bottle of champagne stuffed inside a half-eaten chicken carcass, along with half a pound of raw sausages.

Word of these domestic atrocities quickly got round. On the occasions Mrs Bilby had her girlfriends to visit, they didn't like to decline the champagne but they always politely demurred when offered either chicken or sausages. Her home was in a permanent state of structural disarray, too, owing to the renovations that were continually going on to add chunks to it.

There was always a bit of the house open to the elements, with a tarpaulin pulled down over where an outside wall had been. This only added to the sense of moral and spiritual desolation.

Margaret Teesdale, the housekeeper, despaired.

'I don't care how rich they say she is, she's living in squalor,' she told her husband Bert, as he pulled the feathers off a nice pigeon he had shot. 'She's no better than a scrubber on a housing estate. Spending her dead husband's money and living like a pig. The way she keeps that larder is a disgrace. And those dogs running about the place, defiling the Persian carpets . . . *defiling*, I tell you . . .'

Mrs Teesdale was a religious woman and fond of deploying the word 'defiling' when faced with things that were beyond the pale.

Whenever she got on to the subject of the toilet habits of Mrs Bilby's many dogs, she could only get a few words out before she seized up in apoplexy.

In truth, Mrs Bilby was not a well woman. She was so out of control of her environment it was no wonder it was an unhygienic mess.

'In fact, scrubbers on housing benefit are more dignified,' said Margaret, beginning again when she got her breath back.

'Oh-aye,' said Bert. 'And how's that then?' But he didn't really want to know how that was, then, at all. He just said 'how's that then?' when he couldn't think of anything else to say.

But if anyone else did want to know, the reason Belinda Bilby was so out of control of her environment was that she was out of control of her feelings.

Some seek to impose order on their surroundings to counter the chaos within, while some, like Mrs Bilby, let the chaos spill from within and spread outerwards in ever increasing circles.

Mrs Bilby's circle of chaos started in her heart, in a place and time long before she became an eccentric fifty-something widow living in an absurd country house called Tankards Reach with no apostrophe . . .

27

Mrs Bilby and her lawyer started the morning sitting in a small vestibule outside the courtroom, back to back on a bench, not speaking, Mrs Bilby torturing her phone with her acrylic nails as Madison ate a home-prepared breakfast sandwich. Why? you ask.

Because Madison didn't like to buy breakfast sandwiches at coffee-shop chains, which she considered bad value. She had tried to persuade several of them to lower their prices but they wouldn't listen.

Oh, you mean why were they sitting back to back? Because they had fallen out badly over the subject of Mrs Bilby's outfit.

Mrs Bilby was wearing a Vivienne Westwood suit comprising a mid-thigh-length black astrakhan rah-rah skirt and an astrakhan jacket with an ermine collar, together with lime green tights emblazoned with CND logos, and huge pink Louboutin heels. Arriving at court that morning, she had got out of the car flanked by two bodyguards and lurched past the assembled reporters, here to see Marcus Bilby's widow defend the Bilby shipping fortune against an historic legal challenge by her toyboy husband of only six months, Seth Taylor. When she entered the foyer of the Royal Courts of Justice, her lawyer Madison Flight raised her eyes to the ceiling.

'No, no, no,' she said, as Mrs Bilby staggered towards her, barely able to balance on the six-inch heels when stationary, never mind stay afloat whilst affecting forward momentum – though I think I'm right in saying that, according to the laws of physics, had she gone forward at some considerable speed it might have aided her buoyancy.

As it was, however, she merely staggered a few paces, pulled down her skirt, leaned on her bodyguards and then staggered again. And repeated this process until she had covered the distance of the lobby.

'What do you mean, "No, no, no"?' said Mrs Bilby, panting from the effort as she finally pulled up next to Madison and began picking fluff from her ermine collar. The bodyguards gave Madison a look that said she could be dealt with quite quickly if she wanted to insult their employer.

Madison did not seem to notice the looks. 'I said no, no, no,' she went on. 'I said plain clothes. I will have to send out for something. We need to get you changed.' And she started to call the office to speak to the long-suffering Judith.

'These *are* plain clothes, dear. I am in my slouch wear. How much plainer can you get than a drab little black number and some ghastly old Louboutins I dug out of the back of the closet. I nearly puked when I looked at myself in the mirror, didn't I, Valmir?'

And Valmir nodded.

'Do you want to lose £14 billion in a divorce settlement?' said Madison, being just as awkward and confrontational as her reputation had promised. 'Do you actually contrive to hand over everything your poor long-suffering husband worked for all his life to a two-bit nobody without arguing? Because if so, why don't you just write me a cheque now and I'll see that your useless toyboy gets it and we can save everyone's time including mine because, quite frankly, I don't have even one spare afternoon to waste on an overweight geriatric dressed like a cross between Elizabeth I and Posh Spice unless I'm going to win her case.'

For a few moments, Mrs Bilby couldn't even begin to formulate a response to this impertinence. Valmir slammed his right fist three times into the palm of his left hand and looked sideways at his boss, as if waiting for the nod. Vasilis reached inside his jacket. Mrs Bilby's response then popped out. It was the noise a duck might make if one tied a shoelace around its neck.

Mr Justice Juniper had started the morning sitting in his room sipping from a teacup and doing his deep breathing. In through the nose, out through the mouth. Breathe in hope, breathe out fear. He looked a picture of serenity. You would never have believed that just six months earlier, he had been incarcerated in an institution for alcohol dependency (as well as something called sex addiction, which he refused to believe was an official addiction, even though he clearly had it).

Juniper had always been an addict and had always known he was one. His primary addiction was to butter, truth be told. It started when he was three years old.

Having developed a pretty standard liking for licking out the bowl after his mother made cakes, he was soon licking the Country Life from the packet waiting on the table as she prepared the other ingredients, and then ingesting whole packs of it when her back was turned.

It wasn't long before he progressed to the harder stuff. When he was seven, they found him passed out at the bottom of the stairs, after doing an entire bottle of Chanel No. 5.

It all went completely undiagnosed, of course. In those days children who drank perfume and ate butter were called fat weirdos. But when he reached adulthood he started on the booze and then it was clear to all around him that he had what is commonly known as 'a problem'.

A successful career and a solid marriage kept the thing at bay for many years, however. He hadn't done at all badly, he thought, to get into his sixties before collapsing with a worn-out liver. He only got himself discharged after four weeks by promising to go to AA meetings. These were quite jolly. Breathe in hope, breathe out fear, he chanted, repeating one of the mantras his new AA friends had told him to say when flustered.

Persuading the Attorney General to let him go back to work had not been difficult. If they struck off every judge with a drink, sex and gambling problem, the legal system would grind to a halt.

Now he just had to stay on the straight and narrow, otherwise his wife Lillian would not hesitate to call the police and turn him in for dogging on Wimbledon Common again, of that he had no doubt.

All he had to do was stay off the whiskey, refrain from snorting coke and try not to have too much sex with couples he met in parks. And if he could manage not to lose thousands of pounds in online casinos, so much the better. How difficult could it be?

He looked at his list: Taylor v Taylor. A contested divorce petition. And one of the parties was being represented by Madison Flight.

He breathed in hope and a soothing image instantly materialized in his mind. The Chair-Scraper. She was incredibly attractive in a severe, rather forbidding way. She had, Arthur Juniper thought, a killer figure. The severe pencil skirts set it off very nicely. The spiky black patent-leather stiletto heels . . . Those big brown tortoise-shell glasses perched on her face . . . The long hair she pulled back into a severe ponytail . . .

This was supposed to make her look ordinary but in fact it just made Juniper fantasize about what would happen if the band broke, or was pulled out suddenly, and her hair tumbled down about her shoulders . . .

If he closed his eyes and squinted, she looked a bit like Tippi Hedren in that film where Sean Connery blackmails a mysterious blonde girl into marrying him. What was it called? Damn. Come on, come on. He opened his laptop and started Googling.

'Five minutes, sir,' said the obsequious little clerk, putting his head round the door. Juniper shooed him away.

Marnie! That was it. And he called up the Wikipedia entry and became transfixed by the film poster: 'Alfred Hitchcock's suspenseful sex mystery'!

Grrrr! He slurped the teacup down to the dregs, slammed the laptop shut and stood up.

'Arthur?' The clerk was at the door again.

'Go away, I'm busy.' He wondered what on earth had made such an attractive woman so dour and argumentative.

He heard that she once leapt to her feet 3,148 times during a three-hour hearing.

He wondered if it had anything at all to do with a deep, unquenched desire to enter the darkened offices of an elderly male member of the judiciary and hitch up her pencil skirt and . . .

'They're waiting, Arthur,' nagged the clerk, who had come into the office and was now staring in horror at the can of low-alcohol lager next to the teacup on the judge's desk.

'What? What?'

The clerk shook his head.

'It's just to take the edge off, Gareth. Don't get your knickers in a twist.'

28

If Madison thought she was having trouble with Mrs Bilby's outfit, that was nothing compared to the trouble Elden John had had with Seth's outfit – and, indeed, his own.

He had told Seth to wear a suit, but when he turned up to court for the first day of the hearing he was in his wedding clothes: a tailcoat complete with wilted, almost petrified corsage.

'It's the only suit I've got,' Seth protested, trying to tweak the remains of the rotted orchid in the buttonhole.

'You look like a pillock,' said Elden John.

'You don't look too hot yourself,' said Seth, eyeing Elden's crumpled viscose Primark 'easy-dry' suit (£29.99). 'Where on earth did you get that tie?' It was garishly bright, almost Day-Glo, and unfeasibly kippered.

The pair looked a sorry sight as they sat at their table in court number 38 at the Royal Courts of Justice, Elden's mouth opening and closing soundlessly like a goldfish at feeding time.

Madison, in her sharpest dark suit, white blouse and

black patent-leather stiletto heels, sat at her table with a client dressed in the strangest outfit she had ever seen.

Judge Juniper felt more than a little sorry for the two men as they awaited their fate at the hands of Madison and her mad client. The Chair-Scraper and the man-eater. It was hard to decide which of them was more scary.

He decided there and then, before anyone made any progress, that if at all possible, legally, he would favour the husband and try to get him off as lightly as possible.

And after Miss Flight had done her usual posturing, and after the husband's hopelessly crap lawyer had demonstrated that he wasn't even capable of speaking, Mr Justice Juniper was even more minded to swing this case as far as possible in Seth's direction.

'Miss Flight, I understand your client is defending this petition. Can I ask why?'

'M'Lord, my client's case is very simple,' said Madison. 'She refutes absolutely that her marriage has broken down irretrievably. She also refutes that her behaviour was in any way unreasonable. She fought very hard for this marriage to work, as we will demonstrate, in the face of increasingly eccentric behaviour on the part of Mr Taylor, and we will prove this, also. But despite his behaviour, she was committed to making the marriage work. And having fought so hard, and made so much progress to ensure that this would be a good marriage, and having helped Mr Taylor – a lost soul if ever there was one – in so many ways and being such a loving and supporting wife to him, and being still very much in love with him today, it would be a travesty if my client's efforts ended in a divorce which did not even recognize her side of things or at least give her a chance to urge Mr Taylor to reconsider. He has, sadly, however, refused all offers to enter into mediation, which is especially sad when my client has made it clear that in order to make him happy she is prepared to do, and I quote, "literally anything, if he will only, please, come back home."'

'I see. Very moving, Miss Flight. Mr Johns, what have you to say about your petition, in the light of this?'

Elden John got up and simultaneously dropped all his papers, which had been sitting on his lap. They scattered across the floor and as he bent down to start gathering them, the judge decided he would definitely find in favour of the husband if he possibly could.

'Gareth,' he said, bending down to his clerk. 'Go and help . . .'

And the clerk was despatched. 'Please, Mr Johns, continue.'

'Thank you, M'Lord. I . . .' Gareth was now rummaging around between Elden's feet. 'I would like to say, firstly, that when we lodged this petition we could have used any one of the five facts, because this marriage has broken down so irretrievably that all five grounds for divorce would have been as good as . . .'

'Each other,' said Seth, promptly, without looking up, as if he thought he could perform like a ventriloquist and finish his lawyer's sentences without the judge noticing.

Juniper flinched as if he could tell something was awry, but the illusion of the words coming out of the solicitor's mouth just about held up.

'Well, you've picked one. So continue with it.'

'Mrs Bilby is the most unreasonable woman I have ever come across in all my years as a solicitor. Her behaviour is beyond the bounds of human decency and transgresses all reasonable norms in every way. She was impossible to live with, to the extent that after three years my client was a physical, emotional and mental . . .'

'Wreck,' said Seth, from behind his hand. Judge Juniper frowned. But Elden recovered himself and started again.

'This was a marriage in name only, M'Lord. During the three years that they were living together, in so far as they were co-habiting beneath one roof, they never actually did so as man and er . . . man and . . . er . . .'

'Wife,' said Seth, under his hand.

Madison looked over her glasses at the judge, and then to the people sitting around her in the courtroom. She whispered something to Mrs Bilby.

'Spell it out, Mr Johns,' said Juniper, looking down his nose at Elden. 'Are you saying what I think you're saying?'

'I am, M'Lord. The marriage was not . . . er . . .'

'Consummated.'

There were gasps throughout the courtroom. The odd collection of people watching appeared to be the usual courtside rubberneckers, old people and tramps who had come in out of the cold to enjoy the free heating. But even they appeared to have been stirred from their sleep.

The court artist was also stirred and wrote a note in her pad: 'Husband – gormless daft expression. Hair standing on end. Morning suit like clown outfit. Looks like young Rod Stewart. Wife in shock. Hair also standing on end.'

Later she would swish her charcoal pencil across the page with an enormous flourish to depict this, but for now, court rules banned her from actually drawing anything while the proceedings were in progress.

She would have to submit her drawings for the perusal of the waiting press later, and the inevitable slot in the *Daily Telegraph*. As usual, they would look nothing like the actual people but she didn't even try any more. What was the point in even attempting to draw someone accurately from memory? It was a stupid system. She used to rail against it. Now she took perverse pleasure in making her drawings look as little like the people involved as possible. This was particularly satisfying where famous people were concerned. So she made Paul McCartney look like Harry Potter and John Cleese like the self-portrait by Vincent Van Gogh. She enjoyed aping the styles of great painters. This cheered her up considerably.

She was going to make Mrs Bilby look like a deranged Queen Elizabeth I, posed like the Mona Lisa.

Seth whispered under his breath to Elden: 'You can't say that. It was . . . we did . . . we did . . . we did it . . .'

Elden shushed him.

Madison made a disgusted face and scribbled on a pad.

Elden continued. 'Mr Taylor lived in a separate part of Tankards Reach, in a wing of his own, where he had his own bathroom, kitchen and dining facilities.

'Let me put it another way: Mrs Bilby made my client live in the servants' quarters. She wouldn't let him in the main parts of the house.

'Aside from the times she made certain demands of him, the pair barely met on a daily basis. Mrs Bilby insisted on this arrangement, to Mr Taylor's very great distress, for reasons that became clear to him as the marriage, if you can call it that, wore on.'

'Say something,' Mrs Bilby leaned sideways and hissed at Madison.

'However, my client is not going to pursue the process of obtaining an annulment because he accepts that the time for such a solution has long passed and it would be disingenuous to seek such a remedy now.'

'*That* would be disingenuous?' said the judge, raising an eyebrow and leaning over the bench.

'We do, however, maintain that the lovelessness of the union, if you can call it that, was a motivating factor in Mr Taylor's rather erratic behaviour, which Mrs Bilby will no doubt play upon.

'But his erratic behaviour, which merely extended to his being upset at being treated more like a servant than a husband, is as nothing compared to Mrs Bilby's, which can best be described as three years of mental, emotional and physical abuse – husband battering, if you will – and culminated in the night my client finally fled the marital home because Mrs Bilby slashed his buttocks with a cheese knife . . . like this one . . .'

And he waved a serrated knife in a plastic bag with a tag on it.

'She chased my client from the house and stabbed him, viciously, with this knife while shouting, as witnesses will corroborate . . .'

Elden then began reading from his sheet, in a monotone that did no justice to the drama of what he was saying, '"I'll kill you if you try and leave me, you horrible little man, you're not even a man, you don't deserve to live, people like you should be strangled at birth . . ." and so on and so forth . . .' And then he dropped his papers all over the floor again, only this time he got down on his hands and knees and disappeared under the desk himself.

'Gareth . . . You say "certain services", Mr Johns. What do you mean by that?'

'She clearly considered that she had enlisted his services as a male gigolo. He was meant to simply come out when she summoned him to perform. Is it any wonder he felt unable to?'

'And they say romance is dead,' said Juniper. 'Miss Flight, what do you have to say about this?'

Madison rose and said, very calmly, in her special smooth voice that made everything sound reasonable: 'M'Lord, we do not deny that there was an incident involving a cheese knife on the night leading up to their estrangement. My client was driven to desperation. And the cheese knife was not as sharp as has been made out. It was more like this one . . .'

And she brought out another cheese knife, also in a bag with a tag.

'Hmm,' said the judge, as Gareth passed him the bag.

Seth squeaked. Elden told him to be quiet. He needed to listen. This bit was, he explained in his ear, absolutely crucial. He had a copy of the *Guide to Divorce Law* on his knee under the desk. His brain was at full stretch.

There then followed a very long discussion about the relative properties of the two cheese knives exhibited. A doctor's report was submitted, detailing Seth's puncture wounds. A very embarrassing picture of his rear end was put on general display in the court. And all in all, a horrible few hours were had by Seth Taylor.

At the end of it all, Mr Justice Juniper declared that he had rarely seen an example of breakdown as irretrievable as this one. Nor could he think of a single case so singularly capable of demonstrating the notion of what might be termed unreasonable.

'It seems to me that no marriage can survive the deployment of pronged instruments in the general direction of posteriors, even when the prongs are blunt,' the judge told the sorry-looking pair. 'In fact, irrespective of the relative merits of the prongs of both the knives we have had exhibited in this courtroom, I take a dim view of the thing.

'Mrs Bilby-Taylor, you are lucky not to have been charged with assault and battery. If you were my wife I would have pressed charges. Mr Taylor, I commend your restraint. This petition is granted. I suggest you both start preparing your financial statements.

'I want Form Es submitted swiftly and with no funny business,' said Juniper. 'Court is adjourned.'

29

To those experts involved who understood modern divorce, it was more or less immediately clear after the parties' first day in court that a speedy resolution to the matter of Taylor v Taylor was not going to be possible.

As well as the legal pyrotechnics of the contested petition, the pair then submitted deeply unhelpful details of their assets and liabilities.

Judge Juniper thought it entirely likely that he would have to hold Mrs Bilby in contempt and send her to jail if she didn't start disclosing her net worth properly.

Her contention, in the innocuously entitled Form E, was that she had nothing left in the world following a run of colossal bad business luck. Despite the appearance of immense wealth and prosperity, she was, she claimed, penniless.

'People look at me without compassion and do not understand the financial torments I am suffering. I am my own worst enemy in this respect because of my youthful good looks and effortless style and panache,' she explained.

She had been left shares in her dead husband's company, she admitted, but that was entirely under the control of her three delinquent sons, who had plundered it, partly through lack of brains – 'they inherited their father's stupidity', she explained – but also through the prolonged use of illegal drugs, 'which finished off what little intelligence nature had allowed them'.

The house in Holland Park was in trust for these three delinquents, although she did own the apartment in Monaco and the mansion in Surrey. That was no great shakes, though, she explained. It had been worth an estimated £10 million at the time of purchase a few years ago, but she had re-mortgaged it considerably to meet her costs since Mr Bilby's death, and to do various alterations, none of which had turned out how she had planned, owing to the treachery of various cowboy builders, who would not listen to her when she tried to point out what was going wrong.

She had, for example, during vast renovations to add six bedrooms to the eastern wing, commissioned the installation of solar panels on the roof, which she fervently believed would generate enough energy to power the entire sixteen-bedroomed house and cut her oil bills down to nothing.

The roof was duly covered in said panels, at vast expense, along with a little wind turbine for good measure, but when she got her next oil bill after the completion of the renovations it had inexplicably gone up.

'That's cos your 'ouse is bigger, Mrs B,' the inscrutable electrician, Terry, had explained.

'No, no,' said Belinda. 'These solar panels simply need to be turned on, you know.'

'They're turned on all right,' said Terry, chewing a mouthful of gum. 'The problem you've got is that solar panels do not produce oil.'

'Hmm? What's that you say?'

'Oil, Mrs B. Your heating is oil powered. And the panels are solar. The sun cannot produce oil, no matter what you hook the panels up to. It's simple physixxx.' And he pulled up his trousers as if to emphasize the point.

'No, no,' she insisted, waving a shiny purple-nailed hand full of sparkling jewellery, 'you people have got to realize that we simply cannot go on raping our planet as we are doing. Never mind your physics. We've got to economize, you see. Live more frugally. We must all think of the environment. Now, what I want you to do is to check the connection between the solar panels and the boiler, because something has gone wrong that means they aren't powering the heating properly.'

'Mrs B. You've been 'ad. Whoever told you you could power your oil central 'eating with solar panels was taking you for a ride. There ain't enough sun in the whole of Surrey to keep an 'ouse like this goin'. In fact, you couldn't power one lightbulb in one room with that entire load of panels up there. It don't produce enough 'lectric.'

'Look, you're not listening to me. My heating bills have gone up since my environmentally friendly renovations when, clearly, they should be going down. I need you to sort it out.'

'Your 'eating bills have gone up, Mrs B, because you've added the equivalent of a six-bedroomed 'ouse to the side of your already enormous 'ouse.'

'Good lord, man, don't be ridiculous. I've got solar panels on my roof. Can't you see? Now, I want you to check the connection between the boiler and the panels . . .'

In the end, poor Terry marched out to his van to get his tools, telling Valmir and Vasilis as he passed them – they were sitting on the lawn in their dark suits and dark glasses sunning themselves with a cold beer, as usual – that he couldn't understand a word she was going on about. 'Is she on drugs?' he asked them.

'She on everything,' said Valmir, enigmatically.

In other words, the renovations were a disaster, and Mrs Bilby's financial statement reflected this in spades. The latest valuation of the local estate agent was that the house, post 'improvements', was now worth a mere £2.2 million, far less than the value of the mortgage, and the only person likely to buy it would be an Arab playboy who had the money to simply knock it down and start again. Or else a Premiership footballer who was too stupid to notice that all the rooms were in the wrong place.

In Surrey, it was always possible that she might find just such a buyer. But even if she sold, she would not be able to pay off the mortgage.

What was worse, she had sold everything of value inside the house – all the paintings, the jewellery, the antiques and artefacts – to try to finish the renovations, by putting it on eBay.

In conjunction with her bad selling habit, she still had a bad spending habit, which sucked cash out of her bank accounts as quickly as it poured in from the stuff she was recklessly listing with no reserve.

While her Lowrys went for a song, nothing she had bought while surfing the online marketplace had turned out to be of any use, nor had it risen in price at all. This went for all seventeen vintage Cadillacs she had imported from America. She had, she admitted, the reverse of the Midas touch.

At various points along this financial road to ruin, she had entered into doomed business ventures, sinking her remaining cash into schemes which had turned out to be astonishingly ill fated and stupid.

She had joined a consortium called Cherry Orchard Property Investments Ltd, a group of old business associates of her husband, which bought up disused plots of land in the Surrey green belt and tried to build on them. But Cherry Orchard had not been as fruitful as she would have liked, she explained in her statement, because the local council had stopped them building a thousand starter homes in a meadow just outside Dorking, which just went to show that you couldn't help some people. 'I have tried to do my bit for the poor,' she wrote, 'but I have been thwarted by petty bureaucracy and Nimbys at every turn.' This failed venture alone had cost her £7 million.

Furthermore, she had been a member of another, more sinister consortium involving a billionaire Kazakhstani oil and gas baron called Mogi Beresovskenaziskyaski. There were only two things apparent from Mrs Bilby's statement with regard to this particular business associate. Number one, it was impossible to pronounce her name. No matter which way you tried to tackle it, it was insurmountable, like the north face of Everest. You could only get as far as the middle 'n' – a sort of base camp – then you invariably had to abandon your attempt and climb back down.

The second thing that was apparent was that Mogi Beresovsken-etc-ski, at just twenty-eight years of age, ran an empire that would take the best forensic accountants in the western hemisphere several years to even begin to unravel. Even if the court could devote that much tax-payers' money to keep the case going that long – without sparking a media furore – it was unlikely the investigators would ever get to the bottom of it.

The Mogi Beresovsken-etc-ski venture in which Mrs Bilby had become involved was called Project Bojana. This was an attempt to build an enormous high-class holiday resort on the island of Ada Bojana in Montenegro – or as the excerpt from the business plan called it, 'an unspoilt asset on the Adriatic coast'.

Unfortunately for Miss Beresovsken-etc-ski and Mrs Bilby, just prior to development getting under way, the contractors had discovered a nudist colony living just adjacent to the site of the proposed five-star luxury hotel and spa complex and championship golf course. Because of this they had had to pull the plug, losing their outlay of £239 million, which is what it had cost to buy the entire island in a fire sale from the Montenegrin authorities, who were evidently mad keen to get shot of it.

There are many problems you can get around when building a playground for rich Russians, corrupt Italian politicians and their friends in the British establishment, but the one problem you cannot get around is the resort overlooking a beach used by hairy naked middle-aged suntanners.

They tried to buy the nudists out but it turned out to be a nature reserve and site of special scientific interest. Both the Montenegrin and Albanian governments started cutting up rough because they argued that both the wild birds and the naked people were protected by international laws on species preservation.

So the consortium called Project Bojana simply left its newly acquired island derelict, apart from the nudists who went on happily being nude at their expense. They could have gone on trying to find ways to evict them, but it evidently wasn't worth Miss Beresovsken-etc-ski getting embroiled in a political row with two sovereign nations. It was small change to a Kazakhstani oil baron, Arthur Juniper supposed.

He Googled her and noted that she was at the centre of a brewing international controversy over a new Baltic sea pipeline which could see her company GasCom dominating the European energy market, especially if a proposed merger with Northern Power went through. She was also getting some heat in this country about her friendship with a member of the royal family, who the tabloids had found her kissing in a Mayfair nightclub called Boo-Boos. And there were the usual questions about her tax status, with rumours that she paid everyone with whom she did business, and her employees, in bundles of American dollars, weighed not counted. It was obvious what sort of person this Russian billionairess was. But doubtless Mrs Bilby – who claimed she had lost an estimated £13 million in Project Bojana, some of which 'the Russians' were still chasing her for, she alleged – had joined an obviously corrupt venture in the hope of making a fast buck.

What a greedy, amoral bitch, he thought, as he dragged the last bit of pleasure out of the joint he was smoking. He flicked through the rest of the submission.

In addition to these rather large and geo-political financial disasters, Mrs Bilby had suffered myriad smaller business mishaps, which she detailed as follows:

She lost £250,000 on Stinking Rich, a perfume made from potent secret ingredients that claimed to put you in the right frame of mind to become a successful entrepreneur. (Nobody did, including her.)

She blew £400,000 on a new gastro-pub in Esher called Forage!, which served only food garnered from the flora and fauna of the countryside within a one-mile radius. While customers were happy enough for six months, with several rave reviews, an investigation by an *Evening Standard* journalist, who went undercover by getting a job in the kitchen, soon exposed that the ingredients were actually coming from a nearby Costcutter. She still owed creditors £750,000 for that one.

And she lost every penny of half a million on a range of bespoke pet products launched by a start-up company called Paws for Applause which included Pet Pud – tins of dessert specially formulated for cats and dogs (because why wouldn't your four-legged friend want a little something for afters?) and Dog-Bans – a range of designer sunglasses for dogs.

All of which meant that the bottom line was that Mrs Bilby was in debt to the tune of £32 million. Or so she claimed.

'Lying whore,' Juniper muttered, as he put Mrs Bilby's statement to one side and began to construct another fat roll-up stuffed with very strong skunk.

He puffed on it happily as he turned to the husband's submission.

In his Form E, Seth Taylor declared an annual income of £22,000. He relied on Housing Benefit, Jobseeker's Allowance, disability benefit for a 'long term psychological condition' and only made occasional modest sums of money whenever he sold a painting. A typical work of his currently fetched around £500, and he estimated that he sold one of these every eight or nine months.

'Jesus wept,' said Juniper to himself, going slightly red-eyed as he dragged on his rollie.

To those experts involved who did not understand modern divorce, nothing about Taylor v Taylor was remotely clear at all.

However, now that he had succeeded in having the petition granted, Elden John was still hopeful that he could get Seth a large pay-out that would more than set him up for life. And it would be good for Seth too.

He felt no compunction about fleecing Mrs Bilby. You only got one shot at the big time, and this was his.

A suburban, sole-practice nobody like him was never going to have another chance to feather his nest like this.

And if, in the process of doing said feathering, he succeeded in establishing a legal precedent that young, ambitious, penniless men with only three years of marriage to a rich widow under their belt could still expect a financial settlement to keep them in the manner to which they had recently become accustomed, then wasn't that something to be proud of when recounting one's illustrious legal career to the grandchildren?

He had already had some lucky breaks. Belinda Bilby had not thought to get her husband to sign a pre-nup. Well, according to Seth, she had considered it but had quickly dismissed the idea. The Bilby family solicitor, Lawrence Loonie, had even drafted one and put it down in front of her one day, after storming into the house and demanding to see her.

She had sent him away with a flea in his ear.

'You're making a big mistake,' he had yelled at her, as Valmir and Vasilis showed him to the door in their own inimitable way.

'So unromantic, muffy-woo,' is how she put it to Seth. ''Oo would never leave me, would 'oo?'

Seth was able to reassure her that no, of course he never would.

'Kiss for Blindy!' she said, pushing out her lips.

'You are kidding me?' said Elden.

'No. I'm not,' said Seth. 'That was how she was. She was a sweet lady.'

'She sounds like a total weirdo,' said Elden.

'You don't understand her,' said Seth. 'She's not that bad. She's just had a hard life.'

30

About a year after Mrs Bilby had given birth to her third child, she found a little place near Marylebone High Street to do yoga on Tuesday evenings.

She was bendier then. Bendier in a physical sense, certainly, but also bendier in that she was able to have adventures and consider other possible outcomes for her life as it hurtled along its financially privileged but spiritually redundant course.

After attending the classes for a few months, she signed up for a retreat in Tuscany.

She packed her La Perla yoga trousers and Ralph Lauren tracksuits and designer swimming costumes and two cases full of outfits by her favourite designers for the evenings. It would be the first time she had been away from home on her own, without Marcus, without her sons.

'Why do you want to go on a holiday with a load of bickering old women?' said Marcus, looking cross.

She had to lie and say it was a charity thing she was organizing.

In truth, she was going there to try to get to the bottom of the soul sickness that afflicted her.

When she got there, and walked around the grounds of the Tuscan castello and breathed the warm evening sea air, and did a few sun salutations the next morning, and then drank a lot of white wine for lunch, and chatted with the other women over a good dinner, and smoked roll-up cigarettes with them long into the evening, it was perfectly obvious what the cause of her soul sickness was.

She rang Marcus to tell him a week later, but when he answered the phone he sounded so pleased to hear her voice that she felt quite mean to have to break the news that she wasn't coming home.

She told him she had found herself. She told him that under the guidance of her shivananda guru she had discovered that her inner psychic self was someone different to the person she'd thought she was and that she would now need to explore this new self by staying on for three more weeks.

'In the five-star hotel?' asked Marcus, adroitly.

'Yes,' said Mrs Bilby.

'You're finding yourself in a £300-a-night five-star hotel suite and you want me to go on paying for this?'

'Yes,' said Mrs Bilby. 'Are you trying to say something?'

'No. No. You go on looking for yourself at my expense. But be sure to leave no stone unturned because I want you back here well and truly found in three weeks' time. I'll be at the airport.'

And he slammed the phone down.

You would have thought that would have put a stop to

her nonsense. But you've got to admire the chutzpah of some people. At the end of the three weeks Mrs Bilby rang her husband to say that, unfortunately, she had now lost herself again. Having found herself she had lost herself and needed more time to recommence the search.

After another three weeks she rang to say she had now relocated herself, and needed more time to settle in.

This esoteric deep-soul diving was all very well, but Marcus Bilby had to explain his wife's absence to those who enquired about her whereabouts. This he did by barking: 'She's in Tuscany where she's found her inner innerness, or something, on a godforsaken bloody tofu-munching retreat I'm bloody well paying for.'

But the real treachery was still to come, because three weeks after she found herself for the second time, Belinda rang her husband from the hotel to say that, with regret, she must inform him that her new self wasn't in love with his self and wasn't coming home.

'Of course you're coming home, you silly cow. Look, you've had your fun. You've done your Pilates. But enough's enough. We need you. The boys need you. Come home right now, Belinda. Do you hear me? I demand it!'

But she wouldn't come home. Marcus tried everything. He even sent a private plane to the nearest airstrip, which she refused to get on.

In the end he agreed to a divorce on her terms, through which she would get half of everything.

'Come home and sign the papers, Belinda. I just want this to be over.'

At the airport, Marcus arrived with two men in dark suits. She thought they were just there to carry her luggage.

She didn't realize it was a trap until they got her into the back of the car.

Sitting in the front seat was Mr Bilby's private doctor, who would write out a prescription for anything in return for cash. They drove straight to a building in Harley Street where a psychiatrist with eyes that were too close together and hair that came to a point low on his forehead saw her for the briefest of consultations before writing out the order.

'These inner selves you say you've been discovering – do they talk to you? Hmm?' he said, not even looking at her as he scrawled on a leather-bound Smythson pad.

'What's all this about? Drive me home immediately. I need to speak to my guru. You're damaging my oneness.' She then explained that she was made up of three bodies, physical, subtle and causal, which ought to be united but which were in danger of fracturing due to the stress of being bundled into a car and interrogated in this obnoxious manner.

Paranoid schizophrenia was the diagnosis of Dr Cameron McTavish, who promptly plunged a sedative into her right arm.

She was given the option of committal or treatment at home, so of course she chose home.

She was heavily medicated for weeks, and then put onto a maintenance dose of anti-psychotic drugs that would have knocked out an elephant. They made her gain weight, and brought on diabetes, which plunged her into an actual depression that justified the continued administering of the drugs she hadn't really needed.

And that was how Mrs Bilby really came to have three very uncommunicative children who were hideously rude and unpleasant, lacked any kind of social skills, and displayed quite complex attachment disorders. It was nothing to do with the way they were conceived, or the playing of 'Bohemian Rhapsody' in the background while the act was taking place, and in truth the estate of the late Freddie Mercury should have sued Mrs Bilby for saying it was.

The boys turned out the way they did because their mother discovered the shopping channel after the chlorpromazine their father forced her to take to make sure she didn't leave him stopped her sleeping.

Buying goods in the night soothed her. She crept out of bed when Marcus was asleep and went downstairs to the family room next to the kitchen. She poured herself a glass of sauvignon, which reacted superbly with the drugs, got comfortable on the big sofa and turned the TV to BargainHunter first. Later she would check out QVC, Ideal World and Price Drop.

It was clothes at first, then items for the home, children's toys, craft kits, vacuum cleaners, miracle cleaning products, miracle hair removers, miracle cosmetics, gadgets that took fluff and lint off a multitude of surfaces, electrical systems that stopped pests coming near the boundaries of the house.

Miracle. She liked that word. Every time they said it,

she felt safer. Pretty soon she was sitting up half the night watching show after show, wrapped in her Slanket (£34.99 for a pack of three!).

Better even than the miracles on offer was the fact that the presenters became your friends.

She liked Jeremy Thomas, Julia Barnfield and Lesley Worthington the best.

Jeremy could do anything with a gadget called a Magi-saw, while Julia could change the way you cooked forever with a range of plastic boxes to store food called Fresherware. Lesley, meanwhile, had beautiful hair, which she treated with a product called MiracleTress. Mrs Bilby bought three bottles of this for £49.99 at 3.15 a.m. when it happened to be on special – offer can't last!

Staying up all night with her new friends ordering MiracleTress, Fresherware and tools from the Magi-saw range, as well as everlasting lint rollers and face peels that turned back the hands of time, meant she was even more tired during the day than her medication was already making her.

One morning the housekeeper, Mrs Sajja, found her standing up against the kitchen counter staring into space, a cup of cold coffee in one hand, and in the other a cigarette which had smoked its own way to the end and had two inches of ash still delicately attached as it balanced precariously between her frozen fingers. In front of her glazed eyes, the two eldest boys, Truman and Fitzgerald, their faces painted in vivid felt-tip-pen camouflage, fought each other with ten-inch meat knives from the Magi-knife range, a spin-off from Magi-saw, while the youngest, Ernest, sat on the floor next to the dog bowls scooping Winalot into his mouth.

Mrs Sajja picked him up, held him over the sink and wiped the dog-meat gravy from his sweaty, pink-cheeked, tear-stained little face as he screamed furiously to be put back down by the Winalot – for it was evidently delicious to a baby, especially one who had not yet had breakfast because his heavily medicated mother had forgotten to give him any.

'You cannot go on like this,' she told her boss. 'Something terrible is going to happen. Mrs Bilby is in a world of her own. She is not safe around the children.'

Marcus pondered this. If he took responsibility for the boys away from Bee she would have even less to do and would probably deteriorate further.

Mrs Sajja said that if he left the boys with her, she might very well end up accidentally killing one or more of them, or all of them.

'You will have blood on your hands,' said Mrs Sajja, who loved a crisis that might end in tragedy.

'I don't know why Vineeta is making all this fuss,' said Mrs Bilby, as she sat in bed that evening, filing her nails with a Miracle File while her husband changed out of his suit and prepared not to join her in bed, but to go, instead, into the next-door guest room. 'I only buy extremely good dog food. It's not as if he was eating Chappie, or Pedigree Chum.'

'The point is, Bee, you need to concentrate on getting well. The children are too much for you.'

'This is all your fault,' Mrs Bilby said. 'If you hadn't brought me back from San Gimignano I would have been finding spiritual fulfilment and peace and joy in the simple things by now.'

'Of course you would,' he muttered.

'The most infuriating thing about it all was that I had so nearly found myself. I was this close, Marcus. This close!'

Marcus Bilby sighed. 'The trouble with you, Belinda, is that you've always been so busy looking for yourself you haven't been able to find anyone else.'

'What are you on about now?'

'Nothing. Forget it. I did what I had to do,' he explained wearily, for they'd had this conversation a thousand times. 'What else could I do? I had to get you back. Fitzgerald was crying himself to sleep at night.' Although God knows why. She had never been a hands-on mother even when she was, notionally at least, there.

'Fitzgerald,' she said haughtily, 'might have missed me for a while but eventually he would have been happy to know that his mother was happy. Ernest would never have remembered me; he was too young when I left. And Truman loathes me anyway, as you well know. The boy's quite clearly a psychopath. As for you, you would have moved on and got over it by now.'

'Maybe I would. But have you ever stopped to think that I did it for your own good, too? Those bloody tofu-munchers had kidnapped you. They were brainwashing you with all that nonsense about chakras.'

'They did not kidnap me. They were my friends. And

they were not realigning my chakras. I had that done three years ago by the Chinese lady who lived next door to the knocking shop in Charing Cross and it didn't work, although I wouldn't expect you to remember. This was yoga, Marcus. Y-o-g-a-h.' She spelt it out with dyslexic panache, whilst giving him a look that said he was remedial. 'They were trying to help me reinvent myself as a daughter of Vishnu?' *Obviously*, said the look, and the question mark at the end of the sentence. 'Now I'll never be happy. And neither will you, by the way. It's called karma. K-a-r . . .'

M-a-h. I know, thought Marcus Bilby.

Then Marcus Bilby suddenly found himself spelling another word out in his head. H-a-p-p-y. He was reflecting on whether he had ever been happy. Happy. H-a-p-p-y. He had never before in his entire life ever had this thought.

He stood in front of the wardrobe in his boxer shorts with his shirt unbuttoned to reveal the saggy, worn-out chest that contained his saggy, worn-out heart, feeling thoroughly stunned by the enormity of the question and wondering why he had never asked it of himself before.

It suddenly occurred to him that the answer to that rather important question, which truly he had never once in his entire life considered, was no. What had made him happy was the idea that his loved ones were happy. What had made him work sixteen-hour days since he'd left school at fifteen was the idea that he might be the sort of man his father had been. An honourable man, a provider. What made him build up two companies to the point that their turnover rivalled the GDP of a South American country was the satisfaction of knowing he was doing what men ought to do. Whatever that was. What was it?

He looked at his wife, filing her nails and blowing away the dust.

'I didn't even mind that I wasn't happy because I thought what I was doing was making *you* happy. If you're not happy, what was the point of it all?' But he didn't say this out loud.

A few weeks later, the Bilbys reached an accommodation. Mr Bilby accepted that he could not continue to demand that his wife remain with him in a bondage of misery, drugged up to the eyeballs on an illicit cocktail of repeat private prescriptions. He would agree to a divorce. She could stop taking the pills if she wanted to. He really didn't care any more.

And it was at this precise moment that Mrs Bilby decided she ought to stay married, if only because her husband was not a young or particularly healthy individual and might not last much longer. If she divorced him he would have the best lawyers and she would be portrayed as insane. The Bilby fortune would in all likelihood pass to her sons. Whereas if she remained married, she stood to inherit the lot when her husband sadly succumbed, as he surely must, to the stress of his shallow existence.

She hoped his soul would then commence a healing journey to learn the lessons it needed to learn to atone for its transgressions in this life. Possibly it would enter the body of a sixteenth-century French peasant, or a Russian serf, or a Roman slave, or a dog. (Not a pampered dog, but a stray roaming the streets of Corfu, for example.)

'No, I will not divorce you, Marcus,' she said. 'And I don't need your permission to stop taking the pills, either.'

She had not taken those for months. She had been medicating herself on Herbaleze, £69.75 for a three-month supply, or £160 for six months, or £350 for a great-value pack that lasted a year. It contained a special balance of nutrients and herbs and a miracle ingredient called Alphatrixalon, which literally arrested the ageing process in the tissues and triggered the body's natural ability to rejuvenate by ridding itself of the harmful toxins in air pollutants, which combine with the body's stores of adrenalin, or possibly saturated fat, to form something. Or other. Lesley looked fabulous on it.

As well as informing her husband that she had been flushing all his pills down the loo for months, Mrs Bilby revealed that it was her considered opinion that they might live entirely efficiently from now on by totally ignoring each other.

A house must be bought for her in the country, somewhere near Cobham. She liked the sound of Cobham.

Until such a house could be found, she found a way to channel her inner innerness within the confines of the Holland Park mansion, by standing in the garden surrounded by wind chimes dangling from trees, dressed in Armani sweatpants and chanting: 'Money is evil, my soul runs free like the wind. Om namah shivaya!'

And she banged a native drum (made of genuine Exmoor ponyskin, but perhaps she couldn't have known that).

Mr Bilby instructed the agents to speed up the search for a house in Cobham because he couldn't have her doing that in front of the neighbours. And he went out to work to earn the money she loathed but still managed to spend as if it were going out of fashion, which, to be fair to her, she did state very clearly she wished would happen.

In between house-hunting and shopping and spending money and chanting about how money was evil, Mrs Bilby took guitar lessons, for no good reason that anyone could make out.

And then there was the seduction of the Spanish waiter called José, with whom she began a torrid affair.

But he dumped her when he found out she had no intention of divorcing her husband and was, in fact, awaiting natural processes. Weighing things up with a keen eye for the main chance, he decided that, what with Mr Bilby's access to excellent private healthcare, this was not a good bet.

Happily for the lady herself, his desertion did not matter because it was around this time that Seth walked through the back door of the Bilby residence in Holland Park carrying a huge blank canvas and a big, wide, innocent expression on his handsome young face.

Belinda fell in love. It was a *coup de foudre*. A total eclipse of the heart. The first time ever she saw his face, she thought the sun rose in his eyes, and shone out of his other end. She couldn't eat, she couldn't sleep. She felt like she was the luckiest woman on earth. And so on and so forth.

And this was why, when she asked Seth to marry her several months later, she ignored the advice of Lawrence Loonie, of Loonie, Loos and Leithall, which was to get a watertight, top-of-the-range pre-nuptial agreement. She had been too happy.

31

On the morning of the opening of her financial dispute
resolution hearing at the Royal Courts of Justice, Mrs
Bilby's chakras were so out of sorts it had taken three
phone calls to her yoga guru to unblock them.

She had begun her day by changing out of her favourite
outfit. That had to be a bad omen, she thought.

Madison had sent a trainee at Wilde and Sawyer to
Peter Jones to buy a sombre, navy blue skirt suit, plain
navy blue tights and court shoes, and a white blouse. The
skirt came well below the knee.

'I look like someone's Aunt Fanny,' Belinda Bilby told
Madison, as they sat outside Court 38 waiting to be called.

'I don't even know what that means,' said Madison.
'You look normal to me.'

'Normal?' said Mrs Bilby, as if Madison had labelled
her with a vile insult. 'How can people wear clothes as
dull as this? I feel suicidal. I've seen nuns in sexier shoes
than these.'

'You will feel suicidal,' said Madison, flicking through
a lever-arch file, 'when you lose all your money in ten

minutes flat. Which is what would have happened if I had let you come to court in that Issey Miyake number.'

Madison, who was preparing to pull a major rabbit out of the hat, or rather out of a lever-arch file, had begun her day by arguing with Mrs Bilby about her sartorial ideas. She had had the foresight to demand they meet at the offices of Wilde and Sawyer at 9 a.m. and had ambushed Mrs Bilby with the outfit she had brought for her. Either she put it on, or Madison would resign from the case that morning, leaving her unrepresented as the lawyers went to work on her bank statements.

'Very well, I shall wear it. But if the judge takes against me because I am so ludicrously badly attired, I shall hold you personally responsible.'

'It is an undisputed statistical fact that of those acquitted of murder last year, the highest proportion were wearing navy blue suits, followed by those in dark grey.'

Mrs Bilby was looking at her like she was speaking a foreign language, so she added: 'Judge Juniper will look at you more favourably than he even wants to because you are wearing that outfit, believe me.'

Judge Juniper had begun his day by driving to work, stopping his Mercedes in the back streets of Victoria to let his dealer, Bermondsey Barry, jump into the passenger seat momentarily and put three tightly wrapped lottery tickets full of cocaine in his glove compartment.

'Got big plans for the weekend?' said Barry, showing his horrible yellow teeth.

'Yes, that's right,' said Juniper, pushing the wad of cash at him and hoping he would just get straight back out of the car and go away.

He couldn't be too rude, or Barry might punch him. He was a huge, foul-smelling man covered in tattoos and piercings.

Juniper always sighed with relief when Barry got out of the car without killing him.

With Barry safely divested onto the pavement outside Argos, he drove to the back of the courthouse, leaned over and took one wrap from the glove compartment before getting out and handing over his car to the ever-faithful Gareth, who was waiting to park it.

Elden John had begun his day by practising in front of the mirror. He wanted to get to the end of the most important sentence of the hearing. He knew he could do it if he learned it off by heart. Now, as he stood in the courtroom, he was sweating profusely as he braced himself to begin the crucial section:

'And so,' he concluded very deliberately, his eyes narrowed until they were almost closed with concentration, 'given the nature of the emotional support my client offered to his wife . . .' he took a big, gulping breath ' . . . and given that he helped her . . .' There was a dreadful pause as he forced himself forward '. . . wrest back control of her company from her three sons and . . .' He breathed in again '. . . rebuild it from virtually nothing following their gross mismanagement . . .' He exhaled with relief before beginning the really audacious part 'we are asking for a . . . for a . . .'

In his mind, Elden pictured himself as a child, ice-skating across the frozen lake near his home in the Welsh valleys, his mother calling to him, enticing him to skate towards her. He had started to move, and build up speed, and now he was careering out of control. His legs were skidding out from under him.

As he garbled the last bit of his sentence, he saw himself skedaddle across the ice, feet shooting in every direction, arms windmilling in a bid to get to his mother and grab hold of her before he fell.

'...weareaskingfora5050cleanbreaksettlementinorder-toexpediteaspeedyconclusiontothesematters.'

Madison was on her feet: 'M'Lord, did Mr John just say what I think he said?'

Juniper looked at the clerk. Gareth shrugged.

'M'Lord, this is outrageous. There is no way this marriage can be seen to have endured long enough to warrant a 50-50 split. There are no children. Mrs Bilby is in straightened financial circumstances. Mr Taylor had no role in the company of her ex-husband and has done nothing to warrant a stake in it. There is not a single trace of him in any company business. Furthermore, Mr Taylor has already bled my client dry, which I was about to demonstrate.'

'Go on.'

'We maintain that during the time the couple lived at Tankards Reach – if you can call it that, because Tankards really don't have a reach . . .'

The judge nodded sympathetically. The logic was impeccable.

'. . . Mr Taylor removed valuable items such as antiques and fine art, and family heirlooms.'

'No I didn't!' Seth whispered to his lawyer. But Elden had slumped back into his seat and was sitting there panting and insensible. He had already taken off his ice-skates and had no intention of putting them back on for the foreseeable future.

'We are seeking the return of those items, or a cash payment for the equivalent value, which we estimate to be in the region of £1.2 million.'

'Say something!' hissed Seth as Elden looked at him helplessly, the sweat still pouring down his forehead.

'We submit pictures of the items stolen by Mr Taylor, including, as you will see, a very nice engraving of a sketch by J. M. W. Turner and a bust of Mrs Bilby-Taylor (not sure which way up this should be, actually) by the eminent post-modernist conceptual sculptor Dorian Hunt. It is made entirely of sow's udders. It's terribly clever and detailed, as you can see.' And she clack-clacked dramatically in her high black patent-leather heels across the floor and put the photographs on the judge's bench.

'I would never steal something by Dorian Hunt! The man's a charlatan!' shouted Seth, who could contain himself no longer.

'Silence!' scolded the judge. 'Or I will hold you in contempt and have you removed from this courtroom. Really,

Mrs Bilby-Taylor, this bust is not much of a likeness of you at all. I hope you didn't pay much for it.'

Mrs Bilby shrugged and pursed her lips. In truth, the bust had been done just after her surgery and sadly bore no resemblance to her at all, now that the facelift had worn off.

'Clearly, Mr Taylor's intention all along in targeting my client, then a rich, vulnerable widow,' Madison continued, 'was to infiltrate the Bilby family and remove valuable heirlooms from their possession, possibly to defraud them even more substantially in the long term.'

'Say something!' Seth yelped to Elden.

'And yes, we have no doubt he would have liked a role in the business empire, in order to defraud it. But my client did not allow him one. The police have been notified about the thefts and are in the process of an investigation. They are also investigating my client's claims that Mr Taylor was repeatedly abusive during the marriage. Mr Taylor has approached my client several times since these hearings began to make threatening remarks, and if he continues to do so, we will apply for a restraining order.'

'She chased me with a cheese knife!' Seth shouted, then whimpered at the memory of it, like an animal in agony. 'I'm the one who needs the restraining order. I mean, she is! She needs restraining. I don't need restraining!'

Madison raised her eyebrows.

The judge nodded. 'Please, Mr Taylor, restrain yourself.'

'M'Lord, this is entirely typical behaviour,' said Madison. 'Mr Taylor is a dangerous and unpredictable man.'

'Well, it wasn't long ago, Miss Flight, that your client

was claiming he was Romeo to her Juliet, and they were love's young dream, so I take all that with a pinch of salt.'

'We can explain. My client was traumatized. I have the report of two independent psychiatrists who will testify that when she tried to defend the divorce petition she was suffering from post-traumatic stress disorder.'

'Just get on with it, Miss Flight.'

'M'Lord, far from being an innocent victim, as he claims, Mr Taylor is a callous and aggressive confidence trickster and my client feels she has been the target of an elaborate and cruel hoax. The evidence we shall present will further substantiate our claims to that effect.'

'Say something!' Seth squeaked.

'In addition to the trauma and financial loss from the removal of her valuables, my client suffered a considerable loss of earnings during the period she was married, if you can call it that, to Mr Taylor, because she was too upset by his antics to work.'

'What work? She doesn't work!' Seth said out loud, forgetting he was meant to be quiet.

'Charitable work,' said Madison, censoriously. 'She feels, out of the goodness of her heart, that she ought to repay the various good causes for whom she is patron, the money she feels she would have made for them had not her precious time been diverted by the callous actions of a toyboy husband on the make.'

'Ha!' blurted out Seth. 'She works one morning a week for the Cats Protection Racket. And I'm hardly a toyboy. I'm thirty-nine, you know.'

'Cats' Protection League,' said Madison. 'My client is also a senior figure in the National Society for the Protection of Domestically Kept Miniature Cross-breed Farm Animals.'

'The pig thing?' said Seth, who was jumping about in his seat in agitation.

'Britain's leading charity working to raise awareness of the plight of micro-pigs kept in a home environment,' said Madison.

'Let's move on, Miss Flight,' said the judge, sensing that the Chair-Scraper could milk this one indefinitely.

'She also seeks recompense for the money she spent funding Mr Taylor's many therapies . . .' Madison began an elaborate and entirely bogus shuffling of her papers '. . . psychotherapy, physiotherapy, colonic irrigation therapy . . . M'Lord, I won't bore the court. The list goes on and on. My client has been paying through the nose for an array of treatments for various neuroses, real and imagined, and partaken through every available orifice, so far as I can make out . . .'

Here, Madison pushed her glasses to the end of her nose as she squinted at the papers, which she moved ostentatiously backwards and forwards in front of her face so as to give the impression it was impossible to focus on the words, so convoluted and outrageous were they.

'. . . and for disorders that Mr Taylor claimed he suffered from which he had obviously either been suffering for a good while before he met my client, or had simply invented as another ruse to get money from her.

'For example: seasonal affective dysmorphia, which causes one to imagine one is shrinking during reduced daylight hours; compulsive shoe hoarding; bipolar 3 (personally, I wasn't aware there was a third one); as well as various eating disorders including, does this say . . . bigorexia? The imagined need to become more muscular. A likely story. Then there's "reduplicative paramnesia", imagining that a place or location exists twice, dendrophobia, a fear of trees . . .' she was sounding bored now '. . . and oh, not to forget "arctic hysteria", a propensity to become irrational during winter months, owing to his distant Inuit ancestry, apparently.'

Madison took off her glasses and shrugged. 'Your honour, just a few of the clearly bogus mental disorders from which Mr Taylor claimed to be suffering and for which he demanded his wife fund treatment. We have written statements from the doctors involved.'

Seth leaned in to whisper in his lawyer's ear. 'Say something! She's making all this up!'

'We therefore estimate that Mrs Bilby is out of pocket to the tune of £1.5 million,' Madison continued.

'Say something now – or I will!' Seth whispered desperately to Elden.

'That is a huge sum of money, Miss Flight,' said the judge, 'and you must be aware that Mr Taylor is a jobbing artist and virtually penniless. You cannot surely be suggesting he repay this in any settlement?'

'He can pay it off in monthly instalments. I've done some calculations. Mrs Bilby is prepared to accept payments of

£2,500 a month at 0 per cent APR for fifty years. That's assuming Mr Taylor keeps himself in reasonable health, of course, and doesn't manage to die before her.

'And assuming my client will be deceased first, as per the age gap, she has generously agreed that continuing payments can be made to The Micro-Pig Foundation.'

Seth's mouth was now hanging open and he had assumed a look of rigor mortis. The court artist wrote: 'Husband: Gaping horror mouth.'

'Unless, of course, Mr Taylor wishes to be reasonable and desists with his outrageous pursuit of a 50-50 clean break settlement. In which case I suggest we might be able to knock the £1.5 million off what Mrs Bilby can be reasonably thought to owe Mr Taylor after just three years of marriage, and with no children resulting from it, which – to be generous and show good will – we would hold to be in the region of 2 per cent of her net wealth, which works out as . . . (and here she made another elaborate show of rifling through all the papers in front of her as if the whole thing were incredibly spontaneous) . . . oh, it's £1.4million. One moment . . .'

She whispered in Mrs Bilby's ear.

'My client has told me she will be prepared to waive the £100,000 he still owes her. As another gesture of good will.'

The courtroom was silent. Even the old homeless people in the public gallery who had only come in to use the free heating were dumbfounded by this demonstration of chutzpah.

Seth stared. The court artist wrote: 'Husband: *The Scream*.' She was definitely going to go with a Munch theme for this one.

Madison sat back down and all eyes turned to Seth's lawyer for his response. But Seth's lawyer was in a huddle with his client.

'I never had colonic . . . irrigation,' spat Seth in a furious whisper to Elden. He was evidently bothered by this detail more than the fact that unless he agreed to leave with nothing, he might be working for Mrs Bilby for the rest of his natural life. 'Are you sure?' whispered Elden John, eyeing Madison with something like awe. 'I mean, maybe you forgot . . .'

'She was the one who claimed she was descended from Eskimos and had a form of hysteria which caused her to go mad every time it snowed. Or didn't snow. I can't remember which.'

Elden John sat as frozen as an Eskimo himself.

Judge Juniper leaned forward. 'Mr Johns. Do you have anything to say? Mr Johns?'

The court artist leaned forward. The judge said: 'Mr Johns! Speak up if you're going to!' Seth stamped on Elden's foot under the table and whispered far too loudly, to gasps from all around the courtroom: 'I thought we were meant to be taking her to the cleaners!'

Whereupon Elden John's mouth opened and the inevitable popped out.

'C***!' he shouted. And although it upset the judge no end, Elden wasn't far wrong.

32

Judge Juniper sat in his rooms, blowing the smoke from his roll-up towards the open window and thinking about ringing his dealer.

He had searched his drawer to see if there was any cocaine stashed there but he couldn't find a single one of those tightly folded lottery tickets that Barry had given him. All he had been able to find was a wrap of what the ugly brute called whiz. He was never very sure what this actually was but he emptied it into a small tumbler full of whiskey and slugged it back and for a few minutes it made him feel like he could do anything.

Then, a few minutes after that, he started feeling really quite devastatingly panic-stricken, which was why he'd had to roll himself a joint.

The Bilby divorce was testing his already threadbare emotional resources to the very limit. The husband's solicitor was making heavy weather of it. And the Chair-Scraper was on particularly infuriating form.

Juniper had had to rule both Taylor and Elden John in contempt after the King Cnut incident and the police had dragged them both from the court in handcuffs. They had sat in a cell together beneath the Royal Courts of Justice during the lunch recess, looking very sorry for themselves. He had let them sit there for an hour and a half, then ordered them to be released without charge, because he felt so touched by their obvious incompetence and imbecility.

Juniper had a lot of sympathy in general with people who blurted things out at inopportune moments.

Whenever he was in court these days it was a bit of a struggle not to say the wrong thing.

During hearings he would drift off as someone was banging on about their hard life and then he would snap out of his reverie suddenly, aware of a captive audience waiting for him to speak, and say: 'Er, ahem! My name's Arthur and I'm an alcoholic.'

And then, when the embarrassed courtroom murmur alerted him to that being the wrong thing to say, or the clerk kicked him, he would add:

'Sorry, that's not what I meant. I thought I was somewhere else.'

Later, at AA meetings, he would drift off as some unfortunate was banging on about their hard life and when someone nudged him he would lurch awake and yell: 'Order! The court will come to order! Oh, sorry, I thought I was somewhere else.'

Thinking he was somewhere else was fast becoming the story of Juniper's life. He leaned further out of the window to blow the smoke clear as it kept coming back in.

He could see the press gathering on the pavement

outside, waiting for the various players to arrive back from lunch. The TV anchormen and women including . . . wasn't that? Yes it was . . . including Karen Fairisle, who appeared to be bringing her *Afternoon Live* show from the steps of the courthouse.

Her perfect, power-bobbed hair glinted in the sun. As the judge watched from his vantage point, a scrum started to form as a car pulled up and Fairisle began running down the steps, microphone in hand, to greet a strange-looking figure getting out of a large black car.

Mrs Bilby, in huge Jackie O dark glasses and outfit that defied belief – a long, garish coat made of strips of material every colour of the rainbow and a pair of bright purple suede platform boots – staggered from the limo.

Juniper dragged harder on his roll-up and waved the dodgy-smelling smoke out of the window with his hands.

The press pack looked as though they were about to close in and set upon the Bilby woman like dogs descending on a hunk of raw meat, but were kept at bay by her fearsome-looking bodyguards.

As she started to ascend the steps, a fracas broke out in the middle of the press pack and it started to bobble about like a rugby scrum as if a fight were going on inside it. Suddenly, a female reporter in a cheap suit was thrust out of the pack, her head on the end of someone's arm.

The arm was attached to a hand containing fingers that were closed tightly around a neck.

'What the . . . ?' Juniper blinked as if the joint were doing more to his brain than it ought to be.

After a few seconds, Karen Fairisle popped out of the press pack, her gleaming red hair uncharacteristically ruffled. And now it was plain to see what was happening. She was throttling the life out of a young female reporter.

'Get out of my shot!' she was screaming. The pair of them squirmed on the steps of the court for a while, until someone pulled the anchorwoman off the reporter by prising her fingers, one by one, from the girl's neck.

Judge Juniper swigged back his whiskey. It was a shame his jurisdiction didn't extend to the smooth conduct of proceedings on the pavement or he would hold Karen Fairisle in contempt of court, right there on *Afternoon Live*.

'What is the matter with women nowadays?' he wondered. They all seemed to be becoming unnaturally aggressive.

As Mr Justice Juniper prepared for the continuation of the Bilby divorce hearing by smoking pot, and as a trainee journalist borrowed a fellow reporter's make-up compact to examine the red weals left on her neck by the hands of *Afternoon Live*'s Karen Fairisle, Madison was having an equally complicated time.

Mrs Bilby had changed out of the sober suit she had sent an assistant out to buy and was now sitting on a stone seat in the waiting area outside the court looking like the ringmaster of a circus.

She was giving Madison a big speech about authenticity. 'I am what I am,' she declared, still wearing her ridiculous dark glasses. Before she could launch into the full Shirley

Bassey, Madison cut her off. She needed to look over her notes.

But all she could hear was Shirley singing about the ace and the deuces and how it was one life with no return and no deposit. Time to open up your closet . . . Which was just what Mrs Bilby was doing, she supposed.

She saw Shirley standing in the vaulted halls, urging her to see things from a different angle.

'It's no good. I need a coffee,' said Madison, getting up.

'I'll have a decaf soya mocha . . .' began Mrs Bilby.

But she was gone.

Madison did not want the first coffee the café across the street offered her. She wanted it made again.

'What's wrong with this one, madam?' said the pretty Latvian girl behind the counter, holding the take-away cup that Madison had just handed back.

'It's too weak. There's too much water in it and not enough coffee. And the cup's too full. Please don't just empty some of it out and put another shot in it because then it will be too strong. I don't want to be shaking like a leaf all day.'

'Maybe coffee is not a good idea if you don't want caffeine, madam.'

'Maybe putting customers off coffee is not a good idea if you want to keep your job in a coffee shop.'

'I make you another one, madam. Is no problem.'

And the barista made another coffee, which was exactly the same, only she did take care to leave an inch of it missing this time.

After paying with the exact money, Madison walked out of the coffee shop and headed back to the Royal Courts of Justice, and even at that point things might have carried on pretty much as they always had in Madison's life if there hadn't been roadworks right outside.

But there were roadworks, across two lanes of traffic, and improvements to the paved areas all around the courthouse entrance.

There was a pedestrian crossing which would have taken her safely to the other side of the road, and then into a fenced-off area which took her a long way around the roadworks and finally into the courthouse.

She had used it happily enough earlier, but now she decided she was running late and she didn't see why she should have to go round.

'Stupid bloody roadworks. Where are the workmen, anyway? They're not doing anything. And this will be costing the taxpayer a fortune . . .'

She stood in front of the mess of barriers and cones, grumbling and pulling faces.

She weighed it all up and decided to cross where the entrance was. She would climb the barriers and dodge across the traffic.

Some might say that this was asking for trouble. But Madison was not one of those people who bought into the theory that if you did what you were told you were likely to stay safe and out of trouble.

And so ignoring the signs directing her around the roadworks, she hitched her skirt up and swung her leg over the first set of barriers. A man in a white van beeped his horn and whistled through his open window.

She waited for a gap in the traffic before darting across the first lane. Cars beeped as they swerved, a cyclist who was almost unseated gave her the finger.

She waited by the barriers in the middle of the road for a few seconds to get her breath. More traffic was coming on the other side. She waited for a gap and then climbed another barrier by swinging her leg over it, waist high, in one swift movement. A workman wolf-whistled.

Now she was over the barrier but the traffic was coming again, fast and furious. She grasped the barrier and held on while she waited for another gap in the traffic. She barely had room for her feet as she clung on. The wind from the traffic whipped her face and kept knocking her off balance.

She waited for what seemed like ages. Her hands started to ache. She waited until she started to have doubts about her strategy of not using the designated crossing. Why am I doing this again? she thought, suddenly struck by the absurdity of the situation. She was on the verge of feeling a fool, of realizing that her pig-headed determination to pick a fight with the system was not a clever way to carry on.

But then she saw a gap coming in the traffic after a double-decker bus. As the bus passed her with a tremendous whoosh, she let go and ran.

Her right foot struck out but her left foot tripped on something. Her shoe came off. She made it a few steps in one shoe before stumbling again. For a second she steadied herself and thought she was all right. 'I'll have to go back for the shoe,' she was thinking, 'because they're my favourite scary stilettos . . .' Then she toppled over completely, knocked sideways by some unseen force.

It all happened too fast for her to know why it happened exactly, but later they told her she had been hit by a car.

The first thing that went was her hearing. The long, sonorous beep of a car horn faded into nothing and then all was silent. She didn't hear herself hitting the road. The world had become a totally soundless place. For a few seconds, she only had vision. Cars, careering around her in strange patterns. Lights flashing.

The last thing she saw, right by her head, was a piece of gnawed chewing gum stuck on the hard grey surface of the road. She saw it from a strange sideways angle, for a split second, in incredible detail. She wondered why she was looking at it from this angle, as the corners of her vision darkened like an old silent movie screen with a border round the edges. Then the border crept inwards and the scene – a sideways-on road and a piece of chewing gum – simply blinked into darkness.

She lay in darkness for a few seconds, listening to the silence getting thicker and thicker. She tried to move her legs and arms but was unable to. She felt queasy at first, and then the sickness faded and she felt a wave of tiredness come over her.

And then a wonderful feeling of lightness and letting go. Then a sensation of being lifted, and carried. She had not been carried since she was a child. It was not just enjoyable because her body became weightless, but because it was as if, in the process of being lifted up and carried, all her cares were being taken from her too.

She had the idea she was being carried at shoulder height through a garden of long grasses and wildflowers. Everything was golden. The wildflowers, the sun. She felt the warmth of the sun on her face and her arms. The feeling of lightness was exquisite. She floated in a sea of golden, almost blinding, light and silence.

Total silence. Silence like she had never heard silence before. And then deeper silence.

And then nothing.

And then she was having the most peculiar dream . . .

33

She was standing at the bottom of Shirley's garden in an overgrown vegetable patch surrounded by strange-looking weeds. She was pulling up the weeds. Her hands were bleeding because there were thick thorns amongst them.

What on earth was she doing? Then she remembered: her mother had been taking an afternoon nap when she crawled through the gap in the hedge into the next-door garden.

Then she scrambled back. In the kitchen, listening for any sign of her mother waking up, she placed a chair against the units, clambered up and bashed the greenery she had collected with a large meat knife into a finely chopped pile that could have been parsley, or mint. This she mulched in a bowl with water and sugar and then put the mixture into a flask with hot water and a tea bag.

It was not difficult to persuade her mother to let her go with Shirley to the hospital that evening. Cynthia said she had one of her heads on her – strange phrase, that, as if we had more than one head to put on – and could do with the house to herself for a bit.

After a dinner of heated-up leftover beef stroganoff (people were always eating beef stroganoff in the eighties, they couldn't get enough of it), she despatched Madison next door, telling her she was a very thoughtful girl indeed to want to go and see Ralph.

Madison noted her mother's ironic smile. No doubt she thought the tea would taste horrible.

But the tea tasted really good. Ralph loved it. He drank three cups. Slightly trickier was the task of getting him to look at the pornographic magazines she had brought with her in her knapsack.

She wanted to ensure he was not stuck in all eternity. She had to get him to commit a mortal sin just before he died, with no chance to confess. Then he wouldn't be in any danger of living forever and having to listen to harp music.

She had had to sneak off to the newsagents on her bike and ask Mr Roberts to get them down from the top shelf for her. Luckily, the practice of letting ten-year-old children buy porno mags with their pocket money was a lot more prevalent in the 1980s than it is now. People tended not to worry so much about things like that then.

Mr Roberts had tried to talk her out of it but Madison argued that a) she needed the magazines for a school project and b) the law was intended to prohibit only young boys from seeing them, and she wasn't a young boy. And that seemed logical enough to him.

The day after Madison's visit to the hospital, Shirley came round, very excited. Ralph had perked up, she said. He was asking for Madison to visit again, and the ward

sister had specifically asked if she would bring him some
more of her herbal tea, which was having a wonderfully
calming effect.

It was a lot of trouble. Making the tea with the stuff
at the bottom of Shirley's garden and going to the hospital with Shirley every Saturday. Sitting by the bedside,
listening as Ralph went on and on about the tea being
a terrific pick-me-up. Then when Shirley went to the loo
or to the nurses' station to complain about something, he
would lean towards her and whisper: 'Have you got the
magazines?' And she would slip them under the covers.

Poor Madison. Her career as a mercy killer had not got
off to a good start. Killing people certainly was a lot more
complicated than killing rabbits. Each evening, she would
leave the ward carrying her empty flask dejectedly.

It took five visits before Ralph succumbed.

The nurse found him with a copy of *Penthouse* in his
hands. After a life of unrelenting dissatisfaction and misery, Ralph Perkins died with a smile on his face. Happy
at last.

She saw Ralph Perkins' happy smiling dead face.

Then the face of a huge smiling rabbit.

Then nothing.

Then silence.

And then out of the silence a faint noise coming from
infinitely far away.

Madison . . .

. . . Maaaadison . . .

. . . Maaaaaaaaaaaaaadisssson . . .

Don't wake me. Go away. Don't wake me. I don't want to wake up.

But the noise persisted, like a bird flapping at her cheek.

She opened her eyes slightly. She could see the wheat still waving at the corners of her vision. But in the centre, a blurry face was standing over her, its mouth moving silently. Was it Ralph Perkins, come back to life? Or the rabbit she had killed? She hoped not.

'Maaaadison,' it was saying. 'Maaaadisssson.'

Who was Madison?

'Madison!' The mouth saying it was a person's, but not Ralph Perkins'. She could see that now. She could see a blurry face.

'Madison!'

Was that her name?

How strange that she should be called Madison. Like the avenue in New York.

What sort of person is named after a street? she wondered. What sort of person kills a man in his hospital bed, as if he were a rabbit needing to be put out of his misery.

What sort of person? What sort of person?

'Sssssssssssssssssssssilly . . .' said the voice in the wheat field.

'S-s-s-s-s-s-s-s-s-illy . . .'

'S-s-s-s-s-silly. S-s-s-s-s-silly.'

The voice started vibrating. And getting louder. Her head was aching. She didn't feel nice any more. She felt tired, and in pain.

'D-d-d-don't be so s-s-s-s-silly,' was what the voice was saying.

'Are you OK?' said another voice, belonging to another blurred face. She saw a circus ringmaster in front of her, complete with top hat. She hoped she wasn't going to be fed to the lions.

And then another voice shouted: 'MISS FLIGHT!'

Her head jerked forward and flopped against her chest. The motion brought her back to full consciousness and she was horrified to find she was lying on her side in the road with a crowd including Seth, Elden John and Mrs Bilby standing over her.

Two lanes of traffic were swerving around them, beeping their horns.

Mrs Bilby was fanning her with a file of papers and shouting: 'She's not dead. Look, she's opening her eyes. Wake up, you stupid girl! Have you never heard of the green cross code?' And she poked her in the bottom, with her enormous purple boot.

The strangest thing about that was, Madison didn't really feel like she minded.

'Even if she's not dead she might be brain damaged,' said Mrs Bilby. 'And I don't want a lawyer who's brain damaged. We must ask for the case to be adjourned . . . I *will* not be represented by a vegetable.'

'Let's get her off the street and inside,' said Elden.

Mrs Bilby fluttered a manicured hand at him as if to say this was a superfluous exercise. The only thing that interested her now was the procurement of another solicitor as this one was clearly broken. As such it could easily be left lying in the street.

They had all run out from the courthouse when they saw the commotion outside – Mrs Bilby, Elden John and Seth, who was making himself useful by trying to direct traffic around the incident.

The cars beeped their horns at him and every few seconds he shouted after them: 'Yeah? Well, fuck you too! Asshole!' He didn't normally swear. He felt stressed.

Madison rolled over and tried to get up. Elden shouted at her not to move. Seth stopped directing traffic for a second and knelt down on the ground with them to see if he could help.

'Can you move your arms and legs?' he asked, more for something to say than anything else.

He looked at her. And she, who had been looking at her ankle and rubbing it, looked up at him. And smiled.

And said: 'Yes. Thank you.' And looked at him with huge, deep, vulnerable eyes.

'That's good,' he said, feeling like the world was going into slow motion.

They had been sitting in the entrance lobby waiting to be called when Mrs Bilby had rushed up to them fretting about how she couldn't find her lawyer. She had only nipped out for a coffee. Maybe she had done a runner. The hearing would have to be postponed.

Then they had heard someone talking about an accident outside and Seth had gone out into the street, followed by Elden and Mrs Bilby. The press pack had run after them, Karen Fairisle in the lead, running and screaming, 'Get me on air! Tell Gerry we need to go live! Now!' and the cameras were filming them now as they tried to revive Madison.

'Do you suspect sabotage, Miss Flight? Were you pushed?' shouted Fairisle, as Seth and Elden helped her up.

She began limping. Her ankle was sprained.

Fairisle turned to the camera: 'And so, another dramatic twist in this extraordinary divorce saga here at the High Court today. We'll be bringing you all the updates from the hearing as they unfold. Tune in for my *Afternoon Live* show for all the latest in the Bilby divorce, as well as the very latest news and weather. But for now, Bob, back to you in the studio.'

And she smiled the most devastatingly beautiful smile, which she held for slightly longer than seemed feasible. Then the smile suddenly vanished.

'Are we off?' she said to the cameraman, before pulling her earpiece out and turning to a frightened-looking boy with a clipboard and headphones. 'You fucking useless little turd, Brian. We should have got the whole accident on tape. What were you doing? Eating a sandwich? We don't pay you to eat . . .' And she stormed off into the court building to fix her make-up in the ladies'.

As she did so, she pushed a small huddle of people out of her way, including Seth and Elden, who were trying to help Madison up the steps. Karen Fairisle seemed not to be interested in them now the cameras were turned off.

Mrs Bilby had run on ahead and was flapping around inside the courthouse, telephoning Christopher on her mobile phone to demand he send another lawyer and then, when she couldn't get Christopher, leaving messages on Lawrence Loonie's voicemail to demand he get her the Pirana woman.

But when Madison was seated outside the courtroom with a bottle of mineral water, even Mrs Bilby had to admit that she had begun to look as though she hadn't been hurt after all.

'Are you sure you're all right?' asked Juniper, who had been informed of the accident and had interrupted a particularly good game of online bingo to come out to assess the situation.

'Yes,' said Madison, smoothing her hair and her skirt. 'I'm embarrassed, obviously. But I don't think there's anything wrong with me. Honestly, apart from a few scratches, I'm as good as new.'

And, strangely, she really did feel it.

34

Elden John was on a roll, and that didn't happen very often. In fact, to his knowledge, it had never happened before in his entire life. Finally, he was having a breakthrough. He was grabbing life by the throat. He was peaking.

All his life he had known he was capable of great things if only he could get the breaks. If he only found his true element he would take off and become something big. His mother had often said this to him. 'Elden, you know your trouble? You're punching below your weight. You're not going to show the world what you're made of until you're mixing with people of your own calibre.'

And now he was in the ring with the big boys, the heavy-weights. He had moved up into the world he was meant to be in. He was surrounded by the best in the business, his true peers. He had risen to the occasion. He was flying. He was like a man reborn. And if he was not very much mistaken, his sentences were finishing themselves like a dream.

'Mrs Bilby has assets, we estimate, in the region of £12billion. She is hiding most of these offshore, currently, and misleading this court about the true nature of the arrangements her husband made with their sons over property.'

In his mind's eye, he saw himself as Lawyer of the Year. He was giving interviews to *The Times*. He was on the steps of the High Court after winning his client a record-breaking settlement. He was the toast of the legal establishment. Better than that, he was a maverick – a dangerous maverick, and was treated with just a little bit of envy and fear.

And then he realized that he had just dropped a huge sheaf of papers. He fumbled, apologized, picked some of them up, dropped them again, picked them up, dropped some others . . .

Juniper sighed and said: 'Is there much more of this?' which only made Elden John drop the papers he was holding again.

Madison appeared not to notice any of this. She was sitting with her jaw cupped in her hands and a smile on her face, as if finding it all wonderfully entertaining.

'Are you sure you don't want to describe all this as a circus, Miss Flight? Your client certainly looks like she's just run away from one . . .'

Madison just smiled. It really was most peculiar but it was also very convenient. Juniper realized that if things went on like this he would be able to conclude the hearing before tea time and get to an early-evening meeting. Perhaps he would try NA tonight. See if he couldn't knock that crack habit on the head once and for all.

Juniper looked at Elden John throwing paper all over

the place. He had been talking for an hour now, making all sorts of outrageous claims that had gone unchallenged.

He was evidently enjoying himself so much that he had clean forgotten to stutter as he straightened up and concluded by announcing triumphantly:

'We therefore seek a cash settlement of £23 million and maintenance of £8,000 a month.'

Nevertheless, he looked nervously across at the wife and her solicitor as he sat down, because surely there were now going to be some fireworks.

But Madison Flight sat staring into space. Mrs Bilby nudged her.

In the end, Juniper prompted her: 'Miss Flight. Are you sure you wouldn't like to tell me that everything Mr Johns has just said is a travesty?'

Madison sat with her head propped on one hand dreamily staring out into space, or so it seemed. If you had followed her eyeline, you would have seen that it went all the way across the courtroom to the right of her, until it alighted on Seth, and there it stayed.

To Madison, it seemed that Seth was like some kind of angel. Blond, blue-eyed, his face slightly weather-beaten from all the time he spent outdoors painting, he was the most beautiful man she had ever seen.

Of course, it all made sense to her now. That was why he had been so entirely passive. That was why he just sat politely without arguing and let Mrs Bilby do her worst. What a terrible person she had been to even think about trying to cheat him out of his divorce settlement. He was

a saint. A quiet, uncomplaining hero. And she was a terrible person. A terrible, terrible—'

'Miss Flight?' said the judge.

'Oh my God, she's a vegetable,' said Mrs Bilby. 'I told
you this would happen. I'm calling for another one.' And
she pulled out her mobile phone.

'Put that away in my courtroom!' yelled Juniper. 'Miss
Flight?' And he sent Gareth over to her table. The clerk
shook her and waved a glass of water under her nose.

'Hmm?' said Madison.

Juniper leaned forward and spoke slowly: 'I'm assuming that you are sitting still at the very moment we are all
expecting you to jump up and argue as part of some ruse?'

'Hmmm? No, no. I'm just thinking.'

The clerk made a camp face. 'She doesn't look at all
well, Arthur. I don't like her colour.'

'I'm fine,' insisted Madison, shuffling papers as if to
prove she was functioning normally.

Belinda Bilby dug Madison in the ribs again and hissed:
'Stand up. Say something. They're going to take all my
money.'

'Yes,' said Madison, half to Mrs Bilby, half to the court.
'Yes, I hear that. But really, I wouldn't worry about it.
I mean, what did you ever do with it anyway? Except
buy those hideous clothes and do a lot of extremely silly
things.' Mrs Bilby's mouth was open. But nothing, as yet,
was coming out.

'We will respond to Mr John in due course, M'Lord,
when I have attended to other more serious matters.'

'Which are?' said Juniper.

Madison stood up, gripped the edge of the table, took a deep breath and said, in a brisk, businesslike tone: 'I wish to confess that I have killed someone. It's been on my conscience for a long time and I cannot stay silent a moment longer.'

Now everyone had their mouths wide open. Except Mrs Bilby, who seemed to come to suddenly.

'What the fucking hell is wrong with you?' she screeched.

As Mrs Bilby was led away to the holding cell and jailed for contempt, Madison slumped at the table, put her head in her arms, and began to snore very loudly.

35

'Mitchell. Mitchell!' shouted Cynthia up the stairs. 'We need to leave this house right now!'

She had packed the car with their things, including a lunch of ham sandwiches and Victoria sponge cake to eat on the way. It was a two-hour drive to Madison's house and if they left now they would make it before rush hour hit the city. Her baby was in trouble and they had to get to her. But Mitchell was refusing to entertain the notion of a mad dash. Not without completing all the necessary mad dash pre-checks. Cynthia's response to bad news involved making sandwiches. Fair enough. But Mitchell had a system for emergencies too. Family emergencies were much like mid-flight emergencies. You followed procedure. No need for drama or heroics. Just work calmly through your checklist. Remember your training.

'I'm coming, I'm coming,' he said wearily as he came down the stairs. 'We're not going to get there any faster if you shout. I can't find my keys.'

'I told you ten minutes ago, I've got your keys! Christ

on a bike, Mitchell, you'd test the patience of a saint. Can we go now, please?'

'Just a moment. I need to check everything's locked up.'

'I've locked the back door, for crying out loud – I told you that ten minutes ago.'

'You seem to have been very busy ten minutes ago,' muttered Mitchell, wandering about the house checking doors and window locks. 'Did you do anything else ten minutes ago? Read *War and Peace*? Reinvent nuclear fission?'

This sarcasm didn't bother Cynthia much because she had moved on to something else that was bothering her much more.

'What on earth are you wearing?'

'I'm wearing clothes.'

'Yes, but what clothes? Aren't those the trousers you were gardening in earlier?'

Mitchell, in his view, had not had time to change. They had got the call from Christopher as he was mowing the lawn. Cynthia picked it up and then ran out into the garden and started shrieking at him to turn off the mower.

Madison had collapsed in court.

'What do you mean collapsed?' said Mitchell, with customary reasonableness and calm.

'After being hit by a car!' said Cynthia. 'The doctors can't find anything wrong. Not even concussion. She's been released from hospital but she's at home on her own and Christopher thinks someone should be with her. She might get delayed concussion. I said we'd leave now.'

Mitchell started wandering slowly around, casting off gardening gloves and wellies and picking up random items he might need for the journey as Cynthia stood in the middle of the kitchen watching him with wild eyes and thinking back over the strange conversation she had just had with Christopher, who had sounded as unfocused as ever:

'It's strange they can't find anything wrong. Maybe she wasn't hit by a car at all. Maybe she just fell over in the road and passed out. Maybe she's just a bit run down or something.'

'Yes, she's a bit run down! Run down by a car. Christ on a bike. I'm on my way.'

'Wait. You should know she's been acting a bit strangely,' Christopher had said, before she put the phone down. 'It's nothing you can really put your finger on. It's just that she's not quite the same as she was before.'

'This is terrible. What are you trying to do to me? The more you tell me the more panic-stricken I'm becoming.'

'No, no. It's not bad. In fact, if anything, she's sort of better than she was.'

'What are you talking about?'

'I don't know how to put this. But you know how Madison has always been a little, well, argumentative?'

'I do. She's her mother's daughter. But even I've struggled with her over the years. I always say she came out arguing. She argued from the first second she drew breath. I just thank God she found a profession where she could put it to good use.'

'Well, quite. The thing is . . . and I'm telling you now

so you're prepared . . . your daughter has . . . well . . . the thing is . . .'

'The thing is what? For heaven's sake, man, spit it out.'

'She's stopped arguing.'

That sent Cynthia into a tailspin. She slammed down the phone without even saying goodbye.

'I don't care what they say, I want a second opinion,' she said to Mitchell as he disappeared upstairs.

'On what? Whether she's stopped arguing or not?' he called back.

'This is no time to be philosophical, Mitchell. They're saying the effect of the trauma has exacerbated pre-existing problems. But I don't trust those London doctors. She didn't have any pre-existing problems.'

'She had nothing but pre-existing problems,' said Mitchell, as they got into the car.

As he drove his big red BMW saloon very slowly, they sat in silence for a while, staring ahead, and then she turned to him and said: 'Thank God *you* didn't pick the phone up. Hello, Mr Flight, your daughter's a vegetable. Oh, that's nice. Thank you for letting me know. She was always a bit strange, so not to worry.'

'That's not what I said.'

Silence. The houses of Little Fougham flew past with their ever-hopeful gnomes and windmills. And then he couldn't resist saying:

'But if the only symptom of this blow to the head, or whatever it was, is that she's lost the ability to argue, then it might be a blessed relief. For everyone.'

More silence. Cynthia sat staring out of the window, pursing her lips first one way then the other, before replying:

'It's bloody typical of you to look on the bright side.'

Madison stood in her bathroom staring in the mirror at her forehead. Where the pulsing temple vein had been, her barometer of stress and tension, there was now, well, the opposite. Where there had once been a lump sticking out of her temple, there was now a tiny, almost invisible dent.

She hadn't noticed it earlier. She supposed it was where her head had collided with a bump in the road, or the kerb, or maybe a stone. Miraculously, the skin had not been broken and there was no mark. Not even a scratch.

She put her finger in the dent. She hoped it would not be permanent. Even though it was a small dent, and she was not vain, no one liked to have a dent in their head.

She wondered briefly what was behind the dent, what part of her brain. And then she pushed this from her mind as she sank down onto the bathroom floor and fell asleep again.

She didn't wake until the door-knocking got really insistent. Her mobile phone was ringing as well. She pulled herself off the floor and dragged herself into the kitchen. The word 'Mother' was flashing on her BlackBerry.

Someone banged on the door again. A voice shouted. She could hear her mother now, or what passed for her mother – the muffled sound of a huge fuss on the other side of the front door: '. . . she could be dead! . . . I told you this would happen! . . . We need to call the police!'

She sloped towards the front door, yawning, pulled it open and said: 'Oh, it's so nice to see you. What a lovely surprise.'

And the strangest thing was, she meant it.

As her mother pushed straight past her and into the house, swearing, she didn't feel the least bit annoyed. She thought how wonderful it was to have a mother. And a father . . .

'Daddy!' she exclaimed, as she caught sight of Mitchell humping bags towards the threshold. And she threw her arms around her father, who flinched at the strangeness of the feeling for truly, he couldn't remember when he had last been hugged.

'Hello, dear,' said Mitchell. 'Mind if I bring these in? We've brought rather a lot of stuff, I'm afraid. Your mother seems to think we're going to be staying for the next thirteen years. Or until man lands on Mars, whichever is sooner.'

'Oh, let me help you with those,' said Madison, and started bringing bags in. 'You look well, Daddy. Really well. Have you been out in the garden? You've got a lovely sun tan.'

'Your mother wants less lawn and more decking. So I've been—'

'Mitchell! What are you doing? Have you brought the

bags in yet? Dear God, if I'm not behind you every second of the live-long day you go to pieces.'

Cynthia rushed back down the hallway, having, in less than a minute, deposited her handbag on the kitchen table, found a strange poem on a piece of scrap paper, which she filed in her handbag to worry about later, put the kettle on, checked the contents of the fridge and started a bath running.

'Right, madam, let's get you back to bed.' And she grabbed hold of Madison and started manhandling her into the bedroom.

She pushed Madison under the duvet and looked at her face intently. She stared into her eyes.

'What are you doing? You're frightening me.'

'Your pupils are dilated.'

'I feel sleepy. Why are you here?'

'You had an accident. Remember?'

'Oh, it was only a little thing. I slipped over in the road. Christopher brought me home. He's such a sweet man. He says I've to take a few days off. But I need to get back to work soon because I've got a big case. I'm trying to help a poor old lady get divorced, which is so sad.'

'You're not going anywhere. You'll stay where you are until I say so.'

'Oh, well, all right then. If you think it's best.'

Cynthia stopped smoothing the duvet and stood up straight. 'What did you say?'

'If you think it's best I don't go back to work, I won't. I'll stay here.' And then Madison reached out for her mother's hand.

'Have you ever noticed how wonderful the world is, Mummy? I have. I've been lying here thinking about how lucky I am to have such a wonderful life and wonderful friends. And you. And Daddy. And then just as I'm thinking it, here you are . . .' Madison squeezed Cynthia's hand tighter, and beamed. 'Here you are! And I just feel luckier and happier than ever and I want to tell you how much you mean to me.'

Cynthia smiled sweetly, nodded, and told Madison to get some sleep. Then she walked out of the bedroom, shut the door softly and stood for a moment still holding onto the handle, breathing in and out rapidly. She pulled her inhaler out of her pocket and took a big drag.

Then she staggered into the living room where her husband was already sitting with his head back against the sofa, eyes shut, feet up, TV on, and said: 'Mitchell, wake up. Quick. We need to call a doctor.'

Once she had shaken her husband awake, Cynthia started: 'It's worse than I thought. She's really sick. In fact, she's worse than sick. She's gone ga-ga.' She had shut the living room door and was speaking low with the TV on so Madison didn't hear them.

'She seems all right to me.'

'You would say that. You don't notice anything. But she's really lost it this time.'

'If anything,' said Mitchell, carrying on as if he hadn't even heard Cynthia's last comment, 'she seems happier than I've seen her in a long time.'

'That's just the point. Madison isn't happy. She's not meant to be happy. Happy isn't normal for her. So why is she happy now, coincidentally, after hitting her head? I've read about these sudden personality changes following an accident. It's a head injury. Oh dear lord, my baby's brain damaged.'

'Don't reach for the worst-case scenario before you know what's happened. Maybe the accident just moved things around a bit. Maybe it's improved things. We all need a shake-up now and again.'

Cynthia squawked, in a whisper: 'A shake-up? Have you seen the dent in her head, just here?' Cynthia prodded her own face. 'No, you wouldn't have. Well, there's a dent. A dent, Mitchell! I think we should take her to A&E. And if they won't do anything we'll demand they refer her to a specialist.'

'She doesn't need a specialist. She's just a bit dazed, that's all.'

'She said she was lucky and life was wonderful. It put chills up my spine. And that you can just sit in here, watching *Countdown* . . .'

'I like *Countdown*.'

'Do you think she's had a stroke? I said she was over-doing it. She never takes a holiday. Works all the hours God sends. Never stops. I told her to slow down. She takes after me, of course.'

Cynthia glanced at herself in the mantelpiece mirror, noticing her hair was awry. She smoothed it, and by the time she looked back at Mitchell, he had his eyes shut again.

She would have to sort this out. Like she sorted out everything.

36

The offices of Pirana and Clutterbuck were reassuringly terrifying. They were on the thirteenth floor of an ugly steel and glass monstrosity in the middle of the financial district. The building was called The Shaft, because it was meant to look like the long, narrow stem of a spear or arrow, or a shaft of light, perhaps. But whatever it looked like, the name was appropriate because people got shafted there. In fact, some of those who had been shafted had taken to referring to the firm as Pirana and Clusterfuck.

The staff certainly did not mess about. Within seconds of arriving on the euphemistically titled fourteenth floor – it was really the thirteenth but they didn't want to worry anyone – Belinda Bilby had been shown into Anna Pirana's vast corner office with its wall-to-ceiling windows overlooking St Paul's Cathedral.

The artwork on the walls was in a different league to the gentle, amateurish sketches at Wilde and Sawyer: enormous modern oil paintings depicting unfathomably violent themes.

One of them was simply a vivid puke-green back-ground covered in splashes of bright red paint, like blood spatter. It was horrible. Mrs Bilby thoroughly approved. Something in the painting cried out to her. You might say it spoke to her. She was feeling rather grim since spending a day in a cell, although the judge had ultimately shown mercy and decided not to jail her properly for contempt of court. When Valmir came to pick her up after they told her she could go, he pronounced the cell 'very nice. Is not like jail back home. No chains on wall.' Even so, she felt hard done by.

She sat staring at the pleasing depictions of violence and horror screaming out from every canvas.

By the time her new lawyer walked in, she was ready to sign on the dotted line. The busty, red-haired, brightly dressed woman burst through the door like a whirlwind, making spurious apologies about traffic and preposterous-sounding things happening to various chil-dren she owned. She grabbed Mrs Bilby's hand, shook it so hard she nearly dislocated it, and finally came to rest around the other side of her desk, but remained standing.

She placed her hands on the desk, without sitting down. With the City of London spread out behind her, Miss Pirana was an imposing figure indeed.

You could see from the way she stood that, in her opinion, she bestrode the world of matrimonial law like a colossus. Her perfectly salon-blowdried big hair sat firmly on her broad shoulders as she stood in front of her big desk with her arms gripping the edges like Boadicea on her chariot. The colour was up in her cheeks.

There was nothing that got her juices flowing more than a client defecting to her from another firm. It gave her a very special frisson.

A few moments earlier, a shiver of pleasure had coursed through her as she walked along the corridor to her office knowing the widow of Marcus Bilby, the shipping magnate, was sitting in there waiting for her, having sacked a rival firm. That Madison Flight was the solicitor who had been handling her case was too delicious for words. Pirana loved to steal clients from the Flight woman almost more than she loved divorce itself – but not quite, because there was nothing on God's earth she loved more than divorce.

She loved divorce so much, she was fond of saying, she had had three of them herself.

The Flight woman was positively frigid by comparison. But she clearly thought she had class. Anna saw the looks she gave her. Snooty, scornful looks that said she thought she was in another league. But she wasn't. Oh, she might have a better law degree from a better university. And a more serious face, and a more boring dress sense. But when it came right down to it, she wasn't classier or more ethical at all. She was just a mean, uptight bitch who was as cold as ice – and about as interesting as ice, when it came right down to it.

Oh yes, she would enjoy stealing the Bilby account.

Standing behind her desk, stilettos planted, leaning forward, she launched dramatically into her well-rehearsed opening spiel: 'Congratulations. You have taken the first step towards seizing control of your destiny. Today is the first day of the rest of your life.'

Mrs Bilby crinkled her nose. Even she could tell that this was hooey.

37

When Madison opened her eyes, she was alarmed to see that the late-afternoon sun, which had been dropping through the sky when she dozed off, had gone backwards into a morning position. She called her mother. After a few minutes, Cynthia came down the corridor with coffee.

'What day is it?'

'You've been sleeping.'

'Have I been sleeping since you arrived yesterday? You did arrive yesterday, didn't you?'

'Yes. Don't worry. I didn't wake you for dinner last night because I thought it was best to let you sleep through. Here, I've brought you your coffee – made strong, just how you like it.'

Madison sat up and took the cup and sipped it. Cynthia looked at her anxiously.

'Mmmm. Lovely. That *is* just how I like it.'

'Oh, Christ, I was hoping you might have slept it off,' muttered Cynthia.

'Where's Daddy?'

'I've sent your father out to buy cleaning products.'

'The cleaner came yesterday.'

'Well, then, you need to get rid of her. She hasn't cleaned under the sink and the fridge is filthy. You might be vulnerable to infection and there's goodness knows how many germs hanging around that salad drawer. The whole place needs a proper deep clean.'

Cynthia was already going at 680 miles an hour. She was wearing yellow Marigold rubber gloves and an apron, and she had her hair tied back in a scarf.

Madison normally hated it when her mother arrived and insinuated she was incapable by immediately changing into old clothes and getting to work. 'My mother pushes all my buttons,' she used to tell her friends. 'I have to put boundaries down because if I let her, she will infantilize me and make me feel inadequate.'

She had a vague memory of saying these things, but what a mouthful it all sounded now.

Now she said: 'Oh, Mum. Thank you,' with tears in her eyes. 'I don't know what I would do without you. You've always been the rock in my life.'

Cynthia pulled a disgusted face. Lip curled, peering at Madison, she said: 'Are you on something?'

'What do you mean?'

'Have you been taking things? Come on, you can tell me. I know the pressure you're under. I always said you weren't cracked up for it. That job has been getting on top of you, hasn't it? I'm not surprised. No one can live like that. Eating dinner at the office. This has been coming for some time, young lady. I'm not going to judge you, although I will say you brought it on yourself by not listening to me. I just want to know the truth. What is it you've been taking? Did one of those other lawyers get you hooked on it?'

'Mother?'

'Is it crack cocaine?'

'What are you on about?'

'Non-crack cocaine?'

'No!'

'LCD? Speedo? Skunk?'

'Mother!'

'Vicodin? Percodan? Valium? Oh my God – it's not Nurofen Plus, is it? Rita Finkelstein's daughter got hooked on that. They found her wandering around the heritage motor museum high as a kite. They had to detox her in a secure rehab unit in Arizona. And then she ran off with one of the counsellors. The police found them hiding at the Oasis Motel in Tucson. Apparently, they'd rented a convertible Thunderbird and were planning to drive off the edge of the Grand Canyon like Thelma and Louise. She's never been right since.'

'Mother. I need to get out of this bed. I want to go for a walk. It's such a glorious day. I want to feel the sun on my face. And I thought, maybe you could take me into town to do some shopping.' And she picked up one of the women's magazines that Cynthia had brought for her and pointed to an advertisement page.

'Look, there's this face cream that combats the seven signs of ageing. Can we see if we can get it? Can we? There are lots of other things too. There are so many things I want to buy. There's the face cream, and then there's a shampoo that makes your hair thicker and more manageable . . .' And she started flicking through the magazine, trying to find it.

Cynthia backed towards the door as if afraid to take her eyes off her daughter.

'Can we go and see if they've got some? Can we?'

'The doctor's coming at eleven. You're going nowhere.'

Cynthia got the name of the private specialist from Christopher, who got it from Madison, who got it from Belinda Bilby, strangely enough. 'There is this psychiatrist in Harley Street who will prescribe anything if you give him £200 for a consultation,' said Mrs Bilby to Madison, and then Madison to Christopher. Belinda Bilby thought it might be useful to Madison if she ever decided to do something about her obvious personality disorder. Madison thought it might be useful to Christopher in case he went through one of his barefoot crises again.

Dr Cameron McTavish arrived at Madison's apartment in his silver Audi R8.

'Blunt-force trauma head injury,' was his diagnosis. It was imperative Madison be X-rayed and MRI-scanned at the earliest opportunity to check for bleeds or swelling. He would ring the private hospital he dealt with now and if her parents could get her there tonight, he would make sure there was a team waiting.

Cynthia was delighted. 'Dr McTavish, you speak my

language,' she said. '*He* is an action man,' she whispered to Mitchell, as the doctor made the necessary phone calls.

They dressed Madison in a tracksuit and warm coat and helped her out to the car.

Cynthia and Mitchell argued all the way to Harley Street, firstly about the congestion charge hours, and whether they would get fined or not, then about the way the satnav was sending them, via Oxford Street, which Cynthia didn't agree with but Mitchell did.

In road tests, the BMW 3-series navigation system was rarely wrong, he reminded her, as she threatened to pull it out of the dashboard and throw it through the window.

Madison, meanwhile, stared out of the window oblivious to the constant rowing, admiring absolutely everything that went past: 'Oh, look at that huge store with the lights all over it! Oh, wow! Look at the pretty street lamps! Selfridges! I'd love to go in there! Ha ha! Look at that man's hat, with the Union Jack on the front – that's so funny! Nike Air! I want some trainers. Can we stop?'

At the Princess Alice Hospital a team was waiting to take Madison straight to the X-ray department. A nurse came out with a wheelchair.

'Everyone is so nice! Isn't it wonderful that people are being so nice?' said Madison, as a man took her bags and the nurse helped her into the chair.

'Isn't it wonderful what you can get if you're prepared to pay for it?' said Cynthia, acidly.

'I'm with you on that. I would have thought the NHS should have done all this,' said Mitchell.

'I've always said it. You get what you pay for,' said Cynthia, who was secretly pleased as Punch that her daughter was only going to get cured at an exclusive, private medical establishment, even if she had no idea at this precise moment in time how on earth they were going to pay for it.

When the scans were done, the specialist McTavish had arranged to be called in from home – lord knows at what cost – came out into the waiting area where Mitchell and Cynthia were sitting sipping weak tea from plastic cups and invited them into his office. Various frightening-looking images of the inside of Madison's head were pinned on the wall. Madison herself was sitting smiling and swinging her legs in a big chair.

The specialist held out his hand to Mitchell. 'Hello, I'm Dr Nicolaas Labuschagne.'

Mitchell thought: Christ, I hope they haven't flown him in from Cape Town specially. The bill is going to be horrendous.

Before they had even sat down, and as if Madison weren't there, the specialist walked over to the scans hanging on the wall and said: 'This is your problem.'

Cynthia and Mitchell squinted at the scan as he pointed to various parts of it and explained:

'There is swilling, here and here. And this particular area of swilling is prissing on the limbic lobe, here, blocking the flow of neurons in the cingulate gyrus, here, inhibiting its ability to transmit messages to and from the inner limbic system.'

'Say what?' said Mitchell.

'The swilling is prissing on a part of the brain that governs certain emotional and behavioural responses. We see this sort of thing all the time in subtle head injuries. There's nothing you can do but wait for it to go down.'

Mitchell wished that the workings of Madison's brain had parallels with aerospace engineering, then he might be able to offer something informed. As it was, all he could say was: 'Is she going to be all right?'

'She's in no danger. She can go home. She can live a normal laaf, more or liss.'

The couple looked over at their daughter. Madison was still swinging her legs in the chair, whilst reading a leaflet entitled 'Head Injury? – Injurylawyers4U!' She kept laughing, as if amused by something.

Cynthia did not look convinced. 'Mr . . . Ragushagme . . .'

'Labuschagne.'

'Sorry. I do beg your pardon. Mr . . . ehem. What I want to know is, when will my daughter get back to normal, in herself? She's been acting very strangely. Her personality hasn't just changed slightly. It has completely changed. She's gone from being a very difficult person, very . . .' Cynthia was struggling for the word.

'Obstreperous,' said Mitchell.

'Obstreperous, yes. To being sunny and positive and pleasant to be around.'

'I can see how that would be disconcerting.'

'It is. Personally, I liked her the way she was. At least we knew where we stood. Now it's all sunshine and daisies and wanting to rush out and buy face creams because she believes they're going to stop the seven signs of ageing.'

'That must be awkward.'

'Very awkward. My daughter is a top divorce lawyer, Mr Lagushagme. She relies on her innate cynicism every day in her professional life. If this injury robs her of her career the person who hit her in that car is going to have a lot to answer for.'

'Certainly, one should think seriously about a personal injury suit. I could supply you with adequate medical reports.'

'Unfortunately, the car drove off. They examined the CCTV but couldn't see the plates. We just need to know how we can get her back to normal.'

'In my opinion, Mrs Flight, this personality change will continue so long as the swilling persists. Which is to say, it's fair to assume that your daughter won't be her old silf again until the swilling goes down. And we have no option here but to allow the swilling to go down of its own accord.'

'And how long will that take?'

'With head injuries like this it's hard to say. It could be months, or even years. Sometimes, in extreme cases, the swilling never goes down. What you've got, you've got, as they say.'

'Well, I say, that's terrific news,' said Mitchell, who declared as they left the doctor's office that he wanted to celebrate by going out for a slap-up meal.

Madison was in full agreement. As they made their way down the wheelchair ramp to where Mitchell had parked the car, she said she was all for a night out on the tiles.

'Oh, let's go to that new place on Monmouth Street,' she cried, clasping her hands together with unbridled glee.

'We need to get you home and keep you quiet,' said Cynthia.

'Screw quiet,' said Mitchell. 'How about an Argentinian steakhouse? I fancy a big piece of meat. Then we could go take in a show. How about it, old girl?'

'Oh, Daddy, let's!' said Madison, with childlike abandon.

Cynthia grimaced. Both her husband and her daughter seemed to have discovered, rather late on in life, their innate sense of joy and optimism, which was the last thing she needed.

They drove to the restaurant in silence as Cynthia brooded.

When they pulled up on a single yellow line outside the restaurant she took against the Cattle Grid at first sight because there was a huge life-size model of a cow next to the entrance.

To make matters worse, a drunk girl with her skirt hitched up to her knickers was sitting on it. And as the Flights entered, she shouted out: 'Yee-ha!' at Cynthia.

Madison loved all the food on the menu so it took a long time to force her to choose what to have. In the end, she opted for prawn cocktail followed by T-bone steak because she wanted to be 'just like Daddy'.

'Excuse me while I puke into my handbag,' said Cynthia, not very politely.

After ordering, when Madison excused herself to go to the ladies', Mitchell called the waitress over and ordered champagne. 'A little surprise,' he twinkled.

'What is the matter with you?' Cynthia hissed.

'Don't you see? My daughter's finally happy. All my life I've wanted her to be happy. I've blamed myself for the fact that she wasn't happy. I've asked myself a thousand times: Was I to blame? Was I away too often?'

Cynthia muttered, 'Yes,' in a bored voice, as if this were obvious.

'Was I too distant . . . ?'

'Yes.'

'Too unavailable . . . ?'

'Yes.'

'Too focused on my job . . . ?'

'Yes. Yes, yes, yes.' Cynthia was still sitting in her coat, something she did whenever she was not pleased with a place, as if to signal she would not be staying long. She had, however, taken her glasses out of her bag so she could peruse the menu with a look of unbridled disapproval.

'But now it doesn't matter,' said Mitchell, knocking back the contents of a whiskey tumbler. 'Because now it turns out that she is happy, after all. And I want to make the most of it.'

Cynthia slammed down the menu. 'I want her to be happy too. But not like this. Not by losing her marbles. Jesus Christ on a bike, Mitchell. Our daughter's a vegetable!'

Mitchell shushed her as the other diners looked round. 'Maybe it doesn't matter how it happened. Maybe it's fate that she found happiness after a blow to the head. Maybe she is, in a way, a bit limited. So what? That's an act of God, isn't it? Maybe the big man upstairs just couldn't bear to see her fighting any longer and he sent that car to knock some sense into her. I mean out of her.

'Or maybe there was no car.' Mitchell leaned in close. 'What if she was knocked off her feet . . .' He leaned in closer still. Cynthia leaned back, grimacing, as if he were giving off a bad smell. '. . . by the hand of God?'

'You're drunk.' And Cynthia was about to launch into one of her speeches about how he always drank too much at crucial junctures requiring sobriety. And her views about a certain air stewardess called Cheryl were about to be raised, but then weren't, because Madison was coming back from the ladies', beaming from ear to ear at the sight of the waitress at the table with the bottle of bubbly.

'Oh, Daddy, champagne! You shouldn't have, how exciting!'

As the cork popped, Madison started giggling. And she didn't stop giggling until the giggles got mixed up with the T-bone steak and turned to hiccups. Even Mitchell looked a bit worried at this point. Then she fell asleep at the table. So they had to drag her out to the car. And she lay across the back seat all the way home, snoring loudly.

Anna Pirana was Britain's Best Divorce

38

Anna Pirana was Britain's Best Divorce Lawyer. It said so on her website.

Her website also displayed, without irony, the two main pillars of her company's service in two vertical columns headed, respectively, Safeguarding Your Assets and Getting What You Deserve.

The former explained in 250 words how the firm she ran with her partner Claudia Clutterbuck would help wealthy individuals hide their money from their greedy, grasping ex-spouses; and the latter explained, also in 250 words, how the firm would help the underdogs find assets that their mean ex-partners were concealing.

Why customers never seemed to read both columns was a mystery. If they had, they might so easily have seen through the veneer of Pirana and Clutterbuck – or P&C, as it was known – to the abject moral redundancy beneath, but as they only ever read one column or the other, they didn't.

Another mysterious thing was that once you had Googled Anna Pirana, even once, you could never escape from her.

One Google of her name would set up a Trojan horse in

your computer that meant you were thereafter constantly bombarded with adverts for her. Whenever you Googled any other site on the internet, the page you wanted would open up and for a few seconds all would be fine, but then a huge window would pop up on the page with a picture of Anna Pirana's big, glossy-haired, red-lipsticked head and the words:

'Britain's Best Divorce Lawyer!' Just in case you had forgotten. She wasn't so much a divorce lawyer as a computer virus.

But let us not be too harsh on P&C. Because a divorce firm is, in effect, offering the reverse service to a dating agency, then perhaps it was appropriate that Pirana and Clutterbuck used glossy, seductive, dating agency speak.

With unbridled vulgarity, it advertised six different levels of service depending on how much you either wanted to 'protect' or 'get because you deserved it'.

It went all the way from a basic no-frills service called Discovery, for those of modestly wealthy means: ordinary professionals or their spouses (with assets of £0.5 million to £2million), through Executive, for the moderately wealthy, like executives and company owners (£2 million–£10 million), Executive Plus, for the properly wealthy – bankers and fund managers, for example (£10 million–£25 million), Executive SuperPlus for the aspiring super-rich: footballers, minor pop stars and so on (£25 million–£250 million), Premier, for the properly super-rich: aristocracy, major celebrities, heirs and heiresses (£250 million–£2 billion) and Premier Plus for disgustingly, revoltingly rich industrial magnates, Russian oligarchs and media moguls, or their partners (£2billion upwards).

Mrs Bilby perused the menu of options whilst sipping a glass of crisp white wine served to her by an office junior. 'I think I'll take the Premier,' she said, haughtily.

She easily qualified for the Premier Plus but she figured it was probably almost exactly the same as Premier, just more expensive.

'An excellent choice, Mrs Bilby,' said Anna Pirana, who was sitting behind her desk in an outfit with shoulder pads so big they were blocking out half the London skyline. St Paul's Cathedral ought to have been visible through the window behind her but the dome was almost entirely obscured by the vast bulk of her vintage 1980s jacket.

'I'm sure you will find the service you receive here will put the provincial solicitors at Wilde and Sawyer to shame.'

'Yes, well, the poor girl was a bit out of her depth after she suffered a serious head injury.'

'The way I heard it, she wasn't doing so well before she hit her head. No, no. Here at P&C, I think you will find we move ahead with all due expediency, and, going forward, as it were, start getting you some tangible results very quickly. The first thing we must do is get your financial statement, your Form E, in better order.'

'Yes, well, I've been thinking about that,' said Mrs Bilby, puffing herself up as she prepared to tell her new lawyer how she wanted to play it. 'I've decided I want to liquidize my assets.'

'You mean liquidate?'

'I mean liquidize.'

'You mean liquidate. Unless you want to put your money in a blender and make a milkshake out of it.' And Anna Pirana laughed a hideously grating laugh, which sounded like a handsaw going through plywood.

As Anna Pirana was serving Mrs Bilby with an extra helping of shtick, Madison was feeling as perky as you like after a good night's sleep following her hectic evening of brain scans and T-bone steak.

Cynthia took her to the supermarket where she wandered the aisles like a child at Disney World, admiring every single one of the products. 'Gets clothes seven shades whiter than the other leading brands . . .' she said, as she put two enormous cartons of soap powder into the trolley.

'Leaves clothes feeling soft, smelling fresh and looking great!' she exclaimed as she added three giant bottles of fabric softener.

'Won't dry your skin like soap can . . . that's amazing . . .' She was in the bath and hair products aisle.

'Two for one on all shampoos and conditioners . . . what a good deal . . . and this shampoo says it promotes the seven signs of healthy-looking hair!'

Cynthia realized her daughter had not just lost her ability to argue, she had lost her ability to differentiate between truth and bullshit. No wonder she was happy.

Whatever part of her brain was malfunctioning was the part that contained both her arguing powers and her powers of discernment.

The world was a nicer place because she was literally unable to see anything wrong with it.

She was experiencing the world afresh and seeing the good in everything, God help her. She was as vulnerable as a baby crawling towards an open fire because she had no idea what could possibly go wrong.

As such, she was going to require even more worrying about than when she had been a cynical misery-guts.

'Actively lowers cholesterol . . . one of your five a day . . .' her daughter cried out, examining a yoghurt with fruit compote corner.

'Nutella spread, full of the goodness of hazelnuts and milk chocolate!' as they moved on to the jams and spreads aisle.

'That's pure sugar and fat. It's not good for you at all. Put it back,' said Cynthia, trying to rain on her parade.

'But it says here that it *is* good for you. Look: "Nutritious and wholesome. Make Nutella part of your breakfast for a healthy source of energy and protein! Kids love it!"'

'Put it back.'

'The strange thing is, I don't know why I've never bought this before. It's chocolate. And it says you can eat it on toast for breakfast. Why haven't I been doing that? It doesn't make any sense that I haven't been eating it every single day. Maybe I've had it before and I just can't remember.' And she shrugged and put three jars of it into the trolley.

Cynthia tried to guide her towards the checkout with her packed trolley, but she was having an epiphany in the cereal aisle: 'Ooh, look! Harvest Time. Crunchy clusters of oats with pieces of real strawberries. That looks yummy . . .

'. . . Cheese Chasers, the snack that won't leave you hungry . . . Hey, the ketchup's on offer! And it's buy one get one half price on all tins of own-brand chopped tomatoes! Maybe we should make spaghetti Bolognese tonight. Or chilli con carne. Or something else completely! Using Quorn mince, the healthy protein source – as eaten on TV by Mo Farah!'

The bean curd stew that Madison prepared that evening was truly tasteless, although Mitchell, most unhelpfully, thoroughly enjoyed it. Afterwards they settled down to watch the television together and Cynthia tried to interest Madison in a programme featuring a celebrity she knew she didn't like.

She thought it might awaken some of her former cynicism.

'Look, it's that man you hate. The one you always say makes you want to punch the TV set.'

'Oh, but he's really funny. I love his silly sticky-uppy hair.'

'I know what might help,' said Cynthia, reaching for the remote. 'Let's watch *EastEnders*.'

But by the time the cliffhanger end came, Madison was on the edge of her seat, with tears in her eyes, declaring that the episode of unrelenting misery said a lot about the triumph of community spirit over adversity.

'It's hopeless,' Cynthia said, after her daughter had gone to bed, exhausted, as she always was now by 9 p.m. 'Our daughter may be happy, but she's a total moron.'

39

Mr Justice Juniper was sitting in his rooms, snorting coke off the top of Belinda Bilby's financial statement through a rolled-up twenty.

He had told himself he would stop with the Charlie if he ever got himself into a position where he was snorting it through five-pound notes. He had seen someone doing that in the loo of a club in Soho once and had decided that was going to be his bottom line.

As it was, he was holding everything together very nicely – including, as it happened, the inside of his nostrils. He assumed that was a horror story put about by scaremongers and people in the media who didn't know how to do drugs properly.

He did know how to do them properly. In fact, he was doing a particularly bloody brilliant job of doing them.

His wife had no idea that his worsening three-quarter-life crisis had moved from whiskey, gambling and porn to class A narcotics. It was incredible the way he kept the various parts of his world separate, and everyone in each part completely in the dark. He took his hat off to himself.

As long as he checked in at his meetings every night he seemed to be able to maintain the fiction that he was dealing with his demons. What demons? He felt as invincible as a prize bull.

The girl he had found on the internet had just left. It was better than looking at porn all day. This way, the taxpayer only had to foot the bill for twenty minutes, tops, of lost court time when he was otherwise engaged in his office. Before he hit upon the idea of ordering in, he had been wasting hours and hours on the internet, which wasn't an efficient use of public resources.

Yes, he had cracked it all right. He had finally worked out how it all fitted together. Never mind all those other suckers who had to stay clean and sober all their lives. He, Arthur Juniper, could handle it. For that to be so, according to the people at his meetings, he would have to be the first addict in history to be able to handle it, but in his heightened state, he thought that entirely possible.

After licking the stray coke off the front cover, he opened Mrs Bilby's file.

The pages of figures were dizzying. But the long and the short of it appeared to be that she was both denying she had any money at all and claiming she needed £5,000 a week to live on. It was a version of the same story in the other file. The husband was claiming he had nothing, but was used to everything, and therefore needed £25,000 a month.

The husband's solicitor, who was turning out to be something of a quiet genius, had cleverly turned round the accusations made by the Flight woman in court and was now admitting that his client was a basket case who required extensive round-the-clock care, including help to tie his own shoelaces.

Whether he would get it was another thing, as Mrs Bilby's amazing disappearing assets had shrunk even further. Her late husband's shipping company was being put into receivership with bad debts.

Tankards Reach now appeared to be in the name of the housekeeper, Mrs Margaret Teesdale, while someone called Bert Teesdale – her husband, the judge presumed – had found himself the owner of an apartment in Monaco. It transpired that it had been Marcus Bilby's dying wish that his wife sign over large amounts of property to their trusted household staff, a wish he had voiced in person to her on his deathbed, but owing to her extreme grief at the time, she had only just remembered it.

Bert Teesdale was probably the first gamekeeper in history to own a £5 million seafront apartment in Monte Carlo. Or maybe he wasn't. Who knows? Maybe the rich have been doing this sort of thing under our noses for as long as there have been very small, fiendishly expensive apartments in Monte Carlo for tax purposes – or gamekeepers, or divorces, thought Juniper, cutting himself another fat line.

In any case, the husband's increasingly shrewd solicitor had evidently got wind of the amazing disappearing Bilby fortune, and had appointed a team of forensic accountants to find it again.

As well as an order to freeze Mrs Bilby's remaining assets, Elden John applied for an interim maintenance order to fund the spiralling costs of the case. Juniper, who actively loathed Mrs Bilby now, eagerly granted both the orders.

Juniper could have jailed the wife for six months for contempt of court to frighten her into declaring her assets properly, if he so chose. But wouldn't that rather spoil things?

He greatly looked forward to the fun and games that would undoubtedly ensue as the husband's legal team started spending Mrs Bilby's money to try to find Mrs Bilby's money. It was not a move, in his very great experience, that was inclined to produce straightforward results.

40

Mitchell carried the tea tray into Madison's room with trembling hands.

She was sleeping, so he placed it gently down on the dressing table and began tiptoeing to the door.

Madison stirred and opened her eyes. 'That smells nice, what is it?'

'Something your mother's cooked. Shepherd's pie, I think. Or it could be lasagne. You know what her cooking's like, it's all the same.'

'I'm sure it's delicious.'

'Oh yes, I'm sure it's delicious too. Really delicious.' Mitchell had forgotten for a second that Madison was a new person now. He had thought he might have a quick jibe at Cynthia and they could bitch a little.

Instead his daughter pulled herself up under the covers and smiled beatifically. 'Stay, please. I wanted to talk to you.'

'Oh, what about?' Mitchell stayed standing.

'Mitchell! What are you doing in there?' Cynthia was yelling from the kitchen. 'Your dinner's getting cold.'

'What have you been up to?'

'Helping your mother in the kitchen. I made the salad. So that bit's safe.'

'No, I mean . . .' And Madison paused, as if puzzled herself by what she was about to say. 'I mean, all these years.'

'All these years?'

'Yes, you know, I've never really asked you what you've been doing. Ever.'

'Well, the usual. Gardening, pottering, I've some inventions I'm working on in the shed. Of course your mother's pretty cross about it since they're making an awful mess.'

'But what have you been doing, apart from that? Before you started pottering, I mean.'

'Well, I worked as an airline pilot, as you know . . .'

Mitchell wasn't at all sure any more if she did know. She was looking increasingly vague. Maybe her memory had gone now too.

'Oh, that's right!' she said, as if being reminded of a quaint fact she had long ago forgotten. 'And did you do that until very recently?'

'No, that came to an end a while ago now. When I was . . .'

And Mitchell stopped himself. Why remind his daughter about the bad things if she didn't remember them? So he said: 'When I took early retirement, after fifty years of service. They threw me a party and made me pilot of the decade.' He paused, before getting into his stride:

'It reminded me of when I was decorated for bravery. When I was a fighter pilot.'

Mitchell had always thought he was due a bit more adoration from his daughter. She had never really been as in awe of him as he would have liked.

'Oh, Daddy, you are wonderful,' said Madison, beaming from ear to ear.

Mitchell felt a warm glow and he fully intended to enjoy it. 'Now, eat your dinner, or your mother will get cross.' And he put the tray down on her lap.

Outside the door, Cynthia collared him. He should have known. She was usually listening behind doors, even if you thought she was at the other end of the house.

'What do you think you're playing at? You were barely alive during the Second World War. If she is seriously losing her memory and needs reminding of things then I am going to be here to tell her that you weren't awarded pilot of the decade, you were sacked for drink-driving.'

When they were seated at the kitchen table, the door shut and the burnt shepherd's pie in front of them, Mitchell broke the silence: 'It's not called drink-driving. I wasn't a driver, I was a pilot. And I wasn't drunk. I was tired. I hadn't slept for three days because of Royal Atlantic's barely legal shift patterns. All I had was one whiskey to take the edge off.'

'Yes, take the edge off your pension. I can't believe you would lie like that. To your own daughter.'

'It was a sting operation, as you well know. They wanted to make cutbacks so they randomly tested a hundred pilots and found half of us over the limit.'

'Yes. And why couldn't you have been in the half that

wasn't over the limit? Hmm? Because you had to have a whiskey to take the edge off. The edge off what, exactly? The misery I put you through, I suppose that's what you're imply-ing. And now you can't even face up to what you've done and tell the truth to your own amnesiac, brain-damaged daughter. What sort of man are you?'

Mitchell threw his knife and fork down and gave up all pretence that he was going to eat the shepherd's pie.

'Who is it harming? The truth wasn't doing any of us any good. Starting again with the slate clean is making all of us happy. Except you.'

'Yes,' said Cynthia, 'how like me to be awkward and want to get to the truth of the situation. Like the time I rang that hotel in Africa and a woman picked up the phone in your room.'

'You did what?'

'Yes, I found out. You didn't think I was capable of ringing the airline and asking what your schedule was, where you were flying to and what hotel you were staying in, did you?'

Cynthia pointed her fork at her husband. 'I find out about everything, Mitchell. I'm a truth-seeking missile. Where do you think Madison gets it from?'

'This is terrible. You mustn't tell Madison.' Mitchell was staring down into his plate. He felt so bad now he was considering eating the burnt shepherd's pie, just to take his mind off it.

'I don't think she would care if I did. In her current state she seems determined to look on the bright side of everything. If I told her her father ran away to the Horn of Africa – oh, the irony – with a trolley dolly called Cheryl in 1974, and God knows how many times since, she would probably ask you what the swimming pool was like. It was baby's first holiday, Mitchell. How could you miss it?'

'We did not run away together. It was one night. I only did it because you made it perfectly clear you didn't want me to come to Benidorm with you. And she was not a trolley dolly.'

'What was she, then?'

Mitchell thought about it. It was a good question. Cheryl was a very attractive but very unhinged middle-aged woman who had lived her entire life in the air. She never put down any roots and had absolutely no life at all outside of her job. In between flights she slept. As soon as she got home she climbed into bed, swallowed various kinds of benzodiazepines and went to sleep for days on end. It started as a way of getting over jet lag, she told him, but after twenty-five years covering long haul she had become a sleep addict. When she wasn't flying, and serving rich, bad-tempered, leering businessmen, she was barely ever conscious.

But she had evidently felt something of a newfound zest for life after her night in the Horn of Africa with Mitchell. She had wanted him to leave Cynthia for her. She had fallen in love with him. 'You make me want to stay awake,' she said.

No one had ever told him something deep and meaningful like that before. It was rather nice. But he didn't want to leave Cynthia and all the kerfuffle that would entail. So he went home and thought no more about it, until he realized one day that he hadn't seen Cheryl on a flight for over a year.

When he made enquiries he found out that she had put herself to sleep for the last time. Not intentionally, they said. She had bought a new brand of sleeping pills called Zopidan whilst on a stopover in the States and she had taken too many by mistake. Possibly with a glass or two of wine, which proved fatal. They found her all tucked up in her room at the Hotel Minneapolis, a tray of dinner with the empty wine glass by the bed and the TV still on. He felt bad. But at the time he didn't really see there was anything he could have done.

Now he thought about it again, he wondered whether he should have called her.

Mitchell pushed the lumpy mashed potato around his plate. Perhaps it was best he had left things as they were. Especially given what happened to his career. Cheryl might not have stuck with him the way Cynthia had.

Cynthia snatched his plate away just as he was about to put a forkful of lumps into his mouth. He watched her sweep his half-eaten dinner into the bin in that impatient, unforgiving way of hers, but he didn't argue.

He didn't argue because as well as being divested of his pilot's wings, he had also lost his place in the competitive world of processed pig-meat after Mitchell's Meats – Best of British! went bust after health and safety checks found horsemeat in the pork pies.

It was viewed in the media as a shocking scandal, but in truth the demise of Mitchell's Meats had been a long time coming, given its many unconventional practices in mechanical food processing. Still, it left Mitchell feeling aggrieved. Despite having spent a lot of his life wanting nothing to do with his father's business, after joining it as a desperate middle-aged man with a family who was unemployable in his chosen career, he felt a deep respect for it – the sort of respect one feels for an embarrassing fat friend who stands by you when no one else will.

And now it had been destroyed he felt a pang of grief.

Thank goodness his parents, Mitchell Senior and Doris, were both gone now. It was a mercy they had not lived to see the inspectors invading the place dressed in protective suits and brandishing forceps. By this time the company had been all but sold out to a larger firm, but Mitchell had retained a share.

He could have taken a place on the board and it would have been something to stave off retirement.

Sadly, that turned out not to be possible. There are many things the public will put up with when it comes to food quality, but pony pies is not one of them. The story made the *Daily Mail* and the game was up for Mitchell's Meats.

Cynthia was furious and would not listen to reason.

'A bit of horsemeat never killed anyone . . . The horses were dead already . . . They only found traces of phenylbutazone . . . A bit of phenylbutazone never hurt anyone . . . At least we'd changed the slogan from "Food You Can Trust" to "Best of British". It *was* the best of British horsemeat. We never lied to our customers . . .' These were just a few of the excuses Mitchell used to try to pacify his wife, but she was mortified and beyond consolation.

She was even more beyond consolation when Mitchell was suddenly at home all day and every day.

Forced together for the first time in their married lives, they discovered that they liked each other as little as they had often suspected.

They argued about everything, including where Mitchell put his feet whilst he had his shoes on, and where Cynthia put the milk, at the back of the fridge where he couldn't find it.

This went on and on relentlessly until they both got thoroughly bored of it. Sick and tired of being sick and tired of each other, they collapsed into a state of utter exhaustion.

Cynthia declared to Rita Finkelstein that they were both simply waiting for death now. 'That's it. My life's over,' she said, as Rita perched on the settee eating from a luncheon spread laid out on lace doilies on the marble coffee table.

'Well, I must say, it's a relief to be able to come over here again without worrying about the pork. Pass me another savoury roll, will you, dear? These are delicious. Are you sure they're vegetarian?'

And then, one day, Mitchell got out of bed and came downstairs to the kitchen to find Cynthia cooking breakfast with a determined look on her face.

'I thought we might go and pick up some more bedding

plants for the front garden today,' she said, as she cracked an egg smartly into the pan.

And Mitchell, not wanting to interfere with whatever plan his wife had hatched to get them out of the bind they were in, for he was at his wits' end, said: 'That's a good idea, dear.'

And so it was. They had a very pleasant day, including lunch at the café at the garden centre and a quick look round the heritage motor museum on the way back because Mitchell said he hadn't been for years and fancied seeing it again.

And when they got home, he took care to take his shoes off before he put his feet up on the sofa to watch *Countdown*.

Which had a profound effect on Cynthia, who, while she made dinner, unilaterally decided to rearrange the refrigerator.

Kneeling in front of it, she reached to the back and gingerly, as if slightly afraid of the enormity of what she was doing, moved the milk to the front, so that Mitchell would be able to put his hands on it quickly if he fancied pouring himself a glass before he turned in that night.

Yes. They had come to an arrangement. Mitchell reflected on it now, as he sat at the table while Cynthia crashed around the kitchen and then slammed a fruit cobbler, or whatever it was, onto the table.

Yes. The arrangement had kept the peace but it had meant that since the day of the garden centre trip he had never really told her what he thought.

Stung by her mentioning Cheryl after all these years, he decided to have a go. As she manhandled fruit cobbler into bowls and violently dolloped cream on top, he said quietly:

'Have you ever thought that Madison might be the way she is because of you?'

'What are you talking about,' said Cynthia, shoving the bowl under his nose as if it were the most normal thing in the world to persist with serving a fruit cobbler minutes after accusing your husband of having an affair.

'You blame me, and the fact that I was away too much. And maybe you're right. I should have been around more. But maybe she's unhappy because you taught her to be unhappy. You filled her with cynicism. Maybe if you'd pretended things were all right, she would have grown up a bit happier.'

Cynthia thought for a minute, her face darkening. He wondered if he had gone too far. Maybe she would put the fruit cobbler on his head. But she simply stood up and cleared away the untouched bowls – as if clearing away pudding a few seconds after serving it was completely normal – and starting washing up, looking out of the window by the sink as she said: 'It's been a nice day but it's coming on to rain. It always rains in the end.'

41

'Call me,
I long to
Hear your voice
W'

This was the note that Cynthia had found on the kitchen table. But she had put it in her bag, and so no one ever did call W and tell him that the woman with whom he had been having an affair, on and off, for five years, had hit her head. They couldn't have called him even if Cynthia had remembered to show Madison the note, because Madison no longer remembered who W was. Or that he existed in her mobile phone between Wayne, the tree surgeon who pollarded her limes, and Wu, the local Chinese take-away.

W had fallen out of her head along with a few other random facts and figures, her sense of cynicism and her ability to argue.

So when W let himself into the house one evening, with a bottle of good wine and some Japanese food, he got short shrift from Cynthia. She had been watching television, Madison was asleep and Mitchell was snoozing. And so, as a key turned in the door, Cynthia didn't even bother to try to wake her husband. I'll deal with this myself, just like I deal with everything, she thought, taking up a defensive position behind the door with a poker.

The man who came through the doorway was about sixty, she guessed, but a prosperous, well-preserved sixty. He was dressed in a very expensive suit, pink striped shirt and what looked like a Hermès tie. He had good hair and good shoes, she noted approvingly, as she decided whether to smash the poker straight down on his head or give him a chance to explain himself.

On the basis that he was wearing monogrammed cuff-links, she decided to let him enter a plea.

When she had W pinned against the wall on the other side of the door, poker to his throat, she asked him the very straightforward question, 'Who are you?' but he looked as though he really didn't know.

'Why have you got a key?'

Half strangled by the threat of the poker, W said Madison had given him a spare key so that he could '. . . er . . . feed the cat! Is Madison here?'

Poor W. Cynthia took his key, told him his services were no longer needed, and sent him away with a flea in his ear.

When she went in to tell Madison that she had dealt with a strange man who claimed to be supplying her with pet-minding services, Madison seemed perfectly content with the action her mother had taken.

'I can't think who that can have been. Unless I gave the key to someone at work. How odd.'

Later, with Cynthia sitting by the bed reading her book, Madison suddenly put down her magazine and said: 'Do you know, I've never felt better. I feel like a weight has been lifted off me. Everything is so much easier this way. But the thing I'm most relieved about is getting it off my chest about killing Ralph Perkins.'

'What are you talking about?' said Cynthia. The judge had ignored her daughter's courtroom murder confession, naturally. He had seen it for what it was: the ramblings of a person who had just hit her head.

'Do you remember Ralph Perkins?' Madison said.

'No. I'd forgotten him.' Cynthia looked tight-lipped and sounded dismissive.

This was apt, thought Madison. Since he had been forgotten so completely when he was alive, there was no reason why Ralph Perkins should be remembered in death.

Madison felt a terrible pang in her heart.

'That poor man. All those years he was treated so badly by Shirley.'

'Ralph? Ralph Perkins?' said her mother, putting down her book. 'Are we talking about the same Ralph Perkins? Womanizer Ralph Perkins? Had about three on the go at any one time? And men too. What a dark horse he turned out to be.'

Madison didn't know what to say to that. Surely her mother had made some mistake.

'No mistake. Ralph Perkins. Ralph. Perkins. Who tried to gas himself with the exhaust because he'd been arrested by the police in the car park at Fougham Common and charged with doing *what they do* with a heating engineer in a Transit van. Not for the first time either. Lost his job because he spent so much time there.

'He told Shirley he was confused and thought he might be gay. Then one of the girls turned up on her doorstep to tell her she was expecting. What a mess. He had to be hospitalized after the suicide attempt.'

'I remember.'

'Of course you do. You went and visited him and took him puzzle books. You could be a very thoughtful child when you wanted to be.'

'I thought I'd killed him with the deadly nightshade from Shirley's garden. I picked it and made it into mint tea.'

'Don't be ridiculous. That *was* mint tea. You're imagining things, you silly girl.'

Cynthia was talking to her like she was a child again now. 'Ralph Perkins took an overdose of tranquillizers. He'd been storing them up under his pillow.'

'Oh.'

'Poor Shirley. I must ring her. She's not been having a good time of it lately. She picked another wrong'un after Ralph, if you ask me.'

Madison was staring into space. After a long pause, during which Cynthia had disappeared into her book again – a romance called *The Costermonger's Daughter* by Genevieve Sanderson – she said: 'I think I may have got everything completely wrong.'

Cynthia kept reading. 'Hmm?'

'I think I've been wrong. About everything. About what I thought I'd done, and why I'd done it. And other people. And what they'd done. And why they'd done it.'

Cynthia said: 'That's right, dear.' The costermonger's daughter was about to say yes to a proposal of marriage from the blacksmith's apprentice.

'I thought Ralph was unhappy because Shirley didn't love him. I thought you and Daddy were unhappy too.'

This made Cynthia look up from her romance.

'Your father and me? Oh no. We've have had our moments. But we wouldn't be without each other. Would we, Mitchell?' She called out of the door towards the living room.

'What's that, dear?' Mitchell called back, over the sound of a *Countdown* repeat.

'You and me. We wouldn't be without each other.'

Mitchell popped his head around the door. 'Are you two all right? Can I get you anything?' Madison's face was a picture of shock and disbelief.

'Daddy, is it true? Are you and Mummy happy?'

42

Elden John was going to need the best forensic accountants in the business to find Mrs Bilby's money and so he
appointed Costello and Wolfson, global financial dispute
specialists.

They did not come cheap. Their elite service was £500
an hour and they estimated it would take a large team
several weeks working round the clock, in several coun-
tries, before they even scratched the surface of the truth of
where the Bilby fortunes had disappeared to.

An all-expenses-paid trip to Africa was going to be
part of this investigation, because to the many bizarre
money-confiscating business ventures Mrs Bilby had
already detailed in her first financial statement, she now
added the fabulous revelation that a cargo ship owned
by her dead husband's company had been captured by
pirates.

The MV *Feisty Lady* went off the radar ninety nauti-
cal miles off the east coast of Somalia. Bilby, Bilby and
Bilby (Logistics) paid $700,000 to a representative of the
pirates in Mombasa, but the ship never materialized again,

although the crew turned up safe and well in Mogadishu a few days after the ransom handover.

Worse, according to Mrs Bilby, the insurance had not paid out, leaving the firm liable for lost cargo amounting to nearly a billion pounds. The insurance company's contention, for what it was worth, was that the ship had been scuttled, or sunk on purpose.

Needless to say, the notorious Bilby brothers were inept at handling the situation – being more than a little distracted by a pending prosecution for possession with intent to supply – and the company was wound up with crippling losses as a result.

As Taylor v Taylor assumed global proportions, with implications for international shipping, Anna Pirana announced that the legendary Roderick Howler QC, head of Vortex Chambers, author of *The Divorce Game* and *How to Get Ahead in Matrimony* would now represent Mrs Bilby in all future court appearances.

Elden John was notified that the other side had instructed counsel in a letter from Pirana and Clutterbuck that was so terrifying it gave him a peptic ulcer, instantly.

After reading the letter, he Googled Howler and then had palpitations at his desk all morning as he worked out how to respond.

He could play the arms race, he thought, as he sipped from a glass of milk. It wasn't a question of money, because since the maintenance order, Mrs Bilby was incurring his costs. He could appoint a top QC if he wanted to. But he didn't want to.

He had got the bit between his teeth, even if his teeth were, at this precise moment, chattering violently.

He wanted to see if he could stand up to the big guys on his own. He was possessed by the idea that he had to prove himself. He was in a David and Goliath battle and if he won this battle on his own, with just his trusty sling full of rocks, he would go down in history.

'What a Howler!' would be the headline in the *Sun*. Whilst the *Croydon Sentinel* would pay tribute to the triumph, against all odds, of 'Local have-a-go hero solicitor!'

Who knew? Maybe Elton John himself would be moved to say something about his nearly namesake when the case was internationally famous. Perhaps he would perform a special version of 'Rocket Man' as a tribute.

Elden saw himself floating through space, a lone warrior for truth and justice, a space cowboy . . .

Mother, he thought, conjuring an image of the late Doris John, floating beside him, holding his hand, what shall I do?

Doris smiled through the visor of her astronaut's helmet and gave a thumbs-up sign. He couldn't be sure of the words she mouthed, but they looked a lot like 'Go get 'em, cowboy.'

Madison was floating through space snoozing when the cautious, barely audible knock on her bedroom door brought her gently out of her slumber.

She recognized that knock.

'Can I come in?' said Christopher, poking his head around the door.

He didn't know what was more disconcerting, the smile on her face as he disturbed her or the fact that she didn't snap his head off when he told her about Mrs Bilby retaining Pirana.

'Oh well, never mind,' she said, obviously trying to disguise her hurt feelings. 'I suppose she'll do a good job. It might be for the best.'

Christopher didn't know what to say. But in the end he thought he might as well plough on and say everything he had not dared to say in nineteen years. He decided to tell Madison the whole lot, before the swelling went down in her brain.

He told her about the deficit in this year's accounts, and he told her about the harassment case from the young office junior he had got drunk and propositioned after the Christmas party, and he told her about the prawn sandwich he'd dropped down the back of the radiator of his office in 1993.

And he was just about to tell her he loved her and always had when her mother burst in with a lunch tray.

'Isn't it time you were leaving?' she said, looking at Christopher suspiciously. It was uncanny how that woman knew everything, including what you were about to say before you said it.

'But I had something important to tell Madison,' he said, making a face.

'Well maybe it had better wait. Until she's better. And can handle it.'

Cynthia did not want Christopher, whose intentions she

knew only too well, proposing to Madison in her weakened state. A dishevelled divorcé with one shirt button permanently burst open was not what she wanted for her daughter, and although there wasn't exactly an orderly queue forming at the door, she still believed that a rich, handsome man of the world might be found who would whisk Madison away from it all, very much in the vein of the department store owner who had swept the costermonger's daughter off her feet.

'You ought to join a tennis club,' was Cynthia's everlasting refrain. For some reason, she believed that all the men who were capable of making women offers they couldn't refuse hung out at lawn tennis clubs, even though Madison said she had tried it and this was a myth.

In any case, Cynthia sensed that Madison was very vulnerable and might capitulate romantically right now to virtually any man who offered himself to her, or indeed any man she met randomly, on the street. If she could fall for a face cream so unequivocally then she could easily fall for just about anything, God help her.

'I'll be leaving, then,' said Christopher, doing his disappointed face.

'Right. It was nice to see you,' said Cynthia, pushing him out the door.

'I'll text you later. Maybe,' he said, sticking his head back round the door briefly before she bundled him back out again.

Cynthia picked up Madison's phone from the bedside table. 'I'll take that, thank you. Make sure you get some rest.'

Christopher walked the short distance from Madison's flat to the station and rode the Tube balefully back to the office. All these years later, he reflected, it still smelt ever so slightly of fish.

43

Anna Pirana fixed Belinda Bilby with a withering stare.

'Unless you stop saying the word "liquidize" in relation to your assets, I am going to refuse to represent you.'

'How rude!' said Mrs Bilby, smoothing her purple Versace skirt which, in an attempt at modesty, almost came as far as her knobbly knees.

She had been explaining to Pirana how, if all else failed, she thought the best possible route was to liquidize everything that remained, including all the stocks and shares and furniture and paintings. Everything that could be sold should be sold, right down to the micro-pigs. Well, liquidized. 'All I'm saying,' she now repeated, 'is that it wouldn't harm to do a little more liquidizing because—'

'Stop! No more liquidizing, do you understand me? In fact, even if you remember that the word is liquidate, I don't want to hear it. When we go in, just sit quietly and say nothing. Let me do all the talking. Until you are called as a witness, do not speak. And when you are called as a witness, say only the answers we have rehearsed. Do you understand?'

'Stop speaking to me like a child. I don't appreciate it. It's befuddling.'

'You mean belittling.'

'I mean befuddling. I know what I mean.'

'No you don't. That's the problem,' said Pirana, through tight lips.

They were sitting in the gothic vaulted atrium of the Royal Courts of Justice, waiting for their case to be called. Mrs Bilby had already tortured her lawyer by noticing the signs for the 'Health and Wellbeing Centre', a small gym and recreation area the court service laid on for staff.

'Ooh, look, there's a spa!' she said. 'How long have we got? I might get my nails done.'

'It's not a spa.'

'It says it's a spa.'

'Well it's not a spa.'

'How do you know? Have you ever been there?'

'Fine, it's a spa. But you're not going to get your nails done in it. Sit still and practise looking hurt and rejected.'

Mrs Bilby grimaced.

'Is that the best hurt and rejected face you can do? Because you look constipated. Do you need to use the facilities?'

'I could use the loo in the spa.'

'You cannot use the spa. You'll use the ladies' like a normal nervous person about to get divorced. When we get in there, if you pull a face like that, I'm going to stop representing you.'

'Are you going to threaten to sack me as a client every few minutes? Because it's very disconfibrulating.'

'Discombobulating.'

'Yes. And that too. When's the barrister person coming?'

'Soon.'

'He's late.'

'He's not late.'

They sat in silence for a few seconds. Then Mrs Bilby started noticing celebrities who weren't there. 'I'm sure that's Clint Eastwood over there,' she said. 'I wonder what he's done.'

'Nothing. It's not him.'

'My God! Isn't that Colonel Gaddafi?'

'Nope. He's been executed.'

'Where's the barrister? He's late.'

'He's not late.'

And so it went on until a lady in an apron came with a trolley and set up a tea tray outside the court they were about to go into.

It was like a little cottage industry, the Taylor v Taylor divorce. After a few minutes, various people, translators and forensic accountants who were on the list to give evidence, came to buy teas and coffees.

Valmir and Vasilis, who had been sitting gloomily on a stone seat in a recess, appeared to buy themselves cans of Dr Pepper.

The Russian translator, who was there to help make sense of various witnesses being called to expose the business dealings of Mogi Beresovskenaziskyaski, mooched up and purchased a Twix.

Seth and Elden John were sitting a good distance away

on the other side of the gothic atrium, with their noses in a big file. They didn't come and buy refreshments. They looked strangely focused and businesslike. Seth had even bought a suit that looked halfway decent. The knot in Elden's kipper tie looked a little less kipper-like, Pirana noticed, feeling a sense of foreboding she didn't like.

She was glad when she saw Roderick Howler QC sweeping along the stone floor towards them, in his long black gown, like a bat swooping.

'Anna. Mrs Taylor,' he said, curtly acknowledging them.

'Mrs Bilby,' said Mrs Bilby.

'Yes, well, we're working on that.' And then he added, 'Ha ha,' in a voice that was so devoid of amusement that the effect was quite chilling.

He sat down, opened a file and began reading while ignoring them.

And moments after that, the camp clerk appeared and told them all it was 'Show time!'

Everyone but the witnesses filed into the courtroom and took up their places on the big, raised, oversized benches in front of oversized tables and the Mad Hatter's tea party scene from *Alice in Wonderland* began again.

Judge Juniper was already in his seat, reading something through half-rimmed specs. He didn't look up until everyone was quiet.

'Mr Johns,' he said, 'please call your first witness.'

'Thank you, M'Lord. I call Mrs . . . er . . .' said Elden.

Anna Pirana smiled a devilish grin and nudged Mrs Bilby. She had promised her client that they would have the best of the day as the court heard testimony about the couple's assets and the nature of their marriage. They would call a long line of credible people who would blow Seth Taylor's version of events out of the water. Mrs Bilby's friends, her neighbours, her former business associates, and most importantly her household staff were all absolutely tight. They had been nailed down and made irreversibly loyal with various methods, some legitimate. They would all appear to support her version of events.

The incompetent fool representing her husband was about to discover that his beginner's luck had run out.

'Mrs, er . . .' said Elden. Pirana laughed out loud. The judge frowned. She checked herself. Howler appeared not to notice anything, but simply sat reading.

And then Elden John shut his eyes, took a breath and said: 'M'Lord . . . I would like to call . . . Margaret . . . er . . .'

And Seth whispered, 'Teesdale' and Elden shouted, 'Teesdale!'

Gareth the camp clerk pushed open the swinging door of the court and called back into the waiting area: 'Margaret Er Teesdale!'

And a little lady in a tweed suit entered, leaning half her weight on an old shooting stick.

44

Cynthia was dismayed to discover, as the weeks following the accident wore on, that Madison was overcome with remorse for absolutely everything she had ever done that she could remember before banging her head.

It took her a great deal of effort to try to persuade her daughter that she had not murdered Ralph Perkins, although the more she thought about it, the more she started to wonder. Perhaps her daughter *had* enjoyed a short career as a mercy killer as a child. She really had taken her eye off the ball there. Rita Finkelstein would have a field day if she found out about that. Well, it was too late to worry about it now. The important thing was to convince her Ralph had taken an overdose of his medication or they would never hear the end of it until she had got herself put behind bars.

There seemed to be no controlling Madison's conscience now she had started seeing the world through rose-tinted glasses.

It didn't help that she was on gardening leave from Wilde and Sawyer, so she spent her days fretting.

She made endless lists with people's names and a summary of what she thought she might have done to them.

She rummaged through boxes and files and photo albums and papers in her study, as if trying to piece together a picture of the person she had been. She also walked around the apartment, picking up pictures in frames and staring at them quizzically, or else she would just stand, frozen, in front of an object or book on a shelf, frowning, as if it brought back half a memory she couldn't make sense of.

The called-off wedding to Simon Pugh, the management consultant who had wanted to whisk her away to live happily ever after in Surbiton, seemed to particularly stick in the craw.

'Poor Simon, I must ring him and apologize,' she said, biting her nails, something she had never done before.

'Christ on a bike! That was twenty years ago,' said Cynthia. 'The poor man's moved on, you must leave him alone. I'm sure he has a very nice wife and a family by now. He doesn't need to hear from the runaway bride who made a fool of him in front of hundreds of people. You'll only bring it all back if you ring him again now.'

'Mmm, maybe,' said Madison. 'But I feel the need to say something. Maybe I should write him a letter.'

Cynthia harrumphed. This all sounded suspiciously like the time Rita Finkelstein's daughter started doing all those errands when she got back from the treatment centre in Arizona.

She went around Little Fougham bringing shame on her poor parents – who had already been through enough, having a daughter who was addicted to barbiturates, and then ran off with the rehab counsellor – by confessing all sorts of misdeeds to all and sundry and asking their forgiveness.

'You're not doing some sort of step, or whatever it's called, are you?' said Cynthia.

'I don't know what you're talking about,' said Madison.

'Thank goodness. That's the last thing I need. I can cope with most things, as you know, but a daughter who suddenly declares herself to be "in recovery" would be too much at my time of life.'

'No, I just feel I should call Simon, and his mother, and father, and perhaps the rest of the wedding guests and tell them how sorry I am for leading them down the garden path . . .'

'And up the aisle.'

'And up the aisle. Yes.'

In fact, Madison insisted on handwriting a long letter of apology to Simon Pugh and an open letter of apology to all the guests at the wedding, which Cynthia had to promise to pin up on the noticeboard in Little Fougham village hall, which, of course, she would not.

She sat at her laptop in the study of her apartment writing this, before printing it out so that it would be clearly legible to the elderly folk of the Foughams. It was headed: 'To Whom It May Concern. An Apology.' And was a comprehensive grovel covering not only the inconvenience of the wasted journey to and from the church, petrol expended, and so on, but also promised, rather rashly, to reimburse anyone who had bought a new outfit for the occasion. In today's prices. No receipts needed.

'That can go straight in the bin,' muttered Cynthia as she crumpled it into a ball when Madison wasn't looking and stuffed it into her handbag. 'Today's prices indeed. That June Harcourt will be putting in for her old fur coat.'

But it wasn't over yet. Not by a long chalk.

Because then Madison started fretting about the man who had come to feed the cats and who had been thrown out by her mother after having a poker held to his throat.

'I feel I do know who that person at the door might have been,' she said, 'only I can't quite get my head around it. I have a distant memory of someone coming here a lot and . . . no, I can't get it. Every time I think I'm remembering it fades away.'

'I'm sure it will come back in time,' said her mother, hoping to God it didn't, because she hadn't liked the look of the cat man. He'd had a very shifty expression on his face. Even if he had also had expensive hair and a nice suit and a (possibly) Hermès tie.

'Is it possible I was involved with this man? Romantically, I mean. I feel I might have been,' said Madison.

'No, quite impossible,' said Cynthia. 'You weren't involved with anyone. I can promise you that. You weren't capable of it. I often used to ask myself what I had done wrong to inflict such a cynical, stubborn, self-righteous person on the world. But I came to the conclusion long ago that I didn't do anything wrong at all. You just came out that way.'

'How awful.'

'I remember when I was pregnant, you used to kick an awful lot. I got the impression even then that you were complaining. I used to joke that you had an opinion before you even came out.'

'How odd. I don't think,' said Madison, looking downcast, 'I can have been a very nice person.'

'Nonsense. You were . . . well, you were . . . very . . . well, it's hard to think of a word when you need one.'

'I feel a tremendous sense of wanting to put an awful lot of things right. I have something in particular I have to put right, face to face. I'm going to have to go and meet someone and tell them I have done them a terrible wrong before the consequences of what I have done make things even worse for them.'

'Oh dear,' said Cynthia, alarmed, thinking this did indeed sounded like Charmaine Finkelstein-type behaviour. She was already wondering how she could follow Madison and make sure she didn't do something she regretted. There was no telling what Simon Pugh might do if she went to find him. Probably, he would punch her in the face.

But as Mitchell said later, Cynthia couldn't keep Madison behind closed doors forever. At some point, they would have to unleash the nice version of their daughter on an unsuspecting world.

45

'Mrs Teesdale,' said Elden John, shuffling his files in front of him as pretentiously as he could. He had bought a pair of half-moon specs with clear glass and he tried to put them on now, but the arms didn't fit properly and they fell straight off his face again and clattered onto the floor.

He didn't bother to bend down and pick them up. Seth was already looking for them.

'Mrs Teesdale,' he began again.

'Call me Margaret, dear.'

'I will. Thank you. Mrs Teesdale . . .'

'Margaret.'

'Sorry. Margaret.'

'M'Lord.' Howler was on his feet. 'This could go on indefinitely, but before it does, may I point out that counsel . . . ha ha (there was that laugh again. It really was horrific) . . . I mean, Mr John, must address the witness as Mrs Teesdale, whatever her preference may be.'

Juniper frowned. 'Mr Howler, you will kindly refrain from mocking Mr Johns. Sarcasm does not become you.

Mr Johns, you will kindly address the witness as Mrs er Teesdale. I mean Teesdale.'

'Sorry, M'Lord.' Elden looked around the court apologetically. 'Come on, Elden,' said Doris, appearing briefly beside Juniper on the bench. She was eating a bag of her favourite chocolate éclairs, as if enjoying a movie at the cinema.

'Mrs Teesdale!' he managed, bolstered by this visitation. 'Would you please describe for the court the nature of the relationship between your employer and her husband?

'Well, they didn't really get on, dear,' said Mrs Teesdale. 'Mrs Bilby, well, she's a handful at the best of times. She's a nightmare to live with. She gave her first husband a terrible time. In fact . . . she killed poor Mr Bilby, God rest his soul.'

'M'Lord, we object to this line of questioning most strongly,' said Howler, leaping to his feet. 'The witness is speculating wildly . . .'

'The witness is giving the court her opinion based on twenty years of working for Mrs Bilby as her housekeeper and having witnessed much of this relationship,' said Elden.

Juniper nodded. 'I agree. Please continue, Mrs Teesdale.'

'Mr Bilby was allergic to dogs, see. Oh, she knew that. But she let those dogs run amok in the London house just like she did when she moved to Tankards after the poor man died. She wouldn't hear of her precious Wonky-Poo and Diddly-Dums being rehomed to save him from his allergies. He suffered dreadfully. And the day he passed on, the coroner said, he sneezed and sneezed until his heart gave up. Either that or . . .'

'Or?' said Elden.

Margaret Teesdale leaned forward.

'They do say that when you sneeze, the devil flies down your throat unless someone says God bless you. Well, she never said God bless you once. There you have it! She killed him! As sure as if she'd taken a dagger to his heart!'

Mrs Bilby could take it no longer and, leaping to her feet, screamed, 'You horrible old harridan. After everything I've done for you!'

Roderick Howler stood up and pleaded: 'M'Lord, this is desperate stuff. We demand that these absurd allegations are struck from the record.'

Juniper shrugged. 'Oh, go on then. Gareth, see to it. Mr Howler, kindly restrain your client. One more outburst and I will have her locked up. Again. Mr Johns, continue. I was just starting to enjoy myself.'

Elden prompted his witness. 'Mrs Teesdale, please try to describe the nature of the marriage between Mr and Mrs Taylor, as you saw it.'

'Well, it's very simple. Mrs Bilby likes things her way. In every respect. Including in the bedroom. I really can't say any more. There were a lot of rows about it. I had to block my ears, as you will understand. At my age . . .'

'Mrs Teesdale,' continued Elden, 'will you please describe for the court the events of the evening that led up to Mr Taylor fleeing the house, Tankards Reach, on a motorbike that didn't have a seat?'

There was a gasp from the courtroom. The court artist

started drawing a seat-less motorbike, more to amuse herself than for publication.

'Well, Mrs Bilby was nagging him for one of her early nights. I was doing the dishes and he just looked like he couldn't take another minute of it. So he tried to explain to her that he was having second thoughts about the marriage and wanted a break. And the next thing I knew she grabbed a knife and chased him around the kitchen then out into the garden and he had to escape on this motorbike of his that didn't have a saddle because she'd told Valmir to remove it so he had no way of ever leaving her. She locked the gates at night, you know. But luckily this was just before 6 p.m. so they were still on automatic open and Mr Taylor, well, he just got on that bike and he left. I ran back to the staff quarters to get out of the way in case she got any ideas about turning the knife on me, but I saw it all from an upstairs window.'

'And what did Mrs Bilby shout at him?'

'She shouted, "Nobody leaves me, you miserable little worm. I'm going to ruin you. You will never get a penny out of me." Personally,' said Mrs Teesdale, looking all around the court and then to the judge, 'I think he should get the lot. She can't manage her money anyway. And the less said about the way those properties are run the better. She lets her dogs do their business all over the house. Have you ever tried to get dog poo out of an Axminster deep shag? I tried everything, all the leading-brand carpet cleaners. I even had Mrs Bilby buy a professional carpet shampoo machine. In fact, she bought two of them . . .'

'M'Lord, is all this detail really necessary? Frankly, I find it a little superfluous, not to mention distasteful.'

'Quite so,' said Juniper. 'Mr Johns, you will ensure your witness steers clear of canine defecatory matters. It will put me off my lunch.'

'I've only a few more questions M'Lord, if you can bear with me. Mrs Teesdale, I'm guessing from your description that you find working for Mrs Bilby very difficult?'

'Frankly, I'm at my wits' end. A few weeks ago, quite out of the blue, she gave me and Bert Tankards, and the house in Monaco, for no good reason we could make out, although we have been very loyal to her. Bert's made up but, to be honest, I'd rather go without the £30 million worth of prime real estate and not have to chase llamas down the driveway. Did I mention she keeps llamas? I say "keep", she doesn't so much keep them as let them roam about terrorizing people. They spit, you know. Filthy things.'

'M'Lord, all of this is completely irrelevant,' said Howler, languidly.

'Er, thank you, Mrs Teesdale,' said Juniper, before turning to Howler and Pirana. 'Would you like to question this witness?'

'No, I most certainly would not,' said Pirana.

Howler added: 'M'Lord, at this time, we have no questions for this witness.'

'What are you two doing?' said Mrs Bilby, when they had left the court after Juniper called a recess for lunch. 'Why on earth are you not asking more questions?'

'When you're in a hole, stop digging,' said Pirana, marching from the court through the corridors back to the entrance. Howler had already disappeared, seemingly into thin air. Either he had swooped back up to the belfry, or gone down into the basement to have a snooze in his coffin.

'Where are you taking me for lunch?'

'I'm not taking you anywhere. You can take yourself. I'm going to meet another client. I don't have time to listen to you now. I will see you back here at 2 p.m. sharp and I don't want you to ring me for the next hour either.'

Mrs Bilby was furious. She clattered after her lawyer across the stone floor, almost falling off her heels several times.

Outside, the press pack were milling about drinking coffee out of plastic cups and eating chocolate bars.

As Pirana exited the swing doors, they leapt into action, raising TV cameras to their shoulders, thrusting microphones in her direction.

Karen Fairisle snapped shut a make-up compact, flicked her hair into place, and led the charging scum forwards, like a warrior queen taking her marauding troops into battle.

Anna Pirana realized instantly that she should have come out of the side exit, because she wasn't in the mood for giving sound bites. Normally, she would relish this confrontation with the world's media, but right now she felt deflated.

She was being outmanoeuvred by a dimwit, and this gave her a strange sensation in her inner core. It felt like the time she'd gone skating as a child and had fallen face-forwards onto the ice, smashing her ribs on the rock-hard surface.

She had got up and for a few minutes, longer than she had thought possible, little Anna had not been able to speak, but simply opened and shut her mouth with no words coming out. Not being able to make the sound of her own voice, which she liked immensely, had been a terrifying experience.

As she stood frozen on the top step, Mrs Bilby suddenly came up behind her and poked her on the shoulder with one overmanicured finger.

She turned. 'Don't you dare walk away from me,' said Mrs Bilby. 'I've got something to say to you. I've made a decision.'

Anna opened her mouth, but nothing came out.

'I've decided that you're sacked,' said Mrs Bilby, with great finality. 'You're useless. You're even more useless than the lawyer who hit her head. And don't you even dare to put in a bill for today. Now clear off.'

The TV cameras rolled, devouring every second. The photographers snapped their shutters like hungry alligators.

Karen Fairisle turned to her runner and hissed: 'Are we live? Are they getting all this?'

And then she thrust her mike into Pirana's face as the stunned lawyer began to come down the steps and shouted: 'What's your reaction to this bombshell? Is this the first time a client has sacked you?'

Pirana opened and shut her mouth but nothing came out. Oh, the horror.

Karen Fairisle turned her back on her and ran in the opposite direction towards Mrs Bilby.

'Can you tell us why you've sacked your lawyer, Mrs Taylor?' shouted Fairisle, sounding completely hysterical. 'Are you able to divulge what went on in court this morning?'

'It's Mrs Bilby,' said Mrs Bilby, 'and yes, I can tell you everything about what went on in court this morning. How long have you got?'

'Why did you sack your lawyer?' shouted another news outlet.

'Who will represent you now? How are you going to find another lawyer?' shouted another.

Mrs Bilby drew herself up and uttered the immortal words: 'Plenty more fish in the sea!'

'Great headline,' said one newsman to another. And they all scribbled and started phoning their editors.

And so it was a great headline. And Anna Pirana's reputation as Britain's Best Divorce Lawyer never recovered from it.

46

When Cynthia helped Madison get dressed the next day and sent her on her way to work, she felt more frightened than when she had put her on the school bus, aged five, for her first day at St Ignatius.

There goes my baby, thought Cynthia, as Madison strode out into the street. Her first day in the real world as a vulnerable person with feelings. God help her.

It took Madison a while to get her bearings. She thought it was a bit odd when she came out of her house and a parking warden who was in the middle of issuing a ticket suddenly ripped it up and scarpered down the street.

At the station, the ticket office clerk reached for his 'Closed' shutter when he saw her coming. He didn't quite get it down in time.

'The sign wasn't me,' he snapped, as she put her money on the counter.

'What?'

'The sign. I know what you're going to say. But it wasn't me. Someone else did it. We hadn't seen you for a while and we thought you might have moved. Well, we were hoping you'd moved. And one of the lads thought he would celebrate by putting up a sign.'

Madison looked round and saw a big white announcement board covered in amateurish black marker pen. It said:

> Love the life you live
> Live the life you love
> — Bob Marley

'I don't have a problem with that,' said Madison. 'Can I have a return to Blackfriars, please?'

The man behind the counter smirked, as if this were a hoax.

'I get it. Day Return by overland only? Like the one that's not on the home screen of the ticket machine, right? You want an argument about it?'

'Not really. Just the ticket. Thanks.'

He scowled and began keying in the ticket details. Then, as he pushed the ticket under the partition, and took her money, he said: 'You sure you don't want to argue about Bob Marley?'

'Not really,' said Madison, frowning. Obviously, she concluded, the man was having a bad day. 'Hope your day gets better,' she added cheerfully.

He narrowed his eyes. As she walked away, she heard him pull down his shutter and lock the kiosk door from the inside.

On the train a group of school kids shouted, 'Hey, you!'

She decided to ignore them and opened a book she had brought to pass the time.

'I said hello, bitch,' said the gang leader, who was now standing next to her seat.

She kept reading.

'Ain't you gonna threaten to call someone? Or put us in a young offenders' institution.'

She looked up, terrified. 'Why on earth would I do that?'

The boy sat down. 'I don't know. It's something you do. We kind of look forward to it.' He put his feet up on the opposite seat. 'It breaks up the monotony of the morning, you know. Otherwise it's just us harassing people and them running away, which is boring.'

Madison shifted over and made room, then went back to her book.

The boy turned his iPhone music up very loud. She flinched.

He put on his best gangster voice. 'Ain't you gonna akkks me to turn the music down?' he said, over the din.

'It's very good,' said Madison, trying to diffuse the situation. 'Can I buy it in the shops?'

'You don't buy it in the shops, bitch. You download it, innit.'

'Fine. I'll download it. Thanks for the tip.'

He shrugged and went back to his friends.

'What did she say?'

'She says she ain't bovvered, man.'

'Man, dat is well bad, innit?' said one of the girls.

'Why don't you dis her some more, bro?'

'I already tell her she is a rude ass white bitch. I can't do no more.'

The girls shook their heads sorrowfully.

They were not the only people that day to suffer an anti-climax on account of Madison.

At the coffee shop near her office, Madison ordered a black Americano from a nervously smiling waitress.

'Mmm, lovely,' she said, as she sipped the finished result.

'I make it again. Is no problem,' said the waitress, the colour draining from her face.

'Why would I want you to make it again? It's fine.'

As she walked out, she looked back and saw that the girl was standing with her mouth open, trying to serve another customer while holding a jug of hot milk at an angle and pouring its contents onto the floor.

At the office, a tall dark Amazonian beauty looked up and rudely said, 'Oh, you're back.'

'Good morning! How are you?' Madison replied, as cheerfully as she could, hoping the girl wouldn't notice she didn't remember who she was.

'No need for sarcasm,' the girl muttered as she walked past.

She made her way down the corridor, which was thankfully familiar, to a door that had her name on it.

She shut herself in and stood with her back to the door, staring around her office and hoping something would trigger the neurons in her brain and all the loose ends would start falling into place.

She had only been standing there a few seconds when

there was a knock at the door. It started to move against her back and a thin, bespectacled woman with childlike bobbed hair pushed her way in with freakish strength.

'Oh my goodness, what are you doing back here?' she said. 'You should never have tried to come to work. Shall I call a taxi to get you home? Oh, you don't look well. You're not a good colour. My golly gosh, you've lost weight. Look at the bags under your eyes. Mind you, you always did have dark circles . . .'

'Do I know you?' And then as soon as she said it, she realized she did know who this was. It was all coming back to her now. 'Judith?'

'Oh dear, they didn't tell me you had amnesia as well. Do you have amnesia? Long term or short term? I don't suppose you can remember. They say it's almost always permanent if it's the long term kind. Oh dear, it's going to be very difficult being a lawyer if you can't remember things. How will you ever memorize a brief . . . ?'

'STOP!'

Judith gulped. She had never been shouted at by Madison before. 'Can I get you a coffee? Or a green tea, perhaps? You don't actually like green tea, but you might not remember so maybe this is a good moment to try it because it's very cleansing.'

'You can leave me to it, Judith. I don't need anything. I'm fine.' And she started rifling through drawers, looking for the papers she needed which she thought must be in there.

But Judith lingered. 'Since you're here,' she said, 'I don't suppose you could help me with that letter to the council?

About the neighbours and the littering? I woke up this morning and there were two Mars bars wrappers actually on my front pathway. You haven't forgotten about the littering problem, have you? You did promise.'

'Oh dear.' Madison was still rifling through the drawer and pulling papers out all over the place, throwing some on the floor and some on the desk.

'It's wrong, you see, isn't it? Given the council tax we pay? You said you were going to help me draft a letter.'

'Well, I would, obviously, but the thing is I'm quite busy with other things right now and I don't want to get distracted. Also, it might be a bit of a waste of time, don't you think?'

'Oh?'

'I don't really fancy it. Fighting causes such negative energy. After all, it's such a nice day outside. Why don't you go and sit in the garden for a bit and soak up some sun. Always makes me feel better!' She straightened up and beamed suddenly. She looked weird.

'Soak up some sun?' said Judith, dreamily.

Madison grabbed a folder and shouted: 'Gotcha!'

'B-but . . .'

'I've found it! I've got to fly!'

'Fly? Fly where? I don't think you're in any fit state to see clients.'

'I've got to go and see a man about a dog,' said Madison, and she ran out the door, waving the file.

47

Sadly, after the glory of despatching a lawyer who had withstood sustained intellectual onslaughts from thousands of people a million times cleverer than she, Mrs Bilby then did something incredibly stupid.

She decided that she would represent herself.

'I can't do any worse than Batman and Fish Woman,' she explained to Mr Justice Juniper when she returned to her place in court alone after a very dreary lunch in a scandalous place called Pret A Manger, where they had made her carry her own sandwich to her table.

She had asked to see the manager and been told that the person in charge was called the Head Barista. 'More lawyers!' she cried, before a very complicated discussion ensued in which she and the head barista were entirely at cross purposes.

When she got back to court she had the two words quite horribly confused.

'That barista,' she told Juniper, 'was £700 an hour and all he did was tell the other side to call my housekeeper by her surname. That's £2,800 to get *him*' she nodded at Elden John 'to say Mrs T-T-T-T-T-Teesdale.'

'I think you mean barrister,' said Juniper. 'But I do see your point.'

'I think you will find one can pronounce it either way.'

'Well, off you go. If you struggle, as I suspect you will, I will allow you to have an appointed person or associate of your own to sit with you, as a McKenzie Friend. Do you understand?'

'But I don't have any friends called McKenzie,' said Mrs Bilby.

'That's not what I mean. "McKenzie Friend" is a legal term. It's a concept named after someone in a trial. Like when you're arrested and read your Miranda Rights.'

'I don't have any friends called Miranda, either.'

'Forget it. Let's move on. Please do whatever it is you intend to do.'

'Your honour, I call my first witness. Me,' said Mrs Bilby.

'Oh, go on, then,' said Juniper, feeling grateful he had just dropped acid, and would shortly, all being well, not be experiencing any of this anyway.

A few moments later, Juniper thought that acid had to be kicking in already when Mrs Bilby walked theatrically to the witness box, sat down in it, then got straight back up and climbed out again. Then she made a huge hoo-hah of striding backwards and forwards in front of it with her hands in her lapels.

'Mrs Bilby,' she said, looking sternly at the space where she would have been sitting in the witness box if she hadn't been trying to interrogate herself, 'I would like to ask why you married the accused, Seth Taylor.'

'You may refer to your husband as Mr Taylor, not the accused,' said Juniper. Was any of this really happening? He couldn't be sure. It looked like the start of a bad trip, but then again he had sat through some seriously nightmarish divorce hearings in his time.

'Thank you, I shall. Now, Mrs Bilby, why did you marry Mr Taylor?' And Mrs Bilby then scuttled back into the witness box and sat down again.

'M'Lord, do we really h-have to continue with this p-p-p-pointless sh . . . sh . . . sh . . .' Elden's arms shot out in front of him in a massive explosion of frustration.

'Charade,' said Juniper.

'Thank you. Pointless charade?'

'Yes, we do. I'm enjoying it. Mrs Taylor, or whatever you're called: continue.'

'I married him because I hadn't had any decent sex in a very long time,' said Mrs Bilby, dabbing her eyes. 'My ex-husband, Marcus Bilby, now deceased, God rest his soul wherever it is burning in hell for all eternity, was a very cruel man. Not to mention a raging homosexual. So you see, your honour, I was a desperate woman.'

Mrs Bilby put down her handkerchief and ran back around the other side of the witness box, grasped her lapels and started pacing up and down again, as a giant squid fell down from the ceiling onto her head.

Now the acid was definitely kicking in.

The only disguise Madison could find at short notice was a baseball cap in a souvenir shop. It said 'I heart London'.

She also bought a pair of cheap sunglasses from the same shop, which she wore with the plastic price tag hanging down from one arm because it was fastened on with a piece of improbably strong black cord which she couldn't pull off. She teamed these accessories with a Union Jack scarf, also from the souvenir shop, which she wound round her neck and pulled up over the lower half of her face. She belted her coat round her tightly with the collar up.

Catching sight of herself in a shop window as she walked down Fleet Street she laughed out loud. What she was about to do could spectacularly backfire, but she didn't mind somehow. Maybe if I do the right thing, everything will be all right in the end, she thought. It felt like this was a tremendous epiphany.

She stood outside the Royal Courts of Justice and waited. Shortly after 1 p.m., the man she recognized as her former client's adversary emerged with his lawyer and the pair of them started walking away from her down Fleet Street.

She followed a little way behind until they turned into a pub advertising 'Good Food Served All Day!'

After a few minutes she entered the pub and clocked the lawyer by the bar, and the client in a window seat.

She walked past the lawyer with her head down and took up a position at the opposite end of the room, where she installed herself in a booth and looked at the menu. Unfathomably, she became quite excited at the thought of ordering a steak and ale pie.

I don't know why I haven't ever tried one of these before, she thought.

She ordered at the bar when the coast was clear. It was slammed down by a waitress with a scowl a suspiciously short amount of time later, and she sat in her hat and coat eating. The steak and ale pie was not good food at all, even if it was served all day, but try as she might to summon the energy to complain about it she just couldn't seem to. 'Ah well,' she found herself thinking, 'one must be grateful.'

She kept her eye on her targets and when they had finished their meal, she decided to make her move.

She paid for her lunch, left a huge tip, which felt both wrong and satisfying in one go, and walked across the bar towards them.

When she got up close, she said to the lawyer in a deep voice so as to disguise her own: 'I have important information for you about Belinda Bilby. Can I sit down?'

'Please do,' said Elden John, looking extremely nervous as he offered her a chair.

She hadn't been sitting down, stiffly in her scarf and sunglasses, for more than a few seconds when Seth said: 'Good lord! You're Mrs Bilby's old lawyer. Are you all right? You look different somehow.'

She sighed and began to take off her disguise. She unravelled the scarf and pulled off the glasses.

'I need to talk to you. It's about Mrs Bilby.'

'What about Mrs Bilby?' said Elden.

'She's completely deranged.'

'We know,' said Elden. 'She's been questioning herself in court all morning.'

'I bet that went down well with the judge.'

'Actually, he didn't mind at all,' said Elden, slurping from his pint of beer. 'He was too busy ducking all the squid that were falling down from the ceiling.'

'I beg your pardon?'

'And the killer laser beams coming out of Mrs Bilby's eyes. Which were glowing red and emitting death rays. According to him, she's a She-Devil who drinks llama blood. He was telling us all about it. But then some men in uniforms came and took him away.'

Madison was sorry she was missing all this.

'Well, I have some information for you that will help you defeat the She-Devil. She's trying to cheat you and I don't think it's fair. So I'm going to tell you some things that will help you. Including some information about the people who work for your wife and the sorts of trouble they're in. She told me everything. And what I know about them will make them putty in your hands. You will have more witnesses spilling the beans on Mrs Bilby than you know what to do with.'

'Oh,' said Seth, looking serene. Even now, she noticed, he was constitutionally incapable of getting worked up about anything.

He didn't even get angry when she had finished telling them the dirt.

Instead, after Madison had divulged all the information she had been able to find hidden in the recesses of her brain, and the recesses of her office desk drawers, Seth sat staring at the table with a look of absolute tranquillity on his face.

He looked so lovely she found herself gazing at him through a thick, impenetrable silence.

Then he looked straight into her eyes, and smiled. And the pair of them gazed at each other.

In the end, Elden John, who had been fidgeting wildly throughout, jumped up and said he had to leave.

'I need to get moving on this straight away.' Then he paused: 'I'll leave you two lovebirds together.'

'What do you mean?' said Seth, looking clueless.

Elden John shrugged. 'Oh, nothing.' He motioned at the waitress. 'Can I have the . . .'

'Bill,' said Seth.

When he was gone, Madison turned to Seth and her face had a strange flush. Seth had seen that look before. Instinctively, he thought: Oh dear.

'I'm glad he's gone,' said Madison. 'Because there's something else I've got to tell you. Another confession.'

'Oh dear,' said Seth, staring out of the window again.

'You know, when we were in court that day, after the accident, after you helped carry me in off the street and sat me down and gave me a bottle of water and looked after me, well . . . I felt something.'

Seth gulped a big mouthful of Diet Coke and then started slurping it like a child while looking out of the window, avoiding Madison's eyes as if what was happening might stop happening if he didn't look straight at it.

'It was something I don't think I've ever felt before. I'm not altogether sure what it was, but I've been thinking about it ever since.'

'Oh, right.' Seth stood up. 'Well, I've got to be going . . .'

'Did you feel it too?'

'I don't think so.' He looked at a random crack in the ceiling as he put his coat on.

'Come on. You must have felt something. After you all carried me in off the street, we exchanged a look. You must remember it. Didn't you feel the electricity between us?'

'I don't know. I did feel something. But I think it might have been indigestion. The whole accident thing was very stressful and I'd eaten a fried breakfast that morning. Bacon always plays havoc with my colon.'

'Oh, don't try and hide it. You can feel it too, I know you can. We're meant to be together.'

Seth looked doubtful. Then suddenly resigned. 'Well, I need to pay the bill first.'

'Not now, silly. Eventually. One day. Or even just metaphorically.'

'Meta . . . ?' said Seth, looking more and more puzzled.

'Look, will you just agree to have dinner with me. Please?'

'Well, all right, so long as it's not Greek food. I'm not good with hummus.'

'I'll take you anywhere. Anywhere in the world you want to go. Just name it.'

So they made arrangements to meet at Nando's on Croydon High Street.

Oh dear, thought Seth, as he mooched back down Fleet Street. Oh dear, oh dear, oh dear. Had he done it again? How many times did he have to fall into the clutches of a powerful woman and get done over before he learned his lesson?

But it wasn't going to be like that.

48

Elden John burst into the office building of Costello and Wolfson, global financial dispute specialists, and stood panting in front of the list of firms named on a plaque in the empty lobby.

The building was a big soulless office block in a dirty street in the less salubrious part of the financial district, the kind of area where bits of paper blew about unchallenged by dustmen because no one in authority had any intention of spending any money on keeping it nice.

Elden had never been here before. He would not have come here now if the blasted staff at C&W had answered the phone. But after ringing and ringing for over an hour, desperate to impart his exciting news, he decided he had no choice but to go down there. He had been expecting something smarter, more befitting of the world leaders in forensic accountancy; something swankier, with security.

Instead, this place looked like it housed temporary offices for people who ran firms that weren't quite legitimate. There was an Indian visa agency listed, with a piece of paper stuck next to it saying, 'Ring bell. If no answer leave passport under mat.'

He found Costello and Wolfson listed on the fifth floor and took the lift.

On his way up he thought back through the dynamite pieces of information he was about to pass on to his forensic accountancy team.

'Information,' he said dramatically to himself as the lift climbed upwards, creakily. 'In-forrrr-mation!' And then practising what he would say to the flashy accountants: 'I have some in-for-mation I think you will find very—'

The lift crashed to a halt and the doors wobbled open.

When he got out, there was a sign pointing him to the end of the corridor, where there was a door displaying another battered sign saying Costello and Wolfson.

He rapped on it and a surprised male voice said, 'Come in?'

Upon entering he realized there was no secretary and only one room. Sitting at a ramshackle old partners desk in the middle of it, surrounded by heaped-up files and overflowing filing cabinets and a huge old dinosaur of a computer, was a little man with a comb-over in a nylon suit.

'Can I help you?' he said, somewhat irritably.

'I'm Elden John. Of Elden John Associates. I retained your firm recently to investigate the finances of Belinda Bilby? Taylor v Taylor? I would like to speak to whoever is in the lead on my case.'

The man smoothed the strands of hair nervously over his head and straightened his tie. Standing up, he offered his hand. 'Oh. Yes. Pleased to meet you. I'm Alf Bird.'

'Alf?'

'Alf Bird. Global financial dispute specialist.'

Elden John looked once more around the office. If he'd had the nerve he would have moved the filing cabinets to see if more people weren't hiding behind them.

'Where're the rest of you?'

'Rest?'

'The team? The team I hired. For £500 an hour. The team who were sent to Mombasa to investigate the ransom money paid to the pirates and the disappearing cargo ship?'

'Yes, that will be me.'

'Please tell me you're not working here on your own.'

'I get this all the time,' said Bird wearily, sitting back down. 'You think the word team implies more than one person, don't you? That it's some kind of plural term.'

'That's because it is. A team of people means more than one person.'

'No, it doesn't.'

'Yes, it does.'

Elden felt like Dorothy in *The Wizard of Oz*. Having finally tracked the wizard down to his headquarters he had found an old man standing behind the curtain working the special effects.

He stared in disbelief at Alf Bird before declaring sarcastically: 'Oh, this is brilliant. This is the icing on the cake.'

Alf Bird stared back. 'What's the matter, Elden? Thought you were the only one-man band pretending to be something you're not?'

Evidently, Alf Bird had done some homework. Elden sat down. Maybe he would give him the benefit of the doubt.

'Coffee?' Alf Bird started rummaging around. 'Or something stronger?' He produced a half-empty bottle of cheap whiskey.

Two hours later, anaesthetized by drink, Elden was sufficiently relaxed to be able to see that he had not made too hasty a judgement.

It turned out that Alf Bird had made no progress whatsoever in investigating the Somalian piracy scam, and had also totally stalled in tracking down one of the bank accounts containing the proceeds of the Project Bojana deal, which was quite obviously an incredibly elegant Ponzi scheme, from which Mrs Bilby had made millions before selling all the other investors down the river.

'I gotta hand it to you, Bird,' said Elden, who was properly sozzled, 'I would never have believed a funny little fella like you could scale such heights of incompetence.'

'The feeling,' said Bird, slurping back the contents of his glass, 'is mutual.'

49

On Croydon High Street, one hot June evening, over a plate of Nando's peri-peri chicken – half medium hot, half lemon and herb – Madison and Seth got to know each other quite well.

I say quite well, because it was impossible to get to know Seth very well, on account of him not really knowing himself very well, never mind being able to explain himself very well to anyone else.

Still, he made a good stab of answering Madison's questions and told her as much as he could remember of what his father had told him about the way his mother had abandoned him at the bus stop.

She seemed incredibly interested in every last detail of this episode, as if it held the key to everything. In a sense, it was the most interesting thing about him, but she delved so deeply into it he couldn't help thinking she was looking for something that wasn't there.

Women were like this, he pondered, as she rattled on and on about how abandoned he must still feel, with tears welling up in her eyes.

He zoned out as she started using words like 'intimacy', 'attachment' and 'inner child'.

He had heard this so many times before, from every woman who had ever tried to fix him.

Seth sometimes felt like a run-down property. Women wandered around him poking into every nook and cranny saying: 'Ooh, I could do wonders with this. There's so much potential.'

But in truth, he suspected he was a bit like a 1970s dormer bungalow. There was nothing you could do to give it depth and character. Your best bet, depending on planning permission, was to knock it down and throw up a nice glass and wood Huf Haus. That's what he would do anyway.

'Have you?'

Madison was staring at him. What was she talking about? She was asking him a question.

'Huh?'

'Have you ever seen your mother again?'

'Oh, no. Never.'

'Tragic. Did you search for her and not find her?'

'No. I never really looked.'

'Why on earth not?'

'Well, I don't know really, it just never occurred to me. What would be the point?'

Silence. Seth stared at the table. Madison interpreted the silence as heart-rending evidence of his inner child's inner turmoil. But Seth was looking at the chicken. 'Do you want that last piece of medium hot, or can I have it?'

There was a tragic edge to his simplicity. Madison decided she had definitely fallen in love. It was weird. She rather liked it. But on another level she didn't like it at all because it gave her indigestion, even though she couldn't eat because she had butterflies in her stomach.

The fact that they were both artists clinched it. Maybe she would give up doing the law and become a full-time sketcher of charcoal nudes. Or paint sunsets. They could live at the cottage together and grow their own vegetables. They wouldn't need much money to survive. For the first time in her life she knew what it was like to daydream.

'So this is what it's like,' she murmured. 'Finally, I'm experiencing the real thing.'

'It's good, isn't it?' said Seth, gnawing through the last medium hot chicken leg. 'But I'm surprised you've never been to Nando's before.'

He dropped her off by walking her to the taxi rank. He didn't have a car, only the seat-less motorbike, which now actually did have a seat. He had been able to fix it with some of the interim maintenance money Elden John had squeezed out of Mrs Bilby. A cool £8,000 had been deposited in his bank account that month and now £7,723 sat there, because he had spent all he wanted to spend at the Honda spare parts stockist.

But Madison had insisted she hadn't wanted to ride on the motorbike. She said it was tainted.

So she'd come by taxi and when it was time to say goodnight he put her back in one.

'Come back with me, to my place, if you like?' she said, looking nervous. 'My parents went home today so I have the place all to myself.'

'My place is nearer,' he said.

So he took her back to his flat to see his portraits of cats and dogs and ferrets. 'I like this one,' she said, pointing to a picture of a startled-looking tabby. 'That one was stuffed. They should have had the portrait done earlier, really,' he said. And then a silence ensued that left them with no other option.

Lying in bed afterwards, he found the forceps scars behind her ears.

'What are these red marks?'

'It's where I got stuck. You know, when I was being born. Actually, I didn't want to come out. They squished my head with forceps. Some babies get dropped on their heads; I got my head squished with a pair of gigantic tongs. My mother says it's why I am how I am.'

'Oh,' said Seth, before explaining that she had to go now because he had an early start the next day.

'I'm being cross-examined by Mrs Bilby.'

Outside she hailed a cab.

'Where to, guvnor? I hope it ain't far, only I'm on me way back home.'

'Oh, don't worry then,' said Madison. 'I'll walk to the station. I wouldn't want to put you out.'

50

Valmir Krasniqi had not been in a court since the unfortunate business with the AK47 in his home village of Vratnica. He shifted nervously in his seat, his eyes darting from his former employer to the lawyer about to interrogate him.

He sensed that something was about to go very badly wrong, but that he was powerless to prevent it.

'Please tell the court, if you would, Mr Krasniqi, what a typical day with Mrs Taylor, by which I mean the woman known to you as Mrs Bilby, involves?'

Valmir looked down at his shoes. Everyone was staring at him. Mrs Bilby was sitting in front of him with Lawrence Loonie next to her. Juniper had insisted on her having him as her McKenzie Friend in the hope that this might stop her tying herself totally in knots.

Valmir had always been afraid that his past might catch up with him. And now he was sitting in a big courtroom, and might incriminate himself at any moment if he said the wrong thing.

He had only been shooting it in the air in an act of exuberance. But unfortunately NATO forces had assumed this was a declaration of hostilities and a small, though by no means unenjoyable rebellion had broken out.

As a consequence, he had been charged with insurgency alongside his seven brothers and several dozen other villagers.

He had escaped before his trial began and come to Britain to start a new life. And he had started a fabulous new life, after running into Mrs Bilby on Kensington High Street. He had been doing some building work for a man called Ken, who had smuggled him across the channel to pay him slave wages.

Mrs Bilby had been struggling out of a fancy interiors store laden down with bags full of luxury linen and candles and soaps and towels. Valmir had been up a ladder, helping Ken to fix the roof of the shop next door.

As she dropped a bag full of scented candles, which spilled out over the pavement, he leapt down the ladder and started picking them up.

'I help you,' he said, as he looked quizzically at the bags of candles. She had roped him into helping her to the car with it all. Then he had gone back with her to the shop because, she said, 'If you trot along with me, darling, I can pick up those Egyptian cotton duvet covers and the Provencal linen baskets and the scatter cushions . . .'

As he carried them back to her car, he told her all about his predicament as a penniless refugee. 'But my darling, that's too awful! Those NATO forces sound like such meddlers. How completely typical of the overbearing state. Why, if you want to fire a Kalashnikov into the air, shouldn't you be able to, in the comfort of your own village? I expect they would be just as pernickety in Kensington, with all the tax we pay.' And she offered him a job as a sort of gofer. Which was just as well because when he climbed back up the ladder after an hour of carrying candles and linen baskets, Ken fired him.

As such, he had always felt a deep sense of loyalty to her. She had rescued him as she rescued all creatures she came across who she took a fancy to. She had taken him in, and now proposed to let him range freely about the house and grounds just as graciously as if he were a llama.

After a few weeks, he asked Mrs Bilby if she and her husband would consider employing another villager, Vasilis, who had also made it to Britain after doing a runner from spurious genocide charges and was even now being overworked for cash in hand by Ken.

Val and Vas, as Mrs Bilby called them, became indispensable arms of the Bilby empire, as security guards and general handymen. They lived in generous staff accommodation and were paid lavish wages, cash in hand.

The only thing Mrs Bilby insisted on that was slightly tiresome was that they dressed in suits at all times, including when doing DIY because, as she said, she never knew when she might need them to drop everything and drive her to Harrods, or Harvey Nicks, or Waitrose. As such, they looked a lot like the Blues Brothers, because they were often in sunglasses and dark suits with the sleeves rolled up because they were midway through painting a wall.

'Is difficult for me,' Valmir said, looking up at the

judge from under his huge bushy black eyebrows, like a Bond villain. 'I work long time for Mrs Bobi and she very nice lady.'

'Mrs Bobi?'

'Yes. Mrs Bobi. Like number plate.' And he spelt it out: 'B-O-B-1. Mrs Bobi give me much champagne. Much, much champagne . . .' And he mimed the act of imbibing. 'Every day. Champagne, champagne . . . and vodka. And sometimes champagne with vodka. You know this thing? Is called Stolly Brolly.' And he grinned a huge, gap-toothed grin. 'Is good, yes?'

'Please try and answer the question,' said Elden, wondering when the last time was he had drunk champagne, or if he ever would. 'What does your day consist of?'

'I take Mrs Bobi shop, because she like shop very much. She buys much thing. We come home, she make cheese cracker. She open champagne. She read magazine. *OK!*, *Hello!*, *Take a Break*. You know these? Very good. I like. In afternoon we feed pigs. This very funny.' And he made pig noises to illustrate. 'Sometime, we go more shop. We buy much thing. We come back. We drink Stolly Brolly . . .'

'I think we get the idea. And does Mrs Bilby talk about having to cut back?'

'Cut back? With knife, you mean? No. She don't cut no one's back. She cut backside one time . . .'

'Indeed. I think we've covered that. No. I mean, does she economize? To make ends meet?'

'Ends meet? What is this, please?'

Elden John was beginning to wonder whether he should have splashed out an extra £50,000 of Mrs Bilby's money on an Albanian translator after all.

'Is she poor?'

'Poor?' Valmir drew himself up. 'Mrs Bilby not poor. Mrs Bilby has much money. Much, much money. Much, much, much . . .'

Lawrence Loonie groaned and put his head in his hands.

'What are you doing, Val?' Mrs Bilby was on her feet. 'I thought we agreed you would help me.'

Valmir leaned forward: 'I sorry, boss. But they tell me I must tell everything or they send me to Holland to be in big trial for war crimes! They say I leader of Albanian National Army. They say I make big massacre of 800 civilians.'

'Never mind that!' shrieked Belinda. 'What about me?'

At this point, Loonie could bear it no longer.

'M'Lord, this witness is simply expressing wild opinions. It is entirely his own conjecture that Mrs Taylor is rich. And might I add, it's all relative if you are used to living in a war-torn village where people are so desperate they will happily eat cats and dogs.'

'Never!' shouted Valmir. 'I never eat cat. And only once dog. Is very tough.'

Juniper would have intervened at this point to move the proceedings on but he was hallucinating again. He saw the cats and dogs, being chased by Valmir.

Round and round the courtroom they went, followed by Mrs Bilby, who was brandishing a cheese knife. After

her went a giant squid, who was trying to pull them all
into its clutches.

'M'Lord, might I have a go now?' said Mrs Bilby, who
was suddenly not running around the court but standing
looking at him expectantly.

'A go? Hmm?' Juniper was busy keeping his eye on the
squid, which *was* still running round and which seemed to
have got hold of the cheese knife.

'I want to have a go at questioning the witnesses.' Mrs
Bilby was on her feet. Juniper blinked to make sure he
was not still hallucinating because she was dressed very
strangely. She was wearing a Christian Dior dinner jacket
for women, teamed with tight black satin trousers, white
shirt and black bow tie. Evidently she had gone through
her wardrobe and found something that she thought made
her look the part.

'I'm not sure that's wise,' said Loonie, trying to stand
up. But Mrs Bilby pushed him back down into his seat.

'Shut up, Lawrence! I will not tell you again! I've seen
Law and Order. I know exactly how to do this. Your honour, I wish to commence my cross.'

'Yes, yes, by all means,' said Juniper. 'Argh!' And he
ducked, because the squid was swooping down from the
ceiling with a cheese knife in every tentacle.

Mrs Bilby straightened herself and put on a pompous
voice. 'Valmir. I mean, Mr Kraqnisi.'

'Krasniqi.'

'That's what I said. Kraqnisi.'

'But is not Kraqnisi. Is Krasniqi.'

'Yes. That's what I said. Now, Mr Kraqinski, would you describe me as the sort of person who would hide money?' And she smiled around the court as if assured that an answer was about to come which would seal her innocence in everyone's minds forever.

But instead of answering instantly, Valmir screwed up his forehead and spent a long time thinking, and repeating the question quietly to himself, before suddenly looking like he had become inspired with the correct answer. 'Yes,' he said, decisively.

Mrs Bilby was already smiling as if he had said, 'No,' when the smile fell off her face. 'Are you sure? Only I was rather hoping you might say the opposite, Val, darling.'

Loonie slumped forward and let his forehead bang against the table.

'Yes, I sure. You told me you hid money under bread bin, for cleaner.'

'That's different. Look, let's try another one. Do you remember me ever being violent or abusive to this man here?' And she indicated Seth.

'You mean like the time you put cheese knife in his—'

'Yes! Like that time. Only please do be an angel and don't go on and on about that. It makes it sound so much worse than it was.'

Loonie intervened again. 'M'Lord, I think Mrs Taylor has become confused about her line of questioning. May I request a short recess so that I can advise her?'

Mr Justice Juniper was only too pleased to say yes. He desperately wanted to get out of the courtroom because there were now seven giant squids hanging from the ceiling, all of them brandishing a cheese knife in every tentacle.

'How did it go?' Madison asked Seth, when they met that evening for pizza on Streatham High Road.

'All right. I'm nearly a free man.'

The case was coming to a conclusion. After his client's cack-handed examination of Valmir, Elden John had stepped in to prevent Mrs Bilby questioning Seth on the grounds that it would retraumatize him.

Mr Justice Juniper had agreed, on the basis that 'more importantly, it will retraumatize me.'

He had then informed them that he had heard enough anyway and was going to deliver his judgement the next day.

'But that's wonderful! Shall we celebrate your impending wealth? Shall we have champagne? If they sell it here.' Madison looked around.

'I think,' said Seth, perusing the menu, 'I'm just going to have a Diet Coke. And a margherita.'

'I assume you mean the pizza, not the cocktail?'

'There's a drink made of tomato and cheese?'

Even if Seth had been the sort to celebrate, there wasn't all that much to pop corks about. This was because no matter how much of Mrs Bilby's money his legal team spent trying to find Mrs Bilby's money, they simply couldn't work out where she had put it all.

When push came to shove, Mrs Bilby's outlandish excuses about her ridiculous failed business ventures and wildly mismanaged finances – from Kazakhstani Ponzi scheme to Somalian pirate hijack – were simply too ludicrous to be disproved.

So all in all, spending vast sums of money tracking down even vaster sums of money was really not what you would call cost-effective.

Nevertheless, they did manage to locate a few hundred thousand, the tail end of her fortune, hanging out of various bank accounts like so many shirtsleeves from a wardrobe door. This was divided up by Judge Juniper so that Seth had enough to buy a two-bedroom apartment in Thornton Heath, while Mrs Bilby affected to buy herself somewhere modest in Surrey, saying she only wanted to live a simple life in her dotage.

Seth reflected that with only £365,928 after tax to show for his trouble, it was just as well he had a new woman looking after him.

51

Excerpts from the ruling of Mr Justice Juniper in the matter of Taylor v Taylor:

1. This final hearing concerns the application by Seth Taylor ("the husband") for financial provision against Belinda Bilby-Taylor ("the wife").

2. The hearing took place over six fucking horrendous days of utter insanity and chaos between 11 and 18 June 2014 when, to be perfectly honest, I wasn't feeling at all well. The wife was at first represented by a string of ludicrously expensive lawyers. Then she sacked them all and represented herself, unbelievably badly, assisted by several McKenzie Friends, including her poor dead husband's long-suffering attorney Lawrence Loonie of Loonie, Loos and Leithall, who didn't get a word in edgeways so may as well not have been there. The husband was represented by a total twat from Croydon who turned out to be rather good, actually.

3. Given that the parties couldn't even decide prior to the start of the final hearing whether they wanted to be divorced or not, or at least one of them couldn't, this load of old bollocks of a case was always going to be a pain in the arse to sort out. It's no wonder I didn't manage to stay sober or clean for its duration, and, in fact, it drove me to greater depths of depravity than I normally sink to. I estimate my own costs in this matter to be around £65,000

in drugs, alcohol, hotels and dry cleaning bills, but that's another matter.

17. In his Form E letter, the husband stated that his reasonable needs to maintain himself required some ludicrous sum or other. Well, he can whistle for it, as my old mum used to say. Guess what? The money isn't there.

19. So far as I can make out, the wife has either spent almost all of the vast fortune she was left by her deceased former husband because she is the biggest loon ever to walk the planet, or she's lost it, or she's hidden it. I really couldn't care less. If she has hidden it, then good on her. Maybe she isn't as big a fool as she looks. In any case, by my reckoning, there's only about half a million kicking about so the husband will have to make do with that.

45. The wife asks the court "to place a significant monetary value on compensation for loss of earnings" suffered by her time being taken up with the husband's various demands on her when she could have been attending to her business. Is she having a laugh? The only business she ever attended to was spending her dead husband's hard-earned money. If she's asking me to take seriously the so-called charity work she does on behalf of micro-pigs which aren't even micro, she can forget it.

47. The husband asks the court to compensate him for emotional trauma and loss of earnings because the wife impaled him on a cheese knife. I see no reason why he cannot carry on working with a puncture wound to his backside. He can stand up and paint, can't he?

117. Never in all my years as a high court judge dealing in high-value divorces have I seen a case where so much money has evaporated into thin air so pointlessly. Mr Johns' costs seem to have spiralled disproportionately with no thought given to the consequences of such profligate spending. I have assumed throughout this case that he is not actually related to Elton John but if he were I would not be surprised.

349. In conclusion, I would like to say to the husband and wife that I hope they are both thoroughly ashamed of themselves. But in the absence of shame, which I have a feeling will not materialize, even now, I hope they will both encounter profound and everlasting regret when they wake up tomorrow and realize that they are both in a far worse position now, after this monumental fuck-up of a divorce, than they ever were when they were in their strange marriage.

350. As for me, I quit. I can't do this any more. I'm seventy-one and I'm not getting any younger. Who cares which greedy swine gets what? I've spent the last thirty years listening to one whining couple after another. It used to be spoilt women demanding pay-outs so they could sit on their arses for the rest of their lives and do nothing, claiming they only wanted the money for the sake of the kiddies. Now it's men who want to be kept in the lifestyle to which they have become accustomed. House husbands. They say what's good for the goose is good for the gander. But have they no balls? No shame? And as for all this whingeing by the wife about finding herself and wanting to be happy . . . Ye gods. Was marriage ever meant to be about being happy? It used to be a perfectly respectable logistical living arrangement. Now everyone wants to get happiness and fulfilment out of it. Not so long ago, people were perfectly happy to be unhappy in the cause of remaining respectable. If it got that bad, there was always suicide. Why, my father manfully topped himself when my mother drove him round the bend. But not for the husbands and wives of today the dignified art of the slow, silent, living death. Or the brave, noble exit of the trusty exhaust pipe. Oh no. Now we all have to be happy. Happy. God, what a sordid, selfish little world we live in. No wonder I drink. And take drugs. And gamble. And have sex with hookers. I'm driven to it by the ceaseless greed, pettiness and self-obsession I am forced daily to witness. Is this what life is all about? It simply cannot be. There's a ticket to the Bahamas with my name on it. I intend to check into the world's most luxurious rehab and spend the rest of the year sipping virgin margaritas on

the beach. After which, who knows? Lillian, if you're read-
ing this, I'm not coming home. You can have everything.
Please forward my mail to Serenity Palms, Paradise Bay,
Nassau, Bahamas.'

It wasn't the most conventional of judgements, but it
would, perhaps, go down in legal history as the most
honest.

52

A few months later, Madison was enjoying a lovely night out with her new boyfriend.

They ordered a whole chicken with three sides – fries, coleslaw and corn on the cob – because Seth was feeling flush now he had a couple of hundred thousand pounds in the bank.

It wasn't enough to go mad and buy a house but that suited him fine. He liked living in digs. Sometimes he stayed over with Madison at her flat and sometimes she went to stay with him, at his flat in Thornton Heath. This suited them both fine. They were happy as sand boys doing an afternoon's shopping in the Whitgift Centre in Croydon. At weekends, they went to Madison's cottage in the country and played at planting vegetables. They sat sketching each other and then turned their pages round to reveal terribly bad likenesses, with Hitler moustaches and other comic touches, and then laughed themselves silly.

Seth was a simple soul and Madison was an uncompli- cated sort of girl. 'Isn't this wonderful?' she said, hugging his arm and beaming as they stood at the counter in Nando's.

'You're easily pleased,' Seth said, as he handed her a Diet Coke and they found themselves a table. 'Are you sure you wouldn't have liked to go somewhere else? We could always try Pizza Express.'

'Oh no,' smiled Madison, sweetly, 'I just love being with you, Pooks. As long as you're happy, I'm happy. You know me!'

They ate in silence, because Madison didn't really have anything to say. There was nothing to say. She was perfectly satisfied. She had spent the day shopping, and had come home with three pairs of jeans, four pairs of wedged sandals and a fantastic haul of new beauty products, most of them on a two-for-one deal. Mind you, when you bought all the offers it soon mounted up. But it didn't matter. She could afford it. She had looked in her bank account and there was so much money in there she couldn't believe she had not spent it before.

She couldn't imagine what on earth she might have been saving it up for. What a waste of time when there were so many wonderful things to buy in the shops nowadays.

And there was no chance of the money running out because she had such a great job. There was hardly anything difficult to do.

She had gone back to work at Wilde and Sawyer but for reasons known only to him, Christopher had kept her working on his cases, doing background research, as if she were an office junior. She didn't mind. She liked not having too much responsibility. And she got to finish work early and meet Seth, who was never very busy because all he did was paint the odd portrait of a neighbour's cat.

Ah yes, life was good. Life was really good. In fact, she couldn't imagine in her wildest dreams how life could be any more perfect.

Seth dropped her home and said he wouldn't come in because he had to be up early in the morning for work.

'This has been the most amazing evening,' said Madison, as he walked her to her door and pecked her on the cheek.

'Has it?' he said, looking puzzled.

'It has. Are you sure you don't want to come in?'

'No, I've got to get an early night. Busy day tomorrow. Mrs Pargetter wants me to paint a picture of her Afghan hound.'

'All right, Pookie. Sweet dreams.'

'Bye.'

'Never goodbye, Pooks. Remember? Always "See you later!"'

'See you later,' he said, and blew her the regulation kiss she insisted on.

After shutting the door, she walked to the bathroom singing to herself.

She was standing in her knickers and bra at the sink, about to brush her teeth, when she suddenly noticed all the pots and tubes on the shelf.

'What the fuck are these?' she heard herself muttering.

She picked up each one and examined it. Then she read

the labels. Then she heard herself saying: 'Seven signs of ageing? Seven signs of a gullible idiot, more like. Damn cosmetics companies, fleecing people . . .'

Then she looked into the mirror and saw the vein. It was standing out on the side of her head. Only slightly. But it was there.

'Oh no! Oh no no no no!' she cried. And then she added, in a different voice: 'Yes! Thank God! Yes!'

Cynthia and Mitchell had only just got home from a day out at the Market Fougham Horticultural Society Royal Show when Madison rang and told them what was happening.

Cynthia took the call on the phone in the hallway and didn't even take off her coat. Mitchell had already gone upstairs to change into his gardening trousers so he could start putting the new mould-resistant water lilies into the pond before Cynthia accused him of dragging his feet. But he had barely got one leg in his trousers when she was screaming the news up the stairs at him and telling him to stop messing around and come quickly.

'In the circumstances,' said Mitchell, tripping down the stairs with a Post-it note on which he had already written an emergency checklist, 'it might just be best if we got straight in the car and went back down there now.'

'Christ on a bike!' screamed Cynthia. 'Of course we're going back now! Hurry up, Mitchell, or we'll get stuck in rush hour on Fougham High Street!' And she began emitting various expletives, which we will not repeat here for quality-control purposes.

'I'm going to have to put my proper clothes back on, at least,' said Mitchell. But Cynthia wouldn't hear of it. She pushed him out of the door in his gardening trousers. Again.

Madison was laughing and crying at the same time.

It was very alarming. One second she was ecstatic, the next moment weeping inconsolably.

They took her straight back to the Princess Alice Hospital.

Cameron McTavish met them there and together they sat before the consultant he had called in from home, telling him it was a desperate emergency.

The consultant said it did not look good. He immediately ordered X-rays and a nurse wheeled Madison to the X-ray suite. She was gabbling schizophrenically, as if she were two distinct people.

'Oh, I love it in this hospital! Everyone is so nice here! The whole thing is a darn cheek. I pay my taxes and here I am, pouring money into the private health sector when I ought to be able to get a consultant to X-ray me in my local A&E.'

When the X-rays were done, they were all called back into the consulting room where a grim-faced brain specialist told them the bad news. 'I'm afraid the swelling is going down.'

Madison, who had been sitting in silence with a very dark look on her face, now burst into tears, then wiped her eyes and started laughing. 'Thank goodness!' she said. Then she started crying again.

'Can't you do something?' said Mitchell, a distraught look on his face. 'There must be something?'

'Not really,' said the consultant, sitting back in his chair. 'There is a technique, experimental, which we might use to reinflame the brain tissue but there are huge risks. Other than pushing her in front of another car and hoping for the same result, which I'm guessing you won't find a satisfactory option, there really is nothing we can do. You're stuck with it.'

'Spell it out, Doctor,' said Cynthia, crossly. 'What exactly are you saying?'

'I'm saying,' said the consultant, leaning forward, 'that I'm afraid your daughter is going to become herself again. I'm sorry.'

Cynthia and Mitchell took Madison home and kept her quiet, as Cameron McTavish had ordered. They called Christopher and told him she wouldn't be coming to work for the foreseeable future because she needed urgent rest. But it was no good. She was definitely on the mend.

For a while, the two personalities were present in equal parts, fighting each other for control, and this was a very distressing time indeed. Madison would sit in front of the television set muttering:

'I love this show, turn it up! Turn it over, you mean. Load of overblown nonsense. Daddy, wake up, it's that show we like! You'll never wake him; he's just done four straight episodes of *Countdown*. He's on a major *Countdown* comedown.'

Then one day, she woke up, stormed into the kitchen where Cynthia and Mitchell were eating cereal and reading the *Telegraph* and grumpily told them to turn down Radio 4 because it was making a racket and she was late for work, before adding:

'Isn't it about time you two went back to Fougham?' And she pronounced it Fuck'em, just to rub it in. 'I don't need you. You're getting under my feet.'

Cynthia and Mitchell gave each other a look. Cynthia smiled.

Two hours later, Madison slammed into the offices of Wilde and Sawyer and stormed past Christopher, who didn't get the point of what was happening until he took her to lunch.

Suddenly, as they sat in The Lobster Pot looking at the menu, the Italian waitress chewing gum in front of them, pencil poised on pad to take their order, Madison started.

'Where is the minestrone?' The waitress stopped chewing. She knew that voice.

'Minestronez finish. We have nice leek and potatoes soup. You like?'

Madison didn't stop for breath until the waitress went to the Costcutter down the street.

Then she argued all the way through her soup, nearly choking on it on several occasions.

She started with the decline in service standards, as evidenced by the disappearance, yet again, of her favourite starter from the specials board, which led on to the decline in moral standards in society in general, which led in turn to a general discourse about how the country was, as she put it, 'going to the dogs'.

'And another thing!' she kept gasping, through mouthfuls of soup, as Christopher ate his meal in silence, nodding his head as he had learned to do, to try to pacify her.

Sometimes she sprayed bits of soup across the table, which wasn't a pretty sight, and not something a woman should have countenanced doing. But she had no control over herself. She was firing on all cylinders.

'This is typical. Typical!' she spat, sending a noodle and a piece of carrot in opposite directions.

At one point Christopher tried to say something, but this made her emit a panic-stricken squeak, as if she would explode if he even so much as hinted that he was taking an opposing position.

'Is this what we have come to in this country?' she ranted. 'Is this what civilized society is reduced to? The mother of all democracies. England. England! This green and pleasant land . . .'

People were beginning to stop eating their lunches and look round. Christopher had to settle the bill quickly and get her out of there.

As they stood on the pavement, he turned to her and smiled: 'It's good to have you back. The world wasn't the same without you.'

Madison screwed up her nose: 'Well, I'm glad to be back. It was horrible being happy. I have a vague memory of buying a lot of face creams.'

The call from Seth had come in as she was walking back from The Lobster Pot. What the hell did he want? Then, she remembered. Oh lord. They had a date tonight. What had she been thinking? She would have to meet him and let him down abruptly. She obviously couldn't be dating a man with all the drive and enthusiasm of a piece of wet lettuce.

'Listen,' she would say, 'you're getting on my nerves. You need to get a grip and take control of your life. You're so passive. You let things happen to you and you never take the initiative. You're a drifter. No. It's worse than that. You're a loser.'

In the end, she didn't have to say anything, which was a shame because she had been looking forward to it. They had only been sitting in Nando's for five minutes, with Madison barking orders at the waitresses and arguing about why their table had a wobbly leg, when Seth could bear it no longer.

'What is the matter with you?'

'Nothing. I've nothing the matter with me. Not now, anyway. The matter was the way I was before. I'm back to normal. I'm the way I'm meant to be.'

'I don't think I like you the way you're meant to be.'

'I don't think I like you the way you're meant to be

either. If indeed you are meant to be like that, which I find hard to believe.'

'I suppose that's that then.'

53

A love of the confessional is usually fostered in early child-hood. For Madison it was the weekly trips to see the priest at St Ignatius that had left her with an indelible confidence in the art of tortured regret. It was superstition, really, but throughout her life she had always loved a good session of self-torment.

As a child, she really looked forward to her visits to the little room behind the school chapel: 'Bless me, Father, for I have sinned. It's been a week since my last confession . . .'

The priest enjoyed her visits too because all the other children had very little of any import to beat their chests about and his job had been somewhat limited until Madison came along with her wide-ranging array of juve-nile sins.

'I've been horrid to the other children . . . didn't do what I was told . . . spat my shepherd's pie out . . . said, "Christ on a bike" seven times . . .'

'Say five Our Fathers and five Hail Marys . . .'

'Are you sure? Only last week I did all that *and* flushed Sally Dickenson's homework down the toilet to serve her right for pulling my hair, and you said three Our Fathers then.'

In many ways, the regrets Madison had now about the time she had spent as a nice person were much more tricky than the regrets she had had when she was rude and obstructive.

As soon as the swelling in her brain had gone down completely, she realized that she had caused all sorts of mayhem by being optimistic.

The trickiest thing she had to do was go to see Mrs Bilby and apologize for being of no use to her in her hour of need and then betraying her completely to Seth's defence team through some misplaced sense of guilt and idealism.

This could not have been more out of character. It was Madison's profound belief that everyone deserved a defence, even a breathtakingly selfish woman with unforgivably purple hair.

After a bit of investigative work, she tracked her former client down to an address in Chessington, not far from the eponymous World of Adventures.

She had reverted to her maiden name, for some reason. The entry on the electoral register said B.O. Montagu-Santos-DuLally-Gaseuse, 34 Leatherhead Road.

When she arrived, Madison found a neat little three-bedroom semi with a picket fence around a postage-stamp lawn lined with tulips, and a huge black Mercedes limousine parked slightly askew on the narrow driveway.

The door was answered by Vasilis, who ushered her into a tiny living room stuffed to the ceiling with ornate antique

furniture evidently imported from Tankards. In addition to
the elegant antiquities, there were a lot of tribal ornaments
and things that looked like native American dream-catch-
ers hanging from the walls. A faint tinkling of wind chimes
could be heard, apparently coming from the garden.

'Please to be waiting here,' said the bodyguard, who
was dressed rather absurdly in a butler's uniform. 'The
mistress of the house coming shortly. I get you drink?'

'Tea, please.'

'Chinese or Indian?'

'Er, Indian.'

'Darjeeling or Assam?'

'Either.' Vasilis backed out of the room deferentially,
knocking a palm off a tall stand that was wedged between
a lamp and a campaign chest.

Whilst he was in the kitchen, a noisy kettle boiling and
the sound of clattering crockery drowning out the wind
chimes, she appeared.

She was wearing a long kaftan; her red hair was loose
but held back from her face with an Alice band, and she
wore flip-flops on her large feet. As she entered she put her
hands together in the prayer position and bowed her head.

'*Namaste*,' she said, eyes closed, before whooshing into
the room, her kaftan flowing behind her, and sitting down
cross-legged in an armchair.

When she was comfortable she laid her hands across
her knees, fingers interlaced, palms upwards, and smiled
serenely at her guest.

Madison looked around. 'I'm sorry you have had

to move to such a small house, Mrs . . . I mean Miss Montagu-Santos . . .'

'Oh no! None of that long-winded business, please. I've shortened it down for everyday usage. Most of the names were perfectly ridiculous, so I've chosen just one. Call me Miss DuLally. Or Belinda, if you prefer. After all, we are old friends.'

'Well, yes. Although . . .' Madison paused, gulped. The lady herself smiled calmly and shut her eyes for a few seconds as if praying. Madison ploughed on. 'I'm sorry to say that after I suffered that bang to the head, I was not quite myself. And I divulged certain pieces of information about you that were client-privileged, which led to you losing all your money.'

'Darling,' said Belinda, 'do not dare to apologize. It has all worked out perfectly. I am beyond happiness.'

And she explained that, after forty years of ceaseless searching, whilst living in some of the most luxurious venues money could buy, she had finally found herself, improbably enough, in Chessington. In these functional surrounds, she had discovered that she wasn't really Belinda Bilby at all. And neither was she Ananda Anadi Ambika, her yoga name – joyous, eternal mother. She had never been anywhere close to that, she realized.

No. When it came down to it she was plain old Belinda Ophelia Montagu-Santos-DuLally-Gaseuse, or Bee DuLally for short. It came to her when she was sitting under the wind chimes one breezy day, blissed out on the sound of the jingly-jangly. She had not looked back since.

She was as happy as could be in her suburban heaven, with everything she needed within a few rooms.

'This semi-detached business has been a revelation,' she told Madison now. 'I had no idea such compact and bijou places existed. Do you know, you come in through the front door and you've got everything you need in three little rooms to the left and right of you. Living room here, kitchen there. The teensiest little dining room you could imagine. Perfectly adorable in every way. And upstairs there are three more little rooms, in a sort of descending order of size. You would think Mummy Bear, Daddy Bear and Baby Bear were living here. It's completely divine. One need only ever walk ten paces to do anything. You can't possibly get lost on the way to the kitchen and end up in the fitness suite – or the ballroom, for heaven's sake, as if anyone really needs one of those – and there is simply nothing one can do to spend too much money. It's virtually pennies to run. We have mains gas, you know. None of that business with a man driving a tanker down the driveway. The heating and hot water comes from a darling little company called British Gas. Have you heard of them? My last bill was something ludicrous like £900. Can you believe it?'

She had even come to terms with her horrid sons, who came to visit occasionally now that they were on parole. 'Ernest insists on the box room. He says it reminds him of HMP Wandsworth. We never got on when we had all that space to lose ourselves in. But now we are forever having exciting little arguments about who's using the bathroom. So as you can see, it has all worked out wonderfully!'

She didn't reveal, exactly, whether she had lied about the money or not, but she did intimate that if there had been a hidden fortune, it was now in trust for the sons, or possibly the piggies, or possibly had simply vanished into the ether indefinitely, as something that had only brought her bad luck. In any case, she waved her hand like a magician and declared, enigmatically: 'Do not ask me about the money. I have put it away.'

After tea and biscuits, Mrs Bilby showed her the garden. 'It's 100 feet, you know. And the pièce de résistance . . . a shed,' she boasted, as if she had invented the concept of suburban living. 'I can do my yoga out here. But best of all, there's somewhere for Wendy and Peter to play.'

Madison looked around. 'You've had more children?' She imagined Mrs Bilby coming back from a trip to India impregnated with twins by one of those controversial fertility doctors who put donated eggs and sperm into the wombs of ageing women who then turned up in the *Daily Mail* nine months later under the headline 'Miracle Baby of Mum, 67!' inevitably followed, a year later, by 'Britain's Oldest Mother Speaks of Regrets'. But Mrs Bilby looked at her as if the actual answer was quite obvious.

'The pigs, my dear. The llamas had to be rehomed, which was probably just as well. The spitting was getting silly. But the piggies are happy as, well, pigs in you know what. Darling creatures. It makes me weep to think how people could try to keep them in tower blocks. There was a man in Peckham recently who was taking one up to his flat in the lift, you know. I've said it once, and I'll say it again: we must undertake nothing less than a sea change in our attitude to the keeping of miniature farm animals as pets in this country. It is the number one issue facing our democracy. I work full time now for The Micro-Pig Foundation, from the little box room office upstairs.' And she clapped her hands together in delight. 'Isn't that too much!'

Vasilis appeared with Valmir at his side. 'We go now, Miss DuLally. Is OK?'

'Oh yes, run along, my dear, dear boys. Toodle pip and remember – God favours the brave! They're going to see the female vicar at the local C of E church down the road, to see if she'll tie their knot, as it were. They're Muslims, of course, but the Imam won't hear of it.'

'They're getting married?'

'Oh yes. Such a lovely story. They've been potty about each other for years. I always knew it but I never let on. I expect it was very difficult for them, in their culture, to come down the stairs.'

'You mean come out of the closet.'

'That's it! Now they want to make it official with a big church wedding. I've bought the most marvellous medieval-themed see-through tartan shift dress from Vivienne Westwood's spring collection. Or then again, I might go in a sari. Did I mention I was a Hindu now? It was terribly difficult to get in. I had to pretend I was related to George Harrison. Would you like another cup of tea? I'm sure I could manage to make one myself. Val and Vas have left me a crib sheet on the kitchen wall of how to do everything with tea. It all hinges on boiling water, I'm told. So clever.

Dear Val and Vas. Won't you come to the wedding? Oh, you must. I'm doing a marquee on the lawn with a string quartet and circus performers.'

At least, thought Madison, as they made their way back across the crazy paving to the double-glazed French windows, someone is living happily ever after.

54

When Madison took up her post at her desk the next morning, Christopher burst into her office with his socks dangerously close to the edges of his heels.

'Thank God you're in early. You've got to start looking through the backlog.'

He was carrying a huge heap of files that were spilling random papers onto the floor as he shambled in.

'Problem?' she said, refusing to look up at him.

'Yes, problem,' he said, slumping down into a chair. 'Have you any idea how much money this firm lost when you were happy? I couldn't let you loose on anything. I had to make up tasks for you to do that you couldn't ruin with your half-baked idealism. In the end I gave you the cleaning rota timesheets to fill in. I was on my own completely – unless you count that useless Judith you call a paralegal, and she went to pieces because you weren't helping her with her noise abatement order – the result being seven clients are threatening to sue us for negligence and the Law Society have been on about the billing – oh, God, I can't even go into that, it's too stressful . . .'

And he slammed the huge heap of cases down on her desk, then looked up at her pitifully.

'If you could get cracking on this lot it might just get everyone off my back. Can you get cracking on them now? We really need the money. We've practically gone under since you hit your head. Did I tell you another problem is that I haven't submitted any billing since you went funny? It's my weak spot, you know that. Without you breathing down my neck it just didn't get done. Now the accountant's foaming at the mouth. And the Law Society has been on, did I tell you that? Christ, I didn't mean to. Oh well, you know now. Add it to the long list of things I've done wrong including the prawns down the radiator. Which might, now I think about it, be to blame for the meat flies. I mean, they could be fish flies. Just an idea. Anyway, the bastard sons of bitches at the Law Society are being totally unreasonable about a perfectly understandable oversight with a tiny little insignificant multi-million-pound account. So I put the clock on during a phone call and fell asleep and went on timing three hours after the silly bitch put the phone down. So shoot me. Four hours, forty hours – it's all the same in the end. Time passes me by, you know that. I'm shit at my job no matter how long I spend on things. I'm burnt out. I need a holiday. About fifty years in the Caribbean should do it.'

He broke off to put his head on the table like a child and then continued moaning as he lay there. 'You've got to help me. It's all going tits-up. And the kids are coming over tonight for a long weekend. It's the only time I get with them. If I'm not there when the she-he who must be obeyed drops them off the she-he'll stop me having access and I don't know how I'll cope if the she-he does that. It's all I've got in life. I mean, if you'd consider sleeping with me I'd have that. But you won't. So I don't. This is it. This is all I've got: this firm, and the thought of losing it makes me suicidal. I don't even think it's worth going to the doctor for some Prozac. I don't think it's going to work this time.' And then he got back up suddenly and started pulling at his socks.

Madison shouted: 'All right! All right!' and started leafing through the files. After a while she said: 'Maybe we can sort all this out. But then again maybe we can't.'

'What do you mean can't? Why can't?'

'Because this represents a sudden increase in my workload.' And she pushed the case files back across the desk towards him.

'Not on the workload you did before. Maybe it's more than the workload you did when you were Lady fucking Gaga, but you couldn't do anything then.' And he pushed them back.

'No, but then I don't suppose a tribunal will look at it like that. Of course we could keep it out of a tribunal. Which is to say, I'm going to need a raise. Let's see, what am I on now? Share of profits. How about full equity partner?'

Christopher popped a second button open on his shirt. 'You know I can't afford to do that.'

The files shot back towards him. 'Come on, come on, I'm going to need your answer. Otherwise these cases are going to have to leave my desk right now. I need the space so I can open up all the files of the cases I'm thinking of taking on when I leave next month to set up my own firm. I've seen some nice premises just opposite St Paul's Cathedral, funnily enough.'

'Fine. I agree.'

Madison smiled and pulled the caseload back towards her. Christopher wiped the sweat off his brow. 'Phew! That was a close one. Quite exhilarating. I'd missed that feeling. You know, I used to think it would be the best thing in the world if you softened up, but then it happened and it just wasn't right at all. I prefer you as a cantankerous bitch. You make more sense that way.'

'Are you trying to flatter me? Because if you are, I've no time for it. Come on, out. I need to get on with expanding our legal practice.' And she pushed him towards the door.

Christopher allowed himself to be bundled out into the corridor, then stuck his head back round the door as she tried to shut it. 'I'm not a religious man, as you know, but all the time you were happy, I used to pray to God he would turn you back into the weirdo we all knew and loved.'

'Well, now your prayers are answered,' said Madison, eyeing his half-done-up fly censoriously before slamming the door in his face.

'Yes,' called Christopher from the corridor. 'Hallelujah!'

As Madison got down to business there was another knock on the door, a very faint, timid one.

'Come in, Judith,' she called.

'Is it all right if I come in? Only I don't want to disturb you if you're in a bad mood. Christopher said you were in a bad mood. If you've got a lot on I can come back.'

'Judith, for God's sake stop faffing about. What have I told you? Nothing is too much trouble for you. Come in. I've missed your unerring pessimism. Your lack of confidence is majestic, your failure to believe in the nonsensical fallacy that it will all be all right, a fallacy cruelly put about by those with a vested interest in keeping the masses cowed, is nothing short of heroic. Sit down. I would rather spend an idle hour with you than almost anyone else I know.'

'Thank you. I think,' said Judith, sitting down on the very edge of the seat and folding her hands primly in her lap. 'Did you manage to, er, you know, find out about the thingy?'

'If you mean did I get the details from the council about how to do the noise abatement order application, then yes. I rang them this morning. And if that doesn't work we can try an ASBO. Hit those ne'er-do-wells with the only language they understand.'

'An ASBO? That sounds a bit drastic. Are you sure the people next door won't find out and come and bang on my door and try to kill me? One of them has the word Hate tattooed on his knuckles.'

'No, I can't be sure. But that's a chance we're just going to have to take. And if they do cut up rough, you can be sure I will make a very stirring speech at your send-off.'

'Oh dear. So much could go wrong, couldn't it?'

'That's the spirit.'

'Well, if you're sure. I know this is a little thing in the grand scheme of things.'

'Nonsense. The grand scheme of things is made up of little things. If no one fought over the little things then what would the grand scheme of things look like? Not very grand, in all probability.'

55

Quite evidently, the world is a vale of tears. Men and women cannot be trusted to be nice to each other for two seconds, and the misery and torment of love continues unabated unto the gates of insanity.

That being said, everyone loves a good wedding. On this particular occasion, Madison and Christopher were huddled together outside the entrance to a very swish hotel and country club on a sunny day, as a jubilant throng milled around them, waiting for the happy couple to arrive for their reception.

'Thanks for coming with me,' said Christopher. 'The prospect of my debonair younger brother getting married and me not even having a girlfriend to bring to the wedding was making me suicidal.'

'That's all right,' said Madison. 'You owe me. I will be calling in the debt with interest. I haven't decided what medium you will be repaying me in but it could be anything, including actual blood. Or I may force you to return the favour by accompanying me to the Vivienne Westwood-themed wedding of two ethnic Albanian rebel leaders in Chessington.'

'Well, whatever, just let me know.' Christopher pretended to smile as other guests recognized him and waved, but really he was struggling to breathe inside his rented morning suit. It hadn't even been worth renting a morning suit in the end because it turned out he was one of ten ushers and could easily have not bothered turning up at all for all anyone would have noticed. He didn't even bother sitting in the front row so he could do his ushering – whatever that was – but rather sat with Madison in a pew towards the back of the church throughout the ceremony, hoping the head usher wouldn't notice he was shirking his duties.

For her part, Madison was finding the occasion not nearly as traumatic as Christopher was.

Whilst it couldn't exactly be said that she was enjoying the wedding itself, she was enjoying the discomfort on Christopher's face, the garish outfits worn by the women guests and the fact that the main cavalcade was late because one of the five preposterously long stretch limos carrying the wedding party with its ten ushers (well, ten minus Christopher, though no one had noticed) and ten bridesmaids had sprung a flat tyre, so the calculated slickness of the occasion had been well and truly punctured.

This boded ill, she decided, cheerfully. So far as she could make out, the couple were quite unsuited to each other.

If *Schadenfreude* is the enjoyment of others' misfortune, there should surely be a word for the enjoyment of ill-fated weddings? *Schadenhochzeitgefreude*, perhaps.

This is what Madison felt as she waited with Christopher, grimacing as he tried to breathe in his suit, watching the giggling wedding guests cavort, the women tottering on heels, outside the ostentatious five-star hotel and country club, catering staff circulating with champagne on trays and canapés that had cost a small fortune but were probably toxic from being left out of the fridge too long.

'Thank God we're together,' said Christopher, trying to undo a button of his shirt. 'I would never have coped with this alone. Damn things are stuck fast. I think I'll have to be cut out of this. Did you bring scissors in your overnight bag.'

'It doesn't matter whether I did or I didn't,' said Madison, 'because if you think I'm coming to your room later to cut you out of your morning suit because you've managed to get yourself stuck in it by being overweight then you must think I was born yesterday. I've heard that one before.'

At this moment, a series of long white Cadillacs began to appear down the drive and eventually pulled up amid much squealing from the lady guests. As the happy couple got out, there was an 'Aaaah!' from the crowd and everyone – except Madison and Christopher, naturally – threw their confetti.

The happy couple, hand in hand, beaming with relief and joy now the formalities of the service were over, ducked as the confetti fell on their heads like a cascade of dandruff, then made their way through the crowd, embracing well-wishers.

The two chisel-jawed, tanned, dark-haired men, dressed immaculately in matching white tuxedos, with red roses on their lapels, came towards them looking like a double helping of Cary Grant. Madison and Christopher painted on smiles.

Christopher embraced his brother and shook the hand of his new brother-in-law. Just my bloody luck, he thought. Now I've got two of them to compare myself to.

Inside, Madison waited until they were seated at their white-satin-draped table, surrounded by an assortment of aged aunts and spare-part twentysomethings, before she leaned in to Christopher and, mouth full of tuna sandwich, said: 'You were right about your brother. He really is the sexiest man I've ever seen. He looks like Alec Baldwin in his younger days.'

'Ouch,' said Christopher. 'By the way, why are you eating a sandwich from your handbag? There will be a huge meal.'

'They always leave the food out too long before serving it. Your chances of getting food poisoning at these things are through the roof. In any case, wedding lunches make me nervous. I need to eat before the horror starts or I get nauseous.'

An aged aunt was tutting as Madison crammed the sandwich into her mouth.

'Well,' said Christopher, 'so long as you didn't bring a flask of minestrone soup . . . oh, you did. Excellent.'

Madison was unloading a Thermos from her bag as he spoke.

'Excuse me,' said the aged aunt, 'do you mind? We're about to have lunch. This isn't a picnic area.'

'I'm sorry, I didn't realize you were from the wedding

reception police,' said Madison. 'Have you got your badge of identification?'

And suddenly, Madison had everything she needed to make for a very enjoyable occasion.

But she had changed. She hardly knew it. She didn't acknowledge it until Christopher rose to go to the desert buffet and asked her if she would like a bowl of tiramisu.

'Go on then.'

'Are you sure? You don't want to tell me you hate tiramisu? That you'd prefer cheese and biscuits?'

'No. I'll have whatever you're having.'

'That's not the sort of thing you normally say. It's a bit mellow for you.'

'Well, maybe I'm just a little bit mellower. After all, I did take a vicious knock to the head. I might not be completely recovered. There might be particles of optimism still floating about left over from when my brains were swimming in fluid.'

'Will you marry me?'

'No.'

'I might try again later. Maybe the particles of optimism come and go.'

Later, during the disco dancing part of the reception, they became horribly drunk. Slumped in their chairs at the table, pristine cloth now askew and spattered with red wine, gravy and trifle, the pair of them watched the guests embarrassing themselves.

One of the bridesmaids had hitched up her gown and was mounting a man from behind to the tune of Van Halen's 'Why Can't This Be Love'.

'If you could have anything on your tombstone, what would it be?' shouted Madison, over the din. She had on her wedding face. After a day and night of non-stop drinking, with a too-long walk to the nearest proper bathroom with a mirror, her lipstick had bled over her lips and her mascara had gone south, giving her panda eyes.

'I don't know. Why do you ask?' slobbered Christopher, slurping the dregs of a glass of red wine.

'I was just thinking, I know what I would have: *I told you it was going to end badly.*'

'I don't get how that's clever.'

'Because at some point, I'm going to be proved right. When the world ends, the aliens will come to pick over the remains, like you would if you came across a derelict house full of antiques, and they will find my grave and finally someone will realize I was right. About everything.'

'You really are deranged.'

There was a long pause while he attempted to refill his glass from an empty bottle, then discovered it was empty, stared into it to check, found another bottle with some dregs in it, poured again, slurped again, before saying:

'I think I'd have *I told you I was ill*, the old Spike Milligan defence, or *I hope you're satisfied now, you bitch*. In case the ex ever pops by to lay flowers.'

'She won't.'

'No.'

'And even if she did, she would be a he. So the bitch part would be wrong.'

'Yes.'

They settled back to watch the action on the dance floor. Earlier, Madison had had to furiously blink back tears and pretend she wasn't moved at all as Christopher's brother and his new husband slow danced the first number. Now the pair took to the dance floor again, their ties pulled loose, and boogied with the other guests. They looked ecstatically happy.

Madison felt that pang again. A few stray particles of hope were obviously swimming about.

She squinted as if studying zebras at a zoo: 'Isn't it incredible, how there is always someone willing to give love a try? Good job for our business.'

'God bless the gays,' said Christopher. 'How long do you think it will take them to work it out?'

'Could be years. Serves them right for being so damn hopeful.'

Madison suddenly grabbed her glass. 'A toast: to gay marriage, and the customers of tomorrow.'

They clinked their glasses and Christopher looked at her longingly and said: 'This is our song.'

'We don't have a song. Unless you count the theme tune to *The Munsters*.'

'You don't get it, do you? You and me – we *are* going to end up together, one day. It's only a matter of time. It's inevitable.'

'It's inconceivable.'

'Semantics.' They sat in silence for a few minutes.

'Want to dance?'

'Not really.'

'You do realize that it's bad luck not to dance at weddings?'

'Good. I could do with some bad luck. Things have been going suspiciously well recently. It makes me nervous.'

They were silent again for a while, until Christopher said, 'It's quite depressing that you don't want to dance with me, actually. Not even one dance. For old times' sake.'

And he pushed his chair back so Madison could see that he was rubbing his feet together, working loose his socks. She gasped with exasperation.

'Fine, I'll dance with you. But don't expect me to like it.'

Postscripts

Seth Taylor ran out of money after a few years and took up with a nice lady called Janice who worked at the Citizens Advice Bureau.

Not the one who put him in touch with Elden John when he was divorcing Mrs Bilby, but another lady who was there one afternoon when he went in to ask for advice on claiming incapacity benefit because painting whilst in a standing position had put his back out.

Elden John's reputation was catapulted into the stratosphere after being praised by the judge in the legendary final settlement of the Taylor v Taylor divorce.

Although his career as a TV pundit never quite took off as they had to do too many takes, he wrote regularly for the *Guardian* and *The Times* Law Supplement. He revamped his law firm, with a website featuring his famous endorsement:

Elden John Associates – 'Rather good, actually'.

He went into partnership with Alf Bird and the pair still work out of offices close to Lunar House in Croydon, the headquarters of the UK Border Agency. They make a huge contribution to society by helping those who have been wrongly accused of terrorism, and quite a few who have not been. Wrongly accused, I mean.

Judith Simmons won her battle with her noisy neighbours after securing an anti-social behaviour order, which led to their eviction. Unfortunately, it was a Pyrrhic victory because after the louts left, a nice middle-class couple moved in and had a baby which screamed day and night and couldn't be silenced owing to this being 'normal domestic noise'. So Judith had to sell up and move. She now lives in a nunnery in Nepal.

'W' went back to his wife, who decided to forgive him for his affair with Madison on the basis that she had always known it was an infatuation that would eventually burn itself out. He acted contritely for a few months and then found himself another single, emotionally illiterate woman twenty years younger than him, who gave him a key to her apartment. When she wasn't there, he left haikus on the kitchen table.

Karen Fairisle secured an exclusive interview with Belinda DuLally, live from Chessington, which broke all records for afternoon current affairs show audience figures and led to her being made the channel's lead anchorwoman, and even more horrible to deal with. Her ego continued to grow until a sound engineer called Dennis Reid bludgeoned her to death with a boom mike one day after she ordered him to make her voice sound younger. Reid was convicted of involuntary manslaughter and sentenced to five years in an open prison after the country's best criminal defence solicitor managed to swing a plea of diminished responsibility.

As this leading lawyer declared on the steps of the court, 'That's showbiz, baby!'

Acknowledgements

I owe so many people thanks but especially: Robyn Allardice-Bourne, Sarah Green-Sutton, Matthew d'Ancona, Aaron Sands, James Gurbutt and Eryl Humphrey Jones. You've all helped me more than I know how to tell you and if I tried in this small space it wouldn't be seemly.